P9-EKJ-816

DOVER·THRIFT·EDITIONS

Humorous American Short Stories

SELECTIONS FROM MARK TWAIN TO OTHERS MUCH MORE RECENT

Edited by Bob Blaisdell

DOVER PUBLICATIONS, INC.
Mineola, New York

DOVER THRIFT EDITIONS

GENERAL EDITOR: MARY CAROLYN WALDREP
EDITOR OF THIS VOLUME: BOB BLAISDELL

ACKNOWLEDGMENTS: SEE P. XI

Copyright

Bibliographical Note

Humorous American Short Stories: Selections from Mark Twain to Others Much More Recent, first published by Dover Publications, Inc., in 2013, is a new anthology of short stories reprinted from standard sources. A new introductory Note has been specially prepared for this edition.

Library of Congress Cataloging-in-Publication Data

Humorous American short stories : selections from Mark Twain to others much more recent / edited by Bob Blaisdell Dover Publications, Inc.
    pages cm — (Dover Thrift Editions)
 ISBN-13: 978-0-486-49988-8
 ISBN-10: 0-486-49988-X
 1. Humorous stories, American. 2. Short stories, American. 3. American wit and humor. I. Blaisdell, Robert, editor of compilation.
 PS648.H84H86 2013
 817—dc23

                                                                                        2013008657

Manufactured in the United States by Courier Corporation
49988X01   2013
www.doverpublications.com

Contents

iii

NOTE

THE LAST THING an editor of a book of humor stories wants to hear about any of his selections is "That's not funny." Accusations of poor taste, ridiculousness, broadness, childishness, absurdity . . . those are *great*. That means the reader laughed but has decided to feel bad for having laughed. Speaking of which, if "Uncle Remus" weren't so funny, I would've chickened out and jettisoned it from this anthology for all of its complicated political and racial incorrectnesses. In the post-Civil War South, Joel Chandler Harris's presentation of Uncle Remus was a complicated balancing act, which even Harris didn't seem fully conscious of performing: he simultaneously confirmed and mocked stereotypes. A sense of humor, it's clear, allows us to get closer to the truth of our common humanity than our public opinions do.

American humor is as distinctive as any culture's, but I would be hard-pressed to describe what that distinctiveness is. Is it Ben Franklin's satirical impersonations of various Philadelphia "types"? Is it Washington Irving's post-revolutionary New York tall tales? Mark Twain is our most famous funny-man; he was so funny he could amuse us even as we *expected* amusement, which is a comedian's most marvelous trick. He provided us with so many examples of humor, because everywhere he looked, all over the world (he was a real traveler), he was amazed and exasperated by the damned human race's self-defeating lies and its verbal ingenuity in doing so. A recent commentator suggests that the distinctiveness of American humor is we are particularly good at making fun of ourselves, but that quality, it seems to me, is simply the *universal* basis of humor. Humor is humor because it shows us how mistaken-ridden we *all* are, how unconscious we are of our fallibilities, how blind we are to our own limitations, how *serious* we are and how ridiculous such posturing is. Humor tricks us into laughing with self-recognition.

All jesters face the ax: *Be funny or die!* says the Reader King. Yet the comic tone usually assures us that nobody, at least in the story, is going to die, or if there *is* death, we readers or listeners will not be wrenched by it. The characters will face many troubles and will, to our reassurance, overcome them or at least end up exactly where he or she started, ready to face another "situation." Dorothy Parker's unfortunate first-person narrator of "A Telephone Call," for example, dramatizes and satirizes a particular anxiety better than any representation before or since: "You see, God, if You would just let him telephone me, I wouldn't have to ask You anything more. I would be sweet to him, I would be gay, I would be just the way I used to be, and then he would love me again. And then I would never have to ask You for anything more. Don't You see, God? So won't You please let him telephone me? Won't You please, please, please? Are You punishing me, God, because I've been bad? Are You angry with me because I did that? Oh, but, God, there are so many bad people—You could not be hard only to me. And it wasn't very bad; it couldn't have been bad. We didn't hurt anybody, God. Things are only bad when they hurt people. We didn't hurt one single soul; You know that. You know it wasn't bad, don't You, God? So won't You let him telephone me now?" We know, just as the Eternal One knows, that in spite of improved technology, our lonely souls haven't moved a single step since 1928, when Parker wrote that story. Why comic revelations about human nature seem to me reassuring, I don't know.

Some of the characters in these stories became stars of recurring comedies—notably Lucretia P. Hale's Peterkin family, John Kendrick Bangs's Idiot, Marietta Holley's Samantha Allen and Langston Hughes's Jesse B. Simple. When readers asked for more, those writers discovered the versatility of their clowns. Simple's creation gave Langston Hughes the fullest range Hughes ever had for his genius; he could step out and let loose on topics that were otherwise too infuriating for readers or too controversial, among them race and social injustice. Comedy gave opportunities to many of these writers to play around and regain the ability to surprise us. Comedy freed the authors and readers from arguments and proofs about the human condition and gave everyone instead a point of view of those edges where humans act consistently inconsistently—like humans.

One of the most poignant of characters is Howard Kaplan's ever-super-conscious protagonist in "How to Fight with Your Wife," which was the title of the 1990s newspaper column that chronicled in the finest psychological detail the social and marital dilemmas of a New Jersey husband. Kaplan's hero makes James Thurber's Walter Mitty seem comparatively slow-witted: "I threw a quick glance at Jean. She looked quite normal. It was I, rather, for just a second, who didn't look himself. I was suddenly in the position of a man who comes to the realization he might have just accidentally poisoned his wife. I'm not often in this predicament. Was this the first time in fact? The alarm I could have predicted, but not the degree of furtiveness. The furtiveness was there in equal measure to the alarm. And then shame at my furtiveness: I wasn't going to warn her. Either everything was absolutely fine—as I was sure it was—or something really was the matter, in which case it was too late. In either case, it seemed to me best to keep quiet." How Kaplan got away with writing so well, so comically, for so long, in a modern periodical remains a happy mystery.

While I intended to include only independent short stories, I found I couldn't draw the line at the excerpts I discovered in earlier anthologies. There was a hey-day of humor anthologies from the 1880s (when Twain edited a great grab-bag volume of American humorous skits, stories, and poems) to the 1910s, when dozens of collections gathered material from the many American magazines that published short fiction or from excerpts the anthologizers quietly made from novels. I myself have not made any excerpts but, less guiltily, have accepted earlier excerpts as faits accompli, among them the marvelous "Selecting the Faculty" by Robert Carlton (Baynard Rush Hall).

The span of time from Benjamin Franklin to Simon Rich is almost three hundred years, but it looks like a lively skip and a jump rather than a leap. Franklin, forever inventive in the sciences as well as in literature, never stopped writing skits and stories of bugs and aliens and underappreciated left hands, while Rich, the cleverest and funniest of contemporary writers, has taken turns through the consciousness of various characters, from ants to chickens to God, Socratically pondering life's everyday problems. Franklin would've immediately grasped and enjoyed Rich's faux-naïve fancies.

I have arranged the stories chronologically, by date of original publication, and at the end of each story have credited the source. The stories and tales, I have trusted, create their own contexts, so I have noted only the skimpiest of background details about the authors or their works. I thank my friends Max Schott, Enid Stubin, and Jack Wolkenfeld for their suggestions of material.

ACKNOWLEDGMENTS

Langston Hughes: "Wooing the Muse" from *The Best of Simple* by Langston Hughes. Copyright © 1961 by Langston Hughes. Copyright renewed 1989 by George Houston Bass. Reprinted by permission of Hill and Wang, a division of Farrar, Straus and Giroux, LLC. Reprinted by permission of Harold Ober Associates Incorporated.

Howard Kaplan: "How to Fight with Your Wife" by Howard Kaplan, reprinted with permission of the author. Howard Kaplan's work has appeared most recently in *The New England Review*.

Dorothy Parker: "A Telephone Call" from *Dorothy Parker: Complete Stories* by Dorothy Parker, copyright 1924–29, 1931–34, 1937–39, 1941, 1943, 1955, 1958, 1995 by The National Association for the Advancement of Colored People. Used by permission of Penguin, a division of Penguin Group (USA) Inc. and by permission of Gerald Duckworth & Co. Ltd.

Kia Penso: "The Gift" by Kia Penso, reprinted with permission of the author.

Simon Rich: "Center of the Universe" by Simon Rich. Copyright © 2012 Condé Nast. From *The New Yorker*. All rights reserved. Article by Simon Rich. Reprinted by permission.

Philip Roth: "The Conversion of the Jews" from *Goodbye, Columbus* by Philip Roth. Copyright © 1959, renewed 1987 by Philip Roth. Reprinted by permission of Houghton Mifflin Harcourt Publishing Company. All rights reserved.

Jervey Tervalon: "Flight Control" by Jervey Tervalon, reprinted with permission of the author.

James Thurber: "The Secret Life of Walter Mitty" from *My World—And Welcome to It* by James Thurber. Copyright © 1942 by Rosemary A. Thurber. Reprinted by arrangement with Rosemary A. Thurber and The Barbara Hogenson Agency. All rights reserved.

Kurt Vonnegut, Jr.: "Harrison Bergeron" from *Welcome to the Monkey House* by Kurt Vonnegut, Jr., copyright © 1961 by Kurt Vonnegut, Jr. Used by permission of Dell Publishing, a division of Random House, Inc. and the Trust U/W of Kurt Vonnegut, Jr. Any third party use of this material, outside of this publication, is prohibited. Interested parties must apply directly to Random House, Inc., and to the Trust U/W of Kurt Vonnegut, Jr. for permission.

ALICE ADDERTONGUE (1732)

Benjamin Franklin

The most famous American who was never President, Franklin (1706–1790) was not only an important printer, publisher, inventor, and diplomat; he was also America's first great popular writer. He often composed witty articles about topical issues from the point of view of various characters. Here, his Alice Addertongue speaks up for gossip, human nature, and women's rights.

Mr. Gazetteer,

I was highly pleased with your last Week's Paper upon SCANDAL, as the uncommon Doctrine therein preach'd is agreeable both to my Principles and Practice, and as it was published very seasonably to reprove the Impertinence of a Writer in the foregoing Thursday's *Mercury*, who at the Conclusion of one of his silly Paragraphs, laments, forsooth, that the Fair Sex are so peculiarly guilty of this enormous Crime: Every Blockhead ancient and modern, that could handle a Pen, has I think taken upon him to cant in the same sense-less Strain. If to scandalize be really a Crime, what do these Puppies mean? They describe it, they dress it up in the most odious frightful and detestable Colours, they represent it as the worst of Crimes, and then roundly and charitably charge the whole Race of Womankind with it. Are they not then guilty of what they condemn, at the same time that they condemn it? If they accuse us of any other Crime, they must necessarily scandalize while they do it: But to scandalize us with being guilty of Scandal, is in itself an egregious Absurdity, and can proceed from nothing but the most consummate Impudence in Conjunction with the most profound Stupidity.

1

This, supposing, as they do, that to scandalize is a Crime; which you have convinc'd all reasonable People, is an Opinion absolutely erroneous. Let us leave then these Ideot Mock-Moralists, while I entertain you with some Account of my Life and Manners.

I am a young Girl of about thirty-five, and live at present with my Mother. I have no Care upon my Head of getting a Living, and therefore find it my Duty as well as Inclination, to exercise my Talent at Censure, for the Good of my Country folks. There was, I am told, a certain generous Emperor, who if a Day had passed over his Head, in which he had conferred no Benefit on any Man, used to say to his Friends, in Latin, *Diem perdidi,* that is, it seems, I have lost a Day. I believe I should make use of the same Expression, if it were possible for a Day to pass in which I had not, or miss'd, an Opportunity to scandalize somebody: But, Thanks be praised, no such Misfortune has befel me these dozen Years.

Yet, whatever Good I may do, I cannot pretend that I first entred into the Practice of this Virtue from a Principle of Publick Spirit; for I remember that when a Child, I had a violent Inclination to be ever talking in my own Praise, and being continually told that it was ill Manners, and once severely whipt for it, the confin'd Stream form'd itself a new Channel, and I began to speak for the future in the Dispraise of others. This I found more agreable to Company, and almost as much so to my self: For what great Difference can there be, between putting your self up, or putting your Neighbour down? Scandal, like other Virtues, is in part its own Reward, as it gives us the Satisfaction of making our selves appear better than others, or others no better than ourselves.

My Mother, good Woman, and I, have heretofore differ'd upon this Account. She argu'd that Scandal spoilt all good Conversation, and I insisted that without it there could be no such Thing. Our Disputes once rose so high, that we parted Tea-Table, and I concluded to entertain my Acquaintance in the Kitchin. The first Day of this Separation we both drank Tea at the same Time, but she with her Visitors in the Parlor. She would not hear of the least Objection to any one's Character, but began a new sort of Discourse in some such queer philosophical Manner as this; I am mightily pleas'd sometimes, says she, when I observe and consider that the World is not so bad as People out of humour imagine it to be. There is something amiable, some good Quality or other in every body. If we were only to speak of People that are least respected, there is such a one is very dutiful to her Father, and methinks has a fine Set of Teeth; such a one is very respectful to her Husband; such a one is very kind to her poor Neighbours, and besides has a very handsome Shape; such a one is always ready to serve a Friend, and in my Opinion there is not a Woman in Town that has a more agreeable Air and Gait. This fine kind of Talk, which lasted near half an Hour, she concluded by saying, I do not doubt but every one of you have made the like Observations, and I should be glad to have the Conversation continu'd upon this Subject. Just at that Juncture I peep'd in at the Door, and never in my Life before saw such a Set of simple vacant Countenances; they looked somehow neither glad, nor sorry, nor angry, nor pleas'd, nor indifferent, nor attentive; but, (excuse the Simile) like so many blue wooden Images of Rie Doe. I in the Kitchin had already begun a ridiculous Story of Mr. ————'s Intrigue with his Maid, and his Wife's Behaviour upon the Discovery; at some Passages we laugh'd heartily, and one of the gravest of Mama's Company, without making any Answer to her Discourse, got up to go and see what the Girls were so merry about: She was follow'd by a Second, and shortly after by a Third, till at last the old Gentlewoman found herself quite alone, and being convinc'd that her Project was impracticable, came her self and finish'd her Tea with us; ever since which Saul also has been among the Prophets, and our Disputes lie dormant.

By Industry and Application, I have made my self the Center of all the Scandal in the Province, there is little stirring but I hear of it. I began the World with this Maxim, That no Trade can subsist without Returns; and accordingly, whenever I receiv'd a good Story, I endeavour'd to give two or a better in the Room of it. My Punctuality in this Way of Dealing gave such Encouragement, that it has procur'd me an incredible deal of Business, which without Diligence and good Method it would be impossible for me to go through. For besides the Stock of Defamation thus naturally flowing in upon me, I practice an Art by which I can pump Scandal out of People that are the least enclin'd that way. Shall I discover my Secret? Yes; to let it die with me would be inhuman.—If I have never heard Ill of some Person, I always impute it to defective Intelligence; for there are none without their Faults, no not one. If she is a Woman, I take the first Opportunity to let all her Acquaintance know I have heard that one of the handsomest or best Men in Town has said something in Praise either of her Beauty, her Wit, her Virtue, or her good Management. If you know any thing of Humane Nature, you perceive that this naturally introduces a Conversation turning upon all her Failings, past, present, and to come. To the same purpose, and with the same Success, I cause every Man of Reputation to be praised before his Competitors in Love, Business, or Esteem on Account of any particular Qualification. Near the Times of Election, if I find it necessary, I commend every Candidate before some of the opposite Party, listning attentively to what is said of him in answer: (But Commendations in this latter Case are not always necessary, and should be used judiciously;) of late Years I needed only observe what they said of one another freely; and having for the Help of Memory taken Account of all Information & Accusations received, whoever peruses my Writings after my Death, may happen to think, that during a certain Term, the People of Pennsylvania chose into all their Offices of Honour and Trust, the veriest Knaves, Fools and Rascals in the whole Province. The Time of Election used to be a busy Time with me, but this Year, with Concern I speak it, People are grown so good natur'd, so intent upon mutual Feasting and friendly Entertainment, that I see no Prospect of much Employment from that Quarter.

I mention'd above, that without good Method I could not go thro' my Business: In my Father's Life-time I had some Instruction in Accompts, which I now apply with Advantage to my own Affairs. I keep a regular Set of Books, and can tell at an Hour's Warning how it stands between me and the World. In my Daybook I enter every Article of Defamation as it is transacted; for Scandals receiv'd in, I give Credit; and when I pay them out again, I make the Persons to whom they respectively relate Debtor. In my Journal, I add to each Story by Way of Improvement, such probable Circumstances as I think it will bear, and in my Ledger the whole is regularly posted.

I suppose the Reader already condemns me in his Heart, for this particular of adding Circumstances; but I justify that part of my Practice thus. 'Tis a Principle with me, that none ought to have a greater Share of Reputation than they really deserve; if they have, 'tis an Imposition upon the Publick: I know it is every one's Interest, and therefore believe they endeavour, to conceal all their Vices and Follies; and I hold, that those People are extraordinary foolish or careless who suffer a Fourth of their Failings to come to publick Knowledge: Taking then the common Prudence and Imprudence of Mankind in a Lump, I suppose none suffer above one Fifth to be discovered: Therefore when I hear of any Person's Misdoing, I think I keep within Bounds if in relating it I only make it three times worse than it is; and I reserve to my self the Privilege of charging them with one Fault in four, which, for aught I know, they may be entirely innocent of. You see there are but few so careful of doing Justice as my self; what Reason then have Mankind to complain of Scandal? In a general way, the worst that is said of us is only half what might be said, if all our Faults were seen.

But alas, two great Evils have lately befaln me at the same time; an extream Cold that I can scarce speak, and a most terrible Toothach that I dare hardly open my Mouth: For some Days past I have receiv'd ten Stories for one I have paid; and I am not able to ballance my Accounts without your Assistance. I have long thought that if you would make your Paper a Vehicle of Scandal, you would double the Number of your Subscribers. I send you herewith Account of 4 Knavish Tricks, 2 crackt M—n—ds, 5 Cu—ld—ms, 3 drub'd Wives, and 4 Henpeck'd Husbands, all within this Fortnight; which you may, as Articles of News, deliver to the Publick; and if my Toothach continues, shall send you more; being, in the mean time,

Your constant Reader,
ALICE ADDERTONGUE

I thank my Correspondent Mrs. Addertongue for her Good-Will; but desire to be excus'd inserting the Articles of News she has sent me; such Things being in Reality no News at all.

SOURCE: *The Pennsylvania Gazette*. September 12, 1732.

RIP VAN WINKLE: A POSTHUMOUS TALE OF DIEDRICH KNICKERBOCKER
(1819–1820)

Washington Irving

Born in New York, Irving (1783–1859) was educated to become a lawyer but instead became famous for his comic A History of New York *(1809). "Rip Van Winkle" appeared in Irving's* The Sketchbook of Geoffrey Crayon, Gent., *and while its outline is well-known, the fine story itself is too rarely read.*

NOTE: The following Tale was found among the papers of the late Diedrich Knickerbocker, an old gentleman of New York, who was very curious in the Dutch history of the province, and the manners of the descendants from its primitive settlers. His historical researches, however, did not lie so much among books as among men; for the former are lamentably scanty on his favorite topics; whereas he found the old burghers, and still more their wives, rich in that legendary lore so invaluable to true history. Whenever, therefore, he happened upon a genuine Dutch family, snugly shut up in its low-roofed farmhouse, under a spreading sycamore, he looked upon it as a little clasped volume of black-letter, and studied it with the zeal of a book-worm.

The result of all these researches was a history of the province during the reign of the Dutch governors, which he published some years since. There have been various opinions as to the literary character of his work, and, to tell the truth, it is not a whit better than it should be. Its chief merit is its scrupulous accuracy, which indeed was a little questioned on its first appearance, but has since been completely established; and it is now admitted into all historical collections as a book of unquestionable authority.

The old gentleman died shortly after the publication of his work; and now that he is dead and gone, it cannot do much harm to his memory to say that his time might have been much better employed in weightier labors. He, however, was apt to ride his hobby his own way; and though it did now and then kick up the dust a little in the eyes of his neighbors, and grieve the spirit of some friends, for whom he felt the truest deference and affection, yet his errors and follies are remembered "more in sorrow than in anger," and it begins to be suspected that he never intended to injure or offend. But however his memory may be appreciated by critics, it is still held dear by many folk whose good opinion is well worth having; particularly by certain biscuit-bakers, who have gone so far as to imprint his likeness on their new-year cakes; and have thus given him a chance for immortality, almost equal to the being stamped on a Waterloo Medal, or a Queen Anne's Farthing.

Whoever has made a voyage up the Hudson must remember the Kaatskill Mountains. They are a dismembered branch of the great Appalachian family, and are seen away to the west of the river, swelling up to a noble height, and lording it over the surrounding country. Every change of season, every change of weather, indeed, every hour of the day, produces some change in the magical hues and shapes of these mountains, and they are regarded by all the good wives, far and near, as perfect barometers. When the weather is fair and settled, they are clothed in blue and purple, and print their bold outlines on the clear evening sky; but, sometimes, when the rest of the landscape is cloudless, they will gather a hood of gray vapors about their summits, which, in the last rays of the setting sun, will glow and light up like a crown of glory.

At the foot of these fairy mountains, the voyager may have descried the light smoke curling up from a village, whose shingle-roofs gleam among the trees, just where the blue tints of the upland melt away into the fresh green of the nearer landscape. It is a little village of great antiquity, having been founded by some of the Dutch colonists, in the early times of the province, just about the beginning of the government of the good Peter Stuyvesant (may he rest in peace!), and there were some of the houses of the original settlers standing within a few years, built of small yellow bricks brought from Holland, having latticed windows and gable fronts, surmounted with weather-cocks.

In that same village, and in one of these very houses (which, to tell the precise truth, was sadly time-worn and weather-beaten), there lived many years since, while the country was yet a province of Great Britain, a simple good-natured fellow of the name of Rip Van Winkle. He was a descendant of the Van Winkles who figured so gallantly in the chivalrous days of Peter Stuyvesant, and accompanied him to the siege of Fort Christina. He inherited, however, but little of the martial character of his ancestors. I have observed that he was a simple, good-natured man; he was, moreover, a kind neighbor, and an obedient, hen-pecked husband. Indeed, to the latter circumstance might be owing that meekness of spirit which gained him such universal popularity; for those men are most apt to be obsequious and conciliating abroad, who are under the discipline of shrews at home. Their tempers, doubtless, are rendered pliant and malleable in the fiery furnace of domestic tribulation; and a curtain lecture is worth all the sermons in the world for teaching the virtues of patience and long-suffering. A termagant wife may, therefore, in some respects, be considered a tolerable blessing; and if so, Rip Van Winkle was thrice blessed.

Certain it is that he was a great favorite among all the good wives of the village, who, as usual with the amiable sex, took his part in all family squabbles, and never failed, whenever they talked those matters over in their evening gossipings, to lay all the blame on Dame Van Winkle. The children of the village, too, would shout with joy whenever he approached. He assisted at their sports, made their playthings, taught them to fly kites and shoot marbles, and told them long stories of ghosts, witches and Indians. Whenever he went dodging about the village, he was surrounded by a troop of them, hanging on his skirts, clambering on his back, and playing a thousand tricks on him with impunity; and not a dog would bark at him throughout the neighborhood.

The great error in Rip's composition was an insuperable aversion to all kinds of profitable labor. It could not be from the want of assiduity or perseverance; for he would sit on a wet rock, with a rod as long and heavy as a Tartar's lance, and fish all day without a murmur, even though he should not be encouraged by a single nibble. He would carry a fowling-piece on his shoulder for hours together, trudging through woods and swamps, and up hill and down dale, to shoot a few squirrels or wild pigeons. He would never refuse to assist a neighbor even in the roughest toil, and was a foremost man at all country frolics for husking Indian corn, or building stone-fences; the women of the village, too, used to employ him to run their errands, and to do such little odd jobs as their less obliging husbands would not do for them. In a word, Rip was ready to attend to anybody's business but his own; but as to doing family duty, and keeping his farm in order, he found it impossible.

In fact, he declared it was of no use to work on his farm: it was the most pestilent little piece of ground in the whole country; everything about it went wrong, and would go wrong, in spite of him. His fences were continually falling to pieces; his cow would either go astray, or get among the cabbages; weeds were sure to grow quicker in his fields than anywhere else; the rain always made a point of setting in just as he had some outdoor work to do; so that, though his patrimonial estate had dwindled away under his management, acre by sere, until there was little more left than a mere patch of Indian corn and potatoes, yet it was the worst con-ditioned farm in the neighborhood.

His children, too, were as ragged and wild as if they belonged to nobody. His son Rip, an urchin begotten in his own likeness, promised to inherit the habits with the old clothes of his father. He was generally seen trooping like a colt at his mother's heels, equipped in a pair of his father's cast-off galligaskins, which he had much ado to hold up with one hand, as a fine lady does her train in bad weather.

Rip Van Winkle, however, was one of those happy mortals, of foolish, well-oiled dispositions, who take the world easy, eat white bread or brown, whichever can be got with least thought or trou-ble, and would rather starve on a penny than work for a pound. If left to himself, he would have whistled life away in perfect content-ment; but his wife kept continually dinning in his ears about his idleness, his carelessness and the ruin he was bringing on his family. Morning, noon and night her tongue was incessantly going, and everything he said or did was sure to produce a torrent of house-hold eloquence. Rip had one way of replying to all lectures of the kind, and that, by frequent use, had grown into a habit. He shrugged his shoulders, shook his head, cast up his eyes, but said nothing. This, however, always provoked a fresh volley from his wife; so that he was fain to draw off his forces, and take to the outside of the house—the only side which, in truth, belongs to a hen-pecked husband.

Rip's old domestic adherent was his dog Wolf, who was as much hen-pecked as his master; for Dame Van Winkle regarded them as companions in idleness, and even looked upon Wolf with an evil eye, as the cause of his master's going so often astray. True it is, in all points of spirit befitting an honorable dog, he was as courageous an animal as ever scoured the woods—but what courage can with-stand the ever-enduring and all-besetting terrors of a woman's tongue? The moment Wolf entered the house his crest fell, his tail dropped to the ground, or curled between his legs, he sneaked about with a gallows air, casting many a sidelong glance at Dame Van Winkle, and at the least flourish of a broom-stick or ladle, he would fly to the door with yelping precipitation.

Times grew worse and worse with Rip Van Winkle as years of matrimony rolled on; a tart temper never mellows with age, and a sharp tongue is the only edged tool that grows keener with constant use. For a long while he used to console himself, when driven from home, by frequenting a kind of perpetual club of the sages, philoso-phers, and other idle personages of the village; which held its ses-sions on a bench before a small inn, designated by a rubicund portrait of His Majesty George the Third. Here they used to sit in the shade through a long lazy summer's day, talking listlessly over village gossip, or telling endless sleepy stories about nothing. But it would have been worth any statesman's money to have heard the profound discussions that sometimes took place, when by chance an old newspaper fell into their hands from some passing traveler. How solemnly they would listen to the contents, as drawled out by Derrick Van Bummel, the schoolmaster, a dapper, learned little man, who was not to be daunted by the most gigantic word in the dictionary; and how sagely they would deliberate upon public events some months after they had taken place!

The opinions of this junto were completely controlled by Nicholas Vedder, a patriarch of the village, and landlord of the inn, at the door of which he took his seat from morning till night, just moving sufficiently to avoid the sun and keep in the shade of a large tree; so that the neighbors could tell the hour by his movements as accurately as by a sun-dial. It is true he was rarely heard to speak, but smoked his pipe incessantly. His adherents, however (for every great man has his adherents), perfectly understood him, and knew how to gather his opinions. When anything that was read or related displeased him, he was observed to smoke his pipe vehemently, and to send forth short, frequent and angry puffs; but when pleased, he would inhale the smoke slowly and tranquilly, and emit it in light and placid clouds; and sometimes, taking the pipe from his mouth, and letting the fragrant vapor curl about his nose, would gravely nod his head in token of perfect approbation.

From even this stronghold the unlucky Rip was at length routed by his termagant wife, who would suddenly break in upon the tranquility of the assemblage and call the members all to naught; nor was that august personage, Nicholas Vedder himself, sacred from the daring tongue of this terrible virago, who charged him outright with encouraging her husband in habits of idleness.

Poor Rip was at last reduced almost to despair; and his only alternative, to escape from the labor of the farm and clamor of his wife, was to take gun in hand and stroll away into the woods. Here he would sometimes seat himself at the foot of a tree, and share the contents of his wallet with Wolf, with whom he sympathized as a fellow-sufferer in persecution. "Poor Wolf," he would say, "thy mistress leads thee a dog's life of it; but never mind, my lad, whilst I live thou shalt never want a friend to stand by thee!" Wolf would wag his tail, look wistfully in his master's face, and if dogs can feel pity, I verily believe he reciprocated the sentiment with all his heart.

In a long ramble of the kind on a fine autumnal day, Rip had unconsciously scrambled to one of the highest parts of the Kaatskill Mountains. He was after his favorite sport of squirrel shooting, and the still solitudes had echoed and re-echoed with the reports of his gun. Panting and fatigued, he threw himself, late in the afternoon, on a green knoll, covered with mountain herbage, that crowned the brow of a precipice. From an opening between the trees he could overlook all the lower country for many a mile of rich woodland. He saw at a distance the lordly Hudson, far, far below him, moving on its silent but majestic course, with the reflection of a purple cloud, or the sail of a lagging bark, here and there sleeping on its grassy bosom, and at last losing itself in the blue highlands.

On the other side he looked down into a deep mountain glen, wild, lonely and shagged, the bottom filled with fragments from the impending cliffs, and scarcely lighted by the reflected rays of the setting sun. For some time Rip lay musing on this scene; evening was gradually advancing; the mountains began to throw their long blue shadows over the valleys; he saw that it would be dark long before he could reach the village, and he heaved a heavy sigh when he thought of encountering the terrors of Dame Van Winkle.

As he was about to descend, he heard a voice from a distance hallooing, "Rip Van Winkle! Rip Van Winkle!" He looked round, but could see nothing but a crow winging its solitary flight across the mountain. He thought his fancy must have deceived him, and turned again to descend, when he heard the same cry ring through the still evening air; "Rip Van Winkle! Rip Van Winkle!"—at the same time Wolf bristled up his back, and giving a low growl, skulked to his master's side, looking fearfully down into the glen. Rip now felt a vague apprehension stealing over him; he looked anxiously in the same direction, and perceived a strange figure slowly toiling up the rocks, and bending under the weight of something he carried on his back. He was surprised to see any human being in this lonely and unfrequented place, but supposing it to be some one of the neighborhood in need of his assistance, he hastened down to yield it.

On nearer approach he was still more surprised at the singularity of the stranger's appearance. He was a short, square-built old fellow, with thick bushy hair, and a grizzled beard. His dress was of the antique Dutch fashion—a cloth jerkin strapped round the waist—several pair of breeches, the outer one of ample volume, decorated with rows of buttons down the sides, and bunches at the knees. He bore on his shoulder a stout keg, that seemed full of liquor, and made signs for Rip to approach and assist him with the load. Though rather shy and distrustful of this new acquaintance, Rip complied with his usual alacrity; and mutually relieving one another, they clambered up a narrow gully, apparently the dry bed of a mountain torrent. As they ascended, Rip every now and then heard long rolling peals like distant thunder, that seemed to issue out of a deep ravine, or, rather, cleft, between lofty rocks, toward which their rugged path conducted. He paused for an instant, but supposing it to be the muttering of one of those transient thundershowers which often take place in mountain heights, he proceeded. Passing through the ravine they came to a hollow, like a small amphitheatre, surrounded by perpendicular precipices, over the brinks of which impending trees shot their branches, so that you only caught glimpses of the azure sky and the bright evening cloud.

During the whole time Rip and his companion had labored on in silence; for though the former marveled greatly what could be the object of carrying a keg of liquor up this wild mountain, yet there was something strange and incomprehensible about the unknown, that inspired awe and checked familiarity.

On entering the amphitheatre, new objects of wonder presented themselves. On a level spot in the center was a company of odd-looking personages playing at nine-pins. They were dressed in a quaint outlandish fashion; some wore short doublets, others jerkins, with long knives in their belts, and most of them had enormous breeches, of similar style with that of the guide's. Their visages, too, were peculiar: one had a large beard, broad face, and small piggish eyes: the face of another seemed to consist entirely of nose, and was surmounted by a white sugar-loaf hat set off with a little red cock's tail. They all had beards, of various shapes and colors. There was one who seemed to be the commander. He was a stout old gentleman, with a weather-beaten countenance; he wore a laced doublet, broad belt and hanger, high-crowned hat and feather, red stockings and high-heeled shoes, with roses in them. The whole group reminded Rip of the figures in an old Flemish painting, in the parlor of Dominie Van Shaick, the village parson, and which had been brought over from Holland at the time of the settlement.

What seemed particularly odd to Rip was, that though these folks were evidently amusing themselves, yet they maintained the gravest faces, the most mysterious silence, and were, withal, the most melancholy party of pleasure he had ever witnessed. Nothing interrupted the stillness of the scene but the noise of the balls, which, whenever they were rolled, echoed along the mountains like rumbling peals of thunder.

As Rip and his companion approached them, they suddenly desisted from their play, and stared at him with such fixed statue-like gaze, and such strange, uncouth, lack-lustre countenances, that his heart turned within him, and his knees smote together. His companion now emptied the contents of the keg into large flagons, and made signs to him to wait upon the company. He obeyed with fear and trembling; they quaffed the liquor in profound silence, and then returned to their game.

By degrees Rip's awe and apprehension subsided. He even ventured, when no eye was fixed upon him, to taste the beverage, which he found had much of the flavor of excellent Hollands. He was naturally a thirsty soul, and was soon tempted to repeat the draught. One taste provoked another; and he reiterated his visits to the flagon so often that at length his senses were over powered, his eyes swam in his head, his head gradually declined, and he fell into a deep sleep.

On waking, he found himself on the green knoll whence he had first seen the old man of the glen. He rubbed his eyes—it was a bright sunny morning. The birds were hopping and twittering among the bushes, and the eagle was wheeling aloft, and breasting the pure mountain breeze. "Surely," thought Rip, "I have not slept here all night." He recalled the occurrences before he fell asleep: the strange man with a keg of liquor—the mountain ravine—the wild retreat among the rocks—the woebegone party at nine-pins—the flagon—"Oh! that flagon! that wicked flagon!" thought Rip—"what excuse shall I make to Dame Van Winkle!"

He looked round for his gun, but in place of the clean, well-oiled fowling-piece, he found an old firelock lying by him, the barrel incrusted with rust, the lock falling off, and the stock worm-eaten. He now suspected that the grave roisters of the mountain had put a trick upon him, and, having dosed him with liquor, had robbed him of his gun. Wolf, too, had disappeared, but he might have strayed away after a squirrel or partridge. He whistled after him and shouted his name, but all in vain; the echoes repeated his whistle and shout, but no dog was to be seen.

He determined to revisit the scene of the last evening's gambol, and if he met with any of the party, to demand his dog and gun. As he rose to walk, he found himself stiff in the joints, and wanting in his usual activity. "These mountain beds do not agree with me," thought Rip, "and if this frolic should lay me up with a fit of the rheumatism, I shall have a blessed time with Dame Van Winkle." With some difficulty he got down into the glen: he found the gully up which he and his companion had ascended the preceding evening; but to his astonishment a mountain stream was now foaming down it, leaping from rock to rock, and filling the glen with babbling murmurs. He, however, made a shift to scramble up its sides, working his toilsome way through thickets of birch, sassafras and witch-hazel and sometimes tripped up or entangled by the wild grapevines that twisted their coils or tendrils from tree to tree, and spread a kind of network in his path. At length he reached to where the ravine had opened through the cliffs to the amphitheatre; but no traces of such opening remained. The rocks presented a high impenetrable wall over which the torrent came tumbling in a sheet of feathery foam, and fell into a broad deep basin, black from the shadows of the surrounding forest. Here, then, poor Rip was brought to a stand. He again called and whistled after his dog; he was only answered by the cawing of a flock of idle crows, sporting high in air about a dry tree that overhung a sunny precipice; and who, secure in their elevation, seemed to look down and scoff at the poor man's perplexities. What was to be done? the morning was passing away, and Rip felt famished for want of his breakfast. He grieved to give up his dog and gun; he dreaded to meet his wife; but it would not do to starve among the mountains. He shook his head, shouldered the rusty firelock, and, with a heart full of trouble and anxiety, turned his steps homeward.

As he approached the village he met a number of people, but none whom he knew, which somewhat surprised him, for he had thought himself acquainted with every one in the country round. Their dress, too, was of a different fashion from that to which he was accustomed. They all stared at him with equal marks of surprise, and, whenever they cast their eyes upon him, invariably stroked their chins. The constant recurrence of this gesture induced Rip, involuntarily, to do the same, when, to his astonishment, he found his beard had grown a foot long!

He had now entered the skirts of the village. A troop of strange children ran at his heels, hooting after him, and pointing at his gray beard. The dogs, too, not one of which he recognized for an old acquaintance, barked at him as he passed. The very village was altered; it was larger and more populous. There were rows of houses which he had never seen before, and those which had been his familiar haunts had disappeared. Strange names were over the doors—strange faces at the windows—everything was strange. His mind now misgave him; he began to doubt whether both he and the world around him were not bewitched. Surely this was his native village, which he had left but the day before. There stood the Kaatskill Mountains—there ran the silver Hudson at a distance—there was every hill and dale precisely as it had always been—Rip was sorely perplexed—"That flagon last night," thought he, "has addled my poor head sadly!"

It was with some difficulty that he found the way to his own house, which he approached with silent awe, expecting every moment to hear the shrill voice of Dame Van Winkle. He found the house gone to decay—the roof had fallen in, the windows shattered, and the doors off the hinges. A half-starved dog that looked like Wolf was skulking about it. Rip called him by name, but the cur snarled, showed his teeth, and passed on. This was an unkind cut indeed—"My very dog," sighed poor Rip, "has forgotten me!"

He entered the house, which, to tell the truth, Dame Van Winkle had always kept in neat order. It was empty, forlorn, and apparently abandoned. This desolateness overcame all his connubial fears—he called loudly for his wife and children—the lonely chambers rang for a moment with his voice, and then all again was silence.

He now hurried forth, and hastened to his old resort, the village inn—but it too was gone. A large rickety wooden building stood in its place, with great gaping windows, some of them broken and mended with old hats and petticoats, and over the door was painted, "The Union Hotel, by Jonathan Doolittle." Instead of the great tree that used to shelter the quiet little Dutch inn of yore, there now was reared a tall naked pole, with something on the top that looked like a red night-cap, and from it was fluttering a flag, on which was a singular assemblage of stars and stripes—all this was strange and incomprehensible. He recognized on the sign, however, the ruby face of King George, under which he had smoked so many a peaceful pipe; but even this was singularly metamorphosed. The red coat was changed for one of blue and buff, a sword was held in the hand instead of a scepter, the head was decorated with a cocked hat, and underneath was painted in large characters, "General Washington."

There was, as usual, a crowd of folk about the door, but none that Rip recollected. The very character of the people seemed changed. There was a busy, bustling, disputatious tone about it instead of the accustomed phlegm and drowsy tranquility. He looked in vain for the sage Nicholas Vedder, with his broad face, double chin, and fair long pipe, uttering clouds of tobacco-smoke instead of idle speeches; or Van Bummel, the schoolmaster, doling forth the contents of an ancient newspaper. In place of these, a lean, bilious-looking fellow, with his pockets full of handbills, was haranguing vehemently about rights of citizens—elections—members of Congress—liberty—Bunker's Hill—heroes of Seventy-six—and other words, which were a perfect Babylonish jargon to the bewildered Van Winkle.

The appearance of Rip, with his long grizzled beard, his rusty fowling-piece, his uncouth dress, and an army of women and children at his heels, soon attracted the attention of the tavern politicians. They crowded round him, eyeing him from head to foot with great curiosity. The orator bustled up to him, and, drawing him partly aside, inquired "on which side he voted?" Rip stared in vacant stupidity. Another short but busy little fellow pulled him by the arm, and, rising on tiptoe, inquired in his ear, "Whether he was Federal or Democrat?" Rip was equally at a loss to comprehend the question; when a knowing, self-important old gentleman, in a sharp cocked hat, made his way through the crowd, putting them to the right and left with his elbows as he passed, and planting himself before Van Winkle, with one arm akimbo, the other resting on his cane, his keen eyes and sharp hat penetrating, as it were, into his very soul, demanded in an austere tone, "what brought him to the election with a gun on his shoulder, and a mob at his heels, and whether he meant to breed a riot in the village?"—"Alas! gentlemen," cried Rip, somewhat dismayed, "I am a poor quiet man, a native of the place, and a loyal subject of the king, God bless him!"

Here a general shout burst from the by-standers—"a Tory! a Tory! a spy! a refugee! hustle him! away with him!" It was with great difficulty that the self-important man in the cocked hat restored order; and, having assumed a tenfold austerity of brow, demanded again of the unknown culprit what he came there for, and whom he was seeking? The poor man humbly assured him that he meant no harm, but merely came there in search of some of his neighbors, who used to keep about the tavern.

"Well—who are they?—name them."

Rip thought himself a moment, and inquired, "Where's Nicholas Vedder?"

There was a silence for a little while, when an old man replied, in a thin piping voice, "Nicholas Vedder! why, he is dead and gone these eighteen years! There was a wooden tombstone in the church-yard that used to tell all about him, but that's rotten and gone too."

"Where's Brom Dutcher?"

"Oh, he went off to the army in the beginning of the war; some say he was killed at the storming of Stony Point—others say he was drowned in a squall at the foot of Antony's Nose . . . I don't know—he never came back again."

"Where's Van Bummel, the schoolmaster?"

"He went off to the wars too, was a great militia general, and is now in Congress."

Rip's heart died away at hearing of these sad changes in his home and friends, and finding himself thus alone in the world. Every answer puzzled him too, by treating of such enormous lapses of time, and of matters which he could not understand: war—Congress—Stony Point—he had no courage to ask after any more friends, but cried out in despair, "Does nobody here know Rip Van Winkle?"

"Oh, Rip Van Winkle!" exclaimed two or three, "Oh, to be sure! that's Rip Van Winkle yonder, leaning against the tree."

Rip looked, and beheld a precise counterpart of himself, as he went up the mountain: apparently as lazy, and certainly as ragged. The poor fellow was now completely confounded. He doubted his own identity, and whether he was himself or another man. In the midst of his bewilderment, the man in the cocked hat demanded who he was, and what was his name?

"God knows," exclaimed he, at his wit's end; "I'm not myself—I'm somebody else—that's me yonder—no—that's somebody else got into my shoes—I was myself last night, but I fell asleep on the mountain, and they've changed my gun, and every thing's changed, and I'm changed, and I can't tell what's my name, or who I am!"

The by-standers began now to look at each other, nod, wink significantly, and tap their fingers against their foreheads. There was a whisper, also, about securing the gun, and keeping the old fellow from doing mischief, at the very suggestion of which the self-important man in the cocked hat retired with some precipitation. At this critical moment a fresh, comely woman pressed through the throng to get a peep at the gray-bearded man. She had a chubby child in her arms, which, frightened at his looks, began to cry. "Hush, Rip," cried she, "hush, you little fool; the old man won't hurt you." The name of the child, the air of the mother, the tone of her voice, all awakened a train of recollections in his mind. "What is your name, my good woman?" asked he.

"Judith Gardenier."

"And your father's name?"

"Ah, poor man, Rip Van Winkle was his name, but it's twenty years since he went away from home with his gun, and never has been heard of since—his dog came home without him; but whether he shot himself, or was carried away by the Indians, nobody can tell. I was then but a little girl."

Rip had but one question more to ask; but he put it with a faltering voice:

"Where's your mother?"

"Oh, she too had died but a short time since; she broke a blood-vessel in a fit of passion at a New-England peddler."

There was a drop of comfort, at least, in this intelligence. The honest man could contain himself no longer. He caught his daughter and her child in his arms. "I am your father!" cried he—"Young Rip Van Winkle once—old Rip Van Winkle now! Does nobody know poor Rip Van Winkle?"

All stood amazed, until an old woman, tottering out from among the crowd, put her hand to her brow, and peering under it in his face for a moment, exclaimed, "Sure enough! It is Rip Van Winkle—it is himself! Welcome home again, old neighbor—why, where have you been these twenty long years?"

Rip's story was soon told, for the whole twenty years had been to him as one night. The neighbors stared when they heard it; some were seen to wink at each other, and put their tongues in their cheeks: and the self-important man in the cocked hat, who, when the alarm was over, had returned to the field, screwed down the corners of his mouth, and shook his head, upon which there was a general shaking of the head throughout the assemblage.

It was determined, however, to take the opinion of old Peter Vanderdonk, who was seen slowly advancing up the road. He was a descendant of the historian of that name, who wrote one of the earliest accounts of the province. Peter was the most ancient inhabitant of the village, and well versed in all the wonderful events and traditions of the neighborhood. He recollected Rip at once, and corroborated his story in the most satisfactory manner. He assured the company that it was a fact, handed down from his ancestor the historian, that the Kaatskill Mountains had always been haunted by strange beings; that it was affirmed that the great Hendrick Hudson, the first discoverer of the river and country, kept a kind of vigil there every twenty years, with his crew of the Half-Moon, being permitted in this way to revisit the scenes of his enterprise, and keep a guardian eye upon the river, and the great city called by his name; that his father had once seen them in their old Dutch dresses playing at nine-pins in a hollow of the mountain; and that he himself had heard, one summer afternoon, the sound of their balls, like distant peals of thunder.

To make a long story short, the company broke up, and returned to the more important concerns of the election. Rip's daughter took him home to live with her; she had a snug, well-furnished house, and a stout cheery farmer for a husband, whom Rip recollected for one of the urchins that used to climb upon his back. As to Rip's son and heir, who was the ditto of himself, seen leaning against the tree, he was employed to work on the farm; but evinced an hereditary disposition to attend to anything else but his business.

Rip now resumed his old walks and habits; he soon found many of his former cronies, though all rather the worse for the wear and tear of time; and preferred making friends among the rising generation, with whom he soon grew into great favor.

Having nothing to do at home, and being arrived at that happy age when a man can be idle with impunity, he took his place once more on the bench at the inn door, and was reverenced as one of the patriarchs of the village, and a chronicle of the old times "before the war." It was some time before he could get into the regular track of gossip, or could be made to comprehend the strange events that had taken place during his torpor. How that there had been a Revolutionary war—that the country had thrown off the yoke of old England—and that, instead of being a subject of his Majesty George the Third, he was now a free citizen of the United States. Rip, in fact, was no politician; the changes of states and empires made but little impression on him; but there was one species of despotism under which he had long groaned, and that was—petticoat government. Happily that was at an end; he had got his neck out of the yoke of matrimony, and could go in and out whenever he pleased, without dreading the tyranny of Dame Van Winkle. Whenever her name was mentioned, however, he shook his head, shrugged his shoulders, and cast up his eyes; which might pass either for an expression of resignation to his fate, or joy at his deliverance.

He used to tell his story to every stranger that arrived at Mr. Doolittle's hotel. He was observed, at first, to vary on some points every time he told it, which was, doubtless, owing to his having so recently awakened. It at last settled down precisely to the tale I have related, and not a man, woman or child in the neighborhood, but knew it by heart. Some always pretended to doubt the reality of it, and insisted that Rip had been out of his head, and that this was one point on which he always remained flighty. The old Dutch inhabitants, however, almost universally gave it full credit. Even to this day they never hear a thunderstorm of a summer afternoon about the Kaatskill, but they say Hendrick Hudson and his crew are at their game of nine-pins; and it is a common wish of all hen-pecked husbands in the neighborhood, when life hangs heavy on their hands, that they might have a quieting draught out of Rip Van Winkle's flagon.

SOURCE: Washington Irving. *The Sketch Book of Geoffrey Crayon, Gent.* New York: George P. Putnam, 1848.

SELECTING THE FACULTY (1855)

Robert Carlton (Baynard Rush Hall)

Hall wrote The New Purchase: Or, Early Years in the Far West *as a history of the settlement of Monroe County, Indiana, but in his wonderful unsupressible excess of humor, could not help himself from including comical fictionalized episodes, including this one.*

Our Board of Trustees, it will be remembered, had been directed by the Legislature to procure, as the ordinance called it, "Teachers for the commencement of the State College at Woodville." That business, by the Board, was committed to Dr. Sylvan and Robert Carlton—the most learned gentlemen of the body, and of—the New Purchase! Our honourable Board will be more specially introduced hereafter; at present we shall bring forward certain rejected candidates, that, like rejected prize essays, they may be published, and *thus* have their revenge.

None can tell us how plenty good things are till he looks for them; and hence, to the great surprise of the Committee, there seemed to be a sudden growth and a large crop of persons even in and around Woodville, either already qualified for the "Professorships," as we named them in our publications, or who *could* "qualify" by the time of election. As to the "chair" named also in our publications, one very worthy and disinterested schoolmaster offered, as a great collateral inducement for his being elected, *"to find his own chair!"*—a vast saving to the State, if the same chair I saw in Mr. Whackum's school-room. For his chair there was one with a hickory bottom; and doubtless he would have filled it, and even lapped over its edges, with equal dignity in the recitation room of Big College.

22

The Committee had, at an early day, given an invitation to the Rev. Charles Clarence, A. M., of New Jersey, and his answer had been affirmative; yet for political reasons we had been obliged to invite competitors, or *make* them, and we found and created "a right smart sprinkle."

Hopes of success were built on many things—for instance, on poverty; a plea being entered that some thing ought to be done for the poor fellow—on one's having taught a common school all his born days, who now deserved to rise a peg—on political, or religious, or fanatical partisan qualifications—and on pure patriotic principles, such as a person's having been "born in a canebrake and rocked in a sugar trough." On the other hand, a fat, dull-headed, and modest Englishman asked for a place, because he had been born in Liverpool! and had seen the world beyond the woods and waters too! And another fussy, talkative, pragmatical little gentleman, rested his pretensions on his ability to draw and paint maps!—not projecting them in roundabout scientific processes, but in that speedy and elegant style in which young ladies *copy* maps at first chop boarding schools! Nay, so transcendent seemed Mr. Merchator's claims, when his *show* or *sample* maps were exhibited to us, that some in our Board, and nearly everybody out of it, were confident he would do for Professor of Mathematics and even Principal.

But of all our unsuccessful candidates, we shall introduce by name only two—Mr. James Jimmey, A.S.S., and Mr. Solomon Rapid, A. to Z.

Mr. Jimmey, who aspired to the mathematical chair, was master of a small school of all sexes, near Woodville. At the first, he was kindly, yet honestly told, his knowledge was too limited and inaccurate; yet, notwithstanding this, and some almost rude repulses afterwards, he persisted in his application and his hopes. To give evidence of competency, he once told me he was arranging a new spelling-book, the publication of which would make him known as a literary man, and be an unspeakable advantage to "the rising generation." And this naturally brought on the following colloquy about the work:—

"Ah! indeed! Mr. Jimmey?"

"Yes, indeed, Mr. Carlton."

"On what new principle do you go, sir?"

"Why, sir, on the principles of nature and common sense. I allow school-books for schools are all too powerful obstruse and hard-like to be understood without exemplifying illustrations."

"Yes, but Mr. Jimmey, how is a child's spelling-book to be made any plainer?"

"Why, sir, by clear explifications of the words in one column, by exemplifying illustrations in the other."

"I do not understand you, Mr. Jimmey, give me a specimen."

"Sir?"

"An example."

"To be sure—here's a spes-a-example; you see, for instance, I put in the spelling column, C-r-e-a-m, *cream,* and here in the explification column, I put the exemplifying illustration—*Unctious part of milk!*"

We had asked, at our first interview, if our candidate was an algebraist, and his reply was *negative;* but, "he allowed he could '*qualify*' by the time of election, as he was powerful good at figures, and had cyphered clean through every arithmetic he had ever seen, the rule of promiscuous questions and all!" Hence, some weeks after, as I was passing his door, on my way to a squirrel hunt, with a party of friends, Mr. Jimmey, hurrying out with a slate in his hand, begged me to stop a moment, and thus addressed me:—

"Well, Mr. Carlton, this algebra is a most powerful thing—aint it?"

"Indeed it is, Mr. Jimmey—have you been looking into it?"

"Looking into it! I have been all through this here fust part; and by election time, I allow I'll be ready for examination."

"Indeed!"

"Yes, sir! but it is such a pretty thing! Only to think of cyphering by letters! Why, sir, the sums come out, and bring the answers exactly like figures. Jist stop a minute—look here; a stands for 6, and b stands for 8, and c stands for 4, and d stands for figure 10; now if I say $a+b-c=d$, it is all the same as if I said, 6 is 6 and 8 makes 14, and 4 subtracted, leaves 10! Why, sir, I done a whole slate full of letters and signs; and afterwards, when I tried by figures, they every one of them came out right and brung the answer! I mean to cypher by letters altogether."

"Mr. Jimmey, my company is nearly out of sight—if you can get along this way through simple and quadratic equations by our meeting, your chance will not be so bad—good morning, sir."

But our man of "letters" quit cyphering the new way, and returned to plain figures long before reaching equations; and so he could not become our professor. Yet anxious to do us all the good in his power, after our college opened, he waited on me, a leading trustee, with a proposal to board our students, and authorized me to publish—"as how Mr. James Jimmey will take strange students—students not belonging to Woodville—to board, at one dollar a week, and find every thing, washing included, and will black their *shoes* three times a week to *boot,* and—*give them their dog-wood and cherry-bitters every morning into the bargain!*"

The most extraordinary candidate, however, was Mr. Solomon Rapid. He was now somewhat advanced into the shaving age, and was ready to assume offices the most opposite in character; although justice compels us to say Mr. Rapid was as fit for one thing as another. Deeming it waste of time to prepare for any station till he was certain of obtaining it, he wisely demanded the place first, and then set to work to become qualified for its duties, being, I suspect, the very man, or some relation of his, who is recorded as not knowing whether he could read Greek, as he had never tried. And, beside, Mr. Solomon Rapid contended that all offices, from president down to fence-viewer, were open to every white American citizen; and that every republican had a blood-bought right to seek any that struck his fancy; and if the profits were less, or the duties more onerous than had been anticipated, that a man ought to resign and try another.

Naturally, therefore, Mr. Rapid, thought he would like to sit in our chair of languages, or have some employment in the State college; and hence he called for that purpose on Dr. Sylvan, who, knowing the candidate's character, maliciously sent him to me. Accordingly, the young gentleman presented himself, and without ceremony, instantly made known his business thus:—

"I heerd, sir, you wanted somebody to teach the State school, and I'm come to let you know I'm willing to take the place."

"Yes, sir, we are going to elect a professor of languages who is to be the principal, and a professor."

"Well, I don't care which I take, but I'm willing to be the principal. I can teach sifring, reading, writing, joggerfree, surveying, grammur, spelling, definitions, parsin—"

"Are you a linguist?"

"Sir?"

"You of course understand the dead languages?"

"Well, can't say I ever seed much of them, though I have heerd tell of them; but I can soon larn them—they aint more than a few of them I allow?"

"Oh! my dear sir, it is not possible—we—can't—"

"Well, I never seed what I couldn't larn about as smart as any body—"

"Mr. Rapid, I do not mean to question your abilities; but if you are now wholly unacquainted with the dead languages, it is impossible for you or any other talented man to learn them under four or five years."

"Pshoo! foo! I'll bet I larn one in three weeks! Try me, sir,—let's have the furst one furst—how many are there?"

"Mr. Rapid, it is utterly impossible; but if you insist, I will loan you a Latin book—"

"That's your sorts, let's have it, that's all I want, fair play."

Accordingly, I handed him a copy of *Historiae Sacrae*, with which he soon went away, saying, he "didn't allow it would take long to git through Latin, if 'twas only sich a thin patch of a book as that."

In a few weeks to my no small surprise, Mr. Solomon Rapid again presented himself; and drawing forth the book began with a triumphant expression of countenance: "Well, sir, I have done the Latin."

"Done the Latin!"

"Yes, I can read it as fast as English."

"Read it as fast as English!"

"Yes, as fast as English—and I didn't find it hard at all."

"May I try you on a page?"

"Try away, try away; that's what I've come for."

"Please read here then, Mr. Rapid"; and in order to give him a fair chance, I pointed to the first lines of the first chapter, viz: *"In principio Deus creavit coelum et terram intra sex dies; primo die fecit lucem,"* etc.

"That, sir?" and then he read thus, "in prinspo duse creevit kalelum et terrum intra sex dyes—primmo dye fe-fe-sit looseum," etc.

"That will do, Mr. Rapid—"

"Aha! I told you so."

"Yes, yes—but translate."

"Translate!" (eyebrows elevating).

"Yes, translate, render it."

"Render it! how's that?" (forehead more wrinkled).

"Why, yes, render it into English—give me the meaning of it."

"MEANING!" (staring full in my face, his eyes like saucers, and forehead wrinkled with the furrows of eighty)—"MEANING! I didn't know it *had* any meaning. I thought it was a DEAD language!"

Well, reader, I am glad you are *not* laughing at Mr. Rapid; for how should any thing *dead* speak out so as to be understood? And indeed, does not his definition suit the vexed feelings of some young gentlemen attempting to read Latin without any interlinear translation? and who inwardly, cursing both book and teacher, blast their souls "if they can make any sense out of it." The ancients may yet speak in their own languages to a few; but to most who boast the honour of their acquaintance, they are certainly dead in the sense of Solomon Rapid.

Our honourable board of trustees at last met; and after a real attempt by some, and a pretended one by others, to elect one and another out of the three dozen candidates, the Reverend Charles Clarence, A. M., was chosen our principal and professor of languages; and that to the chagrin of Mr. Rapid and other disappointed persons, who all from that moment united in determined and active hostility towards the college, Mr. Clarence, Dr. Sylvan, Mr. Carlton, and, in short, towards "every puss proud aristocrat big-bug, and blasted Yankee in the New Purchase."

SOURCE: Baynard Rush Hall. *The New Purchase: Or, Early Years in the Far West.* New Albany, Indiana: R. Nunemacher, 1855.

"THE JUMPING FROG": IN ENGLISH. THEN IN FRENCH. THEN CLAWED BACK INTO A CIVILIZED LANGUAGE ONCE MORE, BY PATIENT, UNREMUNERATED TOIL (1865 & 1879)

Mark Twain (Samuel Clemens)

America's most famous humorist (1835–1910) first came to national attention for "The Notorious Jumping Frog of Calaveras County" (originally titled "Jim Smiley and His Jumping Frog"). While the story is well known and appreciated, his comic rendering of its French translation back into English is less so. This selection presents his commentary, the original story and then his re-translation of the French version (which may be found in, among other sources, "The Jumping Frog": In English. Then in French. Then Clawed Back into a Civilized Language Once More, by Patient, Unremunerated Toil. New York: Harper and Brothers, 1903).

EVEN A CRIMINAL is entitled to fair play; and certainly when a man who has done no harm has been unjustly treated, he is privileged to do his best to right himself. My attention has just been called to an article some three years old in a French Magazine entitled, *Revue des Deux Mondes* (Review of Some Two Worlds), wherein the writer treats of "Les Humoristes Americaines" (These Humorists Americans). I am one of these humorists Americans dissected by him, and hence the complaint I am making.

This gentleman's article is an able one (as articles go, in the French, where they always tangle up everything to that degree that when you start into a sentence you never know whether you are going to come out alive or not). It is a very good article, and the writer says all manner of kind and complimentary things about me—for which I am sure I thank him with all my heart; but then why should he go and spoil all his praise by one unlucky experiment? What I refer to is this: he says my Jumping Frog is a funny story, but still he can't see why it should ever really convulse anyone with laughter—and straightway proceeds to translate it into French in order to prove to his nation that there is nothing so very extravagantly funny about it. Just there is where my complaint originates. He has not translated it at all; he has simply mixed it all up; it is no more like the Jumping Frog when he gets through with it than I am like a meridian of longitude. In order that even the unlettered may know my injury and give me their compassion, I have been at infinite pains and trouble to re-translate this French version back into English; and to tell the truth I have well-nigh worn myself out at it, having scarcely rested from my work during five days and nights. I cannot speak the French language, but I can translate very well, though not fast, I being self-educated. I ask the reader to run his eye over the original English version of the Jumping Frog, and then read my re-translation from the French, and kindly take notice how the Frenchman has riddled the grammar. I think it is the worst I ever saw; and yet the French are called a polished nation. If I had a boy that put sentences together as they do, I would polish him to some purpose. Without further introduction, the Jumping Frog, as I originally wrote it, was as follows—[after it will be found my re-translation from the French]:

The Notorious Jumping Frog of Calaveras County

In compliance with the request of a friend of mine, who wrote me from the East, I called on good-natured, garrulous old Simon Wheeler, and inquired after my friend's friend, Leonidas W. Smiley, as requested to do, and I hereunto append the result. I have a lurking suspicion that *Leonidas W.* Smiley is a myth; that my friend never knew such a personage; and that he only conjectured that if I asked old Wheeler about him, it would remind him of his infamous *Jim* Smiley, and he would go to work and bore me to death with some exasperating reminiscence of him as long and as tedious as it should be useless to me. If that was the design, it succeeded.

I found Simon Wheeler dozing comfortably by the bar-room stove of the dilapidated tavern in the decayed mining camp of Angel's, and I noticed that he was fat and bald-headed, and had an expression of winning gentleness and simplicity upon his tranquil countenance. He roused up, and gave me good-day. I told him a friend of mine had commissioned me to make some inquiries about a cherished companion of his boyhood named *Leonidas W. Smiley—Rev. Leonidas W.* Smiley, a young minister of the Gospel, who he had heard was at one time a resident of Angel's Camp. I added that if Mr. Wheeler could tell me anything about this Rev. Leonidas W. Smiley, I would feel under many obligations to him.

Simon Wheeler backed me into a corner and blockaded me there with his chair, and then sat down and reeled off the monoto-nous narrative which follows this paragraph. He never smiled, he never frowned, he never changed his voice from the gentle-flowing key to which he tuned his initial sentence, he never betrayed the slightest suspicion of enthusiasm; but all through the interminable narrative there ran a vein of impressive earnestness and sincerity, which showed me plainly that, so far from his imagining that there was anything ridiculous or funny about his story, he regarded it as a really important matter, and admired its two heroes as men of transcendent genius in *finesse*. I let him go on in his own way, and never interrupted him once.

Rev. Leonidas W. H'm, Reverend Le—well, there was a feller here once by the name of *Jim* Smiley, in the winter of '49—or maybe it was the spring of '50—I don't recollect exactly, somehow, though what makes me think it was one or the other is because I remember the big flume warn't finished when he first came to the camp; but any way, he was the curiosest man about always betting on anything that turned up you ever see, if he could get anybody to bet on the other side; and if he couldn't he'd change sides. Any way that suited the other man would suit *him*—any way just so's he got a bet, *he* was satisfied. But still he was lucky, uncommon lucky; he most always come out winner. He was always ready and laying for a chance; there couldn't be no solit'ry thing mentioned but that feller'd offer to bet on it, and take any side you please, as I was just telling you. If there was a horse-race, you'd find him flush or you'd find him busted at the end of it; if there was a dog-fight, he'd bet on it; if there was a cat-fight, he'd bet on it; if there was a chicken-fight, he'd bet on it; why, if there was two birds setting on a fence, he would bet you which one would fly first; or if there was a camp-meeting, he would be there reg'lar to bet on Parson Walker, which he judged to be the best exhorter about here, and so he was too, and a good man. If he even see a straddle-bug start to go anywheres, he would bet you how long it would take him to get to—to wherever he was going to, and if you took him up, he would foller that straddle-bug to Mexico but what he would find out where he was bound for and how long he was on the road. Lots of the boys here has seen that Smiley and can tell you about him. Why, it never made no difference to *him*—he'd bet on *any* thing—the dangest feller. Parson Walker's wife laid very sick once, for a good while, and it seemed as if they warn't going to save her; but one morning he come in, and Smiley up and asked him how she was, and he said she was considable better—thank the Lord for his infinit mercy—and coming on so smart that with the blessing of Prov'dence she'd get well yet; and Smiley, before he thought, says, "Well, I'll risk two-and-a-half she don't anyway."

Thish-yer Smiley had a mare—the boys called her the fifteen-minute nag, but that was only in fun, you know, because of course she was faster than that—and he used to win money on that horse, for all she was so slow and always had the asthma, or the distemper, or the consumption, or something of that kind. They used to give her two or three hundred yards start, and then pass her under way; but always at the fag-end of the race she'd get excited and desperate-like, and come cavorting and straddling up, and scattering her legs around limber, sometimes in the air, and sometimes out to one side amongst the fences, and kicking up m-o-r-e dust and raising m-o-r-e racket with her coughing and sneezing and blowing her nose—and *always* fetch up at the stand just about a neck ahead, as near as you could cipher it down.

And he had a little small bull-pup, that to look at him you'd think he warn't worth a cent but to set around and look ornery and lay for a chance to steal something. But as soon as money was up on him he was a different dog; his under-jaw'd begin to stick out like the fo'-castle of a steamboat, and his teeth would uncover and shine like the furnaces. And a dog might tackle him and bully-rag him, and bite him, and throw him over his shoulder two or three times, and Andrew Jackson—which was the name of the pup—Andrew Jackson would never let on but what *he* was satisfied, and hadn't expected nothing else—and the bets being doubled and doubled on the other side all the time, till the money was all up; and then all of a sudden he would grab that other dog jest by the j'int of his hind leg and freeze to it—not chaw, you understand, but only just grip and hang on till they throwed up the sponge, if it was a year. Smiley always come out winner on that pup, till he harnessed a dog once that didn't have no hind legs, because they'd been sawed off in a circular saw, and when the thing had gone along far enough, and the money was all up, and he come to make a snatch for his pet holt, he see in a minute how he'd been imposed on, and how the other dog had him in the door, so to speak, and he 'peared surprised, and then he looked sorter discouraged-like, and didn't try no more to win the fight, and so he got shucked out bad. He gave Smiley a look, as much as to say his heart was broke, and it was *his* fault, for putting up a dog that hadn't no hind legs for him to take holt of, which was his main dependence in a fight, and then he limped off a piece and laid down and died. It was a good pup, was that Andrew Jackson, and would have made a name for hisself if he'd lived, for the stuff was in him and he had genius—I know it, because he hadn't no opportunities to speak of, and it don't stand to reason that a dog could make such a fight as he could under them circumstances if he hadn't no talent. It always makes me feel sorry when I think of that last fight of his'n, and the way it turned out.

Well, thish-yer Smiley had rat-tarriers, and chicken, cocks, and tom-cats and all of them kind of things, till you couldn't rest, and you couldn't fetch nothing for him to bet on but he'd match you. He ketched a frog one day, and took him home, and said he cal'lated to educate him; and so he never done nothing for three months but set in his back yard and learn that frog to jump. And you bet you he *did* learn him, too. He'd give him a little punch behind, and the next minute you'd see that frog whirling in the air like a doughnut—see him turn one summerset, or may be a couple, if he got a good start, and come down flat-footed and all right, like a cat. He got him up so in the matter of ketching flies, and kep' him in practice so constant, that he'd nail a fly every time as fur as he could see him. Smiley said all a frog wanted was education, and he could do 'most anything—and I believe him. Why, I've seen him set Dan'l Webster down here on this floor—Dan'l Webster was the name of the frog—and sing out, "Flies, Dan'l, flies!" and quicker'n you could wink he'd spring straight up and snake a fly off'n the counter there, and flop down on the floor ag'in as solid as a gob of mud, and fall to scratching the side of his head with his hind foot as indifferent as if he hadn't no idea he'd been doin' any more'n any frog might do. You never see a frog so modest and straightfor'ard as he was, for all he was so gifted. And when it come to fair and square jumping on a dead level, he could get over more ground at one straddle than any animal of his breed you ever see. Jumping on a dead level was his strong suit, you understand; and when it come to that, Smiley would ante up money on him as long as he had a red. Smiley was monstrous proud of his frog, and well he might be, for fellers that had traveled and been every wheres, all said he laid over any frog that ever *they* see.

Well, Smiley kep' the beast in a little lattice box, and he used to fetch him down town sometimes and lay for a bet. One day a feller—a stranger in the camp, he was—come acrost him with his box, and says:

"What might it be that you've got in the box?"

And Smiley says, sorter indifferent-like, "It might be a parrot, or it might be a canary, maybe, but it ain't—it's only just a frog."

And the feller took it, and looked at it careful, and turned it round this way and that, and says, "H'm—so 'tis. Well, what's *he* good for?"

"Well," Smiley says, easy and careless, "he's good enough for *one* thing, I should judge—he can outjump any frog in Calaveras county."

The feller took the box again, and took another long, particular look, and give it back to Smiley, and says, very deliberate, "Well," he says, "I don't see no p'ints about that frog that's any better'n any other frog."

"Maybe you don't," Smiley says. "Maybe you understand frogs and maybe you don't understand 'em; maybe you've had experience, and maybe you ain't only a amature, as it were! Anyways, I've got *my* opinion and I'll risk forty dollars that he can outjump any frog in Calaveras county."

And the feller studied a minute, and then says, kinder sad like, "Well, I'm only a stranger here, and I ain't got no frog; but if I had a frog, I'd bet you."

And then Smiley says, "That's all right—that's all right—if you'll hold my box a minute, I'll go and get you a frog." And so the feller took the box, and put up his forty dollars along with Smiley's, and set down to wait.

So he set there a good while thinking and thinking to hisself, and then he got the frog out and prized his mouth open and took a teaspoon and tilled him full of quail shot—filled him pretty near up to his chin—and set him on the floor. Smiley he went to the swamp and slopped around in the mud for a long time, and finally he ketched a frog, and fetched him in, and give him to this feller, and says:

"Now, if you're ready, set him along side of Dan'l, with his forepaws just even with Dan'l's, and I'll give the word." Then he says, "One—two—three—*git!*" and him and the feller touched up the frogs from behind, and the new frog hopped off lively, but Dan'l give a heave, and hysted up his shoulders—so—like a Frenchman, but it warn't no use—he couldn't budge; he was planted as solid as a church, and he couldn't no more stir than if he was anchored out. Smiley was a good deal surprised, and he was disgusted too, but he didn't have no idea what the matter was, of course.

The feller took the money and started away; and when he was going out at the door, he sorter jerked his thumb over his shoulder—so—at Dan'l, and says again, very deliberate, "Well," he says, *"I* don't see no p'ints about that frog that's any better'n any other frog."

Smiley he stood scratching his head and looking down at Dan'l a long time, and at last he says, "I do wonder what in the nation that frog throwed off for—I wonder if there ain't something the matter with him—he 'pears to look mighty baggy, somehow." And he ketched Dan'l by the nap of the neck, and hefted him, and says, "Why blame my cats if he don't weight five pounds!" and turned him upside down and he belched out a double handful of shot. And then he see how it was, and he was the maddest man —he set the frog down and took out after that feller, but he never ketched him. And—"

[Here Simon Wheeler heard his name called from the front yard, and got up to see what was wanted.] And turning to me as he moved away, he said: "Just set where you are, stranger, and rest easy—I ain't going to be gone a second."

But, by your leave, I did not think that a continuation of the history of the enterprising vagabond *Jim* Smiley would be likely to afford me much information concerning the Rev. *Leonidas W. Smiley*, and so I started away.

At the door I met the sociable Wheeler returning, and he button-holed me and recommenced:

"Well, thish-yer Smiley had a yaller one-eyed cow that didn't have no tail, only jest a short stump like a bannanner, and—"

However, lacking both time and inclination, I did not wait to hear about the afflicted cow, but took my leave.

[Translation of the above back from the French of "La Grenouille Santeuse du Comte de Calaveras," in the *Revue des Deux Mondes*, July 15th, 1872.]

The Frog Jumping of the County of Calaveras

It there was one time here an individual known under the name of Jim Smiley: it was in the winter of '49, possibly well at the spring of '50, I no me recollect not exactly. This which me makes to believe that it was the one or the other, it is that I shall remember that the grand flume is not achieved when he arrives at the camp for the first time, but of all sides he was the man the most fond of to bet which one have seen, betting upon all that which is presented, when he could find an adversary; and when he not of it could not, he passed to the side opposed. All that which convenienced to the other, to him convenienced also; seeing that he had a bet, Smiley was satisfied. And he had a chance! a chance even worthless: nearly always he gained. It must to say that he was always near to himself expose, but one no could mention the least thing without that this *gaillard* offered to bet the bottom, no matter what, and to take the side that one him would, as I you it said all at the hour (*tout a l'heure*). If it was of races, you him find rich or ruined at the end: if it there is a combat of dogs, he bring his bet; he himself laid always for a combat of cats, for a combat of cocks;—by-blue! if you have see two birds upon a fence, he you should have offered of to bet which of those birds shall fly the first; and if there is *meeting* at the camp (*meeting au camp*) he comes to bet regularly for the cure Walker, which he judged to be the best predicator of the neighborhood (*predicateur des environs*) and which he was in effect, and a brave man. He would encounter a bug of wood in the road, whom he will bet upon the time which he shall take to go where she would go—and if you him have take at the word, he will follow the bug as far as Mexique, without himself caring to go so far; neither of the time which he there lost. One time the woman of the cure Walker is very sick during long time, it seemed that one not her saved not; but one morning the cure arrives, and Smiley him demanded how she goes, and he said that she is well better, grace to the infinite misery (*lui demande comment elle va, et il dit qu'elle est bien mieux, grace a l'infinie misericorde*) so much better that with the benediction of the Providence she herself of it would pull out (*elle s'en tirerait*); and behold without there thinking Smiley responds: "Well, I gauge two-and-half that she will die all of same."

This Smiley had an animal which the boys called the nag of the quarter of hour, but solely for pleasantry, you comprehend, because, well understand, she was more fast as that! [*Now why that exclamation?*—M. T.] And it was custom of to gain of the silver with this beast, notwithstanding she was *poussive, cornarde,* always taken of asthma, of colics or of consumption, or something of approaching. One him would give two or three hundred yards at the departure, then one him passed without pain; but never at the last she not fail of herself *echauffer,* of herself exasperate, and she arrives herself *ecartant, se defendant,* her legs *greles* in the air before the obstacles, sometimes them elevating and making with this more of dust than any horse, more of noise above with his *eternumens* and *reniflemens*—crac! she arrives then always first by one head, as just as one can it measure. And he had a small bull dog (*boule dogue!*) who, to him see, no value, not a cent; one would believe that to bet against him it was to steal, so much he was ordinary; but as soon as the game made, she becomes another dog. Her jaw inferior commence to project like a deck of before, his teeth themselves discover brilliant like some furnaces, and a dog could him tackle (*le taquiner*), him excite, him murder (*le mordre*), him throw two or three times over his shoulder, Andre Jackson—this was the name of the dog—Andre Jackson takes that tranquilly, as if he not himself was never expecting other thing, and when the bets were doubled and redoubled against him, he you seize the other dog just at the articulation of the leg of behind, and he not it leave more, not that he it masticate, you conceive, but he himself there shall be holding during until that one throws the sponge in the air, must he wait a year. Smiley gained always with this beast-la; unhappily they have finished by elevating a dog who no had not of feet of behind, because one them had sawed; and when things were at the point that he would, and that he came to himself throw upon his morsel favorite, the poor dog comprehended in an instant that he himself was deceived in him, and that the other dog him had. You no have never see person having the air more *penaud* and more discouraged; he not made no effort to gain the combat, and was rudely shucked.

Eh bien! this Smiley nourished some *terriers a rats*, and some cocks of combat, and some cats, and all sorts of things; and with his rage of betting one no had more of repose. He trapped one day a frog and him imported with him (*et l'emporta chez lui*) saying that he pretended to make his education. You me believe if you will, but during three months he not has nothing done but to him apprehend to jump (*apprendre a sauter*) in a court retired of her mansion (*de sa maison*). And I you respond that he have succeeded. He him gives a small blow by behind, and the instant after you shall see the frog turn in the air like a grease-biscuit, make one summersault, sometimes two, when she was well started, and re-fall upon his feet like a cat. He him had accomplished in the art of to gobble the flies (*gober des mouches*), and him there exercised continually—so well that a fly at the most far that she appeared was a fly lost. Smiley had custom to say that all which lacked to a frog it was the education, but with the education she could do nearly all—and I him believe. *Tenez,* I him have seen pose Daniel Webster there upon this plank—Daniel Webster was the name of the frog—and to him sing, "Some flies, Daniel, some flies!"—in the flash of the eye Daniel had bounded and seized a fly here upon the counter, then jumped anew at the earth, where he rested truly to himself scratch the head with his behind-foot, as if he no had not the least idea of his superiority. Never you not have seen frog as modest, as natural, sweet as she was. And when he himself agitated to jump purely and simply upon plain earth, she does more ground in one jump than any beast of his species than you can know. To jump plain—this was his strong. When he himself agitated for that, Smiley multiplied the bets upon her as long as there to him remained a red. It must to know, Smiley was monstrously proud of his frog, and he of it was right, for so me men who were traveled, who had all seen, said that they to him would be injurious to him compare to another frog. Smiley guarded Daniel in a little box latticed which he carried by times to the village for some bet.

One day an individual stranger at the camp him arrested with his box and him said:

"What is this that you have then shut up there within?"

Smiley said, with an air indifferent:

"That could be a *paroquet*, or a syringe (*ou un serin*), but this no is nothing of such, it not is but a frog."

The individual it took, it regarded with care, it turned from one side and from the other, then he said:

"*Tiens!* in effect!—At what is she good?"

"My God!" respond Smiley, always with an air disengaged, "she is good for one thing, to my notice, (*a mon avis*), she can batter in jumping (*elle peut batter en sautant*) all frogs of the county of Calaveras."

The individual re-took the box, it examined of new longly, and it rendered to Smiley in saying with an air deliberate:

"Eh bien! I no saw not that that frog had nothing of better than each frog." (*Je ne vois pas que cette grenouille ait rien de mieux qu'aucune grenouille*). [*If that isn't grammar gone-to-seed, then I count myself no judge.*—M. T.]

"Possible that you not it saw not," said Smiley, "possible that you—you comprehend frogs; possible that you not you there comprehend nothing; possible that you had of the experience, and possible that you not be but an amateur. Of all manner (*De toute maniere*), I better forty dollars that she batter in jumping no matter which frog of the county of Calaveras."

The individual reflected a second, and said like sad:

"I not am but a stranger here, I no have not a frog; but if I of it had one, I would embrace the bet."

"Strong well!" respond Smiley; "nothing of more facility. If you will hold my box a minute, I go you to search a frog (*j'irai vous chercher*)."

Behold, then, the individual, who guards the box, who puts his forty dollars upon those of Smiley, and who attends (*et qui attend*). He attended enough longtimes, reflecting all solely. And figure you that he takes Daniel, him opens the mouth by force and with a teaspoon him fills with shot of the hunt, even him fills just to the chin, then he him puts by the earth. Smiley during these times was at slopping in a swamp. Finally he trapped (*attrape*) a frog, him carried to that individual, and said:

"Now if you be ready, put him all against Daniel, with their before-feet upon the same line, and I give the signal"—then he added: "One, two, three,—advance!"

Him and the individual touched their frogs by behind, and the frog new put to jump smartly, but Daniel himself lifted ponderously, exalted the shoulders thus, like a Frenchman—to what good? he not could budge, he is planted solid like a church, he not advance no more than if one he in had put at the anchor.

Smiley was surprised and disgusted, but he not himself doubted not of the turn being intended (*mais il ne se doutait pas du tour, bien entendu*). The individual empocketed the silver, himself with it went, and of it himself in going is it that he no gives not a jerk of thumb over the shoulder—like that—at the poor Daniel, in saying with his air deliberate—(*L'individu empoche l'argent, s'en va et en s'en allaut est ce qu'il ne donne pas un coup de pouce pardessus l'epaule, comme ca, au pauvre Daniel, endisant de son air delibere*):

"Eh bien I! *no see not that that frog has nothing of better than another.*"

Smiley himself scratched long times the head, the eyes fixed upon Daniel, until that which at last he said:

"I me demand how the devil it makes itself that this beast has refused. Is it that she had something? One would believe that she is stuffed."

He grasped Daniel by the skin of the neck, him lifted and said: "The wolf me bite if he no weigh not five pounds." He him reversed and the unhappy belched two handfuls of shot (*et le malhereus*, etc.).—When Smiley recognized how it was, he was like mad. He deposited his frog by the earth and ran after that individual, but he not him caught never.

Such is the Jumping Frog, to the distorted French eye. I claim that I never put together such an odious mixture of bad grammar and delirium tremens in my life. And what has a poor foreigner like me done, to be abused and misrepresented like this? When I say, "Well, I don't see no p'ints about that frog that's any better'n any other frog," is it kind, is it just, for this Frenchman to try to make it appear that I said: "Eh bien! I no saw that that frog had nothing of better than each frog?" I have no heart to write more. I never felt so about anything before.

SOURCES: Mark Twain. *Sketches.* Toronto: Belfords, Clarke and Company, 1879.

Mark Twain. *Sketches New and Old.* New York: Harper and Brothers, 1917.

BILL NATIONS (1873)

Bill Arp (Charles Henry Smith)

From the beginning of the Civil War in 1861, Smith (1826–1903) wrote a column for the Atlanta Constitution *in the voice of his invented character Bill Arp.*

YOU NEVER KNOWD Bill, I rekun. Hes gone to Arkensaw, and I don't know whether hes ded or alive. He was a good feller, Bill was, as most all whisky drinkers are. Me and him both used to love it powerful—especially Bill. We soaked it when we could git it, and when we coudent we hankered after it amazingly. I must tell you a little antidote on Bill, tho I dident start to tell you about that.

We started on a little jurney one day in June, and took along a bottle of "old rye," and there was so many springs and wells on the road that it was mighty nigh gone before dinner. We took our snack, and Bill drained the last drop, for he said we would soon git to Joe Paxton's, and that Joe always kept some.

Shore enuff Joe dident have a drop, and we concluded, as we was mighty dry, to go on to Jim Alford's, and stay all night. We knew that Jim had it, for he always had it. So we whipped up, and the old Bay had to travel, for I tell you when a man wants whiskey everything has to bend to the gittin' of it. Shore enuff Jim had some. He was mity glad to see us, and he knowd what we wanted, for he knowd how it was hisself. So he brought out an old-fashend glass decanter, and a shugar bowl, and a tumbler, and a spoon, and says he, "Now, boys, jest wait a minit till you git rested sorter, for it ain't good to take whiskey on a hot stomack. I've jest been readin' a piece in Grady's newspaper about a frog—the darndest frog that perhaps ever come from a tadpole. It was found up in

40

Kanetucky, and is as big as a peck measure. Bill, do you take this paper and read it aloud to us. I'm a poor hand to read, and I want to hear it. I'll be hanged if it ain't the darndest frog I ever hearn of."

He laid the paper on my knees, and I begun to read, thinkin' it was a little short anticdote, but as I turned the paper over *I* found it was mighty nigh a column. I took a side glance at Bill, and I saw the little dry twitches a jumpin' about on his countenance. He was mighty nigh dead for a drink. I warent so bad off myself, and I was about half mad with him for drainin' the bottle before dinner; so I just read along slow, and stopped two or three times to clear my throat just to consume time. Pretty soon Bill got up and commenced walkin' about, and he would look at the dekanter like he would give his daylights to choke the corn juice out of it. I read along slowly. Old Alford was a listnin' and chawin' his tobakker and spittin' out of the door. Bill come up to me, his face red and twitchin', and leanin' over my shoulder he seed the length of the story, and I will never forgit his pitiful tone as he whispered, "Skip some, Bill, for heaven's sake skip some."

My heart relented, and I did skip some, and hurried through, and we all jined in a drink; but I'll never forgit how Bill looked when he whispered to me to "skip some, Bill, skip some." I've got over the like of that, boys, and I hope Bill has, too, but I don't know. I wish in my soul that everybody had quit it, for you may talk about slavery, and penitentiary, and chain-gangs, and the Yankees, and General Grant, and a devil of a wife, but whiskey is the worst master that ever a man had over him. I know how it is myself.

But there is one good thing about drinkin'. I almost wish every man was a reformed drunkard. No man who hasn't drank liker knows what a luxury cold water is. I have got up in the night in cold wether after I had been spreein' around, and gone to the well burnin' up with thirst, feeling like the gallows, and the grave, and the infernal regions was too good for me, and when I took up the bucket in my hands, and with my elbows a tremblin' like I had the shakin' ager, put the water to my lips; it was the most delicious, satisfying luxurius draft that ever went down my throat. I have stood there and drank and drank until I could drink no more, and gone back to bed thankin' God for the pure, innocent, and coolin' beverig, and cursin' myself from my inmost soul for ever touchin' the accursed whisky. In my torture of mind and body I have made vows and promises, and broken 'em within a day. But if you want to know the luxury of cold water, get drunk, and keep at it until you get on fire, and then try a bucket full with your shirt on at the well in the middle of the night. You won't want a gourd full—you'll feel like the bucket ain't big enuf, and when you begin to drink an earthquake couldn't stop you. My fathers, how good it was! I know a hundred men who will swear to the truth of what I say: but you see it's a thing they don't like to talk about. It's too humiliatin'.

But I dident start to talk about drinkin'. In fact, I've forgot what I did start to tell you. My mind is sorter addled now a days, anyhow, and I hav to jes let my tawkin' tumble out permiskuous. I'll take another whet at it afore long, and fill up the gaps.

Yours trooly,
Bill Arp.

SOURCE: Bill Arp (Charles Henry Smith). *Bill Arp's Peace Papers.* New York: G. W. Carleton and Company, 1873.

A JERSEY CENTENARIAN (1875)

Bret Harte

For a time, Harte (1836–1902) was almost as popular a writer as Mark Twain. Born and raised in New York State, he gained his literary reputation in California, where he wrote "Western" poetry and fiction and many comic stories, before returning to the East Coast and then moving to Europe.

I HAVE SEEN her at last. She is a hundred and seven years old, and remembers George Washington quite distinctly. It is somewhat confusing, however, that she also remembers a contemporaneous Josiah W. Perkins, of Basking Ridge, N. J., and, I think, has the impression that Perkins, was the better man. Perkins, at the close of the last century, paid her some little attention. There are a few things that a really noble woman of a hundred and seven never forgets.

It was Perkins, who said to her in 1795, in the streets of Philadelphia, "Shall I show thee General Washington?" Then she said, carelesslike (for you know, child, at that time it wasn't what it is now to see General Washington)—she said, "So do, Josiah, so do!" Then he pointed to a tall man who got out of a carriage, and went into a large house. He was larger than you be. He wore his own hair — not powdered; had a flowered chintz vest, with yellow breeches and blue stockings, and a broad-brimmed hat. In summer he wore a white straw hat, and at his farm at Basking Ridge he always wore it. At this point, it became too evident that she was describing the clothes of the all-fascinating Perkins: so I gently but firmly led her back to Washington.

Then it appeared that she did not remember exactly what he wore. To assist her, I sketched the general historic dress of that period. She said she thought he was dressed like that. Emboldened by my success, I added a hat of Charles II, and pointed shoes of the eleventh century. She endorsed these with such cheerful alacrity that I dropped the subject.

The house upon which I had stumbled, or, rather, to which my horse—a Jersey hack, accustomed to historic research—had brought me, was low and quaint. Like most old houses, it had the appearance of being encroached upon by the surrounding glebe, as if it were already half in the grave, with a sod or two, in the shape of moss, thrown on it, like ashes on ashes, and dust on dust. A wooden house, instead of acquiring dignity with age, is apt to lose its youth and respectability together. A porch, with scant, sloping seats, from which even the winter's snow must have slid uncomfortably, projected from a doorway that opened most unjustifiably into a small sitting-room. There was no vestibule, or locus poenitentiae, for the embarrassed or bashful visitor: he passed at once from the security of the public road into shameful privacy. And here, in the mellow autumnal sunlight, that, streaming through the maples and sumach on the opposite bank, flickered and danced upon the floor, she sat and discoursed of George Washington, and thought of Perkins. She was quite in keeping with the house and the season, albeit a little in advance of both; her skin being of a faded russet, and her hands so like dead November leaves, that I fancied they even rustled when she moved them.

For all that, she was quite bright and cheery; her faculties still quite vigorous, although performing irregularly and spasmodically. It was somewhat discomposing, I confess, to observe that at times her lower jaw would drop, leaving her speechless, until one of the family would notice it, and raise it smartly into place with a slight snap—an operation always performed in such an habitual, perfunctory manner, generally in passing to and fro in their household duties, that it was very trying to the spectator. It was still more embarrassing to observe that the dear old lady had evidently no knowledge of this, but believed she was still talking, and that, on resuming her actual vocal utterance, she was often abrupt and incoherent, beginning always in the middle of a sentence, and often in the middle of a word.

"Sometimes," said her daughter, a giddy, thoughtless young thing of eighty-five—"sometimes just moving her head sort of unhitches her jaw; and, if we don't happen to see it, she'll go on talking for hours without ever making a sound."

Although I was convinced, after this, that during my interview I had lost several important revelations regarding George Washington through these peculiar lapses, I could not help reflecting how beneficent were these provisions of the Creator—how, if properly studied and applied, they might be fraught with happiness to mankind—how a slight jostle or jar at a dinner-party might make the post-prandial eloquence of garrulous senility satisfactory to itself, yet harmless to others—how a more intimate knowledge of anatomy, introduced into the domestic circle, might make a home tolerable at least, if not happy—how a long-suffering husband, under the pretense of a conjugal caress, might so unhook his wife's condyloid process as to allow the flow of expostulation, criticism or denunciation to go on with gratification to her, and perfect immunity to himself.

But this was not getting back to George Washington and the early struggles of the Republic. So I returned to the commander-in-chief, but found, after one or two leading questions, that she was rather inclined to resent his re-appearance on the stage. Her reminiscences here were chiefly social and local, and more or less flavored with Perkins. We got back as far as the Revolutionary epoch, or, rather, her impressions of that epoch, when it was still fresh in the public mind. And here I came upon an incident, purely personal and local, but, withal, so novel, weird and uncanny, that for a while I fear it quite displaced George Washington in my mind, and tinged the autumnal fields beyond with a red that was not of the sumach. I do not remember to have read of it in the books. I do not know that it is entirely authentic. It was attested to me by mother and daughter, as an uncontradicted tradition.

In the little field beyond, where the plough still turns up musket-balls and cartridge-boxes, took place one of those irregular skirmishes between the militiamen and Knyphausen's stragglers, that made the retreat historical. A Hessian soldier, wounded in both legs and utterly helpless, dragged himself to the cover of a hazel-copse, and lay there hidden for two days. On the third day, maddened by thirst, he managed to creep to the rail-fence of an adjoining farmhouse, but found himself unable to mount it or pass through. There was no one in the house but a little girl of six or seven years. He called to her, and in a faint voice asked for water. She returned to the house, as if to comply with his request, but, mounting a chair, took from the chimney a heavily loaded Queen Anne musket, and, going to the door, took deliberate aim at the helpless intruder, and fired. The man fell back dead, without a groan. She replaced the musket, and, returning to the fence, covered the body with boughs and leaves, until it was hidden. Two or three days after, she related the occurrence in a careless, casual way, and leading the way to the fence, with a piece of bread and butter in her guileless little fingers, pointed out the result of her simple, unsophisticated effort. The Hessian was decently buried, but I could not find out what became of the little girl. Nobody seemed to remember. I trust that, in after years, she was happily married; that no Jersey Lovelace attempted to trifle with a heart whose impulses were so prompt, and whose purposes were so sincere. They did not seem to know if she had married or not. Yet it does not seem probable that such simplicity of conception, frankness of expression, and deftness of execution, were lost to posterity, or that they failed, in their time and season, to give flavor to the domestic felicity of the period. Beyond this, the story perhaps has little value, except as an offset to the usual anecdotes of Hessian atrocity.

They had their financial panics even in Jersey, in the old days. She remembered when Dr. White married your cousin Mary—or was it Susan?—yes, it was Susan. She remembers that your Uncle Harry brought in an armful of bank-notes—paper money, you know—and threw them in the corner, saying they were no good to anybody. She remembered playing with them, and giving them to your Aunt Anna—no, child, it was your own mother, bless your heart! Some of them was marked as high as a hundred dollars. Everybody kept gold and silver in a stocking, or in a "chancy" vase, like that. You never used money to buy anything. When Josiah went to Springfield to buy anything, he took a cartload of things with him to exchange. That yaller picture-frame was paid for in greenings. But then people knew jest what they had. They didn't fritter their substance away in unchristian trifles, like your father, Eliza Jane, who doesn't know that there is a God who will smite him hip and thigh; for vengeance is mine, and those that believe in me. But here, singularly enough, the inferior maxillaries gave out, and her jaw dropped. (I noticed that her giddy daughter of eighty-five was sitting near her, but I do not pretend to connect this fact with the arrested flow of personal disclosure.) Howbeit, when she recovered her speech again, it appeared that she was complaining of the weather.

The seasons had changed very much since your father went to sea. The winters used to be terrible in those days. When she went over to Springfield, in June, she saw the snow still on Watson's Ridge. There were whole days when you couldn't get over to William Henry's, their next neighbor, a quarter of a mile away.

It was that drefful winter that the Spanish sailor was found. You don't remember the Spanish sailor, Eliza Jane—it was before your time. There was a little personal skirmishing here, which I feared, at first, might end in a suspension of maxillary functions, and the loss of the story: but here it is. Ah, me! it is a pure white winter idyl: how shall I sing it this bright, gay autumnal day?

It was a terrible night, that winter's night, when she and the century were young together. The sun was lost at three o'clock: the snowy night came down like a white sheet, that flapped around the house, beat at the windows with its edges, and at last wrapped it in a close embrace. In the middle of the night, they thought they heard above the wind a voice crying, "Christus, Christus!" in a foreign tongue. They opened the door—no easy task in the north wind that pressed its strong shoulders against it— but nothing was to be seen but the drifting snow. The next morning dawned on fences hidden, and a landscape changed and obliterated with drift. During the day, they again heard the cry of "Christus!" this time faint and hidden, like a child's voice. They searched in vain: the drifted snow hid its secret. On the third day they broke a path to the fence, and then they heard the cry distinctly. Digging down, they found the body of a man —a Spanish sailor, dark and bearded, with earrings in his ears. As they stood gazing down at his cold and pulseless figure, the cry of "Christus!" again rose upon the wintry air; and they turned and fled in superstitious terror to the house. And then one of the children, bolder than the rest, knelt down, and opened the dead man's rough pea-jacket, and found—what think you!—a little blue-and-green parrot, nestling against his breast. It was the bird that had echoed mechanically the last despairing cry of the life that was given to save it. It was the bird, that ever after, amid outlandish oaths and wilder sailor-songs, that I fear often shocked the pure ears of its gentle mistress, and brought scandal into the Jerseys, still retained that one weird and mournful cry.

The sun meanwhile was sinking behind the steadfast range beyond, and I could not help feeling that I must depart with my wants unsatisfied. I had brought away no historic fragment: I absolutely knew little or nothing new regarding George Washington. I had been addressed variously by the names of different members of the family who were dead and forgotten; I had stood for an hour in the past: yet I had not added to my historical knowledge, nor the practical benefit of your readers. I spoke once more of Washington, and she replied with a reminiscence of Perkins.

Stand forth, O Josiah W. Perkins, of Basking Ridge, N.J.! Thou wast of little account in thy life, I warrant; thou didst not even feel the greatness of thy day and time; thou didst criticise thy superiors; thou wast small and narrow in thy ways; thy very name and grave are unknown and uncared for: but thou wast once kind to a woman who survived thee, and, lo! thy name is again spoken of men, and for a moment lifted up above thy betters.

SOURCE: Bret Harte. *Tales of the Argonauts, and Other Sketches*. Boston: Houghton, Mifflin and Company, 1875.

HOW I KILLED A BEAR (1878)

Charles Dudley Warner

Warner (1829–1900) was a newspaper and magazine editor and a longtime friend of Mark Twain, with whom he collaborated on a novel, The Gilded Age *(1873).*

So MANY CONFLICTING accounts have appeared about my casual encounter with an Adirondack bear last summer, that in justice to the public, to myself and to the bear, it is necessary to make a plain statement of the facts. Besides, it is so seldom I have occasion to kill a bear, that the celebration of the exploit may be excused.

The encounter was unpremeditated on both sides. I was not hunting for a bear, and I have no reason to suppose that a bear was looking for me. The fact is, that we were both out blackberrying and met by chance—the usual way. There is among the Adirondack visitors always a great deal of conversation about bears—a general expression of the wish to see one in the woods, and much speculation as to how a person would act if he or she chanced to meet one. But bears are scarce and timid, and appear only to a favored few.

It was a warm day in August, just the sort of a day when an adventure of any kind seemed impossible. But it occurred to the housekeepers at our cottage—there were four of them—to send me to the clearing, on the mountain back of the house, to pick blackberries. It was, rather, a series of small clearings, running up into the forest, much overgrown with bushes and briers, and not unromantic. Cows pastured there, penetrating through the leafy passages from one opening to another, and browsing among the bushes. I was kindly furnished with a six-quart pail, and told not to be gone long.

Not from any predatory instinct, but to save appearances, I took a gun. It adds to the manly aspect of a person with a tin pail if he also carries a gun. It was possible I might start up a partridge; though how I was to hit him, if he started up instead of standing still, puzzled me. Many people use a shot-gun for partridges. I prefer the rifle: it makes a clean job of death, and does not prematurely stuff the bird with globules of lead. The rifle was a Sharps, carrying a ball cartridge (ten to the pound) —an excellent weapon belonging to a friend of mine, who had intended, for a good many years back, to kill a deer with it. He could hit a tree with it—if the wind did not blow, and the atmosphere was just right, and the tree was not too far off— nearly every time. Of course, the tree must have some size. Needless to say that I was at that time no sportsman. Years ago I killed a robin under the most humiliating circumstances. The bird was in a low cherry-tree. I loaded a big shotgun pretty full, crept up under the tree, rested the gun on the fence, with the muzzle more than ten feet from the bird, shut both eyes and pulled the trigger. When I got up to see what had happened, the robin was scattered about under the tree in more than a thousand pieces, no one of which was big enough to enable a naturalist to decide from it to what species it belonged. This disgusted me with the life of a sportsman. I mention the incident to show, that although I went blackberrying armed, there was not much inequality between me and the bear.

In this blackberry-patch bears had been seen. The summer before, our colored cook, accompanied by a little girl of the vicinage, was picking berries there one day, when a bear came out of the woods and walked towards them. The girl took to her heels, and escaped. Aunt Chloe was paralyzed with terror. Instead of attempting to run, she sat down on the ground where she was standing, and began to weep and scream, giving herself up for lost. The bear was bewildered by this conduct . He approached and looked at her; he walked around and surveyed her. Probably he had never seen a colored person before, and did not know whether she would agree with him: at any rate, after watching her a few moments, he turned about and went into the forest. This is an authentic instance of the delicate consideration of a bear, and is much more remarkable than the forbearance towards the African slave of the well-known lion, because the bear had no thorn in his foot.

When I had climbed the hill, I set up my rifle against a tree, and began picking berries, lured on from bush to bush by the black gleam of fruit (that always promises more in the distance than it realizes when you reach it); penetrating farther and farther, through leaf-shaded cow-paths flecked with sunlight, into clearing after clearing. I could hear on all sides the tinkle of bells, the cracking of sticks, and the stamping of cattle that were taking refuge in the thicket from the flies. Occasionally, as I broke through a covert, I encountered a meek cow, who stared at me stupidly for a second, and then shambled off into the brush. I became accustomed to this dumb society, and picked on in silence, attributing all the wood-noises to the cattle, thinking nothing of any real bear. In point of fact, however, I was thinking all the time of a nice romantic bear, and, as I picked, was composing a story about a generous she-bear who had lost her cub, and who seized a small girl in this very wood, carried her tenderly off to a cave, and brought her up on bear's milk and honey. When the girl got big enough to run away, moved by her inherited instincts, she escaped, and came into the valley to her father's house (this part of the story was to be worked out, so that the child would know her father by some family resemblance, and have some language in which to address him), and told him where the bear lived. The father took his gun, and, guided by the unfeeling daughter, went into the woods and shot the bear, who never made any resistance, and only, when dying, turned reproachful eyes upon her murderer. The moral of the tale was to be, kindness to animals.

I was in the midst of this tale, when I happened to look some rods away to the other edge of the clearing, and there was a bear! He was standing on his hind-legs, and doing just what I was doing—picking blackberries. With one paw he bent down the bush, while with the other he clawed the berries into his mouth—green ones and all. To say that I was astonished is inside the mark. I suddenly discovered that I didn't want to see a bear, after all. At about the same moment the bear saw me, stopped eating berries, and regarded me with a glad surprise. It is all very well to imagine what you would do under such circumstances. Probably you wouldn't do it: I didn't. The bear dropped down on his forefeet, and came slowly towards me. Climbing a tree was of no use, with so good a climber in the rear. If I started to run, I had no doubt the bear would give chase; and although a bear cannot run down hill as fast as he can run uphill, yet I felt that he could get over this rough, brush-tangled ground faster than I could.

The bear was approaching. It suddenly occurred to me how I could divert his mind until I could fall back upon my military base. My pail was nearly full of excellent berries—much better than the bear could pick himself. I put the pail on the ground, and slowly backed away from it, keeping my eye, as beast tamers do, on the bear. The ruse succeeded.

The bear came up to the berries, and stopped. Not accustomed to eat out of a pail, he tipped it over, and nosed about in the fruit, "gorming" (if there is such a word) it down, mixed with leaves and dirt, like a pig. The bear is a worse feeder than the pig. Whenever he disturbs a maple-sugar camp in the spring, he always upsets the buckets of syrup, and tramples round in the sticky sweets, wasting more than he eats. The bear's manners are thoroughly disagreeable.

As soon as my enemy's head was down, I started and ran. Somewhat out of breath, and shaky, I reached my faithful rifle. It was not a minute too soon. I heard the bear crashing through the brush after me. Enraged at my duplicity, he was now coming on with blood in his eye. I felt that the time of one of us was probably short. The rapidity of thought at such moments of peril is well known. I thought an octavo volume, had it illustrated and published, sold fifty thousand copies, and went to Europe on the proceeds, while that bear was loping across the clearing. As I was cocking the gun, I made a hasty and unsatisfactory review of my whole life. I noted that, even in such a compulsory review, it is almost impossible to think of any good thing you have done. The sins come out uncommonly strong.

I recollected a newspaper subscription I had delayed paying years and years ago, until both editor and newspaper were dead, and which now never could be paid to all eternity.

The bear was coming on.

I tried to remember what I had read about encounters with bears. I couldn't recall an instance in which a man had run away from a bear in the woods and escaped, although I recalled plenty where the bear had run from the man and got off. I tried to think what is the best way to kill a bear with a gun, when you are not near enough to club him with the stock. My first thought was to fire at his head; to plant the ball between his eyes: but this is a dangerous experiment. The bear's brain is very small; and, unless you hit that, the bear does not mind a bullet in his head; that is, not at the time. I remembered that the instant death of the bear would follow a bullet planted just back of his foreleg, and sent into his heart. This spot is also difficult to reach, unless the bear stands off, side towards you, like a target. I finally determined to fire at him generally.

The bear was coming on.

The contest seemed to me very different from anything at Creedmoor. I had carefully read the reports of the shooting there; but it was not easy to apply the experience I had thus acquired. I hesitated whether I had better fire lying on my stomach; or lying on my back, and resting the gun on my toes. But in neither position, I reflected, could I see the bear until he was upon me. The range was too short; and the bear wouldn't wait for me to examine the thermometer, and note the direction of the wind. Trial of the Creedmoor method, therefore, had to be abandoned; and I bitterly regretted that I had not read more accounts of off-hand shooting.

For the bear was coming on.

I tried to fix my last thoughts upon my family. As my family is small, this was not difficult. Dread of displeasing my wife, or hurting her feelings, was uppermost in my mind. What would be her anxiety as hour after hour passed on, and I did not return! What would the rest of the household think as the afternoon passed, and no blackberries came! What would be my wife's mortification when the news was brought that her husband had been eaten by a bear! I cannot imagine anything more ignominious than to have a husband eaten by a bear. And this was not my only anxiety. The mind at such times is not under control. With the gravest fears the most whimsical ideas will occur. I looked beyond the mourning friends, and thought what kind of an epitaph they would be compelled to put upon the stone. Something like this:

HERE LIE THE REMAINS
OF _____ _____,
EATEN BY A BEAR
Aug. 20, 1877.

It is a very unheroic and even disagreeable epitaph. That "eaten by a bear" is intolerable. It is grotesque. And then I thought what an inadequate language the English is for compact expression. It would not answer to put upon the stone simply "eaten," for that is indefinite, and requires explanation: it might mean eaten by a cannibal. This difficulty could not occur in the German, where *essen* signifies the act of feeding by a man, and *fressen* by a beast. How simple the thing would be in German!—

HIER LIEGT

HOCHWOHLGEBOREN

HERR _____ _____,

GEFRESSEN

Aug. 20, 1877.

That explains itself. The well-born one was eaten by a beast, and presumably by a bear—an animal that has a bad reputation since the days of Elisha.

The bear was coming on; he had, in fact, come on. I judged that he could see the whites of my eyes. All my subsequent reflections were confused. I raised the gun, covered the bear's breast with the sight, and let drive. Then I turned, and ran like a deer. I did not hear the bear pursuing. I looked back. The bear had stopped. He was lying down. I then remembered that the best thing to do after having fired your gun is to reload it. I slipped in a charge, keeping my eyes on the bear. He never stirred. I walked back suspiciously. There was a quiver in the hind-legs, but no other motion. Still, he might be shamming: bears often sham. To make sure, I approached, and put a ball into his head. He didn't mind it now; he minded nothing. Death had come to him with a merciful suddenness. He was calm in death. In order that he might remain so, I blew his brains out, and then started for home. I had killed a bear!

Notwithstanding my excitement, I managed to saunter into the house with an unconcerned air. There was a chorus of voices:

"Where are your blackberries?"

"Why were you gone so long?"

"Where's your pail?"

"I left the pail."

"Left the pail? What for?"

"A bear wanted it."

"Oh, nonsense!"

"Well, the last I saw of it a bear had it."

"Oh, come! You didn't really see a bear?"

"Yes, but I did really see a real bear."

"Did he run?"

"Yes; he ran after me."

"I don't believe a word of it! What did you do?"

"Oh! nothing particular—except kill the bear."

Cries of "Gammon!" "Don't believe it!" "Where's the bear?"

"If you want to see the bear, you must go up into the woods. I couldn't bring him down alone."

Having satisfied the household that something extraordinary had occurred, and excited the posthumous fear of some of them for my own safety, I went down into the valley to get help. The great bear-hunter, who keeps one of the summer boarding-houses, received my story with a smile of incredulity; and the incredulity spread to the other inhabitants and to the boarders, as soon as the story was known. However, as I insisted in all soberness, and offered to lead them to the bear, a party of forty or fifty people at last started off with me to bring the bear in. Nobody believed there was any bear in the case; but everybody who could get a gun carried one; and we went into the woods, armed with guns, pistols, pitchforks and sticks, against all contingencies or surprises—a crowd made up mostly of scoffers and jeerers.

But when I led the way to the fatal spot, and pointed out the bear, lying peacefully wrapped in his own skin, something like terror seized the boarders, and genuine excitement the natives. It was a no-mistake bear, by George! and the hero of the fight—well, I will not insist upon that. But what a procession that was, carrying the bear home! and what a congregation was speedily gathered in the valley to see the bear! Our best preacher up there never drew anything like it on Sunday.

And I must say that my particular friends, who were sportsmen, behaved very well on the whole. They didn't deny that it was a bear, although they said it was small for a bear. Mr. Deane, who is equally good with a rifle and a rod, admitted that it was a very fair shot. He is probably the best salmon-fisher in the United States, and he is an equally good hunter. I suppose there is no person in America who is more desirous to kill a moose than he. But he needlessly remarked, after he had examined the wound in the bear, that he had seen that kind of a shot made by a cow's horn.

This sort of talk affected me not. When I went to sleep that night, my last delicious thought was, "I've killed a bear!"

SOURCE: *The Atlantic Monthly*. January 1878.

THE PARSON'S HORSE RACE (1878)

Harriet Beecher Stowe

Harriet Beecher Stowe (1811–1896), renowned for the novel Uncle Tom's Cabin *(1852), which indeed deserves credit for shaking America of its complacency with slavery, was a professional author of great skill and conviction, and she wrote with power and comedy for several decades. Among the many surprises a modern reader will find in* Uncle Tom's Cabin, *for instance, are the light and comic episodes. Stowe collected this "used-horse salesman" story in* Sam Lawson's Oldtown Fireside Stories *(1881).*

"WAL, NOW, THIS 'ere does beat all! I wouldn'ta thought it o' the deacon."

So spoke Sam Lawson, drooping in a discouraged, contemplative attitude in front of an equally discouraged-looking horse, that had just been brought to him by the Widow Simpkins for medical treatment. Among Sam's many accomplishments, he was reckoned in the neighborhood an oracle in all matters of this kind, especially by women, whose helplessness in meeting such emergencies found unfailing solace under his compassionate willingness to attend to any business that did not strictly belong to him, and from which no pecuniary return was to be expected.

The Widow Simpkins had bought this horse of Deacon Atkins, apparently a fairly well-appointed brute, and capable as he was good-looking. A short, easy drive, when the Deacon held the reins, had shown off his points to advantage; and the widow's small stock of ready savings had come forth freely in payment for what she thought was a bargain. When, soon after coming into possession, she discovered that her horse, if driven with any haste, panted in a fearful manner, and that he appeared to be growing lame, she waxed wroth, and went to the Deacon in anger, to be met only with the smooth reminder that the animal was all right when she took him; that she had seen him tried herself. The widow was of a nature somewhat spicy, and expressed herself warmly: "It's a cheat and a shame, and I'll take the law on ye!"

"What law will you take?" said the unmoved Deacon. "Wasn't it a fair bargain?"

"I'll take the law of God," said the widow, with impotent indignation; and she departed to pour her cares and trials into the ever ready ear of Sam. Having assumed the care of the animal, he now sat contemplating it in a sort of trance of melancholy reflection.

"Why, boys," he broke out, "why didn't she come to me afore she bought this crittur? Why, I knew all about him! That 'ere crittur was jest ruined a year ago last summer, when Tom, the Deacon's boy there, come home from college. Tom driv him over to Sherburn and back that 'ere hot Fourth of July. 'Member it, 'cause I saw the crittur when he come home. I sot up with Tom takin' care of him all night. That 'ere crittur had the thumps all night, and he hain't never been good for nothin' since. I telled the Deacon he was a gone hoss then, and wouldn't never be good for nothin'. The Deacon, he took off his shoes, and let him run to pastur' all summer, and he's ben a-feedin' and nussin' on him up; and now he's put him off on the widder. I wouldn'ta thought it o' the Deacon! Why, this hoss'll never be no 'good to her! That 'ere's a used-up crittur, any fool may see! He'll mabbe do for about a quarter of an hour on a smooth road; but come to drive him as a body wants to drive, why, he blows like my bellowsis; and the Deacon knew it—musta known it!"

"Why, Sam!" we exclaimed, "ain't the Deacon a good man?"

"Wal, now, there's where the shoe pinches! In a gin'al way the Deacon is a good man—he's consid'able more than middlin' good; gin'ally he adorns his perfession. On most p'ints I don't hev nothin' agin the Deacon; and this 'ere ain't a bit like him. But there 'tis! Come to hosses, there's where the unsanctified natur' comes out. Folks will cheat about hosses when they won't about 'most nothin' else." And Sam leaned back on his cold forge, now empty of coal, and seemed to deliver himself to a mournful train of general reflection. "Yes, hosses does seem to be sort o' unregenerate critturs," he broke out: "there's suthin about hosses that deceives the very elect. The best o' folks gets tripped up when they come to deal in hosses."

"Why, Sam, is there anything bad in horses?" we interjected timidly.

" 'Tain't the hosses," said Sam with solemnity. "Lordy massy! the hosses is all right enough! Hosses is scriptural animals. Elijah went up to heaven in a chari't with hosses, and then all them lots o' hosses in the Ravelations—black and white and red, and all sorts o' colors. That 'ere shows hosses goes to heaven; but it's more'n the folks that hev 'em is likely to, ef they don't look out.

"Ministers, now," continued Sam, in a soliloquizing vein—"folks allers thinks it's suthin' sort o' shaky in a minister to hev much to do with hosses—sure to get 'em into trouble. There was old Parson Williams of North Billriky got into a drefful mess about a hoss. Lordy massy! he wern't to blame, neither; but he got into the dreffulest scrape you ever heard on—come nigh to unsettlin' him."

"O Sam, tell us all about it!" we boys shouted, delighted with the prospect of a story.

"Wal, wait now till I get off this crittur's shoes, and we'll take him up to pastur', and then we can kind o' set by the river, and fish. Hepsy wanted a mess o' fish for supper, and I was cal'latin' to git some for her. You boys go and be digging bait, and git yer lines."

And so, as we were sitting tranquilly beside the Charles River, watching our lines, Sam's narrative began:

"Ye see, boys, Parson Williams—he's dead now, but when I was a boy he was one of the gret men round here. He writ books. He writ a tract agin the Armenians, and put 'em down; and he writ a big book on the millennium (I've got that 'ere book now); and he was a smart preacher. Folks said he had invitations to settle in Boston, and there ain't no doubt he mighta hed a Boston parish ef he'd 'a ben a mind ter take it; but he'd got a good settlement and a handsome farm in North Billriky, and didn't care to move; thought, I s'pose, that 'twas better to be number one in a little place than number two in a big un. Anyway, he carried all before him where he was.

"Parson Williams was a tall, straight, personable man; come of good family—father and grand'ther before him all ministers. He was putty up and down, and commandin' in his ways, and things had to go putty much as he said. He was a good deal sot by, Parson Williams was, and his wife was a Derby—one o' them rich Salem Derbys—and brought him a lot o' money; and so they lived putty easy and comfortable so fur as this world's goods goes. Well, now, the parson wa'n't reely what you call worldly-minded; but then he was one o' them folks that knows what's good in temporals as well as sperituals, and allers liked to hev the best that there was goin'; and he allers had an eye to a good hoss.

"Now, there was Parson Adams and Parson Scranton, and most of the other ministers: they didn't know and didn't care what hoss they hed; jest jogged round with these 'ere poundin', potbellied, sleepy critturs that ministers mostly hes—good enough to crawl around to funerals and ministers' meetin's and 'sociations and sich; but Parson Williams, he allers would hev a hoss as was a hoss. He looked out for blood; and, when these 'ere Vermont fellers would come down with a drove, the person he hed his eyes open, and knew what was what. Couldn't none of 'em cheat him on hoss flesh! And so one time when Zach Buel was down with a drove, the doctor he bought the best hoss in the lot. Zach said he never see a parson afore that he couldn't cheat; but he said the doctor reely knew as much as he did, and got the very one he'd meant to 'a kept for himself.

"This 'ere hoss was a peeler, I'll tell you! They'd called him Tamerlane, from some heathen feller or other: the boys called him Tam, for short. Tam was a great character. All the fellers for miles round knew the doctor's Tam, and used to come clear over from the other parishes to see him.

"Wal, this 'ere sot up Cuff's back high, I tell you! Cuff was the doctor's nigger man, and he was nat'lly a drefful proud crittur. The way he would swell and strut and brag about the doctor and his folks and his things! The doctor used to give Cuff his cast-off clothes: and Cuff would prance round in 'em, and seem to think he was a doctor of divinity himself, and had the charge of all natur'.

"Well, Cuff he reely made an idol o' that 'ere hoss—a reg'lar graven image—and bowed down and worshiped him. He didn't think nothin' was too good for him. He washed and brushed and curried him, and rubbed him down till he shone like a lady's satin dress; and he took pride in ridin' and drivin' him, 'cause it was what the doctor wouldn't let nobody else do but himself. You see, Tam wern't no lady's hoss. Miss Williams was 'afraid as death of him; and the parson he hed to git her a sort o' low-sperited crittur that she could drive herself. But he liked to drive Tam; and he liked to go round the country on his back, and a fine figure of a man he was on him, too. He didn't let nobody else back him or handle the reins but Cuff; and Cuff was drefful set up about it, and he swelled and bragged about that ar hoss all round the country. Nobody couldn't put in a word 'bout any other hoss, without Cuff's feathers would be all up stiff as a tomturkey's tail; and that's how Cuff got the doctor into trouble.

"Ye see, there nat'lly was others that thought they'd got horses, and didn't want to be crowed over. There was Bill Atkins, out to the west parish, and Ike Sanders, that kep' a stable up to Pequot Holler: they was down a-lookin' at the parson's hoss, and a-bettin' on their'n, and a darin' Cuff to race with 'em.

"Wal, Cuff, he couldn't stan' it, and, when the doctor's back was turned, he'd be off on the sly, and they'd hev their race; and Tam he beat 'em all. Tam, ye see, boys, was a hoss that couldn't and wouldn't hev a hoss ahead of him—he jest wouldn't! Ef he dropped down dead in his tracks the next minit, he would be ahead; and he allers got ahead. And so his name got up, and fellers kep' comin' to try their horses; and Cuff'd take Tam out to race with fust one and then another till this 'ere got to be a reg'lar thing, and begun to be talked about.

"Folks sort o' wondered if the doctor knew: but Cuff was sly as a weasel, and allers had a story ready for every turn. Cuff was one of them fellers that could talk a bird off a bush—master hand he was to slick things over!

"There was folks as said they believed the doctor was knowin' to it, and that he felt a sort o' carnal pride sech as a minister oughtn't fer to hev, and so shet his eyes to what was a-goin' on. Aunt Sally Nickerson said she was sure on't. 'Twas all talked over down to old Miss Bummiger's funeral, and Aunt Sally she said the church ought to look into't. But everybody knew Aunt Sally: she was allers watchin' for folks' haltin's, and settin' on herself up to jedge her neighbors.

"Wal, I never believed nothin' agin Parson Williams: it was all Cuff's contrivances. But the fact was, the fellers all got their blood up, and there was hoss-racin' in all the parishes; and it got so they'd even race hosses a Sunday.

"Wal, of course they never got the doctor's hoss out a Sunday. Cuff wouldn'ta durst to do that, Lordy massy, no! He was allers there in church, settin' up in the doctor's clothes, rollin' up his eyes, and lookin' as pious as ef he never thought o' racin' hosses. He was an awful solemn-lookin' nigger in church, Cuff was.

"But there was a lot o' them fellers up to Pequot Holler— Bill Atkins, and Ike Sanders, and Tom Peters, and them Hokum boys— used to go out arter meetin' Sunday arternoon, and race hosses. Ye see, it was jest close to the State-line, and, if the s'lectmen was to come down on 'em, they could jest whip over the line, and they couldn't take 'em.

"Wal, it got to be a great scandal. The fellers talked about it up to the tavern; and the deacons and the tithingman, they took it up and went to Parson Williams about it; and the parson he told 'em jest to keep still, not let the fellers know that they was bein' watched, and next Sunday he and the tithingman and the constable, they'd ride over, and catch 'em in the very act.

"So next Sunday arternoon Parson Williams and Deacon Popkins and Ben Bradley (he was constable that year), they got on to their hosses, and rode over to Pequot Holler. The doctor's blood was up, and he meant to come down on 'em strong; for that was his way o' doin' in his parish. And they was in a sort o' day-o'-jedgment frame o' mind, and jogged along solemn as a hearse, till, come to rise the hill above the holler, they see three or four fellers with their hosses gittin' ready to race; and the parson says he, 'Let's come on quiet, and get behind these bushes, and we'll see what they're up to, and catch 'em in the act.'

"But the mischief on't was, that Ike Sanders see 'em comin', and he knowed Tam in a minit—Ike knowed Tam of old—and he jest tipped the wink to the rest. 'Wait, boys,' says he: 'let 'em git close up, and then I'll give the word, and the doctor's hoss will be racin' ahead like thunder.'

"Wal, so the doctor and his folks they drew up behind the bushes, and stood there innocent as could be, and saw 'em gittin' ready to start. Tam, he begun to snuffle and paw, but the doctor never mistrusted what he was up to till Ike sung out, 'Go it, boys!' and the hosses all started, when, sure as you live, boys! Tam give one fly, and was over the bushes, and in among 'em, goin' it like chain-lightnin' ahead of 'em all.

"Deacon Popkins and Ben Bradley jest stood and held their breath to see 'em all goin' it so like thunder; and the doctor, he was took so sudden it was all he could do to jest hold on anyway: so away he went, and trees and bushes and fences streaked by him like ribbins. His hat flew off behind him, and his wig arter, and got catched in a barberry-bush; but Lordy massy! he couldn't stop to think o' them.

He jest leaned down, and caught Tam round the neck, and held on for dear life till they come to the stopping-place.

"Wal, Tam was ahead of them all, sure enough, and was snorting and snuffling as if he'd got the very old boy in him, and was up to racing some more on the spot.

"That 'ere Ike Sanders was the impudentest feller that ever you see, and he roared and rawhawed at the doctor. 'Good for you, parson!' says he. 'You beat us all holler,' says he. 'Takes a parson for that, don't it, boys?' he said. And then he and Ike and Tom, and the two Hokum boys, they jest roared, and danced round like wild critturs. Wal, now, only think on't, boys, what a situation that 'ere was for a minister—a man that had come out with the best of motives to put a stop to Sabbath-breakin'! There he was all rumpled up and dusty, and his wig hangin' in the bushes, and these 'ere ungodly fellers gettin' the laugh on him, and all acause o' that 'ere hoss. There's times, boys, when ministers must be tempted to swear, if there ain't preventin' grace, and this was one o' them times to Parson Williams. They say he got red in the face, and looked as if he should bust, but he didn't say nothin': he scorned to answer. The sons o' Zeruiah was too hard for him, and he let 'em hev their say. But when they'd got through, and Ben had brought him his hat and wig, and brushed and settled him ag'in, the parson he says, 'Well, boys, ye've had your say and your laugh; but I warn you now I won't have this thing goin' on here any more,' says he; 'so mind yourselves.'

"Wal, the boys see that the doctor's blood was up, and they rode off pretty quiet; and I believe they never raced no more in that spot.

"But there ain't no tellin' the talk this 'ere thing made. Folks will talk, you know; and there wer'n't a house in all Billriky, nor in the south parish nor center, where it wer'n't had over and discussed. There was the deacon, and Ben Bradley was there, to witness and show jest how the thing was, and that the doctor was jest in the way of his duty; but folks said it made a great scandal; that a minister hadn't no business to hev that kind o' hoss, and that he'd give the enemy occasion to speak reproachfully. It reely did seem as if Tam's sins was imputed to the doctor; and folks said he ought to sell Tam right away, and get a sober minister's hoss.

"But others said it was Cuff that had got Tam into bad ways; and they do say that Cuff had to catch it pretty lively when the doctor come to settle with him. Cuff thought his time had come, sure enough, and was so scairt that he turned blacker'n ever: he got enough to cure him o' hoss-racin' for one while. But Cuff got over it arter a while, and so did the doctor. Lordy massy! there ain't nothin' lasts forever! Wait long enough, and 'most every thing blows over. So it turned out about the doctor. There was a rumpus and a fuss, and folks talked and talked, and advised; everybody had their say: but the doctor kep' right straight on, and kep' his hoss all the same.

"The ministers, they took it up in the 'sociation; but, come to tell the story, it sot 'em all a-laughin', so they couldn't be very hard on the doctor.

"The doctor felt sort o' streaked at fust when they told the story on him; he didn't jest like it: but he got used to it, and finally, when he was twitted on't, he'd sort o' smile, and say, 'Anyway, Tam beat 'em: that's one comfort.'"

SOURCE: *The Atlantic Monthly*. Volume 42. October 1878.

THE PETERKINS DECIDE TO LEARN
THE LANGUAGES (1878)

Lucretia Peabody Hale

*Born in Boston, Hale (1820–1900) was the daughter of the nephew of the
American patriot Nathan Hale. The Peterkins were her situation-comedy heroes
and starred in many stories and two collections.*

CERTAINLY NOW WAS the time to study the languages. The
Peterkins had moved into a new house, far more convenient than
their old one, where they would have a place for everything, and
everything in its place. Of course they would then have more time.

Elizabeth Eliza recalled the troubles of the old house; how for a
long time she was obliged to sit outside of the window upon the
piazza, when she wanted to play on her piano.

Mrs. Peterkin reminded them of the difficulty about the table-
cloths. The upper table-cloth was kept in a trunk that had to stand in
front of the door to the closet under the stairs. But the under table-
cloth was kept in a drawer in the closet. So, whenever the cloths were
changed, the trunk had to be pushed away under some projecting
shelves to make room for opening the closet door (as the under table-
cloth must be taken out first), then the trunk was pushed back to
make room for it to be opened for the upper table-cloth, and, after
all, it was necessary to push the trunk away again to open the closet-
door for the knife-tray. This always consumed a great deal of time.

Now that the china-closet was large enough, everything could
find a place in it.

Agamemnon especially enjoyed the new library. In the old house
there was no separate room for books. The dictionaries were kept

64

upstairs, which was very inconvenient, and the volumes of the Encyclopaedia could not be together. There was not room for all in one place. So from A to P were to be found downstairs, and from Q to Z were scattered in different rooms upstairs. And the worst of it was, you could never remember whether from A to P included P. "I always went upstairs after P," said Agamemnon, "and then always found it downstairs, or else it was the other way."

Of course, now there were more conveniences for study. With the books all in one room there would be no time wasted in looking for them.

Mr. Peterkin suggested they should each take a separate language. If they went abroad, this would prove a great convenience. Elizabeth Eliza could talk French with the Parisians; Agamemnon, German with the Germans; Solomon John, Italian with the Italians; Mrs. Peterkin, Spanish in Spain; and perhaps he could himself master all the Eastern languages and Russian.

Mrs. Peterkin was uncertain about undertaking the Spanish; but all the family felt very sure they should not go to Spain (as Elizabeth Eliza dreaded the Inquisition), and Mrs. Peterkin felt more willing.

Still she had quite an objection to going abroad. She had always said she would not go till a bridge was made across the Atlantic, and she was sure it did not look like it now.

Agamemnon said there was no knowing. There was something new every day, and a bridge was surely not harder to invent than a telephone, for they had bridges in the very earliest days.

Then came up the question of the teachers. Probably these could be found in Boston. If they could all come the same day, three could be brought out in the carry-all. Agamemnon could go in for them, and could learn a little on the way out and in.

Mr. Peterkin made some inquiries about the Oriental languages. He was told that Sanskrit was at the root of all. So he proposed they should all begin with Sanskrit. They would thus require but one teacher, and could branch out into the other languages afterward.

But the family preferred learning the separate languages. Elizabeth Eliza already knew something of the French. She had tried to talk it, without much success, at the Centennial Exhibition, at one of the side stands. But she found she had been talking with a Moorish gentleman who did not understand French. Mr. Peterkin feared they might need more libraries if all the teachers came at the same hour; but Agamemnon reminded him that they would be using different dictionaries. And Mr. Peterkin thought something might be learned by having them all at once. Each one might pick up something besides the language he was studying, and it was a great thing to learn to talk a foreign language while others were talking about you. Mrs. Peterkin was afraid it would be like the Tower of Babel, and hoped it was all right.

Agamemnon brought forward another difficulty. Of course, they ought to have foreign teachers who spoke only their native languages. But, in this case, how could they engage them to come, or explain to them about the carry-all, or arrange the proposed hours? He did not understand how anybody ever began with a foreigner, because he could not even tell him what he wanted.

Elizabeth Eliza thought a great deal might be done by signs and pantomime. Solomon John and the little boys began to show how it might be done. Elizabeth Eliza explained how *"langues"* meant both "languages" and "tongues," and they could point to their tongues. For practice, the little boys represented the foreign teachers talking in their different languages, and Agamemnon and Solomon John went to invite them to come out and teach the family by a series of signs.

Mr. Peterkin thought their success was admirable, and that they might almost go abroad without any study of the languages, and trust to explaining themselves by signs. Still, as the bridge was not yet made, it might be as well to wait and cultivate the languages.

Mrs. Peterkin was afraid the foreign teachers might imagine they were invited out to lunch. Solomon John had constantly pointed to his mouth as he opened it and shut it, putting out his tongue, and it looked a great deal more as if he were inviting them to eat than asking them to teach. Agamemnon suggested that they might carry the separate dictionaries when they went to see the teachers, and that would show that they meant lessons, and not lunch.

Mrs. Peterkin was not sure but she ought to prepare a lunch for them, if they had come all that way; but she certainly did not know what they were accustomed to eat.

Mr. Peterkin thought this would be a good thing to learn of the foreigners. It would be a good preparation for going abroad, and they might get used to the dishes before starting. The little boys were delighted at the idea of having new things cooked. Agamemnon had heard that beer-soup was a favorite dish with the

Germans, and he would inquire how it was made in the first lesson. Solomon John had heard they were all very fond of garlic, and thought it would be a pretty attention to have some in the house the first day, that they might be cheered by the odor.

Elizabeth Eliza wanted to surprise the lady from Philadelphia by her knowledge of French, and hoped to begin on her lessons before the Philadelphia family arrived for their annual visit.

There were still some delays. Mr. Peterkin was very anxious to obtain teachers who had been but a short time in this country. He did not want to be tempted to talk any English with them. He wanted the latest and freshest languages, and at last came home one day with a list of "brand-new foreigners."

They decided to borrow the Bromwicks' carry-all to use, besides their own, for the first day, and Mr. Peterkin and Agamemnon drove into town to bring all the teachers out. One was a Russian gentleman, traveling, who came with no idea of giving lessons, but perhaps would consent to do so. He could not yet speak English. Mr. Peterkin had his card-case and the cards of the several gentlemen who had recommended the different teachers, and he went with Agamemnon from hotel to hotel collecting them. He found them all very polite and ready to come, after the explanation by signs agreed upon. The dictionaries had been forgotten, but Agamemnon had a directory, which looked the same and seemed to satisfy the foreigners.

Mr. Peterkin was obliged to content himself with the Russian instead of one who could teach Sanskrit, as there was no new teacher of that language lately arrived.

But there was an unexpected difficulty in getting the Russian gentleman into the same carriage with the teacher of Arabic, for he was a Turk, sitting with a fez on his head, on the back seat! They glared at each other, and began to assail each other in every language they knew, none of which Mr. Peterkin could understand. It might be Russian; it might have been Arabic. It was easy to understand that they would never consent to sit in the same carriage. Mr. Peterkin was in despair; he had forgotten about the Russian war! What a mistake to have invited the Turk!

Quite a crowd collected on the sidewalk in front of the hotel. But the French gentleman politely, but stiffly, invited the Russian to go with him in the first carry-all. Here was another difficulty. For the German professor was quietly ensconced on the back seat!

As soon as the French gentleman put his foot on the step and saw him, he addressed him in such forcible language that the German professor got out of the door the other side, and came round on the sidewalk and took him by the collar. Certainly the German and French gentlemen could not be put together, and more crowd collected!

Agamemnon, however, had happily studied up the German word "Herr," and he applied it to the German, inviting him by signs to take a seat in the other carry-all. The German consented to sit by the Turk, as they neither of them could understand the other; and at last they started, Mr. Peterkin with the Italian by his side, and the French and Russian teachers behind, vociferating to each other in languages unknown to Mr. Peterkin, while he feared they were not perfectly in harmony; so he drove home as fast as possible. Agamemnon had a silent party. The Spaniard at his side was a little moody, while the Turk and the German behind did not utter a word.

At last they reached the house, and were greeted by Mrs. Peterkin and Elizabeth Eliza, Mrs. Peterkin with her llama lace shawl over her shoulders, as a tribute to the Spanish teacher. Mr. Peterkin was careful to take his party in first, and deposit them in a distant part of the library, far from the Turk or the German, even putting the Frenchman and Russian apart.

Solomon John found the Italian dictionary, and seated himself by his Italian; Agamemnon, with the German dictionary, by the German. The little boys took their copy of the *Arabian Nights* to the Turk. Mr. Peterkin attempted to explain to the Russian that he had no Russian dictionary, as he had hoped to learn Sanskrit of him, while Mrs. Peterkin was trying to inform her teacher that she had no books in Spanish. She got over all fears of the Inquisition, he looked so sad, and she tried to talk a little, using English words, but very slowly, and altering the accent as far as she knew how. The Spaniard bowed, looked gravely interested, and was very polite.

Elizabeth Eliza, meanwhile, was trying her grammar phrases with the Parisian. She found it easier to talk French than to understand him. But he understood perfectly her sentences. She repeated one of her vocabularies, and went on with, *"J'ai le livre."* *"As-tu le pain?"* *"L'enfant a une poire."* He listened with great attention, and replied slowly. Suddenly she started, after making out one of his sentences, and went to her mother to whisper, "They have made the mistake you feared. They think they are invited to lunch! *He* has just been thanking me for our politeness in inviting them to *dejeuner*,—that means breakfast!"

"They have not had their breakfast!" exclaimed Mrs. Peterkin, looking at her Spaniard; "he does look hungry! What shall we do?"

Elizabeth Eliza was consulting her father. What should they do? How should they make them understand that they invited them to teach, not lunch. Elizabeth Eliza begged Agamemnon to look out "*apprendre*" in the dictionary. It must mean to teach. Alas, they found it means both to teach and to learn! What should they do? The foreigners were now sitting silent in their different corners. The Spaniard grew more and more sallow. What if he should faint? The Frenchman was rolling up each of his mustaches to a point as he gazed at the German. What if the Russian should fight the Turk? What if the German should be exasperated by the airs of the Parisian?

"We must give them something to eat," said Mr. Peterkin, in a low tone. "It would calm them."

"If I only knew what they were used to eating!" said Mrs. Peterkin.

Solomon John suggested that none of them knew what the others were used to eating, and they might bring in anything.

Mrs. Peterkin hastened out with hospitable intents. Amanda could make good coffee. Mr. Peterkin had suggested some American dish. Solomon John sent a little boy for some olives.

It was not long before the coffee came in, and a dish of baked beans. Next, some olives and a loaf of bread, and some boiled eggs, and some bottles of beer. The effect was astonishing. Every man spoke his own tongue, and fluently. Mrs. Peterkin poured out coffee for the Spaniard, while he bowed to her. They all liked beer; they all liked olives. The Frenchman was fluent about *"les moeurs Americaines."* Elizabeth Eliza supposed he alluded to their not having set any table. The Turk smiled; the Russian was voluble. In the midst of the clang of the different languages, just as Mr. Peterkin was again repeating, under cover of the noise of many tongues, "How shall we make them understand that we want them to teach?"—at this moment the door was flung open, and there came in the lady from Philadelphia, that day arrived, her first call of the season.

She started back in terror at the tumult of so many different languages. The family, with joy, rushed to meet her. All together they called upon her to explain for them. Could she help them? Could she tell the foreigners that they wanted to take lessons? Lessons? They had no sooner uttered the word than their guests all started up with faces beaming with joy. It was the one English word they all knew! They had come to Boston to give lessons! The Russian traveler had hoped to learn English in this way. The thought pleased them more than the dejeuner. Yes, gladly would they give lessons. The Turk smiled at the idea. The first step was taken. The teachers knew they were expected to teach.

SOURCE: *St. Nicholas: Scribner's Illustrated Magazine*. New York: Scribner and Company, December 1878.

UNCLE REMUS AND THE WONDERFUL TAR-BABY STORY (1881)

Joel Chandler Harris

Harris (1848–1908) was a white man born in Georgia who made his name while a copy editor at Atlanta Constitution *as the creator of "Uncle Remus." Uncle Remus was a black man born into slavery, whose tales of clever animals amused the grandson of the plantation owner who used to own him. Harris began writing these stories in 1879, and they became immensely popular, being reprinted in other newspapers and then collected in books. There's no avoiding the squirming these black-face stories cause in their original and Disneyfied versions, but the originals have the advantage of being more complicated and less reducible to stereotypes; for example, Uncle Remus continuously conveys his idiosyncratic personality and distinctiveness in spite of the patronizing point of view of the narrator. Below are presented three short tales; I have altered the original title of the first selection, "Uncle Remus Initiates the Little Boy," to avoid even further nervousness on the part of twenty-first-century readers. If not historically interesting, which they certainly are, they're actually funny. I present three episodes, the second of which provides the overall title (the third is "How Mr. Rabbit Was Too Sharp for Mr. Fox").*

ONE EVENING RECENTLY, the lady whom Uncle Remus calls "Miss Sally" missed her little seven-year-old. Making search for him through the house and through the yard, she heard the sound of voices in the old man's cabin, and, looking through the window, saw the child sitting by Uncle Remus. His head rested against the old man's arm, and he was gazing with an expression of the most intense interest into the rough, weather-beaten face that beamed so kindly upon him. This is what "Miss Sally" heard:

"Bimeby, one day, arter Brer Fox bin doin' all dat he could fer ter ketch Brer Rabbit, en Brer Rabbit bin doin' all he could fer ter

71

keep 'im fum it, Brer Fox say to hisse'f dat Uncle Remus, he'd put up a game on Brer Rabbit, en he ain't mo'n got de wuds out'n his mout twel Brer Rabbit come a lopin' up de big road, lookin' des ez plump en ez fat en ez sassy ez a Moggin hoss in a barley-patch.

"'Hol' on, dar, Brer Rabbit,' sez Brer Fox, sezee.

"'I ain't got time, Brer Fox,' sez Brer Rabbit, sezee, sorter mendin' his licks.

"'I wanter have some confab wid you, Brer Rabbit,' sez Brer Fox, sezee.

"'All right, Brer Fox; but you better holler fum whar you stan'. I'm monstus full er fleas dis mawnin',' sez Brer Rabbit, sezee.

"'I seed Brer B'ar yistiddy,' sez Brer Fox, sezee, "en he sorter rake me over de coals kaze you en me ain't make frens en live naberly; en I tole 'im dat I'd see you.'

"Den Brer Rabbit scratch one year wid his off hine-foot sorter jub'usly, en den he ups en sez, sezee:

"'All a settin', Brer Fox. Spose'n you drap roun' ter-morrer en take dinner wid me. We ain't got no great doin's at our house, but I speck de ole 'oman en de chilluns kin sorter scramble roun' en git up somp'n fer ter stay yo' stummuck.'

"'I'm 'gree'ble, Brer Rabbit,' sez Brer Fox, sezee.

"'Den I'll 'pen' on you,' sez Brer Rabbit, sezee.

"Nex' day, Mr. Rabbit an' Miss Rabbit got up soon, 'fo' day, en raided on a gyarden, like Miss Sally's out dar, en got some cabbiges, en some roas'n years, en some sparrer-grass, en dey fix up a smashin' dinner. Bimeby, one er de little Rabbits playin' out in de back-yard, come runnin' in, hollerin', 'Oh, ma! oh, ma! I seed Mr. Fox a comin'!' En den Brer Rabbit he tuck de chilluns by der years en make um set down; en den him en Miss Rabbit sorter dally roun' waitin' for Brer Fox. En dey keep on waitin', but no Brer Fox ain't come. Atter 'while Brer Rabbit goes to de do', easy like, en peep out, en dar, stickin' out fum behine de cornder, wuz de tip-een' er Brer Fox's tail. Den Brer Rabbit shot de do' en sot down, en put his paws behime his years en begin fer ter sing:

"De place wharbouts you spill de grease,
Right dar youer boun' ter slide,
An' whar you fine a bunch er hay,
You'll sholy fine de hide.

"Nex' day, Brer Fox sent word by Mr. Mink, en skuze hisse'f, kase he wuz too sick fer ter come, en he ax Brer Rabbit fer ter come en take dinner wid him, en Brer Rabbit say he wuz 'gree'ble.

"Bimeby, w'en de shadders wuz at der shortes', Brer Rabbit he sorter brush up en santer down ter Brer Fox's house, en w'en he got dar, he yer somebody groanin', en he look in de do' en dar he see Brer Fox settin' up in a rockin'-cheer all wrop up wid flannil, en he look mighty weak. Brer Rabbit look all 'roun', he did, but he ain't see no dinner. De dish-pan wuz settin' on de table, en close by wuz a kyarvin'-knife.

"'Look like you gwinter have chicken fer dinner, Brer Fox,' sez Brer Rabbit, sezee.

"'Yes, Brer Rabbit, deyer nice en fresh en tender,' sez Brer Fox, sezee.

"Den Brer Rabbit sorter pull his mustarsh, en say: 'You ain't got no calamus root, is you, Brer Fox? I done got so now dat I can't eat no chicken 'ceptin she's seasoned up wid calamus root.' En wid dat, Brer Rabbit lipt out er de do' and dodge 'mong de bushes, en sot dar watchin' fer Brer Fox; en he ain't watch long, nudder, kaze Brer Fox flung off de flannel en crope out er de house en got whar he could close in on Brer Rabbit, en bimeby Brer Rabbit holler out: 'Oh, Brer Fox! I'll des put yo' calamus root out yer on dish yer stump. Better come git it while it's fresh,' an' wid dat Brer Rabbit gallop off home. En Brer Fox ain't never kotch 'imyit, en w'at's mo', honey, he ain't gwineter.''

"Didn't the fox *never* catch the rabbit, Uncle Remus?" asked the little boy the next evening.

"He come mighty nigh it, honey, sho's you bawn—Brer Fox did. One day, alter Brer Rabbit fool 'im wid dat calamus root, Brer Fox went ter wuk en got 'im some tar, en mix it wid some turkentime, en fix up a contrapshun wat he call a Tar-Baby, en he tuck dish yer Tar-Baby en he sot 'er in de big road, en den he lay off in de bushes fer ter see wat de news wuz gwineter be. En he didn't hatter wait long, nudder, kaze bimeby here come Brer Rabbit pacin' down de road—lippity-clippity, clippitylippity—dez ez sassy ez a jay-bird. Brer Fox, he lay low. Brer Rabbit come prancin' long twel he spy de Tar-Baby, en den he fotch up on his behine legs like he was 'stonished. De Tar-Baby, she sot dar, she did, en Brer Fox, he lay low.

" 'Mawnin'!' sez Brer Rabbit, sezee—'nice wedder dis mawnin',' sezee.

"Tar-Baby ain't sayin' nuthin', en Brer Fox, he lay low.

" 'How duz yo' sym'tums seem ter segashuate?' sez Brer Rabbit, sezee.

"Brer Fox, he wink his eye slow, en lay low, en de Tar-Baby, she ain't sayin' nuthin'.

" 'How you come on, den? Is you deaf?' sez Brer Rabbit, sezee. 'Kaze if you is, I kin holler louder,' sezee.

"Tar-Baby stay still, en Brer Fox, he lay low.

" 'Youer stuck up, dat's what you is,' says Brer Rabbit, sezee, 'and I'm gwineter kyore you, dat's w'at I'm a gwineter do,' sezee.

"Brer Fox, he sorter chuckle in his stummock, he did, but Tar-Baby aint' sayin' nuthin'.

" 'I'm gwineter larn you howter talk ter 'specttubble fokes ef hit's de las' ack,' sez Brer Rabbit, sezee. 'Ef you don't take off dat hat en tell me howdy, I'm gwineter bus' you wide open,' sezee.

"Tar-Baby stay still, en Brer Fox, he lay low.

"Brer Rabbit keep on axin' 'im, en de Tar-Baby, she keep on sayin' nuthin', twel present'y Brer Rabbit draw back wid his fis', he did, en blip he tuck 'er side 'er de head. Right dar's whar he broke his merlasses jug. His fis' stuck, en he can't pull loose. De tar hilt 'im. But Tar-Baby, she stay still, en Brer Fox, he lay low.

" 'Ef you don't lemme loose, I'll knock you agin,' sez Brer Rabbit, sezee, en wid dat he fotch 'er a wipe wid de udder han', en dat stuck. Tar-Baby, she ain't sayin' nuthin', en Brer Fox, he lay low.

" 'Tu'n me loose, fo' I kick de natal stuffin' outen you,' sez Brer Rabbit, sezee, but de Tar-Baby, she ain't sayin' nuthin'. She des hilt on, en den Brer Rabbit lose de use er his feet in de same way. Brer Fox, he lay low. Den Brer Rabbit squall out dat ef de Tar-Baby don't tu'n 'im loose he butt 'er cranksided. En den he butted, en his head got stuck. Den Brer Fox, he sa'ntered fort', lookin' des ez innercent ez wunner yo' mammy's mockin'-birds.

" 'Howdy, Brer Rabbit,' sez Brer Fox, sezee. 'You look sorter stuck up dis mawnin',' sezee, en den he rolled on de groun', en laft en laft twel he couldn't laff no mo'. 'I speck you'll take dinner wid me dis time, Brer Rabbit. I done laid in some calamus root, en I ain't gwineter take no skuse,' sez Brer Fox, sezee."

Here Uncle Remus paused, and drew a two-pound yam out of the ashes.

"Did the fox eat the rabbit?" asked the little boy to whom the story had been told.

"Dat's all de fur de tale goes," replied the old man. "He mout, en den agin he mountent. Some say Jedge B'ar come 'long en loosed 'im—some say he didn't. I hear Miss Sally callin'. You better run 'long."

"Uncle Remus," said the little boy one evening, when he had found the old man with little or nothing to do, "did the fox kill and eat the rabbit when he caught him with the Tar-Baby?"

"Law, honey, ain't I tell you 'bout dat?" replied the old darkey, chuckling slyly. "I 'clar ter grashus I ought er tole you dat, but ole man Nod wuz ridin' on my eyeleds 'twel a leetle mo'n I'd a dis'member'd my own name, en den on to dat here come yo' mammy hollerin' after you.

"Wat I tell you w'en I fus' begin? I tole you Brer Rabbit wuz a monstus soon beas'; leas'ways- dat's w'at I laid out fer ter tell you. Well, den, honey, don't you go en make no udder kalkalashuns, kaze in dem days Brer Rabbit en his fambly wuz at de head er de gang w'en enny racket wuz on han', en dar dey stayed. 'Fo' you begins fer ter wipe yo' eyes 'bout Brer Rabbit, you wait en see whar'bouts Brer Rabbit gwineter fetch up at. But dat's needer yer ner dar.

"Wen Brer Fox fine Brer Rabbit mixt up wid de Tar-Baby, he feel mighty good, en he roll on de groun' en laff. Bimeby he up'n say, sezee:

"'Well, I speck I got you dis time, Brer Rabbit,' sezee; 'maybe I ain't, but I speck I is. You been runnin' roun' here sassin' atter me a mighty long time, but I speck you done come ter de een' er de row. You bin cuttin' up yo' capers en bouncin' 'roun' in dis naberhood ontwel you come ter b'leeve yo'se'f de boss er de whole gang. En den youer allers some'rs whar you got no bizness,' sez Brer Fox, sezee. 'Who ax you fer ter come en strike up a 'quaintence wid dish yer Tar-Baby? En who stuck you up dar whar you iz? Nobody in de roun' worril. You des tuck en jam yo'se'f on dat Tar-Baby widout waitin' fer enny invite,' sez Brer Fox, sezee, 'en dar you is, en dar you'll stay twel I fixes up a bresh-pile and fires her up, kaze I'm gwineter bobbycue you dis day, sho,' sez Brer Fox, sezee.

"Den Brer Rabbit talk mighty 'umble.

"'I don't keer w'at you do wid me, Brer Fox,' sezee, 'so you don't fling me in dat brier-patch. Roas' me, Brer Fox,' sezee, 'but don't fling me in dat brier-patch,' sezee.

"'Hit's so much trouble fer ter kindle a fier,' sez Brer Fox, sezee, 'dat I speck I'll hatter hang you,' sezee.

"'Hang me des ez high as you please, Brer Fox,' sez Brer Rabbit, sezee, 'but do fer de Lord's sake don't fling me in dat brier-patch,' sezee.

"'I ain't got no string,' sez Brer Fox, sezee, 'en now I speck I'll hatter drown you,' sezee.

"'Drown me des ez deep ez you please, Brer Fox,' sez Brer Rabbit, sezee, 'but do don't fling me in dat brierpatch,' sezee.

"'Dey ain't no water nigh,' sez Brer Fox, sezee, 'en now I speck I'll hatter skin you,' sezee.

"'Skin me, Brer Fox,' sez Brer Rabbit, sezee, 'snatch out my eyeballs, far out my years by de roots, en cut off my legs,' sezee, 'but do please, Brer Fox, don't fling me in dat brier-patch,' sezee.

"Co'se Brer Fox wanter hurt Brer Rabbit bad ez he kin, so he cotch 'im by de bchime legs en slung 'im right in de middle er de brier-patch. Dar wuz a considerbul flutter whar Brer Rabbit struck de bushes, en Brer Fox sorter hang 'roun' fer ter see w'at wuz gwineter happen. Bimeby he hear somebody call 'im, en way up de hill he see Brer Rabbit settin' cross-legged on a chinkapin log koamin' de pitch outen his har wid a chip. Den Brer Fox know dat he bin swop off mighty bad. Brer Rabbit wuz bleedzed fer ter fling back some er his sass, en he holler out:

"'Bred en bawn in a brier-patch, Brer Fox—bred en bawn in a brier-patch!' en wid dat he skip out des ez lively ez a cricket in de embers."

SOURCE: Joel Chandler Harris. *Uncle Remus: His Songs and His Sayings; the Folk-lore of the Old Plantation*. New York: D. Appleton and Company, 1881.

HIS PA GETS MAD! (1883)

George W. Peck

Peck (1840–1916) was born in New York State but grew up in Wisconsin. A long-time professional editor, he became the governor of Wisconsin in 1890. His "bad boy," featured below, was the starring character of several books.

"I WAS DOWN to the drug store this morning and saw your Ma buying a lot of court-plaster, enough to make a shirt I should think. What's she doing with so much court-plaster?" asked the grocery man of the bad boy, as he came in and pulled off his boots by the stove and emptied out a lot of snow that had collected as he walked through a drift, which melted and made a bad smell.

"O, I guess she was going to patch Pa up so he will hold water. Pa's temper got him into the worst muss you ever see, last night. If that museum was here now they would hire Pa and exhibit him as the tattooed man. I tell you, I have got too old to be mauled as though I was a kid, and any man who attacks me from this out, wants to have his peace made with the insurance companies, and know that his calling and election is sure, because I am a bad man and don't you forget it." And the boy pulled on his boots and looked so cross and desperate that the grocer-man asked him if he wouldn't try a little new cider.

"Good heavens!" said the grocery man, as the boy swallowed the cider, and his face resumed its natural look, and the piratical frown disappeared with the cider. "You have not stabbed your father have you? I have feared that one thing would bring on another, with you, and that you would yet be hung."

"Naw, I haven't stabbed him. It was another cat that stabbed him. You see, Pa wants me to do all the work around the house. The other day he bought a load of kindling wood, and told me to carry it into the basement. I had not been educated up to kindling wood, and I didn't do it. When supper time came, and Pa found that I had not carried in the kindling wood, he had a hot box, and told me if that wood was not in when he came back from the lodge, that he would warm my jacket. Well, I tried to hire someone to carry it in, and got a man to promise to come in the morning and carry it in and take his pay in groceries, and I was going to buy the groceries here and have them charged to Pa. But that wouldn't help me out that night. I knew when Pa came home he would search for me. So I slept in the back hall on a cot. But I didn't want Pa to have all his trouble for nothing, so I borrowed an old torn cat that my chum's old maid aunt owns, and put the cat in my bed. I thought if Pa came into my room after me, and found that by his unkindness I had changed to a torn cat, he would be sorry. That is the biggest cat you ever see, and the worst fighter in our ward. It isn't afraid of anything, and can whip a New Foundland dog quicker than you could put sand in a barrel of sugar.

"Well, about eleven o'clock I heard Pa tumble over the kindling wood, and I knew by the remark he made as the wood slid around under him, that there was going to be a cat fight real quick. He came up to Ma's room, and sounded Ma as to whether Hennery had retired to his virtuous couch. Pa is awful sarcastic when he tries to be. I could hear him take off his clothes, and hear him say, as he picked up a trunk strap, 'I guess I will go up to his room and watch the smile on his face, as he dreams of angels. I yearn to press him to my aching bosom.' I thought to myself, mebbe you won't yearn so much directly. He come up stairs, and I could hear him breathing hard. I looked around the corner and could see he just had on his shirt and pants, and his suspenders were hanging down, and his bald head shown like a calcium light just before it explodes.

Pa went into my room, and up to the bed, and I could hear him say, 'Come out here and bring in that kindling wood or I will start a fire on your base burner with this strap.' And then there was a yowling such as I never heard before, and Pa said, 'Helen Blazes,' and the furniture in my room began to fall around and break. O, *my*! I think Pa took the torn cat right by the neck, the way he does me, and that left the cat's feet free to get in their work. By the way the cat squawled as though it was being choked I know Pa had him by the neck. I suppose the cat thought Pa was a whole flock of New Foundland dogs, and the cat had a record on dogs, and it kicked awful. Pa's shirt was no protection at all in a cat fight, and the cat just walked all around Pa's stomach, and Pa yelled 'police,' and 'fire,' and 'turn on the hose,' and he called Ma, and the cat yowled. If Pa had had presence of mind enough to have dropped the cat, or rolled it up in the mattrass, it would have been all right, but a man always gets rattled in time of danger, and he held on to the cat and started down stairs yelling murder, and he met Ma coming up.

"I guess Ma's night cap or something frightened the cat more, cause he stabbed Ma on the night-shirt with one hind foot, and Ma said 'mercy on us,' and she went back, and Pa stumbled on a hand-sled that was on the stairs, and they all fell down, and the cat got away and went down in the coal bin and yowled all night. Pa and Ma went into their room, and I guess they annointed themselves with vasaline, and Pond's extract, and I went and got into my bed, cause it was cold out in the hall, and the cat had warmed my bed as well as it had warmed Pa. It was all I could do to go to sleep, with Pa and Ma talking all night, and this morning I came down the back stairs, and haven't been to breakfast, cause I don't want to see Pa when he is vexed. You let the man that carries in the kindling wood have six shillings worth of groceries, and charge them to Pa. I have passed the kindling wood period in a boy's life, and have arrived at the coal period. I will carry in coal, but I draw the line at kindling wood."

"Well, you are a cruel, bad boy," said the grocery man, as he went to the book and charged the six shillings.

"O, I don't know. I think Pa is cruel. A man who will take a poor kitty by the neck, that hasn't done any harm, and tries to chastise the poor thing with a trunk strap, ought to be looked after by the humane society. And if it is cruel to take a cat by the neck, how much more cruel is it to take a boy by the neck, that had diphtheria only a few years ago, and whose throat is tender? Say, I guess I will accept your invitation to take breakfast with you," and the boy cut off a piece of bologna and helped himself to the crackers, and while the grocery man was out shoveling off the snow from the sidewalk, the boy filled his pockets with raisins and loaf sugar, and then went out to watch the man carry in his kindling wood.

SOURCE: George W. Peck. *Peck's Bad Boy and His Pa.* Chicago: Belford, Clarke and Company, 1883.

JOHN ADAMS' DIARY (1887)

Bill Nye

Edgar Wilson "Bill" Nye (1850–1896) wrote in his introduction to Remarks, *his book that collected this piece, "It is my greatest and best book. It is the one that will live for weeks after other books have passed away. Even to those who cannot read, it will come like a benison when there is no benison in the house. To the ignorant, the pictures will be pleasing. The wise will revel in its wisdom, and the housekeeper will find that with it she may easily emphasize a statement or kill a cockroach." Nye made his name as a journalist and humorist in Laramie, Wyoming, in the 1880s.*

DECEMBER 3, 1764.—I am determined to keep a diary, if possible, the rest of my life. I fully realize how difficult it will be to do so. Many others of my acquaintance have endeavored to maintain a diary, but have only advanced so far as the second week in January. It is my purpose to write down each evening the events of the day as they occur to my mind, in order that in a few years they may be read and enjoyed by my family. I shall try to deal truthfully with all matters that I may refer to in these pages, whether they be of national or personal interest, and I shall seek to avoid anything bitter or vituperative, trying rather to cool my temper before I shall submit my thoughts to paper.

December 4.—This morning we have had trouble with the hired girl. It occurred in this wise: We had fully two-thirds of a pumpkin pie that had been baked in a square tin. This major portion of the pie was left over from our dinner yesterday, and last night, before retiring to rest, I desired my wife to suggest something in the cold pie line, which she did. I lit a candle and explored the pantry in vain.

80

The pie was no longer visible. I told Mrs. Adams that I had not been successful, whereupon we sought out the hired girl, whose name is Tootie Tooterson, a foreign damsel, who landed in this country Nov. 7, this present year. She does not understand our language, apparently, especially when we refer to pie. The only thing she does without a strong foreign accent is to eat pumpkin pie and draw her salary. She landed on our coast six weeks ago, after a tedious voyage across the heaving billows. It was a close fight between Tootie and the ocean, but when they quit, the heaving billows were one heave ahead by the log.

Miss Tooterson landed in Massachusetts in a woolen dress and hollow clear down into the ground. A strong desire to acquire knowledge and cold, handmade American pie seems to pervade her entire being.

She has only allowed Mrs. Adams and myself to eat what she did not want herself.

Miss Tooterson has also introduced into my household various European eccentricities and strokes of economy which deserve a brief notice here. Among other things she has made pie crust with castor oil in it, and lubricated the pancake griddle with a pork rind that I had used on my lame neck. She is thrifty and saving in this way, but rashly extravagant in the use of doughnuts, pie and Medford rum, which we keep in the house for visitors who are so unfortunate as to be addicted to the doughnut, pie or rum habit.

It is discouraging, indeed, for two young people like Mrs. Adams and myself, who have just begun to keep house, to inherit a famine, and such a robust famine, too. It is true that I should not have set my heart upon such a transitory and evanescent terrestrial object like a pumpkin pie so near to T. Tooterson, imported pie soloist, doughnut maestro and feminine virtuoso, but I did, and so I returned from the pantry desolate.

I told Abigail that unless we poisoned a few pies for Tootie the Adams family would be a short-lived race. I could see with my prophetic eye that unless the Tootersons yielded the Adamses would be wiped out. Abigail would not consent to this, but decided to relieve Miss Tooterson from duty in this department, so this morning she went away. Not being at all familiar with the English language, she took four of Abigail's sheets and quite a number of towels, handkerchiefs and collars. She also erroneously took a pair of my night-shirts in her poor, broken way. Being entirely ignorant of American customs, I presume that she will put a belt around them and wear them externally to church. I trust that she will not do this, however, without mature deliberation. I also had a bottle of lung medicine of a very powerful nature which the doctor had prepared for me. By some oversight, Miss Tooterson drank this the first day that she was in our service. This was entirely wrong, as I did not intend to use it for the foreign trade, but mostly for home consumption.

This is a little piece of drollery that I thought of myself. I do not think that a joke impairs the usefulness of a diary, as some do. A diary with a joke in it is just as good to fork over to posterity as one that is not thus disfigured. In fact, what has posterity ever done for me that I should hesitate about socking a little humor into a diary? When has posterity ever gone out of its way to do me a favor? Never! I defy the historian to show a single instance where posterity has ever been the first to recognize and remunerate ability.

December 6.—It is with great difficulty that I write this entry in my diary, for this morning Abigail thought best for me to carry the oleander down into the cellar, as the nights have been growing colder of late.

I do not know which I dislike most, foreign usurpation or the oleander. I have carried that plant up and down stairs every time the weather has changed, and the fickle elements of New England have kept me rising and falling with the thermometer, and whenever I raised or fell I most always had that scrawny oleander in my arms.

Richly has it repaid us, however, with its long, green, limber branches and its little yellow nubs on the end. How full of promises to the eye that are broken to the heart. The oleander is always just about to meet its engagements, but later on it peters out and fails to materialize.

I do not know what we would do if it were not for our house plants. Every fall I shall carry them cheerfully down cellar, and in the spring I will bring up the pots for Mrs. Adams to weep softly into. Many a night at the special instance and request of my wife I have risen, clothed in one simple, clinging garment, to go and see if the speckled, double and twisted Rise-up-William-Riley geranium was feeling all right.

Last summer Abigail brought home a slip of English ivy. I do not like things that are English very much, but I tolerated this little sickly thing because it seemed to please Abigail. I asked her what were the salient features of the English ivy. What did the English ivy do? What might be its specialty? Mrs. Adams said that it made a specialty of climbing. It was a climber from away back. "All right," I then to her did straightway say, "let her climb." It was a good early climber. It climbed higher than Jack's beanstalk. It climbed the golden stair. Most of our plants are actively engaged in descending the cellar stairs or in ascending the golden stair most all the time,

I descended the stairs with the oleander this morning, though the oleander got there a little more previously than I did. Parties desiring a good, second-hand oleander tub, with castors on it, will do well to give us a call before going elsewhere. Purchasers desiring a good set of second-hand ear muffs for tulips will find something to their advantage by addressing the subscriber.

We also have two very highly ornamental green dogoods for ivy vines to ramble over. We could be induced to sell these dogoods at a sacrifice, in order to make room for our large stock of new and attractive dogoods. These articles are as good as ever. We bought them during the panic last fall for our vines to climb over, but, as our vines died of membranous croup in November, these dogoods still remain unclum.

Second-hand dirt always on hand. Ornamental geranium stumps at bed-rock prices. Highest cash prices paid for slips of black-and-tan foliage plants. We are headquarters for the century plant that draws a salary for ninety-nine years and then dies.

I do not feel much like writing in my diary today, but the physician says that my arm will be better in a day or two, so that it will be more of a pleasure to do business.

We are still without a servant girl, so I do some of the cooking. I make a fire each day and boil the tea-kettle. People who have tried my boiled tea-kettle say it is very fine.

Some of my friends have asked me to run for the Legislature here next election. Somehow I feel that I might, in public life, rise to distinction some day, and perhaps at some future time figure prominently in the affairs of a one-horse republic at a good salary.

I have never done anything in the statesman line, but it does not look difficult to me. It occurs to me that success in public life is the result of a union of several great primary elements, to-wit:

Firstly—Ability to whoop in a felicitous manner.

Secondly—Promptness in improving the proper moment in which to whoop.

Thirdly—Ready and correct decision in the matter of which side to whoop on.

Fourthly—Ability to cork up the whoop at the proper moment and keep it in a cool place till needed.

And this last is one of the most important of all. It is the amateur statesman who talks the most. Fearing that he will conceal his identity as a fool, he babbles in conversation and slashes around in his shallow banks in public.

As soon as I get the house plants down cellar and get their overshoes on for the winter, I will more seriously consider the question of our political affairs here in this new land where we have to tie our scalps on at night and where every summer is an Indian summer.

SOURCE: Edgar W. Nye. *Remarks by Bill Nye*. New York: M. W. Hazen and Company. 1887.

ACTIVE COLORADO REAL ESTATE
(1895)

Hayden Carruth

Not to be confused with the late twentieth-century American poet, this Hayden Carruth (1862–1932) was a journalist and novelist from Minnesota.

"WHEN I WAS visiting at my uncle's in Wisconsin last fall, I went out to Lake Kinnikinnic and caught a shovel-nose sturgeon which weighed eighty-five pounds."

It was Jackson Peters who spoke, and he did it rapidly and with an apprehensive air, for Jones was watching him closely. As he finished, Peters drew a long breath, and seemed much relieved that he had got through the story without an interruption.

"Eighty-five pounds," mused Jones.

"Yes, eighty-five pounds and ten ounces, to be exact, but I called it eighty-five."

"Exactness does not help your story in the least, Jackson," continued Jones. "You might give us the fractions of the ounce, and your story would still remain a crude production. I am in the habit of speaking plainly, and I will do so now. I take it that we are to consider your story simply as an exaggeration—that the fish probably didn't weigh ten pounds. Simple exaggeration, Jackson, is not art, and is unworthy of a man of brains. Anybody can exaggerate—the street laborer as easily as the man in Congress. But artistic storytelling is another thing, and the greatest may well hope for distinction in it. Why did you not, Jackson, tell an artistic lie, and say that when you pulled your fish out of the water the level of the lake fell two feet?"

85

Peters moved about uneasily, but made no reply.

"You never tell fish-stories, Jones?" observed Robinson, in an inquiring tone.

"Seldom, Robinson. The trail of gross exaggeration is over them all. Fish stories have become the common property of the inartistic multitude. Of course I do not for this reason suppress facts having a scientific or commercial value. For instance, last winter I went before the legislative committee on fisheries, and laid before it an account of my experience when I had a farm near Omaha, on the Missouri River bottoms, and baited two miles of barbed-wire fence with fresh pork just before the June rise, and after the water receded removed thirty-eight thousand four hundred fish from the barbs, weighing, in the aggregate, over ninety-six tons. The Legislature passed a special vote of thanks for the facts."

Jones was becoming warmed up. "You have observed, Robinson," he went on, "that I seldom relate the marvellous. That is because it is too easy. I prefer to have the reputation of telling a plain tale artistically to that of telling a fabulous one like a realistic novelist. That is the reason I never told any one of my experience at breaking one hundred and sixty acres of land to ride."

"Tell us, by all means, Jones," said Robinson.

"Yes, go ahead," added Smith. Jackson Peters hid himself behind a cloud of cigar smoke.

"It was an exciting experience," said Jones, thoughtfully, as he gazed into the fire, "and one which I have never mentioned to anybody, although it happened twenty years ago. There is nothing so easy to lose as a reputation for truthfulness. I have my own to maintain. More men have lost their good names by telling the plain, straightforward truth than by indulging in judicious lying. However, I will venture this time. It was, as I said, twenty years ago. There was a great mining boom in Colorado, and I closed my defective-flue factory in Chicago, to the intense joy of the insurance companies, and went out. I saw more money in hens than I did in mines, and decided to start a hen ranch. Eggs sold at five dollars a dozen. The hen, you know, requires a great amount of gravel for her digestion, and she also thrives best at a high altitude; so I went about two miles up Pike's Peak and selected a quarter-section of land good for my purpose. There was gravel in plenty, and I put up a small house and turned loose my three hundred hens. I became so interested in getting settled that I forgot all about establishing my right to the land before the United States Land Office at Colorado Springs.

"One day a large, red-headed man came along and erected a small house on one corner of my ranch, and said that he had as much right to the land as I. He turned out two hundred head of goats, and started for Colorado Springs to file his claim. He had a good horse, while I had none. It was ten miles to the town by the road, and only five in a straight line down the mountain, but this five was impassable on foot or in any other ordinary way. But I did not despair. I had studied the formation of the land, and knew what I could do. I took a half-dozen sticks of giant powder and went over to a small ridge of rocks which held my farm in place. I inserted the powder, gentlemen, and blew those rocks over into the next county. I then lay down on my back and clung to a root while I rode that one hundred and sixty acres of good hen-land down the mountain to Colorado Springs. It felt very much like an earthquake, and I made the five miles in a little over four minutes. Probably ten acres of my farm around the edges were knocked off along on the grand Colorado scenery, and most of the goats jolted off, but the hens, gentlemen, clung, the hens and myself. The corner of my front yard struck the Land Office and knocked it off its foundation. The register and receiver came running out, and I said:

"'Gentlemen, I desire to make claim entry on the northeast quarter of section twenty-seven, township fourteen south, of range sixty-nine, and to prevent mistake I have brought it with me.' The business was all finished by the time the red-headed man came lumbering along, and I gave him ten minutes to get the rest of his goats off my land. He seemed considerably surprised, and looked at me curiously."

Jackson Peters was the first to speak after Jones paused. "It is one of the saddest things in this life," he said, "that the man who always adheres to the exact truth often gets the reputation of being a liar."

"You are right, Jackson," said Jones. "I know of nothing sadder, unless it be, perhaps, to see a young man forget the respect he owes his elders. This life, Jackson, is full of sad things."

SOURCE: Hayden Carruth. *The Adventures of Jones*. New York: Harper and Brothers, 1895.

THE IDIOT'S JOURNALISM SCHEME
(1895)

John Kendrick Bangs

Bangs was born in Yonkers, New York, and while at Columbia University began his writing career. He was an editor at Harper's and a popular novelist. In 1895 he created the character of the Idiot, who was cleverly stupid in dozens and dozens of situations and adventures, many of which stories were collected into books. The episode below, featuring the Idiot himself and two of his foils, is untitled in the original edition.

THE IDIOT WAS unusually thoughtful—a fact which made the School-Master and the Bibliomaniac unusually nervous. Their stock criticism of him was that he was thoughtless; and yet when he so far forgot his natural propensities as to meditate, they did not like it. It made them uneasy. They had a haunting fear that he was conspiring with himself against them, and no man, not even a callous school-master or a confirmed bibliomaniac, enjoys feeling that he is the object of a conspiracy. The thing to do, then, upon this occasion, seemed obviously to interrupt his train of thought—to put obstructions upon his mental track, as it were, and ditch the express, which they feared was getting up steam at that moment to run them down.

"You don't seem quite yourself this morning, sir," said the Bibliomaniac.

"Don't I?" queried the Idiot. "And whom do I seem to be?"

"I mean that you seem to have something on your mind that worries you," said the Bibliomaniac.

"No, I haven't anything on my mind," returned the Idiot. "I was thinking about you and Mr. Pedagog—which implies a thought not likely to use up much of my gray matter."

"Do you think your head holds any gray matter?" put in the Doctor.

"Rather verdant, I should say," said Mr. Pedagog.

"Green, gray, or pink," said the Idiot, "choose your color. It does not affect the fact that I was thinking about the Bibliomaniac and Mr. Pedagog. I have a great scheme in hand, which only requires capital and the assistance of those two gentlemen to launch it on the sea of prosperity. If any of you gentlemen want to get rich and die in comfort as the owner of your homes, now is your chance."

"In what particular line of business is your scheme?" asked Mr. Whitechoker. He had often felt that he would like to die in comfort, and to own a little house, even if it had a large mortgage on it.

"Journalism," said the Idiot. "There is a pile of money to be made out of journalism, particularly if you happen to strike a new idea. Ideas count."

"How far up do your ideas count—up to five?" questioned Mr. Pedagog, with a tinge of sarcasm in his tone.

"I don't know about that," returned the Idiot. "The idea I have hold of now, however, will count up into the millions if it can only be set going, and before each one of those millions will stand a big capital S with two black lines drawn vertically through it—in other words, my idea holds dollars, but to get the crop you've got to sow the seed. Plant a thousand dollars in my idea, and next year you'll reap two thousand. Plant that, and next year you'll have four thousand, and so on. At that rate millions come easy."

"I'll give you a dollar for the idea," said the Bibliomaniac.

"No, I don't want to sell. You'll do to help develop the scheme. You'll make a first-rate tool, but you aren't the workman to manage the tool. I will go as far as to say, however, that without you and Mr. Pedagog, or your equivalents in the animal kingdom, the idea isn't worth the fabulous sum you offer."

"You have quite aroused my interest," said Mr. Whitechoker. "Do you propose to start a new paper?"

"You are a good guesser," replied the Idiot. "That is a part of the scheme—but it isn't the idea. I propose to start a newspaper in accordance with the plan which the idea contains."

"Is it to be a magazine, or a comic paper, or what?" asked the Bibliomaniac.

"Neither. It's a daily."

"That's nonsense," said Mr. Pedagog, putting his spoon into the condensed-milk can by mistake. "There isn't a single scheme in daily journalism that hasn't been tried—except printing an evening paper in the morning."

"That's been tried," said the Idiot. "I know of an evening paper the second edition of which is published at mid-day. That's an old dodge, and there's money in it, too—money that will never be got out of it. But I really have a grand scheme. So many of our dailies, you know, go in for every horrid detail of daily events that people are beginning to tire of them. They contain practically the same things day after day. So many columns of murder, so many beautiful suicides, so much sport, a modicum of general intelligence, plenty of fires, no end of embezzlements, financial news, advertisements, and headlines. Events, like history, repeat themselves, until people have grown weary of them. They want something new. For instance, if you read in your morning paper that a man has shot another man, you know that the man who was shot was an inoffensive person who never injured a soul, stood high in the community in which he lived, and leaves a widow with four children. On the other hand, you know without reading the account that the murderer shot his victim in self-defense, and was apprehended by the detectives late last night; that his counsel forbid him to talk to the reporters, and that it is rumored that he comes of a good family living in New England.

"If a breach of trust is committed, you know that the defaulter was the last man of whom such an act would be suspected, and, except in the one detail of its location and sect, that he was prominent in some church. You can calculate to a cent how much has been stolen by a glance at the amount of space devoted to the account of the crime. Loaf of bread, two lines. Thousand dollars, ten lines. Hundred thousand dollars, half-column. Million dollars, a full column. Five million dollars, half the front page, wood-cut of the embezzler, and two editorials, one leader and one paragraph.

"And so with everything. We are creatures of habit. The expected always happens, and newspapers are dull because the events they chronicle are dull."

"Granting the truth of this," put in the School-Master, "what do you propose to do?"

"Get up a newspaper that will devote its space to telling what hasn't happened."

"That's been done," said the Bibliomaniac.

"To a much more limited extent than we think," returned the Idiot. "It has never been done consistently and truthfully."

"I fail to see how a newspaper can be made to prevaricate truthfully," asserted Mr. Whitechoker. To tell the truth, he was greatly disappointed with the idea, because he could not in the nature of things become one of its beneficiaries.

"I haven't suggested prevarication," said the Idiot. "Put on your front page, for instance, an item like this: 'George Bronson, colored, aged twenty-nine, a resident of Thompson Street, was caught cheating at poker last night. He was not murdered.' There you tell what has not happened. There is a variety about it. It has the charm of the unexpected. Then you might say: 'Curious incident on Wall Street yesterday. So-and-so, who was caught on the bear side of the market with 10,000 shares of J. B. & S. K. W., paid off all his obligations in full, and retired from business with 11,000,000 clear.' Or we might say, 'Superintendent Smithers, of the St. Goliath's Sunday-school, who is also cashier in the Forty-eighth National Bank, has not absconded with $4,000,000.'"

"Oh, that's a rich idea," put in the SchoolMaster. "You'd earn $1,000,000 in libel suits the first year."

"No, you wouldn't, either," said the Idiot. "You don't libel a man when you say he hasn't murdered anybody. Quite the contrary, you call attention to his conspicuous virtue. You are in reality commending those who refrain from criminal practice, instead of delighting those who are fond of departing from the paths of Christianity by giving them notoriety."

"But I fail to see in what respect Mr. Pedagog and I are essential to your scheme," said the Bibliomaniac.

"I must confess to some curiosity on my own part on that point," added the SchoolMaster.

"Why, it's perfectly clear," returned the Idiot, with a conciliating smile as he prepared to depart. "You both know so much that isn't so, that I rather rely on you to fill up."

SOURCE: John Kendrick Bangs. *The Idiot*. New York: Harper and Brothers, 1895.

ROLLO LEARNING TO READ (1897)

Robert J. Burdette

Hailing from Pennsylvania, Burdette (1844–1914) fought for the Union in the Civil War. He was an editor and popular writer of humor pieces in Iowa before becoming a pastor in Pasadena.

WHEN ROLLO WAS five years young, his father said to him one evening: "Rollo, put away your roller skates and bicycle, carry that rowing machine out into the hall, and come to me. It is time for you to learn to read."

Then Rollo's father opened the book which he had sent home on a truck and talked to the little boy about it. It was Bancroft's *History of the United States*, half complete in twenty-three volumes. Rollo's father explained to Rollo and Mary his system of education, with special reference to Rollo's learning to read. His plan was that Mary should teach Rollo fifteen hours a day for ten years, and by that time Rollo would be half through the beginning of the first volume, and would like it very much indeed.

Rollo was delighted at the prospect. He cried aloud: "Oh, papa! thank you very much. When I read this book clear through, all the way to the end of the last volume, may I have another little book to read?"

"No," replied his father, "that may not be; because you will never get to the last volume of this one. For as fast as you read one volume, the author of this history, or his heirs, executors, administrators, or assigns, will write another as an appendix. So even though you should live to be a very old man, like the boy preacher, this history will always be twenty-three volumes ahead of you.

Now, Mary and Rollo, this will be a hard task (pronounced *tawsk*) for both of you, and Mary must remember that Rollo is a very little boy, and must be very patient and gentle."

The next morning after the one preceding it, Mary began the first lesson. In the beginning she was so gentle and patient that her mother went away and cried, because she feared her dear little daughter was becoming too good for this sinful world, and might soon spread her wings and fly away and be an angel.

But in the space of a short time, the novelty of the expedition wore off, and Mary resumed running her temper—which was of the old-fashioned, low-pressure kind, just forward of the fire-box—on its old schedule. When she pointed to "A" for the seventh time, and Rollo said "W," she tore the page out by the roots, hit her little brother such a whack over the head with the big book that it set his birthday back six weeks, slapped him twice, and was just going to bite him, when her mother came in. Mary told her that Rollo had fallen down stairs and torn his book and raised that dreadful lump on his head. This time Mary's mother restrained her emotion, and Mary cried. But it was not because she feared her mother was pining away. Oh, no; it was her mother's rugged health and virile strength that grieved Mary, as long as the seance lasted, which was during the entire performance.

That evening Rollo's father taught Rollo his lesson and made Mary sit by and observe his methods, because, he said, that would be normal instruction for her. He said: "Mary, you must learn to control your temper and curb your impatience if you want to wear low-neck dresses, and teach school. You must be sweet and patient, or you will never succeed as a teacher. Now, Rollo, what is this letter?"

"I dunno," said Rollo, resolutely.

"That is A," said his father, sweetly.

"Huh," replied Rollo, "I knowed that."

"Then why did you not say so?" replied his father, so sweetly that Jonas, the hired boy, sitting in the corner, licked his chops.

Rollo's father went on with the lesson: "What is this, Rollo?"

"I dunno," said Rollo, hesitatingly.

"Sure?" asked his father. "You do not know what it is?"

"Nuck," said Rollo.

"It is A," said his father.

"A what?" asked Rollo.

"A nothing," replied his father, "it is just A. Now, what is it?"

"Just A," said Rollo.

"Do not be flip, my son," said Mr. Holliday, "but attend to your lesson. What letter is this?"

"I dunno," said Rollo.

"Don't fib to me," said his father, gently, "you said a minute ago that you knew. That is N."

"Yes, sir," replied Rollo, meekly. Rollo, although he was a little boy, was no slouch, if he did wear bibs; he knew where he lived without looking at the door-plate. When it came time to be meek, there was no boy this side of the planet Mars who could be meeker, on shorter notice. So he said, "Yes, sir," with that subdued and well pleased alacrity of a boy who has just been asked to guess the answer to the conundrum, "Will you have another piece of pie?"

"Well," said his father, rather suddenly, "what is it?"

"M," said Rollo, confidently.

"N!" yelled his father, in three-line Gothic.

"N," echoed Rollo, in lower case nonpareil.

"B-a-n," said his father, "what does that spell?"

"Cat?" suggested Rollo, a trifle uncertainly.

"Cat?" snapped his father, with a sarcastic inflection, "b-a-n, cat! Where were you raised? Ban! B-a-n—Ban! Say it! Say it, or I'll get at you with a skate-strap!"

"B-a-m, ban'd," said Rollo, who was beginning to wish that he had a rain-check and could come back and see the remaining innings some other day.

"Ba-a-a-an!" shouted his father, "B-a-n, Ban, Ban, Ban! Now say Ban!"

"Ban," said Rollo, with a little gasp.

"That's right," his father said, in an encouraging tone; "you will learn to read one of these years if you give your mind to it. All he needs, you see, Mary, is a teacher who doesn't lose patience with him the first time he makes a mistake. Now, Rollo, how do you spell, B-a-n—Ban?"

Rollo started out timidly on c-a—then changed to d-o—and finally compromised on h-e-n.

Mr. Holiday made a pass at him with Volume I, but Rollo saw it coming and got out of the way.

"B-a-n!" his father shouted, "B-a-n, Ban! Ban! Ban! Ban! Ban! Now go on, if you think you know how to spell that! What comes next? Oh, you're enough to tire the patience of Job! I've a good mind to make you learn by the Pollard system, and begin where you leave off! Go ahead, why don't you? Whatta you waiting for? Read on! What comes next? Why, croft, of course; anybody ought to know that—c-r-o-f-t, croft, Bancroft! What does that apostrophe mean? I mean, what does that punctuation mark between t and s stand for? You don't know? Take that, then! (*whack*). What comes after Bancroft? Spell it! Spell it, I tell you, and don't be all night about it! Can't, eh? Well, read it then; if you can't spell it, read it. H-i-s-t-o-r-y-ry, history; Bancroft's *History of the United States!* Now what does that spell? I mean, spell that! Spell it! Oh, go away! Go to bed! Stupid, stupid child," he added as the little boy went weeping out of the room, "he'll never learn anything so long as he lives. I declare he has tired me all out, and I used to teach school in Trivoli township, too. Taught one whole winter in district number three when Nick Worthington was county superintendent, and had my salary—. . . Look here, Mary, what do you find in that English grammar to giggle about? You go to bed, too, and listen to me—if Rollo can't read that whole book clear through without making a mistake tomorrow night, you'll wish you had been born without a back, that's all."

The following morning, when Rollo's father drove away to business, he paused a moment as Rollo stood at the gate for a final goodbye kiss—for Rollo's daily goodbyes began at the door and lasted as long as his father was in sight—Mr. Holliday said: "Some day, Rollo, you will thank me for teaching you to read."

"Yes, sir," replied Rollo, respectfully, and then added, "but not this day."

Rollo's head, though it had here and there transient bumps consequent upon football practice, was not naturally or permanently hilly. On the contrary, it was quite level.

SOURCE: Robert J. Burdette. *Chimes from a Jester's Bells: Stories and Sketches.* Indianapolis: Bowen-Merrill Company, 1897.

THE WISH AND THE DEED (1903)

Max Adeler (Charles Heber Clark)

Born in Maryland, Clark (1841–1915), fought for the Union in the Civil War. He wrote and published several humorous books in the 1870s and 1880s. Clark took his pen-name from a character in a book he had loved as a boy. This story was later retitled as "The Millionaires."

IT HAD ALWAYS been one of the luxuries of the Grimeses to consider what they would do if they were rich. Many a time George and his wife, sitting together of a summer evening upon the porch of their own pretty house in Susanville, had looked at the long unoccupied country-seat of General Jenkins, just across the way, and wished they had money enough to buy the place and give it to the village for a park.

Mrs. Grimes often said that if she had a million dollars, the very first thing she would do would be to purchase the Jenkins place. George's idea was to tear down the fences, throwing everything open, and to dedicate the grounds to the public. Mrs. Grimes wanted to put a great free library in the house and to have a club for poor workingwomen in the second-floor rooms. George estimated that one hundred thousand dollars would be enough to carry out their plans. Say fifty thousand dollars for purchase money, and then fifty more invested at six percent, to maintain the place.

"But if we had a million," said George, "I think I should give one hundred and fifty thousand to the enterprise and do the thing right. There would always be repairs and new books to buy and matters of that kind."

But this was not the only benevolent dream of these kind-hearted people. They liked to think of the joy that would fill the heart of that poor struggling pastor, Mr. Borrow, if they could tell him that they would pay the whole debt of the Presbyterian Church, six thousand dollars.

"And I would have his salary increased, George," said Mrs. Grimes. "It is shameful to compel that poor man to live on a thousand dollars."

"Outrageous," said George. "I would guarantee him another thousand, and maybe more; but we should have to do it quietly, for fear of wounding him."

"That mortgage on the Methodist Church," said Mrs. Grimes. "Imagine the happiness of those poor people in having it lifted! And so easy to do, too, if we had a million dollars."

"Certainly, and I would give the Baptists a handsome pipe-organ instead of that wheezing melodeon. Dreadful, isn't it?"

"You can get a fine organ for $2,000," said Mrs. Grimes.

"Yes, of course, but I wouldn't be mean about it; not mean on a million dollars. Let them have a really good organ, say for $3,000 or $3,500; and then build them a parsonage, too."

"The fact is," said Mrs. Grimes, "that people like us really ought to have large wealth, for we know how to use it rightly."

"I often think of that," answered George. "If I know my own soul I long to do good. It makes my heart bleed to see the misery about us, misery I am absolutely unable to relieve. I am sure that if I really had a million dollars I should not want to squander it on mere selfish pleasure, nor would you. The greatest happiness any one can have is in making others happy; and it is a wonder to me that our rich people don't see this. Think of old General Jenkins and his twenty million dollars, and what we would do for our neighbors with a mere fraction of that!"

"For we really want nothing much for ourselves," said Mrs. Grimes. "We are entirely satisfied with what we have in this lovely little home and with your $2,000 salary from the bank."

"Almost entirely," said George. "There are some few little things we might add in—just a few; but with a million we could easily get them and more and have such enormous amounts of money left."

"Almost the first thing I would do," said Mrs. Grimes, "would be to settle a comfortable living for life on poor Isaac Wickersham.

That man, George, crippled as he is, lives on next to nothing. I don't believe he has two hundred dollars a year."

"Well, we could give him twelve hundred and not miss it and then give the same sum to Widow Clausen. She can barely keep alive."

"And there's another thing I'd do," said Mrs. Grimes. "If we kept a carriage I would never ride up alone from the station or for pleasure. I would always find some poor or infirm person to go with me. How people can be so mean about their horses and carriages as some rich people are is beyond my comprehension."

It is delightful pastime, expending in imagination large sums of money that you haven't got. You need not regard considerations of prudence. You can give free rein to your feelings and bestow your bounty with reckless profusion. You obtain almost all the pleasure of large giving without any cost. You feel nearly as happy as if you were actually doing the good deeds which are the children of your fancy.

George Grimes and his wife had considered so often the benevolences they would like to undertake if they had a million dollars that they could have named them all at a moment's notice without referring to a memorandum. Nearly everybody has engaged in this pastime, but the Grimeses were to have the singular experience of the power to make their dream a reality placed in their hands.

For one day George came flying home from the bank with a letter from the executors of General Jenkins (who died suddenly in Mexico a week or two before) announcing that the General had left a million dollars and the country-seat in Susanville to George Grimes.

"And to think, Mary Jane," said George when the first delirium of their joy had passed, "the dear old man was kind enough to say—here, let me read it to you again from the quotation from the will in the letter: I make this bequest because, from repeated conversations with the said George Grimes, I know that he will use it aright.' So you see, dear, it was worth while, wasn't it, to express our benevolent wishes sometimes when we spoke of the needs of those who are around us?"

"Yes, and the General's kind remark makes this a sacred trust, which we are to administer for him."

"We are only his stewards."

"Stewards for his bounty."

"So that we must try to do exactly what we think he would have liked us to do," said George. "Nothing else, dear?"

"Why, of course we are to have some discretion, some margin; and besides, nobody possibly could guess precisely what he would have us do."

"But now, at any rate, George, we can realize fully one of our longing desires and give to the people the lovely park and library?"

George seemed thoughtful. "I think, Mary Jane," he said, "I would not act precipitately about that. Let us reflect upon the matter. It might seem unkind to the memory of the General just to give away his gift almost before we get it."

They looked at each other, and Mrs. Grimes said: "Of course there is no hurry. And we are really a little cramped in this house. The nursery is much too small for the children and there is not a decent fruit tree in our garden."

"The thing can just stay open until we have time to consider."

"But I am so glad for dear old Isaac. We can take care of him, anyhow, and of Mrs. Clausen, too."

"To be sure," said George. "The obligation is sacred. Let me see, how much was it we thought Isaac ought to have?"

"Twelve hundred a year."

"H-m-m," murmured George, "and he has two hundred now; an increase of five hundred percent. I'm afraid it will turn the old man's head. However, I wouldn't exactly promise anything for a few days yet."

"Many a man in his station in life is happy upon a thousand."

"A thousand! Why, my dear, there is not a man of his class in town that makes six hundred."

"George?"

"Well?"

"We must keep horses, and there is no room to build a stable on this place."

"No."

"Could we live here and keep the horses in the General's stables across the way, even if the place were turned into a park?"

"That is worth thinking of."

"And George?"

"Well, dear?"

"It's a horrid thing to confess, but do you know, George, I've felt myself getting meaner and meaner, and stingier and stingier ever since you brought the good news."

George tried to smile, but the effort was unsuccessful; he looked half-vexed and half-ashamed.

"Oh, I wouldn't put it just that way," he said. "The news is so exciting that we hardly know at once how to adjust ourselves to it. We are simply prudent. It would be folly to plunge ahead without any caution at all. How much did you say the debt of the Presbyterian Church is?"

"Six thousand, I think."

"A good deal for a little church like that to owe."

"Yes, but—"

"You didn't promise anything, Mary Jane, did you, to Mrs. Borrow?"

"No, for I had nothing to promise, but I did tell her on Sunday that I would help them liberally if I could."

"They will base large expectations on that, sure. I wish you hadn't said it just that way. Of course, we are bound to help them, but I should like to have a perfectly free hand in doing it."

There was silence for a moment, while both looked through the window at the General's place over the way.

"Beautiful, isn't it?" asked Mrs. Grimes.

"Lovely. That little annex on the side would make a snug den for me; and imagine the prospect from that south bedroom window! You would enjoy every look at it."

"George?"

"What?"

"George, dear, tell me frankly, do you really feel in your heart as generous as you did yesterday?"

"Now, my dear, why press that matter? Call it meaner or narrower or what you will; maybe I am a little more so than I was; but there is nothing to be ashamed of. It is the conservative instinct asserting itself; the very same faculty in man that holds society together. I will be liberal enough when the time comes, never fear. I am not going to disregard what one may call the pledges of a lifetime. We will treat everybody right, the Presbyterian Church and Mr. Borrow included. His salary is a thousand, I think you said?"

"Yes."

"Well, I am willing to make it fifteen hundred right now, if you are."

"We said, you remember, it ought to be two thousand."

"Who said so?"

"You did, on the porch here the other evening."

"I never said so. There isn't a preacher around here gets that much. The Episcopalians with their rich people only give eighteen hundred."

"And a house."

"Very well, the Presbyterians can build a house if they want to."

"You consent then to pledge five hundred more to the minister's salary?"

"I said I would if you would, but my advice is just to let the matter go over until tomorrow or next day, when the whole thing can be considered."

"Very well, but, George, sixty thousand dollars is a great deal of money, and we certainly can afford to be liberal with it, for the General's sake as well as for our own!"

"Everything depends upon how you look at it. In one way the sum is large. In another way it isn't. General Jenkins had just twenty times sixty thousand. Tremendous, isn't it? He might just as well have left us another million. He is in Heaven and wouldn't miss it. Then we could have some of our plans more fully carried out." "I hate to be thought covetous," answered Mrs. Grimes, "but I do wish he had put on that other million."

The next day Mr. Grimes, while sitting with his wife after supper, took a memorandum from his pocket and said: "I've been jotting down some figures, Mary Jane, just to see how we will come out with our income of sixty thousand dollars."

"Well?"

"If we give the place across the street for a park and a library and a hundred thousand dollars with which to run it, we shall have just nine hundred thousand left."

"Yes."

"We shall want horses, say a carriage pair, and a horse for the station wagon. Then I must have a saddle horse and there must be a pony for the children. I thought also you might as well have a gentle pair for your own driving. That makes six. Then there will have to be, say, three stable men. Now, my notion is that we shall put up a larger house farther up town with all the necessary stabling. Count the cost of the house and suitable appointments, and add in the four months' trip to Europe which we decided yesterday to take next summer, and how much of that fifty-four thousand do you think we shall have left at the end of the year?"

"But why build the house from our income?"

"Mary Jane, I want to start out with the fixed idea that we will not cut into our principal."

"Well, how much will we have over?"

"Not a dollar! The outlay for the year will approximate fifty-six thousand dollars."

"Large, isn't it?"

"And yet I don't see how we can reduce it if we are to live as people in our circumstances might reasonably be expected to live."

"We must cut off something."

"That is what I think. If we give the park and the library building to the town, why not let the town pay the cost of caring for them?"

"Then we could save the interest on that other hundred thousand."

"Exactly, and nobody will suffer. The gift of the property alone is magnificent. Who is going to complain of us? We will decide now to give the real estate and then stop."

Two days later Mr. Grimes came home early from the bank with a letter in his hand. He looked white and for a moment after entering his wife's room he could hardly command utterance.

"I have some bad news for you, dear—terrible news," he said, almost falling into a chair.

The thought flashed through Mrs. Grimes' mind that the General had made a later will which had been found and which revoked the bequest to George. She could hardly whisper: "What is it?"

"The executors write to me that the million dollars left to me by the General draws only about four percent interest."

"George!"

"Four percent! Forty thousand dollars instead of sixty thousand! What a frightful loss! Twenty thousand dollars a year gone at one breath!"

"Are you sure, George?"

"Sure? Here is the letter. Read it yourself. One-third of our fortune swept away before we have a chance to touch it!"

"I think it was very unkind of the General to turn the four percents over to us while somebody else gets the six percents. How *could* he do such a thing? And you such an old friend, too!"

"Mary Jane, that man always had a mean streak in him. I've said so to myself many a time. But, anyhow, this frightful loss settles one thing; we can't afford to give that property across the street to the town. We must move over there to live, and even then, with the huge expense of keeping such a place in order, we shall have to watch things narrowly to make ends meet."

"And you never were good at retrenching, George."

"But we've *got* to retrench. Every superfluous expenditure must be cut off. As for the park and free library, that seems wild now, doesn't it? I don't regret abandoning the scheme. The people of this town never did appreciate public spirit or generosity, did they?"

"Never."

"I'm very sorry you spoke to Mrs. Borrow about helping their church. Do you think she remembers it?"

"She met me today and said they were expecting something handsome."

Mr. Grimes laughed bitterly.

"That's always the way with those people. They are the worst beggars! When a lot of folks get together and start a church it is almost indecent for them to come running around to ask other folks to support it. I have half a notion not to give them a cent."

"Not even for Mr. Borrow's salary?"

"Certainly not! Half the clergymen in the United States get less than a thousand dollars a year; why can't he do as the rest do? Am I to be called upon to support a lot of poor preachers? A good deal of nerve is required, I think, to ask such a thing of me."

Two weeks afterward Mr. Grimes and his wife sat together again on the porch in the cool of the evening.

"Now," said Grimes, "let us together go over these charities we were talking about and be done with them. Let us start with the tough fact staring us in the face that, with only one million dollars at four percent, and all our new and necessary expenses, we shall have to look sharp or I'll be borrowing money to live on in less than eight months."

"Well," said Mrs. Grimes, "what shall we cut out? Would you give up the Baptist organ that we used to talk about?"

"Mary Jane, it is really surprising how you let such things as that stay in your mind. I considered that organ scheme abandoned long ago."

"Is it worth while, do you think, to do anything with the Methodist Church mortgage?"

"How much is it?"

"Three thousand dollars, I think."

"Yes, three thousand from forty thousand leaves us only thirty-seven thousand. Then, if we do it for the Methodists we shall have to do it for the Lutherans and the Presbyterians and swarms of churches all around the country. We can't make flesh of one and fowl of another. It will be safer to treat them all alike; and more just, too. I think we ought to try to be just with them, don't you, Mary Jane?"

"And Mr. Borrow's salary?"

"Ha! Yes! That is a thousand dollars, isn't it? It does seem but a trifle. But they have no children and they have themselves completely adjusted to it. And suppose we should raise it one year and die next year? He would feel worse than if he just went along in the old way. When a man is fully adjusted to a thing it is the part of prudence, it seems to me, just to let him alone."

"I wish we could—"

"Oh, well, if you want to; but I propose that we don't make them the offer until next year or the year after. We shall have our matters arranged better by that time."

"And now about Isaac Wickersham?"

"Have you seen him lately?"

"Two or three days ago."

"Did he seem discontented or unhappy?"

"No."

"You promised to help him?"

"What I said was, 'We are going to do something for you, Isaac.'"

"Something! That commits us to nothing in particular. Was it your idea, Mary Jane, to make him an allowance?"

"Yes."

"There you cut into our insufficient income again. I don't see how we can afford it with all these expenses heaping up on us; really I don't."

"But we must give him something; I promised it."

George thought a moment and then said: "This is the end of September and I sha'nt want this straw hat that I have been wearing all summer. Suppose you give him that. A good straw hat is 'something.'"

"You remember Mrs. Clausen, George?"

"Have we got to load up with her, too?"

"Let me explain. You recall that I told her I would try to make her comfortable, and when I found that our circumstances were going to be really straitened, I sent her my red flannel petticoat with my love, for I know she can be comfortable in that."

"Of course she can."

"So this afternoon when I came up from the city she got out of the train with me and I felt so half-ashamed of the gift that I pretended not to see her and hurried out to the carriage and drove quickly up the hill. She is afraid of horses, anyhow."

"Always was," said George.

"But, George, I don't feel quite right about it yet; the gift of a petticoat is rather stingy, isn't it?"

"No, I don't think so."

"And, George, to be perfectly honest with ourselves now, don't you think we are a little bit meaner than we were, say, last June?"

George cleared his throat and hesitated, and then he said: "I admit nothing, excepting that the only people who are fit to have money are the people who know how to take care of it."

SOURCE: *The Saturday Evening Post: An Illustrated Weekly Magazine.* Philadelphia: Curtis Publishing Company, March 7, 1903.

SAMANTHA AT THE ST. LOUIS
EXPOSITION (1904)

Josiah Allen's Wife (Marietta Holley)

Holley (1836–1926) was from Upstate New York. She published many collections of "Samantha Smith Allen" adventures, all as penned by "Josiah Allen's Wife," the narrator from Jonesville, New York.

I HAD NOTICED for some time that Josiah Allen had acted queer. He would seem lost in thought anon or oftener, and then seemin'ly roust himself up and try to act natural. And anon he would drag his old tin chest out from under the back stairway and pour over musty old deeds and papers, drawed up by his great-grandpa mebby.

He did this last act so often that I said to him one day, "What under the sun do you find in them yeller old papers to attract you so, Josiah?"

But he looked queer at me, queer as a dog, as if he wuz lookin' through me to some distant view that interested him dretfully, and answered evasive, and mebby he wouldn't answer at all.

And then I'd see him and Uncle Sime Bentley, his particular chum, with their heads clost together, seemin'ly plottin' sunthin' or ruther, though what it wuz I couldn't imagine.

And then they would bend their heads eagerly over the daily papers, and more'n once Josiah got down our old Olney's Atlas and he and Uncle Sime would pour over it and whisper, though what it wuz about I couldn't imagine. And if I'd had the curosity of some wimmen it would drove me into a caniption fit.

And more'n a dozen times I see him and Uncle Sime down by the back paster on the creek pacin' to and fro as if they wuz

measurin' land. And most of all they seemed to be measurin' off
solemn like and important the lane from the creek lot up to the
house and takin' measurements, as queer lookin' sights as I ever see,
and then they would consult the papers and atlas agin, and whisper
and act.

And about this time he begun to talk to me about the St. Louis
Exposition. He opened the subject one day by remarkin' that he
spozed I had never hearn of the Louisana Purchase. He said that the
minds of females in their leisure hours bein' took up by more frivo-
lous things, such as tattin' and crazy bed-quilts, he spozed that I,
bein' a female woman, had never hearn on't.

And my mind bein' at that time took up in startin' the seams in
a blue and white sock I wuz knittin' for him, didn't reply, and he
went on and talked and talked about it.

But good land! I knowed all about the Louisana Purchase; I
knowed it come into our hands in 1803, that immense tract of land,
settlin' forever in our favor the war for supremacy on this continent
between ourselves and England, and givin' us the broad highway of
the Mississippi to sail to and fro on which had been denied us,
besides the enormous future increase in our wealth and
population.

I knowed that between 1700 and 1800 this tract wuz tossted
back and forth between France and Spain and England some as if it
wuz a immense atlas containing pictured earth and sea instead of
the real land and water.

It passed backwards and forwards through the century till 1803
when it bein' at the time in the hands of France, we bought it of
Napoleon Bonaparte who had got possession of it a few years
before, and Heaven only knows what ambitious dreams of foundin'
a new empire in a new France filled that powerful brain, under that
queer three-cornered hat of hisen when he got it of Spain.

But 'tennyrate he sold it in 1803 to our country, the writin's
bein' drawed up by Thomas Jefferson, namesake of our own
Thomas Jefferson, Josiah's child by his first wife. Napoleon, or I
spoze it would sound more respectful to call him Mr. Bonaparte,
he wanted money bad, and he didn't want England to git ahead,
and so he sold it to us.

He acted some as Miss Bobbett did when she sot up her niece,
Mahala Hen, in dressmakin' for fear Miss Henzy's girl would git all
the custom and git rich. She'd had words with Miss Henzy and

wanted to bring down her pride. And we bein' some like Miss Hen in sperit (she had had trouble with Miss Henzy herself, and wuz dretful glad to have Mahala sot up), we wuz more'n willin' to buy it of Mr. Bonaparte. You know he didn't like England, he had had words with her, and almost come to hands and blows, and it did come to that twelve years afterwards.

But poor creeter! I never felt like makin' light of his reverses, for do not we, poor mortals! have to face our Waterloo some time durin' our lives, when we have fought the battle and lost, when the ground is covered with slain Hopes, Ambition, Happiness, when the music is stilled, the stringed instruments and drums broken to pieces, or givin' out only wailin' accompaniments to the groans and cries of the dyin' layin' low in the dust.

We marched onward in the mornin' mebby with flyin' colors towards Victory, with gaily flutterin' banners and glorious music. Then come the Inevitable to crush us, and though we might not be doomed to a desert island in body, yet our souls dwell there for quite a spell.

Till mebby we learn to pick up what is left of value on the lost field, try to mend the old instruments that never sound as they did before. Sew with tremblin' fingers the rents in the old tattered banners which Hope never carries agin with so high a head, and fall into the ranks and march forward with slower, more weary steps and our sad eyes bent toward the settin' sun.

But to stop eppisodin' and resoom. I had hearn all about how it wuz bought and how like every new discovery, or man or woman worth while, the Purchase had to meet opposition and ridicule, though some prophetic souls, like Thomas Jefferson, Mr. Livingstone and others, seemed to look forward through the mists of the future and see fertile fields and stately cities filled with crowds of prosperous citizens, where wuz then almost impassable swamps and forests inhabited by whoopin' savages.

And Mr. Bonaparte himself, let us not forgit in this proud year of fulfilled hopes and achievement and progress how he always seemed to set store by us and his words wuz prophetic of our nation's glorious destiny.

I had knowed all about this but Josiah seemed to delight to instruct me as carefully as a mother would guide a prattlin' child jest beginnin' to walk on its little feet. And some times I would resent it, and some times when I wuz real good natured, for every human bein' no matter how high principled, has ebbs and flows in their moral temperatures, some times I would let him instruct me and take it meekly like a child learnin' its A-B abs. But to resoom. Day by day Josiah's strange actions continued, and at intervals growin' still more and more frequent and continuous he acted, till at last the truth oozed out of him like water out of a tub that has been filled too full, it wuz after an extra good meal that he confided in me.

He said the big celebration of the Louisana Purchase had set him to thinkin' and he'd investigated his own private affairs and had discovered important facts that had made him feel that he too must make a celebration of the Purchase of the Allen Homestead.

"On which we are now dwellin', Samantha," sez he. "Seventy-four acres more or less runnin' up to a stake and back agin, to wit, as the paper sez."

Sez I, "You needn't talk like a lawyer to me, Josiah Allen, but tell me plain as a man and a deacon what you mean."

"Well, I'm tellin' you, hain't I, fast as I can? I've found out by my own deep research (the tin trunk wuzn't more'n a foot deep but I didn't throw the trunk in his face), I've discovered this remarkable fact that this farm the very year of the Louisana Purchase came into the Allen family by purchase. My great-great-grandfather, Hatevil Allen, bought it of Ohbejoyful Gowdey, and the papers wuz signed the very day the other momentous purchase wuz made. There wuz fourteen children in the family of old Hatevil, jest as many as there is States in the purchase they are celebratin' to St. Louis. And another wonderful fact old Hatevil Allen paid jest the same amount for this farm that our Government paid for the Louisiana Purchase."

"Do you mean to tell me, Josiah, that Hatevil Allen paid fifteen millions for this farm. Will you tell me that? You, a member of the meetin' house and a deacon?"

"Well, what you might call the same, it is the same figgers with the six orts left out. Great-granther Allen paid fifteen dollars for this piece of land, it wuz all woods then."

"Another of these most remarkable series of incidents that have ever took place on this continent, Thomas Jefferson wuz a main actor in the Louisana Purchase. He has left this spear some years ago, and who, who is the father of Thomas Jefferson today?"

I didn't say nothin', for I wuz engrossed in my knittin', I wuz jest turnin' the heel of his sock and needed my hull mind.

And sez he, smitin' his breast agin, "I ask you, Samantha, who is the father of Thomas Jefferson today?"

I had by this time turned the heel and I sez, "Why, I spoze he's got the same father now he always had, children don't change their fathers very often as a general thing."

"Well, you needn't be so grumpy about it. Don't you see that these wonderful coincidences are enough to apall a light-minded person. Why, I, even I with my cast iron strength of mind, have almost felt my brain stagger and reel as I onraveled the momentous affair.

"And I am plannin' a celebration, Samantha, that will hist up the name of Allen where it ort to be onto the very top of Fame's towerin' pillow, and keep it in everlastin' remembrance.

"And I, Samantha," and here he smote himself agin in the breast, "I, Josiah Allen, havin' exposed these circumstances, the most remarkable in American history, I lay out to name my show the Exposition of Josiah Allen. And I've thought some times that in order to mate mine with the St. Louis show, as you may say, I'd mebby ort to call myself St. Josiah."

"Saint Josiah!" sez I, and my axent wuz that icy cold that he shivered imperceptibly and added hastily, "Well, we will leave that to the future to decide."

"But," sez he firmly, spruntin' up agin, "if the nation calls on me to name myself thus I shall respond, and expose myself at my Exposition as Saint Josiah."

Sez I anxiously, "I wouldn't expose myself too much, Josiah. You remember the pa that took his weak-minded child to the ball, and told him to set still and not speak or they would find him out. "And they asked him question after question and he didn't say a word, and finally they begun to scoff at him and told him he wuz a fool, and he called out, 'Father, father, they've found me out.'"

Josiah sez snappishly, "What you mean by bringin' that old chestnut up I can't see."

"Well," sez I, "I shan't sew the moral on any tighter." But he kep' on ignorin' my sarcastick allusion.

"To keep up the train of almost miraclous incidents marchin' along through the past connecting the St. Louis and the Allen Purchase like historical twins, I'm goin' to spend on the Exposition of Josiah Allen jest the amount paid for the other original purchase, and I may, for there is no tellin' what a Allen may do when his blood is rousted up, I may swing right out and pay jest the same amount St. Louis is payin' for her Exposition."

"Fifty millions!" sez I with emotions of or—or to think I had a pardner that would tell such a gigantic falsehood, and instinctively I thought of a story I'd hearn Thomas Jefferson tell the evenin' before.

He said three commercial travelers wuz talkin' before an old man from the country whose loose fittin' clothes were gently scattered with hay-seed. The first one told with minute particulars of a Western cyclone that had lifted a house and sot it down in a neighborin' township. The next one said that he wuz knowin' to the circumstances and how the cyclone swep back and brought the suller and sot it down under the house. And the third one remembered vividly how the cyclone went back the second time and brought the hole the suller left and distributed it round under the new site.

The old man listened with deep interest, and said he wuz glad he'd had the privelige of hearin' 'em, for their talk had cleared up a Bible verse he'd long pondered over.

They wuz astounded to think their talk had awakened religious meditations. But the old gentleman said their conversation had cleared up that passage where it said:

"Annanias come forth."

He said it wuz now plain to him that it meant that these three drummers should stand before Annanias, the Prince of Liars, he takin' his place behind 'em, the fourth in the rank of liars.

But this is neither here or there, I only mention it as comin' into my mind instinctively and onbeknown to myself as I hearn Josiah Allen's remark, it came and went, as thoughts will, like a lightning flash, even as I wuz repeatin' the words agin in wonderment and horrow. "Fifty million dollars!"

"No, I said to you, Samantha, that in our conversation we would leave out the orts, fifty dollars wuz what I meant. But as I said this is what I've thought when my brain wuz fired with ambition and glory of histin' the name of Allen up where it ort to be and will be. But when my blood has quieted down and I took a dispassionate view of the affair I have thought it would be more in keepin' with the old traditions of the Allen family to spend jest fifteen, I can do a noble job with Uncle Sime's help and Ury's, with exactly the same sum that wuz paid for these purchases."

I see he wuz jest bound to ignore the millions. But I knowed it wouldn't do any good to keep twittin' him of it. And then he went on to describe more fully the Exposition of Josiah Allen that he'd been plottin' for weeks and weeks. He said that he and uncle Sime had used up two hull pads of writin' paper at a cost of five cents each, plannin' and figurin'. But he didn't begrech the outlay, he said. He wuz layin' out to have the lower paster used as a tentin' ground for the hull Allen race, and the Gowdeys if he decided they wuz worthy to jine in, he hadn't settled on that yet. The cow paster wuz to be used for Equinomical and Agricultural displays and also Peaceful Industries and Inventions, and the lane leadin' up to the barn from the lower paster he laid out to use as a Pike for all sorts of amusements, pitchin' quaits, bull-in-the-barnyard, turnin' hand-springs and summer sets, etc., etc."

Sez I coldly, "It would draw quite a crowd to see you and Deacon Gowdey standin' on your two old bald heads turnin' a summer set."

"Oh, I laid out to have younger people in such thrillin' seens, Ury and others." And then he went on to describe at length his Peaceful Industry Show.

I couldn't sot still to hear it only I felt I wanted to know the worst and cope with it as a surgeon probes to the quick in order to cure.

He thought he could git Aunt Huldy Wood, who wove carpets, to set up her loom for a few days under the big but-nut tree, and be weavin' there before the crowds. He said she wuz a peaceful old critter and would show off well in it. And Bildad Shoecraft, another good-natured creeter, he could bring his shoe-making bench and be tappin' boots. He could not only show off but make money at the same time, for he spozed that many a boot would be wore down to the quick walkin' round viewin' the attractions. And Blandina Teeter he spozed she could run my sewin' machine under the sugar maple. And he thought mebby I would set out under the slippery ellum makin' ginger cookies or fryin' nut-cakes, in either capacity he said I wuz a study for an artist and would draw crowds.

"The wife of Josiah Allen fryin' nut-cakes, what a sound it would have through the world."

"No, Josiah," sez I, "I shan't try to fry nut-cakes in a open lot without ingreents or fire."

"Well, mebby you'd ruther be one of the attractions of the Pike, Samantha. I hain't goin' to limit you to one thing. As the pardner

of the originator of this stupengous scheme you are entitled to
respect. There is where Napoleon, the other great actor in these
twin dramas, missed it, he didn't use his wife as he ort to. But jest
see the wonderful similarity in these cases. He had two stepchil-
dren; the wife of Josiah had two; I am smaller in statute than my
wife; so wuz Napoleon."

"You spoke of your Peaceful Inventions, Josiah," sez I, wantin'
to git his mind off, for truly I begun to fairly feel sick to the stomach
to hear his talk about himself and the Great Conqueror.

"Oh, yes, Samantha, that in itself will be worth double the price
of admission."

"Then you expect to ask pay, Josiah?"

"Certainly, why not? Do they not ask pay at the twin
celebration?"

"But you spoke of inventions; I shall let the rest of the Allens
show off. Lots of 'em have invented things, but of course my inventions will rank number one. There is my button on the suller door
I cut it out of an old boot leg. Who ever hearn of a leather button
before, and it works well if you don't want to fasten the door tight.
Then there is that self actin' hen-coop of mine that lets a stick fall
down and shuts the door when the hen walks up the ladder."

"But no hen has ever clim the ladder yet, Josiah."

"No, perhaps they hain't yet, but I'm expectin' to see 'em every
day, 'tennyrate paint that coop a bright red and yaller and it will
attract a crowd.

"And then there is that travelin' rat trap of brother Henzy's, you
know his grandmother wuz an Allen, I shall mayhap let him appear.
And then there is all my farmin' implements and the rest of the
Allen's I lay out to be just to all, and let 'em all come and show off
in my Agricultural show.

"But of course there has got to be a head to it; Napoleon wuz
the head of the other Purchase, and I'm the head of this. In short,
Samantha, I am *It*."

Oh, how full of pride and vain glory he wuz, and I knowed such
feelin's would have to be brung down for his spiritual good. I realized it as he went on, "I tell you, Napoleon and I would have made
a span, Samantha, if he could been spared till now."

Oh how shamed I wuz to hear such talk, but I sot demute for
reasons named, and he sez agin, "I thought mebby you would want
to be one of the attractions of the Pike, Samantha; I lay out to have

livin' statutes adornin' the side of the lane leadin' up from the bea-
ver medder to the horse trough."

"Livin' statutes!" sez I, coldly, "I don't know what you mean by
them."

"Why, I thought for a few cents I could git a lot of children and
old folks to be white-washed for a day or two and pose as statutes.
It would be a new thing and a crackin' good idee, for livin' statutes
that can wink, and bow, and talk, and walk round some, I don't
believe wuz ever hearn on before." "No indeed," sez I, "but I can
tell you, Josiah Allen, I've played many strange parts in the role of
life at your request, but I tell you once for all I shall never, *never* be
whitewashed and set up for a statute, you can set your mind to rest
on that to once."

"Mebby you'd ruther be a Historical Tabloo, Samantha; I lay out
to have beautiful ones, and I thought I wouldn't confine myself to
the States, but would branch out and have the foreign nations represented figuratively.

"A naval battle between Russia and Japan would draw; if I could
fix some floats on the creek my stun boat could represent Russia,
and Deacon Huffer's Japan, I jest as lives mine would be blowed up
and sunk as not, 'tain't good for much. And if I did have that I
would have the Russian Bear set on the shore growlin', and the
Powers furder back lookin' pleasantly on. You might be a Power,
Samantha, if you wuzn't a female."

"No, thank you, Josiah, I don't hanker after the responsibility for
good or evil that ort to hang onto a Power."

"I'd be the Russian Bear myself, Samantha, with our old buffalo
robe, only I've got everything else to do; I could grasp holt of
things and squeeze 'em tight and growl and paw first rate."

"I wouldn't try to take that Russian Bear's job of graspin' and
growlin' and pawin' onto me, Josiah, if I wuz in your place; it
would tucker anybody out."

"The Eagle of France," sez he dreamily, "could be represented in
reduced form, as artists say, by Solomon Bobbett's old Bramy rooster
with some claws tied on. And Scotland, the land knows there is
thistles enough along the cow path to represent her if they're han-
dled right. And for Ireland I might have two fellers fightin' with
shelalays, Ury could make the shelalays if he had a pattern."

I knit away with a look of cold mockery on my face that I spose
worried him, for he sez, "I wish I could git you interested in my

show, Samantha. Mebby you'd want to represent Britanny scourin' the blue seas, you always thought so much of the Widder Albert. You could enact it in the creek where the water is shaller. You've got a long scrubbin' brush, I always thought you looked some like Britanny, and you do scrub and scour so beautiful, Samantha."

"No, Josiah, you'll never git me into that scrape, not but what Britanny may need help with her scrubbin' brush. But I shan't catch my death cold makin' a fool of myself by tacklin' that job."

"Oh, you could wear my rubber boots. But I shall not urge the matter, I only thought we two countries are such clost friends and I wanted you to have the foremost character, but I can probable git someone else to enact it. But the strain is fearful on me, Samantha, to have everything go on as it should."

His looks wuz strange. I could see that he wuz all nerved up, and his mind (what he had) wuz all wrought up to its highest tension; I knowed what happened when the tension to my sewin' machine wuz drawed too tight—it broke. And my machine wuz strong in comparison to some other things I won't mention out of respect to my pardner. I felt that I must be cautious and tread carefully if I would influence him for his good, so I brought forth the argument that seldom failed with him, and sez I:

"If I hadn't no other reason for jinin' in these doin's, cookin' has got to be done and how can a statute or a Historical Tabloo bile potatoes and brile steak and make yeast emptin's bread perked up on a pedestal or posin' in the creek, and you know, Josiah, that no matter how fur ambition or vain glory may lead a man, his appetite has got to be squenched, and vittles has got to be cooked else how can he squench it."

And to this old trustworthy weepon I held in all his different plans to inviggle me into his preposterous idees and found it answered better than reason or ridicule. But even this failed to break up his crazy plan. His hull mind (what he had) wuz sot on it.

SOURCE: Josiah Allen's Wife (Marietta Holley). *Samantha at the St. Louis Exposition*. New York: J. W. Dillingham Company, 1904.

THE CRIMSON CORD (1904)

Ellis Parker Butler

An Iowa native, Butler (1869–1937) moved to New York to write for trade magazines. Even after having gained a lot of financial success as a writer, he worked as a banker in Queens for ten years. The subtitle in the magazine for this story was "An Adventure of Perkins the Great." Butler's inventive salesman had appeared in an earlier story.

I.

I had not seen Perkins for six months or so and things were dull. I was beginning to tire of sitting indolently in my office with nothing to do but clip coupons from my bonds. Money is good enough, in its way, but it is not interesting unless it is doing something lively— doubling itself or getting lost. What I wanted was excitement and adventure—and I knew that if I could find Perkins I could have both. A scheme is a business adventure, and Perkins was the greatest schemer in or out of Chicago.

Just then Perkins walked into my office.

"Perkins," I said, as soon as he had arranged his feet comfortably on my desk, "I'm tired. I'm restless. I have been wishing for you for a month: I want to go into a big scheme and make a lot of new, up-to-date cash. I'm sick of this tame, old cash that I have. It isn't interesting. No cash is interesting except the coming cash."

"I'm with you," said Perkins, "what is your scheme?"

"I have none," I said sadly, "that is just my trouble. I have sat here for days trying to think of a good practical scheme, but I can't. I don't believe there is an unworked scheme in the whole wide, wide world."

Perkins waved his hand.

"My boy," he exclaimed, "there are millions! You've thousands of 'em right here in your office! You're falling over them, sitting on them, walking on them! Schemes? Everything is a scheme. Everything has money in it!"

I shrugged my shoulders.

"Yes," I said, "for you. But you are a genius."

"Genius, yes," Perkins said smiling cheerfully, "else why Perkins the Great? Why Perkins the originator? Why the Great and Only Perkins of Portland?"

"All right," I said, "what I want is for your genius to get busy. I'll give you a week to work up a good scheme."

Perkins pushed back his hat and brought his feet to the floor with a smack.

"Why the delay?" he queried, "time is money. Hand me something from your desk."

I looked in my pigeonholes and pulled from one a small ball of string. Perkins took it in his hand and looked at it with great admiration.

"What is it?" he asked seriously.

"That," I said humoring him, for I knew something great would be evolved from his wonderful brain, "is a ball of red twine I bought at the ten-cent store. I bought it last Saturday. It was sold to me by a freckled young lady in a white shirtwaist. I paid—"

"Stop!" Perkins cried, "what is it?"

I looked at the ball of twine curiously. I tried to see something remarkable in it. I couldn't. It remained a simple ball of red twine and I told Perkins so.

"The difference," declared Perkins, "between mediocrity and genius! Mediocrity always sees red twine; genius sees a ball of Crimson Cord!"

He leaned back in his chair and looked at me triumphantly. He folded his arms as if he had settled the matter. His attitude seemed to say that he had made a fortune for us. Suddenly he reached forward, and grasping my scissors, began snipping off small lengths of the twine.

"The Crimson Cord!" he ejaculated. "What does it suggest?"

I told him that it suggested a parcel from the druggist's. I had often seen just such twine about a druggist's parcel.

Perkins sniffed disdainfully.

"Druggists?" he exclaimed with disgust. "Mystery! Blood! 'The Crimson Cord.' Daggers! Murder! Strangling! Clues! 'The Crimson Cord'—"

He motioned wildly with his hands as if the possibilities of the phrase were quite beyond his power of expression.

"It sounds like a book," I suggested.

"Great!" cried Perkins. "A novel! The novel! Think of the words 'A Crimson Cord' in blood-red letters six feet high on a white ground!" He pulled his hat over his eyes and spread out his hands, and I think he shuddered.

"Think of 'A Crimson Cord,'" he muttered, "in blood-red letters on a ground of dead, sepulchral black, with a crimson cord writhing through them like a serpent."

He sat up suddenly and threw one hand in the air.

"Think," he cried, "of the words in black on white with a crimson cord drawn taut across the whole ad!"

He beamed upon me.

"The cover of the book," he said quite calmly, "will be white—virgin, spotless white—with black lettering, and the cord in crimson. With each copy we will give a crimson silk cord for a book-mark. Each copy will be done up in a white box and tied with crimson cord."

He closed his eyes and tilted his head upward.

"A thick book," he said, "with deckle-edges and pictures by Christy. No, pictures by Pyle. Deep, mysterious pictures! Shadows and gloom! And wide, wide margins. And a gloomy foreword. One fifty per copy, at all booksellers."

Perkins opened his eyes and set his hat straight with a quick motion of his hand. He arose and pulled on his gloves.

"Where are you going?" I asked.

"Contracts!" he said. "Contracts for advertising! We must boom 'The Crimson Cord.' We must boom her big!"

He went out and closed the door. Presently, when I supposed him well on the way down town, he opened the door and inserted his head.

"Gilt tops," he announced. "One million copies the first impression!"

And then he was gone.

II.

A week later Chicago and the greater part of the United States was placarded with "The Crimson Cord." Perkins did his work thoroughly and well, and great was the interest in the mysterious title. It was an old dodge, but a good one. Nothing appeared on the advertisements but the mere title. No word as to what "The Crimson Cord" was. Perkins merely announced the words and left them to rankle in the reader's mind, and as a natural consequence each new advertisement served to excite new interest.

When we made our contracts for magazine advertising—and we took a full page in every worthy magazine the publishers were at a loss to classify the advertisement, and it sometimes appeared among the breakfast foods, and sometimes sandwiched in between the automobiles and the hot water heaters. Only one publication placed it among the books.

But it was all good advertising, and Perkins was a busy man. He racked his inventive brain for new methods of placing the title before the public: in fact so busy was he at his labor of introducing the title that he quite forgot the book itself.

One day he came to the office with a small, rectangular package. He unwrapped it in his customary enthusiastic manner, and set on my desk a cigar box bound in the style he had selected for the binding of "The Crimson Cord." It was then I spoke of the advisability of having something to the book besides the cover and a boom.

"Perkins," I said, "don't you think it is about time we got hold of the novel—the reading, the words?"

For a moment he seemed stunned. It was clear that he had quite forgotten that book-buyers like to have a little reading matter in their books. But he was only dismayed for a moment.

"Tut!" he cried presently. "All in good time! The novel is easy. Anything will do. I'm no literary man. I don't read a book in a year. You get the novel."

"But I don't read a book in five years!" I exclaimed. "I don't know anything about books. I don't know where to get a novel."

"Advertise!" he exclaimed. "Advertise! You can get anything, from an apron to an ancestor, if you advertise for it. Offer a prize— offer a thousand dollars for the best novel. There must be thousands of novels not in use."

Perkins was right. I advertised as he suggested and learned that there were thousands of novels not in use. They came to us by basketfuls and cartloads. We had novels of all kinds—historical and hysterical, humorous and numerous, but particularly numerous. You would be surprised to learn how many ready-made novels can be had on short notice. It beats quick lunch. And most of them are equally indigestible. I read one or two but I was no judge of novels. Perkins suggested that we draw lots to see which we should use.

It really made little difference what the story was about. "The Crimson Cord" fits almost any kind of a book. It is a nice, non-committal sort of title, and might mean the guilt that bound two sinners, or the tie of affection that binds lovers, or a blood relationship, or it might be a mystification title with nothing in the book about it.

But the choice settled itself. One morning a manuscript arrived that was tied with a piece of red twine, and we chose that one for good luck because of the twine. Perkins said that was a sufficient excuse for the title, too. We would publish the book anonymously, and let it be known that the only clue to the writer was the crimson cord with which the manuscript was tied when we received it. It would be a first-class advertisement.

Perkins, however, was not much interested in the story, and he left me to settle the details; I wrote to the author asking him to call, and he turned out to be a young woman.

Our interview was rather shy. I was a little doubtful about the proper way to talk to a real author, being purely a Chicagoan myself, and I had an idea that while my usual vocabulary was good enough for business purposes it might be too easy-going to impress a literary person properly, and in trying to talk up to her standard I had to be very careful in my choice of words. No publisher likes to have his authors think he is weak in the grammar line.

Miss Rosa Belle Vincent, however, was quite as flustered as I was. She seemed ill-at-ease and anxious to get away, which I supposed was because she had not often conversed with publishers who paid a thousand dollars cash in advance for a manuscript.

She was not at all what I had thought an author would look like. She didn't even wear glasses. If I had met her on the street I should have said: "There goes a pretty flip stenographer." She was that kind—big picture hat and high pompadour.

I was afraid she would try to run the talk into literary lines and Ibsen and Gorky, where I would have been swamped in a minute, but she didn't, and, although I had wondered how to break the subject of money when conversing with one who must be thinking of nobler things, I found she was less shy when on that subject than when talking about her book.

"Well now," I said, as soon as I had got her seated, "we have decided to buy this novel of yours. Can you recommend it as a thoroughly respectable and intellectual production?"

She said she could.

"Haven't you read it?" she asked in some surprise.

"No," I stammered. "At least, not yet. I'm going to as soon as I can find the requisite leisure. You see, we are very busy just now— very busy. But if you can vouch for the story being a first-class article—something, say, like *The Vicar of Wakefield* or *David Harum*—we'll take it."

"Now you're talking," she said. "And do I get the check now?"

"Wait," I said; "not so fast. I have forgotten one thing," and I saw her face fall. "We want the privilege of publishing the novel under a title of our own, and anonymously. If that is not satisfactory the deal is off." She brightened in a moment.

"It's a go, if that's all," she said. "Call it whatever you please, and the more anonymous it is the better it will suit yours truly."

So we settled the matter then and there, and when I gave her our check for a thousand she said I was all right.

III.

Half an hour after Miss Vincent had left the office Perkins came in with his arms full of bundles, which he opened, spreading their contents on my desk.

He had a pair of suspenders with nickel-silver mountings, a tie, a lady's belt, a pair of low shoes, a shirt, a box of cigars, a package of cookies, and a half-dozen other things of divers and miscellaneous character. I poked them over and examined them, while he leaned against the desk with his legs crossed. He was beaming upon me.

"Well," I said, "what is it—a bargain sale?"

Perkins leaned over and tapped the pile with his long fore-finger.

"Aftermath!" he crowed, "aftermath!"

"The dickens it is," I exclaimed, "and what has aftermath got to do with this truck? It looks like the aftermath of a notion store."

He tipped his "Air-the-Hair" hat over one ear and put his thumbs in the armholes of his "ready-tailored" vest.

"Genius!" he announced. "Brains! Foresight! Else why Perkins the Great? Why not Perkins the Nobody?"

He raised the suspenders tenderly from the pile and fondled them in his hands.

"See this?" he asked, running his finger along the red corded edge of the elastic. He took up the tie and ran his nail along the red stripe that formed the selvedge on the back, and said: "See this?" He pointed to the red laces of the low shoes and asked, "See this?" And so through the whole collection.

"What is it?" he asked. "It's genius! It's foresight."

He waved his hand over the pile.

"The aftermath!" he exclaimed.

"These suspenders are the Crimson Cord suspenders. These shoes are the Crimson Cord shoes. This tie is the Crimson Cord tie. These crackers are the Crimson Cord brand. Perkins & Co. get out a great book, 'The Crimson Cord!' Sell five million copies. Dramatized, it runs three hundred nights. Everybody talking Crimson Cord. Country goes Crimson Cord crazy. Result—up jump Crimson Cord this and Crimson Cord that. Who gets the benefit? Perkins & Co.? No! We pay the advertising bills and the other man sells his Crimson Cord cigars. That is usual."

"Yes," I said, "I'm smoking a David Harum cigar this minute, and I am wearing a Carvel collar."

"How prevent it?" asked Perkins. "One way only, discovered by Perkins. Copyright the words 'Crimson Cord' as trade-mark for every possible thing. Sell the trade-mark on royalty; ten percent of all receipts for 'Crimson Cord' brands comes to Perkins & Co. Get a cinch on the aftermath!"

"Perkins!" I cried, "I admire you. You are a genius. And have you contracts with all these—notions?"

"Yes," said Perkins, "that's Perkins' method. Who originated the Crimson Cord? Perkins did. Who is entitled to the profits on the Crimson Cord? Perkins is. Perkins is wide awake all the time. Perkins gets a profit on the aftermath and the math and the before the math."

And so he did. He made his new contracts with the magazines on the exchange plan—we gave a page of advertising in the "Crimson Cord" for a page of advertising in the magazine. We guaranteed five million circulation. We arranged with all the manufacturers of the Crimson Cord brands of goods to give coupons, one hundred of which entitled the holder to a copy of *The Crimson Cord*. With a pair of Crimson Cord suspenders you get five coupons; with each Crimson Cord cigar, one coupon; and so on.

IV.

On the first of October we announced in our advertisement that "The Crimson Cord" was a book; the greatest novel of the century; a thrilling, exciting tale of love. Miss Vincent had told me it was a love story. Just to make everything sure, however, I sent the manuscript to Professor Wiggins, who is the most erudite man I ever met. He knows eighteen languages, and reads Egyptian as easily as I read English. In fact his specialty is old Egyptian ruins and so on. He has written several books on them.

Professor said the novel seemed to him very light and trashy, but grammatically O. K. He said he never read novels, not having time, but he thought that *The Crimson Cord* was just about the sort of thing a silly public that refused to buy his *Some Light on the Dynastic Proclivities of the Hyksos* would scramble for. On the whole I considered the report satisfactory.

We found we would be unable to have Pyle illustrate the book, he being too busy, so we turned it over to a young man at the Art Institute.

That was the fifteenth of October, and we had promised the book to the public for the first of November, but we had it already in type and the young man, his name was Gilkowsky, promised to work night and day on the illustrations.

The next morning, almost as soon as I reached the office, Gilkowsky came in. He seemed a little hesitant, but I welcomed him warmly, and he spoke up.

"I have a girl to go with," he said, and I wondered what I had to do with Mr. Gilkowsky's girl, but he continued: "She's a nice girl and a good looker, but she's got bad taste in some things. She's too loud in hats, and too trashy in literature. I don't like to say this about her, but it's true and I'm trying to educate her in good hats and good literature. So I thought it would be a good thing to take around this *Crimson Cord* and let her read it to me."

I nodded.

"Did she like it?" I asked.

Mr. Gilkowsky looked at me closely.

"She did," he said, but not so enthusiastically as I had expected.

"It's her favorite book. Now, I don't know what your scheme is, and I suppose you know what you are doing better than I do; but I thought perhaps I had better come around before I got to work on the illustrations and see if perhaps you hadn't given me the wrong manuscript."

"No, that was the right manuscript," I said. "Was there anything wrong about it?"

Mr. Gilkowsky laughed nervously.

"Oh, no!" he said. "But did you read it?"

I told him I had not because I had been so rushed with details connected with advertising the book.

"Well," he said, "I'll tell you. This girl of mine reads pretty trashy stuff, and she knows about all the cheap novels there are. She dotes on *The Duchess*, and puts her last dime into Braddon. She knows them all by heart. Have you ever read *Lady Audley's Secret*?"

"I see," I said. "One is a sequel to the other."

"No," said Mr. Gilkowsky. "One is the other. Someone has flim-flammed you and sold you a typewritten copy of *Lady Audley's Secret* as a new novel."

V.

When I told Perkins he merely remarked that he thought every publishing house ought to have some one in it who knew something about books, apart from the advertising end, although that was, of course, the most important. He said we might go ahead and publish *Lady Audley's Secret* under the title of *The Crimson Cord*, as such things had been done before, but the best thing to do would be to charge Rosa Belle Vincent's thousand dollars to Profit and Loss and hustle for another novel, something reliable and not shop-worn.

Perkins had been studying the literature market a little and he advised me to get something from Indiana this time, so I tele-graphed an advertisement to the Indianapolis papers and two days later we had ninety-eight historical novels by Indiana authors from which to choose. Several were of the right length, and we chose one and sent it to Mr. Gilkowsky with a request that he read it to his sweetheart. She had never read it before.

We sent a detective to Dillville, Indiana, where the author lived, and the report we received was most satisfactory.

The author was a sober, industrious young man, just out of the high school, and bore a first-class reputation for honesty. He had never been in Virginia, where the scene of his story was laid, and they had no library in Dillville, and our detective assured us that the young man was in every way fitted to write a historical novel.

The Crimson Cord made an immense success. You can guess how it boomed when I say that although it was published at a dollar and a half, it was sold by every department store for fifty-four cents, way below cost, just like sugar, or Vandeventer's Baby Food, or Q & Z Corsets, or any other staple. We sold our first edition of five million copies inside of three months, and got out another edition of two million, and a specially illustrated holiday edition and an edition de luxe, and *The Crimson Cord* is still selling in paper-covered cheap edition.

With the royalties received from the aftermath and the profit on the book itself, we made—well, Perkins has a country place at Lakewood, and I have my cottage at Newport.

SOURCE: *Frank Leslie's Popular Monthly Magazine,* February 1904.

THE LIFE ELIXIR OF MARTHY (1905)

Elizabeth Hyer Neff

Neff (1857–1942) was from Greenfield, Ohio. In 1876 she married William Byron Neff, who became a Cleveland judge, while she wrote for magazines and published novels and a play.

"AN-NDREW! AN-NDREW!"

"Yes, Marthy."

"Andrew, what be you doin' out there? You've ben sayin' 'Yes, Marthy,' for the last ten minutes."

The patient, middle-aged face of Andrew appeared in the doorway, its high, white forehead in sharp contrast with the deeply tanned features below it.

"I've jest ben takin' your buryin' clothes off the line an' foldin' 'em up. It is such a good day to air 'em for fall—and, then,—I jest hate to tell you!—the moths has got into the skirt of your shroud. I sunned it good, but the holes is there yet."

"Moths!" screamed the thin voice, sharpened by much calling to people in distant rooms. "Then they've got all over the house, I presume to say, if they've got into that. Why don't you keep it in the cedar chist?"

"Because it's full of your laid-by clothes now, and I keep my black suit that you had me git for the funeral in there, too. There ain't room. You told me allus to keep your buryin' clothes in a box in the spare room closet, so's they'd be handy to git if they was wanted in the night. You told me that four or five years ago, Marthy."

"So I did. And I presume to say that my good threeply carpet that mother gave me when we was married is jest reddled with moths—if they're in that closet. If it wasn't for keepin' that spare room ready for the cousins in Maine when they come to the buryin', I'd have you take up that carpet and beat it good and store it in the garret. My, oh, my, what worries a body has when they can't git around to do for themselves! Now it's moths, right on top of Mr. Oldshaw's death after he'd got my discourse all prepared on the text I picked out for him. He had as good as preached it to me, and it was a powerful one, a warnin' to the ungodly not to be took unawares. I advised him to p'int it that way. Then, Jim Woodworth's Mary is leavin' the choir to marry and go west, and I jest won't have Palmyra Stockly sing 'Cool Siloam' over me. I can settle that right now, for I couldn't abide the way she acted about that church fair—and she sings through her nose anyway. An-ndrew!"

"Yes, Marthy."

"You oughtn't to go walkin' off when a body is talkin' to you. You allus do that."

"I c'n hear you, Marthy. I'm jest in the kitchen. I thought the dinner had b'iled dry."

"Are you gittin' a b'iled dinner? It smells wonderful good. What you got in it?"

"Corned beef and cabbage and onions and potatoes and turnips. I've het up a squash pie and put out some of the cider apple sauce that will spile if it isn't et pretty soon. I'll put the tea a-drawin' soon's the kittle b'iles."

Andrew's voice came into the sick room in a mechanical recitative, as if accustomed to recount every particular of the day's doings.

"Well, I guess you can bring me some of it. You bring me a piece of the corned beef and consid'able of the cabbage and potaters and an onion or two. And if that cider apple sauce is likely to spile, I might eat a little of it; bring me a cooky to eat with it. And a piece of the squash pie. What else did you say you had?"

"That's all."

"Don't forgit to put on consid'able of bread. It's a good while till supper, and I don't dast to eat between meals."

Andrew brought the tray to the bedside and propped up the invalid before he ate his own dinner. He had finished it and cleared up the table before the high voice called again: "An-ndrew!"

"Yes, Marthy."

"Is there any more of the corned beef?"

"You brought me such a little mite of a piece."

"Yes, there's plenty more, but I knew you'd object if I brought it first. Like it, did you?"

"Yes, it was tol'able. Them vegetables was a little rich, but maybe they won't hurt me. You might bring me another cooky when you come.—Now, you set down a minute while you're waitin' for my dishes. I've ben worryin' 'bout them moths every minute since you told me, and somethin' has got to be done."

"I know it. I hated to tell you, but I thought you ought to know. I guess I c'n clean 'em out the next rainy spell when I have to stay in."

"No, you can't wait for that. And you can't do it anyway. There's things a man can do, and then again there's things he can't. You're uncommon handy, Andrew, but you're a man."

Andrew's deprecatory gesture implied that he couldn't help it.

"I've thought of that ever so much in the years that I've ben layin' here, and I've worried about what you're goin' to do when I ain't here to plan and direct for you. Those moths are jest an instance. Now, what you goin' to do when you have to think for yourself?"

"I do' know, but you ain't goin' to git up a new worry 'bout that, I hope?"

"No, it is not a new worry. It's an old one, but it's such a delicate subject, even between man and wife, that I've hesitated to speak of it. Andrew, I don't want you to stay single but jest six months—jest six months to the very day after I'm laid away. I've spoken to Hannah Brewster to come in and do for you twice a week, same as she does now, and to mend your socks and underclothes for six months, and then I want you to—git married."

"Why, Marthy!"

"You needn't gasp like you was struck. I presume to say you'd do it anyway without thinkin' it over well beforehand. I've allus planned and thought things over for you till I don't know whether you'd be capable of attendin' to that or not. And I'd go off a sight easier if I knew 'twas all settled satisfactory. I'd like to know who's goin' to keep my house and wear my clothes and sun my bed quilts, and I could have her come and learn my ways beforehand."

"Good gracious, Marthy! There's a limit to plannin'— and directin'—even for as smart a woman as you be. You're not goin' to know whether she'll—consent or not, not while—while you're here, yet. And you're gittin' no worse; it does seem like you're gittin' better all the time. Last time Aunt Lyddy was here she said you was lookin' better'n she ever see you before. I told her you'd picked up in your appetite consid'able. You'll git up yet and be my second wife yourself."

"Yes, Aunt Lyddy allus thinks great things 'bout me; she never would believe how low I've ben, but I guess I know how I be. No, you can't head me off that way, with the moths in my best things and one of my grandmother's silver spoons missin'. If there's one thing a forethoughtful woman ought to plan beforehand, it's to pick out the woman who's to have her house and her things and her husband."

Andrew wriggled uncomfortably. "I shouldn't wonder if the dish water was a-b'ilin', Marthy."

"No, it isn't. You haven't got fire enough. And we'd better settle this matter while we're at it."

"Settle it! Why, Marthy, you talk 's if you wanted me to go 'n' git married on the spot and bring my second wife home to you before—while you're still here. I'm no Mormon. Like's not you've got her selected; you're such a wonderful hand to settle things."

"I can't say's I've got her selected—not the exact one—but I've ben runnin' over several in my mind. We'd better have several to pick from, and then if some refused you, we'd still have a chance."

"But how would you git any of 'em to consent?" asked Andrew with a show of interest.

"How else but ask 'em? They would understand how I feel about you. The hull town knows how I've laid here expectin' every day to be to-morrow, and if I want that thing settled before I go, I don't see how it could make talk."

"Now, who had you sorted out to pick from?" and Andrew leaned back comfortably in his chair. His wife punched up her pillow to lift her head higher.

"Well, there's the widows first. I've sorted them over and over till I've got 'em down to four that ain't wasteful cooks nor got too many relations. There's Widow Jackson—"

"She's weakly," promptly decided Andrew.

"And Mary Josephine Wilson—"

"She don't go to our church. What about the old maids?"

"I don't take much stock in old maids. The likeliest person I know, and I wouldn't call her an old maid, either, is Abilonia Supe. Her mother was counted the best breadmaker in North Sudbury, and Abby was the neatest darner in her class at sewing school."

"But, why, Marthy, isn't Abby promised to Willy Parks?"

"No; I asked Mis' Parks about that yisterday. She said Willy had been waitin' on Abby for four or five years, but they'd had a mis-understandin' this summer, and it was broke off for good."

"He ought to be horsewhipped!" said Andrew warmly. "Abilonia Supe is the finest girl in North Sudbury."

"Ye-es," admitted Marthy reluctantly. "You're sure she wouldn't be too young for you, are you?"

"Too young? For me? I don't want to marry my grandmother, I guess. And I'm not Methusalem myself." and he shook the stoop out of his back and spread the thin hair across his bald spot. His wife looked at him in wondering surprise.

"Abby has had rather a hard time since her mother died," she said weakly.

"Indeed she has, and she deserves to have it easy now. She needs somebody to take care of her if that scamp—and she isn't bad lookin', either—Abby isn't. I tell you, Marthy, there isn't your beat in the hull town for managin' forethoughtedness. Sick or well, you've allus ben a captain at managin'. Now, come to think it over, this isn't a bad idee. But, how'll we git her consent? Maybe I'd better step over and—well—ruther lead up to the sub-ject. I might—"

"That dish water's a-b'ilin', Andrew. It's a-b'ilin' ha'rd. I c'n hear it."

Andrew started briskly for the kitchen, and the dishes clattered merrily. An hour later he framed himself in the doorway in his Sunday clothes.

"I have to go down to the store this afternoon to git that baggin' for the hops, and I can jest as well 's not go round by Supes' and—sort of—talk that over with Abby—and tell her your wishes. I never deny you nothin', Marthy; you know that. If it'll be any comfort to you, I'll jest brace up and do it, no matter how hard it is."

"Well—say, Andrew, wait a minute. Maybe you'd better wait till we talk it over a little more. I might consult with Abby, myself, on the subject—An-ndrew! An-ndrew! That man is gittin' a good deal deafer'n he'll own to."

It was quite supper time when Andrew returned; it was too late to cook anything, so he brought Marthy some of the Sunday baked beans and brown bread, with the cider apple sauce.

"Well, you must'a had a time of it with her," suggested his wife as he placed the tray. "I hope you didn't do more'n make a suppositious case and find out what her sentiments was."

"That was what I set out to do, but she was so surprised an' asked so many questions that I jest had to up and tell her what I was drivin' at. I told her that it was your last wish, and that you'd set your heart on it till you felt like you couldn't die easy unless you knew who was goin' to have your house and your beddin' and— me, and after I'd reasoned with her quite a spell and she'd ruther got used to the idee, she saw how 'twas. I thought you'd like to have it settled, because you allus do, and, as you say, there's no tellin' what day'll be tomorrow. Then, that Willy Parks is likely to come back and spile the hullplan."

"Settle it all? Why, what did she say to it?"

"I guess you may call it settled. I asked her if she'd consider herself engaged to me—"

"What? What's that? Engaged to you?"

"Yes; isn't that what you wanted?"

"What did she say to that?"

"She said yes, she guessed that she would, though she would like to think it over a little."

"I didn't presume to think you'd go and get it all settled without talkin' it over with me, and I calc'lated to— to do the arrangin' myself. What did she say when she consented to it, Andrew?"

Andrew squirmed on the edge of his chair. "I guess my tea is coolin' out there. I'd better go and eat, now."

"A minute more won't make no difference. What did she say?"

"She said—why, she said—a whole lot of things. She said she never expected to marry; that she wanted to give her life to makin' folks happy and doin' for them, folks that had a sorrow— but the Lord hadn't given her any sorrowful folks to do for. It's my opinion that she thought consid'able of that fickle Willy Parks. Then I reasoned with her some, and she come to see that maybe this was the app'inted work for her to do—considerin' you'd set your heart on it so. She said she didn't know but I needed lookin' after and doin' for as much as any one she knew, and it would be a pleasure to—now, Marthy, let me go and have my tea."

"What else did she say?"

"Well, she said I certainly had—that I had—a hard trial this trip, and I'd served my time so faithfully it would be a comfort and a pleasure to—now, Marthy, I know my tea's cold."

It took him so long to have his tea and wash the dishes and bring in the squashes for fear of frost that Marthy had no further opportunity to consider the new position of her husband as an engaged man that night. She resumed the subject early the next morning.

"Andrew, I want you should go and bring Abilonia over here as soon as you git the work done up. There's so much I want to arrange with her, and you never know what day'll be tomorrow. And them moths ought to be seen to right off—"

"What be you goin' up stairs for? You needn't put on your Sunday clothes jest for that. She'll have to see you in your old clothes many a year after you're—ah—when she comes to live here."

"Yes, but that's not now. I'm only engaged to her; I'm only sort of courtin' now, as you might say."

He came back in a little while, bringing a gentle, brown-eyed young woman, who laid away her things and took an apron from her bag with the air of one accustomed to do for others.

"Did you want to see me particularly, Mis' Dobson? I hope you're not feelin' worse?"

"I do' know's I slep' much las' night, and I have an awful funny feelin' round my heart this mornin'. I'm preparin' for the worst. You know 'Two men shall be grindin' at the mill and'—"

"Oh, now, you aren't so bad as all that. You look as smart as a spring robin—you do look wonderful well, Mis' Dobson. Now, what can I do for you?"

"There's a lot of things to look after, Abilonia, now that you— that you—that—"

"Yes, I know there are, and I'll just delight to take hold and do them. I told Mr. Dobson that I wanted to begin to do for you both right away. I'm real glad you thought—of it, Mis' Dobson, for I've nobody else, now, to care for, and I should love to take care of poor Mr. Dobson and try to make him happy—just real happy— the best of anybody in the world. He looked so pleased when I told him so."

"Did he? He did!"

"Yes, his face just lighted up when I told him that we all knew how faithful he'd been to his trust through such a long, hard siege, how kind and patient, and that it would be a privilege to try to make it up to him a little."

"Oh—ah—well, what did he say to that?"

"He just said the hand of the Lord had fallen rather heavy on him, but he'd tried to bear the burden the best he could, and if he held out to the end the Lord would reward him. And he said it was the Lord's mercy to give him such a good, clever wife to take care of—since she was sickly. Now, would you like me to bake you some cookies this morning, or do the mending?"

"I don't know. Did Andrew say that? Well, he has been faithful. You're goin' to git an awful good man, Abilonia. Say, don't you tell him, or it'll scare him, but I'm goin' to do a terrible resky thing. I'm goin' to set up here in the bed a little spell. Go you up to the top bureau drawer in the spare room and git my black shawl. I know I might fall over dead, but I'm goin' to take the resk."

"Why, Mis' Dobson, it isn't safe!"

"Safe or not, I'm goin' to do it. I'm goin' to set up a spell. I never stop for consequences to myself when I set out to do a thing."

The perilous feat was accomplished without tragedy. After she had had a nap, propped up in the bed, Mrs. Dobson's soul rose to greater heights of daring, when Abilonia remarked that Mrs. Dobson's plum-colored silk was the very thing for a lining to her own silk quilt, and as it would not be worn again she might as well take it over and make it up. She was adding that she would like to have a crayon portrait made of Mr. Dobson to hang beside that of his wife which adorned the parlor in antemortem state, when Marthy interrupted: "Abilonia, go you and git me a dress. There ought to be a brown poplin hangin' in the little room closet, unless somebody moved it last spring in housecleanin' time. You bring that down. I want to git my feet onto the floor."

When Andrew came home to get dinner he stopped in the kitchen door, dumb with amazement. Marthy sat by the table in the big wooden chair peeling apples, while Abilonia rolled out the pie crust and told about the church quilting bee.

The next Sunday Andrew did not change his best suit, as usual, after church, and his wife remarked the fact as she sat in a blanketed chair by the living room fire in the evening, with her "Christian Register" in her hand.

"Well, you know—I've ben thinkin'—Abby's settin' over there by herself, and it must be lonesome for the girl. And—if I'm—sort of—engaged to her—don't you see, Marthy? I don't want to leave you—but it's my duty to keep company with her. I want to carry out your wishes exact—every one. You can't ask a thing too hard for me to do."

"Yes, I know that, Andrew. If ever a man done his duty, it's you. And you've had little reward for it, too. I'm tryin' to git you a second wife that'll have her health and—and—yes, I presume to say that Abilonia'll ruther look for you to set a while, now that she is bespoke to you."

"Yes, that's what I guess I ought to do," and he rose briskly.

"Say, Andrew! Don't be in such a hurry. Come back a minute. You gear up ole Jule to the buggy and git down a comforter for me. I c'n walk some, today, and if you help me I c'n git into the buggy. I feel like the air would do me good.—Yes, I presume to say it'll be the death of me, but you never knew me to stop for that, did you? Git my circular cloak and the white cloud for my head. Yes, I'm goin', Andrew. When I git my mind made up, you know what it means."

There was a light in Abilonia's parlor when they drove up, and a man's figure showed through the glass panel of the door as he opened it.

"Willy Parks!" cried Mrs. Dobson in a queer voice.

"Yes, walk right in, Mr. Dobson. That isn't Mrs. Dobson with you—is it possible!—after so many years. Let me help you steady her. Well, this is a surprise! Just walk into the parlor and sit down. Abby's down cellar putting away the milk, but she'll be up in a minute."

"It's consid'able of a surprise to see you here, Willy; it's consid'able of a disapp'intment—to Mis' Dobson. She had set her mind on—on—" ventured Andrew mildly.

"Yes, so I heard—and I thought I'd come home. Abby tells me that she is engaged to you—that she has given her solemn promise."

"That's what she has," said Andrew firmly. "That's what she has, and Mis' Dobson has set her mind on it—and I never refuse her nothin'. I don't want nothin' to reproach myself for. You went off and left that girl—the finest girl in town—and near about broke her heart. You ought to be ashamed to show yourself now."

"I am, Mr. Dobson," said the young man gravely, "and I deserve to lose her. But when I heard that she was engaged to you—as it were—it brought me to my senses, and, since you are my rival, I am going to ask you to be magnanimous. She is so good and true that I believe she will forgive me and take me back if you will release her—you and Mrs. Dobson. You wouldn't hold her while Mrs. Dobson looks so smart as she does tonight—"

"No, Andrew, we won't hold her. It wouldn't be right. She's young—and—and real good lookin', and it would be a pity to spile a good match for her. We oughtn't to hold her—here she is. We will release you from your engagement to—to us, Abilonia—and may you be happy! I'm feelin' a sight better lately; that last bitters you got for me is a wonderful medicine, Andrew. I presume to say I'll be round on my feet yet, before long, and be able to take as good care of you as you have took of me all these years. It's a powerful medicine, that root bitters. We better be goin', Andrew. They've got things to talk about. Good night, Abilonia. Good night, Willy."

SOURCE: *The Reader: An Illustrated Monthly Magazine*. Indianapolis: Bobbs-Merrill Company, August 1905.

THE TALE OF THE TANGLED
TELEGRAM (1905)

Wilbur D. Nesbit

Nesbit (1871–1927), who is best known today for his poetry, was a columnist for
the Chicago Evening Post*, and occasionally wrote as "Josh Wink."*

I.

JAMES TROTTINGHAM MINTON had a cousin who lived in St. Louis.
"Cousin Mary," Lucy Putnam discovered by a process of elimina-
tion, was the one topic on which the reticent Mr. Minton could
become talkative. Mary was his ideal, almost. Let a girl broach the
weather, he grew halt of speech; should she bring up literature, his
replies were almost inane; let her seek to show that she kept abreast
of the times, and talk of politics—then Jimmy seemed to harbor a
great fear in his own soul. But give him the chance to make a few
remarks about his cousin Mary and he approached eloquence. For
this reason Lucy Putnam was wise enough to ask him something
about Mary every so often.

Now, the question arises: Why should Lucy Putnam, or any
other girl, take any interest in a man who was so thoroughly bashful
that his trembling efforts to converse made the light quivering
aspen look like a ten-ton obelisk for calmness? The reason was, and
is, that woman has the same eye for babies and men. The more
helpless these objects, the more interested are the women. The man
who makes the highest appeal to a woman is he whose tongue
cleaves to the roof of his mouth and who does not know what to
do with his hands in her presence. She must be a princess, he a

slave. Each knows this premise is unsupported by facts, yet it is a joyous fiction while it lasts. James Trottingham Mipton was not a whit bashful when with men. No. He called on Mr. Putnam at his office, and with the calmness of an agent collecting rent, asked him for the hand of his daughter.

"Why, Jimmy," Mr. Putnam said good-naturedly, "of course I haven't any objections to make. Seems to me that's a matter to be settled between you and Lucy."

Jimmy smiled confidentially.

"I suppose you're right, Mr. Putnam. But, you see, I've never had the nerve to say anything about it to her."

"Tut, tut. Nothing to be scared of. Nothing at all. What's the matter with you, young man? In my day, if a fellow wanted to marry a girl he wouldn't go and tell her father. He'd marry her first and then ask the old man where they should live."

Mr. Putnam chuckled heavily. Mr. Putnam was possessed of a striking fund of reminiscences of how young men used to do.

"Of course, Mr. Putnam," Jimmy said. "But the girls nowadays are different, and a fel—"

"Not a bit of it. No, sir. Women haven't changed since Eve's time. You mustn't get woman mixed up with dry goods stores, Jimmy. Don't you know there's lots of fellows nowadays that fall in love with the fall styles? Ha, ha!"

It was not all clear to Minton, but he laughed dutifully. His was a diplomatic errand, and the half of diplomacy is making the victim think you are in agreement with him.

"Yes, sir," Putnam chuckled on, "I'll bet that silk and ruffles and pink shades over the lamp have caused more proposals than all the dimples and bright eyes in the world. Eh, Jimmy? But you haven't proposed yet?"

"I did. You gave your consent."

"But you're not going to marry me. You want Lucy. You'll have to speak to her about it."

"Now look, Mr. Putnam, I can come to you and ask you for her, and it's the same thing."

"Not by a hundred miles, my boy. If I told Lucy you had said that, she wouldn't be at home next time you called. The trouble with you is that you don't understand women. You've got to talk direct to them."

Jimmy looked hopelessly out of the window.

"No; what you say to me and what I say to you hasn't any more to do with you and Lucy than if you were selling me a bill of goods. I like you, Jimmy, and I've watched your career so far with interest, and I look for great things from you in the future, and that's why I say to you to go ahead and get Lucy, and good luck to you both."

Mr. Putnam took up some papers from his desk and pretended to be studying them, but from the tail of his eye he gathered the gloom that was settling over Jimmy's face. The elder man enjoyed the situation.

"Well, Mr. Putnam," Jimmy asked, "why can't you just tell Lucy for me that I have asked you, and that you say it's all right? Then when I go to see her next time, it'll all be arranged and understood."

"Let me see. Didn't I read a poem or something at school about someone who hadn't sand enough to propose to a girl and who got another man to ask her? But it wasn't her own father. Why, Jimmy, if you haven't courage enough to propose to a girl, what do you suppose will be your finish if she marries you? A married man has to have spunk."

"I've got the spunk all right, but you understand how I feel."

"Sure! Let me give you some advice. When you propose to a girl, you don't have to come right out and ask her to marry you."

Jimmy caught at the straw.

"You don't?" he asked.

"Certainly not. There's half a dozen ways of letting her know that you want her. Usually—always, I may say—she knows it anyway, and unless she wants you she'll not let you tell her so. But if I wanted a short, sharp 'No' from a girl, I'd get her father to ask her to marry me."

"Then you mean that I've got to ask her myself?"

"To be sure."

"I can't do it, Mr. Putnam; I can't."

"Write it."

"Why, I'd feel as if the postman and everybody else knew it."

"Telephone."

"Worse yet."

"Jim Minton, I'm disgusted with you. I thought you were a young man with some enterprise, but if you lose your courage over such an everyday affair as proposing to a girl—"

"But men don't propose every day."

"Somebody is proposing to somebody every day. It goes on all the time. No, sir; I wash my hands of it. I'll not withdraw my consent, and you have my moral support and encouragement, but getting married is the same as getting into trouble—you have to handle your own case."

"But, Mr. Putnam—"

"You'll only go over the same ground again. Good morning. I don't want to hear any more of this until it is settled one way or the other. I'll not help and I'll not hinder it—It's up to you."

With this colloquial farewell Mr. Putnam waved his hand and turned to his papers. Jimmy accumulated his hat and stick, and left, barren of hope.

That night he took Lucy to see *Romeo and Juliet*. The confidence and enthusiasm of Romeo merely threw him into a deeper despair of his own ability as a suitor, and made him even more taciturn and stumbling of speech than ever. His silence grew heavier and heavier, until at last Lucy threw out her never-failing life-line. She asked him about his cousin Mary.

"By the way," he said, brightening up, "Cousin Mary is going through here one day next week."

"Is she? How I should like to know her. If she is anything like you she must be very agreeable."

"She isn't like me, but she is agreeable. Won't you let me try to bring you two together—at lunch downtown, or something like that?"

"It would be fine."

"I'll do it. I'll arrange it just as soon as I see her."

Then silence, pall-like, fell again upon them. Jimmy thought of *Romeo,* and Lucy thought of—Romeo, let us say. When a young man and a young woman, who are the least bit inclined one to another, witness Shakespeare's great educative effort, the young woman cannot help imagining herself leaning over the balcony watching the attempts of the young man to clamber up the rope ladder.

After he had gone that night, Lucy sat down for a soul communion with herself. Pity the woman who does not have soul communions. She who can sit side by side with herself and make herself believe that she is perfectly right and proper in thinking and believing as she does, is happy. The first question Lucy Putnam put to her subliminal self was: "Do I love Jimmy?" Subliminal self, true to sex, equivocated. It said: "I am not sure." Whereupon Lucy asked: "Why do I love him?" Then ensued the debate. Subliminal self said it was because he was a clean, good-hearted, manly fellow. Lucy responded that he was too bashful. "He is handsome," retorted subliminal self. "But there are times when he grows so abashed that he is awkward." Subliminal self said he would outgrow that. "But there are other men who are just as nice, just as handsome, and just as clever, who are not so overwhelmingly shy," argued Lucy. Whereat subliminal self drew itself up proudly and demanded: "Name one!" And Lucy was like the person who can remember faces, but has no memory at all for names.

II.

Cousin Mary came to town as she had promised, and she made Cousin Jimmy drop his work and follow her through the shops half the morning. Cousin Mary was all that Cousin Jimmy had ever said of her. She was pretty and she was genial. When these attributes are combined in a cousin they invite confidences.

The two were standing on a corner, waiting for a swirl of foot passengers, carriages and street-cars, to be untangled, when Mary heard Jimmy making some remark about "Miss Putnam."

"So, she's the one, is she, Jimmy?"

"Well—er—I—I don't know. You see—"

"Certainly I see. Who wouldn't? Is she pretty, Jimmy?"

Jimmy saw a pathway through the crowd and led his cousin to the farther curb before answering: "Yes, she is very pretty."

"Tell me all about her. How long have you known her? How did you meet her? Is she tall or short? Is she dark or fair? Is she musical? Oh, I am just dying to know all about her!"

All the way down State Street Jimmy talked. All the way down State Street he was urged or aided and abetted by the questions and comments of Cousin Mary, and when they had buffeted their way over Jackson to Michigan Avenue and found breathing room, she turned to him and asked pointedly:

"When is it to be?"

"When is what to be?"

"The wedding."

"Whose wedding?" Jimmy's tone was utterly innocent.

"Whose? Yours and Lucy's, to be sure."

"Mine and Lucy's? Why? Mary, I've never asked her yet."

"You've never asked her! Do you mean to tell me that when you can talk about her for seven or eight blocks, as you have, you have not even asked her to marry you? Why, James Trottingham Minton, you ought to be ashamed of yourself! Where does this paragon of woman live? Take me to see her. I want to apologize for you."

"Won't it be better to get her to come in and lunch with us? She lives so far out you'd miss your train east this afternoon."

"The very thing. Would she come?"

"Why, yes. I asked her the other night and she said she would."

"Then, why have you waited so long to tell me. Where are we to meet her?"

"Well, I didn't know for sure what day you would be here, so I didn't make any definite arrangement. I'm to let her know."

"Oh, Jimmy! Jimmy! You need a guardian, and not a guardian angel, either. You need the other sort. You deserve hours of punishment for your thoughtlessness. Now go right away and send her word that I am here and dying to meet her."

"All right. We'll have lunch here at the Annex. You'll excuse me just a moment, and I'll send her a telegram and ask her to come in."

"Yes, but hurry. You should have told her yesterday. When will you ever learn how to be nice to a girl?"

Jimmy, feeling somehow that he had been guilty of a breach of courtesy that should fill him with remorse, hastened to the telegraph desk and scribbled a message to Lucy. It read:

"Please meet me and Mary at Annex at 2 o'clock."

"Rush that," he said to the operator.

The operator glanced over the message and grinned.

"Certainly, sir," he said. "This sort of a message always goes rush. Wish you luck, sir."

The operator has not yet completely gathered the reason for the reproving stare Jimmy gave him. In part it has been explained to him. But, as Jimmy has said since, the man deserved censure for drawing an erroneous conclusion from another's mistake.

It was then noon, so Jimmy and Mary, at Mary's suggestion, got an appetite by making another tour of the shops. In the meantime a snail-paced messenger boy was climbing the Putnam steps with the telegram in his hand.

III.

Lucy took the telegram from the boy and told him to wait until she saw if there should be an answer. She tore off the envelope, unfolded the yellow slip of paper, read the message, gasped, blushed and turned and left the patient boy on the steps.

Into the house she rushed, calling to her mother. She thrust the telegram into her hands, exclaiming: "Read that! Isn't it what we might have expected?"

"Mercy! What is it? Who's dead?"

"Nobody! It's better than that," was Lucy's astonishing reply.

Mrs. Putnam read the telegram, and then beamingly drew her daughter to her and kissed her. The two then wrote a message, after much counting of words, to be sent to Jimmy. It read: "Of course. Mama will come with me. Telephone to papa."

When this reached Jimmy he was nonplused. He rubbed his forehead, studied the message, reread it, and then handed it to Mary with the suggestion:

"Maybe you can make it out. I can't."

Mary knitted her brows and studied the message in turn. At length she handed it back.

"It is simple," she decided. "She is a nice, sweet girl, and she wants me to meet her mama and papa. Or maybe she wants us to be chaperoned."

So Jimmy and Mary waited in the hotel parlor until Lucy should arrive. Reminded by Mary, Jimmy went to the 'phone and told Mr. Putnam that Lucy was coming to lunch with him.

"Well, that's all right, isn't it, Jimmy?" Mr. Putnam asked.

"Yes. But she told me to telephone you."

"Why?"

"I don't know. But won't you join us?"

"Is that other matter arranged, Jimmy?"

"N-no. Not yet."

"I told you I didn't want to see you until it was. As soon as you wake up, let me know. Good-by."

Jimmy, red, returned to the parlor, and there was confronted by a vision of white, with shining eyes and pink cheeks, who rushed up to him and kissed him and called him a dear old thing and said he was the cleverest, most unconventional man that ever was.

Limp, astounded, but delighted, James Trottingham Minton drew back a pace from Lucy Putnam, who, in her dainty white dress and her white hat and filmy white veil, was a delectable sight.

"I want you to meet Cousin Mary," he said.

"Is she to attend?"

"Of course," he answered.

They walked toward the end of the long parlor where Mary was sitting, but half way down the room they were stopped by Mrs. Putnam. She put both hands on Jimmy's shoulders, gave him a motherly kiss on one cheek, and sighed: "Jimmy, you will be kind to my little girl?"

Jimmy looked from mother to daughter in dumb bewilderment. Certainly this was the most remarkable conduct he ever had dreamed of. Yet, Mrs. Putnam's smile was so affectionate and kind, her eyes met his with such a tender look that he intuitively felt that all was right as right should be. And yet—why should they act as they did?

Into the midst of his reflections burst Lucy's chum, Alice Jordan.

"I've a notion to kiss him, too!" she cried.

Jimmy stonily held himself in readiness to be kissed. If kissing went by favor he was pre-eminently a favored one. But Lucy clutched his arm with a pretty air of ownership and forbade Alice.

"Indeed, you will not. It wouldn't be good form now. After—afterward, you may. Just once. Isn't that right, Jimmy?"

"Perfectly," he replied, his mind still whirling in an effort to adjust actualities to his conception of what realities should be.

The four had formed a little group to themselves in the center of the parlor, Lucy clinging to Jimmy's arm, Mrs. Putnam eyeing them both with a happy expression, and Alice fluttering from one to the other, assuring them that they were the handsomest couple she ever had seen, that they ought to be proud of each other, and that Mrs. Putnam ought to be proud of them, and that she was sure nobody in all the world ever, ever could be as sublimely, beatifically happy as they would be, and that they must be sure to let her come to visit them.

"And," she cried, admiringly, stopping to pat Jimmy on his unclutched arm, "I just think your idea of proposing by telegraph was the brightest thing I ever heard of!"

It is to be written to the everlasting credit of James Trottingham Minton that he restrained himself from uttering the obvious remark on hearing this. Two words from him would have wrecked the house of cards. Instead, he blushed and smiled modestly. Slowly it was filtering into his brain that by some unusual, unexpected, unprecedented freak of fortune his difficulties had been overcome; that some way or other he had proposed and had been accepted.

"I shall always cherish that telegram," Lucy declared, leaning more affectionately toward Jimmy. "If that grimy-faced messenger boy had not gone away so quickly with my answer I should have kissed him!"

"I've got the telegram here, dear," said Mrs. Putnam.

"Oh, let's see it again," Alice begged. "I always wanted to hear a proposal, but it is some satisfaction to see one."

Mrs. Putnam opened her hand satchel, took out the telegram, unfolded it slowly, and they all looked at it, Jimmy gulping down a great choke of joy as he read: "Please meet me and marry at Annex at two o'clock."

His bashfulness fell from him as a garment. He took the message, saying he would keep it, so that it might not be lost. Then he piloted the two girls and Mrs. Putnam to the spot where Mary had been waiting patiently and wonderingly.

"Mary," he said boldly, without a tremor in his voice, "I want you to meet the future Mrs. Minton, and my future mother-in-law, Mrs. Putnam, and my future—what are you to me, anyhow, Alice?"

"I'm a combination flower girl, maid of honor and sixteen bridesmaids chanting the wedding march," she laughed.

"And when," Mary gasped, "when is this to be?"

"At two o'clock," Lucy answered.

"Oh, Jimmy! You wretch! You never told me a word about it. But never mind. I bought the very thing for a wedding gift this morning."

Jimmy tore himself away from the excited laughter and chatter, ran to the telephone and got Mr. Putnam on the wire.

"This is Minton," he said.

"Who? Oh! Jimmy? Well?"

"Well, I've fixed that up."

"Good. And when is it to be?"

"Right away. Here at the Annex. I want you to go and get the license for me on your way over."

"Come, come, Jimmy. Don't be in such precipitate haste."

"You told me that was the only way to arrange these matters."

"Humph! Did I? Well, I'll get the license for you—"

"Good-by, then. I've got to telephone for a minister." The minister was impressed at once with the value of haste in coming, and on his way back to the wedding party Jimmy stopped long enough to hand a five-dollar bill to the telegraph operator.

"Thank you, sir," said the astonished man. "I have been worrying for fear I had made a mistake about your message."

"You did. You made the greatest mistake of your life. Thank you!"

SOURCE: *The Reader Magazine*. Indianapolis: The Bobbs-Merrill Company, May 1905.

THE SET OF POE (1906)

George Ade

Ade (1866–1944) was a farmer's son from Indiana who attended Purdue University. After graduating, he moved to Chicago, where he became famous for his "Fables in Slang" column (which became a book), and then as a popular playwright for Broadway.

MR. WATERBY REMARKED to his wife: "I'm still tempted by that set of Poe. I saw it in the window today, marked down to fifteen dollars."

"Yes?" said Mrs. Waterby, with a sudden gasp of emotion, it seemed to him.

"Yes—I believe I'll have to get it."

"I wouldn't if I were you, Alfred," she said. "You have so many books now."

"I know I have, my dear, but I haven't any set of Poe, and that's what I've been wanting for a long time. This edition I was telling you about is beautifully gotten up."

"Oh, I wouldn't buy it, Alfred," she repeated, and there was a note of pleading earnestness in her voice. "It's so much money to spend for a few books."

"Well, I know, but—" and then he paused, for the lack of words to express his mortified surprise.

Mr. Waterby had tried to be an indulgent husband. He took a selfish pleasure in giving, and found it more blessed than receiving. Every salary day he turned over to Mrs. Waterby a fixed sum for household expenses. He added to this an allowance for her spending money. He set aside a small amount for his personal expenses and deposited the remainder in the bank.

146

He flattered himself that he approximated the model husband.

Mr. Waterby had no costly habits and no prevailing appetite for anything expensive. Like every other man, he had one or two hobbies, and one of his particular hobbies was Edgar Allan Poe. He believed that Poe, of all American writers, was the one unmistakable "genius."

The word "genius" has been bandied around the country until it has come to be applied to a longhaired man out of work or a stout lady who writes poetry for the rural press. In the case of Poe, Mr. Waterby maintained that "genius" meant one who was not governed by the common mental processes, but "who spoke from inspiration, his mind involuntarily taking superhuman flight into the realm of pure imagination," or something of that sort. At any rate, Mr. Waterby liked Poe and he wanted a set of Poe. He allowed himself not more than one luxury a year, and he determined that this year the luxury should be a set of Poe.

Therefore, imagine the hurt to his feelings when his wife objected to his expending fifteen dollars for that which he coveted above anything else in the world.

As he went to his work that day he reflected on Mrs. Waterby's conduct. Did she not have her allowance of spending money? Did he ever find fault with her extravagance? Was he an unreasonable husband in asking that he be allowed to spend this small sum for that which would give him many hours of pleasure, and which would belong to Mrs. Waterby as much as to him?

He told himself that many a husband would have bought the books without consulting his wife. But he (Waterby) had deferred to his wife in all matters touching family finances, and he said to himself, with a tincture of bitterness in his thoughts, that probably he had put himself into the attitude of a mere dependent.

For had she not forbidden him to buy a few books for himself? Well, no, she had not forbidden him, but it amounted to the same thing. She had declared that she was firmly opposed to the purchase of Poe.

Mr. Waterby wondered if it were possible that he was just beginning to know his wife. Was she a selfish woman at heart? Was she complacent and good-natured and kind only while she was having her own way? Wouldn't she prove to be an entirely different sort of woman if he should do as many husbands do—spend his income on clubs and cigars and private amusement, and gave her the pickings of small change?

Nothing in Mr. Waterby's whole experience as a married man had so wrenched his sensibilities and disturbed his faith as Mrs. Waterby's objection to the purchase of the set of Poe. There was but one way to account for it. She wanted all the money for herself, or else she wanted him to put it into the bank so that she could come into it after he—but this was too monstrous.

However, Mrs. Waterby's conduct helped to give strength to Mr. Waterby's meanest suspicions.

Two or three days after the first conversation she asked: "You didn't buy that set of Poe, did you, Alfred?"

"No, I didn't buy it," he answered, as coldly and with as much hauteur as possible.

He hoped to hear her say: "Well, why don't you go and get it? I'm sure that you want it, and I'd like to see you buy something for yourself once in a while."

That would have shown the spirit of a loving and unselfish wife.

But she merely said, "That's right; don't buy it," and he was utterly unhappy, for he realized that he had married a woman who did not love him and who simply desired to use him as a pack-horse for all household burdens.

As soon as Mr. Waterby had learned the horrible truth about his wife he began to recall little episodes dating back years, and now he pieced them together to convince himself that he was a deeply wronged person.

Small at the time and almost unnoticed, they now accumulated to prove that Mrs. Waterby had no real anxiety for her husband's happiness. Also, Mr. Waterby began to observe her more closely, and he believed that he found new evidences of her unworthiness. For one thing, while he was in gloom over his discovery and harassed by doubts of what the future might reveal to him, she was content and even-tempered.

The holiday season approached and Mr. Waterby made a resolution. He decided that if she would not permit him to spend a little money on himself he would not buy the customary Christmas present for her.

"Selfishness is a game at which two can play," he said.

Furthermore, he determined that if she asked him for any extra money for Christmas he would say: "I'm sorry, my dear, but I can't spare any. I am so hard up that I can't even afford to buy a few books I've been wanting a long time. Don't you remember that you told me that I couldn't afford to buy that set of Poe?"

Could anything be more biting as to sarcasm or more crushing as to logic?

He rehearsed this speech and had it all ready for her, and he pictured to himself her humiliation and surprise at discovering that he had some spirit after all and a considerable say-so whenever money was involved.

Unfortunately for his plan, she did not ask for any extra spending money, and so he had to rely on the other mode of punishment. He would withhold the expected Christmas present. In order that she might fully understand his purpose, he would give presents to both of the children.

It was a harsh measure, he admitted, but perhaps it would teach her to have some consideration for the wishes of others.

It must be said that Mr. Waterby was not wholly proud of his revenge when he arose on Christmas morning. He felt that he had accomplished his purpose, and he told himself that his motives had been good and pure, but still he was not satisfied with himself.

He went to the dining-room, and there on the table in front of his plate was a long paper box, containing ten books, each marked "Poe." It was the edition he had coveted.

"What's this?" he asked, winking slowly, for his mind could not grasp in one moment the fact of his awful shame.

"I should think you ought to know, Alfred," said Mrs. Waterby, flushed, and giggling like a schoolgirl.

"Oh, it was you."

"My goodness, you've had me *so* frightened! That first day, when you spoke of buying them and I told you not to, I was just sure that you suspected something. I bought them a week before that."

"Yes—yes," said Mr. Waterby, feeling the saltwater in his eyes. At that moment he had the soul of a wretch being whipped at the stake.

"I was determined not to ask you for any money to pay for your own presents," Mrs. Waterby continued. "Do you know I had to save for you and the children out of my regular allowance. Why, last week I nearly starved you, and you never noticed it at all. I was afraid you would."

"No, I—didn't notice it," said Mr. Waterby, brokenly, for he was confused and giddy.

This self-sacrificing angel—and he had bought no Christmas present for her!

It was a fearful situation, and he lied his way out of it.

"How did you like *your* present?" he asked.

"Why, I haven't seen it yet," she said, looking across at him in surprise.

"You haven't? I told them to send it up yesterday."

The children were shouting and laughing over their gifts in the next room, and he felt it his duty to lie for their sake.

"Well, don't tell me what it is," interrupted Mrs. Waterby. "Wait until it comes."

"I'll go after it."

He did go after it, although he had to drag a jeweller away from his home on Christmas-day and have him open his great safe. The ring which he selected was beyond his means, it is true, but when a man has to buy back his self-respect, the price is never too high.

SOURCE: George Ade. *In Babel: Stories of Chicago.* New York: A. Wessels Company, 1906.

OUR VERY WISHES (1909)

Harriet Prescott Spofford

Spofford (1835–1921) was born in Maine, and, to make money for her struggling family, began writing stories in her twenties for Boston newspapers. She went on to publish hundreds of short stories as well as poems, plays, and novels.

IT WAS NATURAL that it should be quiet for Mrs. Cairnes in her empty house. Once there had been such a family of brothers and sisters there! But one by one they had married, or died, and at any rate had drifted out of the house, so that she was quite alone with her work, and her memories, and the echoes in her vacant rooms. She hadn't a great deal of work; her memories were not pleasant; and the echoes were no pleasanter. Her house was as comfortable otherwise as one could wish; in the very center of the village it was, too, so that no one could go to church, or to shop, or to call, unless Mrs. Cairnes was aware of the fact, if she chose; and the only thing that protected the neighbors from this supervision was Mrs. Cairnes's mortal dread of the sun on her carpet; for the sun lay in that bay-windowed corner nearly all the day, and even though she filled the window full of geraniums and vines and calla-lilies she could not quite shut it out, till she resorted to sweeping inner curtains.

Mrs. Cairnes did her own work, because, as she said, then she knew it was done. She had refused the company of various individuals, because, as she said again, she wouldn't give them house-room. Perhaps it was for the same reason that she had refused several offers of marriage; although the only reason that she gave was that one was quite enough, and she didn't want any boots bringing in mud for her to wipe up. But the fact was that Captain Cairnes had been a mistake; and his relict never allowed herself to dwell upon the fact of her loss, but she felt herself obliged to say with too much feeling that all was for the best; and she dared not risk the experiment again.

Mrs. Cairnes, however, might have been lonelier if she had been very much at home; but she was President of the First Charitable, and Secretary of the Second, and belonged to a reading-club, and a sewing-circle, and a bible-class, and had every case of illness in town more or less to oversee, and the circulation of the news to attend to, and so she was away from home a good deal, and took many teas out. Some people thought that if she hadn't to feed her cat she never would go home. But the cat was all she had, she used to say, and nobody knew the comfort it was to her. Yet, for all this, there were hours and seasons when, obliged to stay in the house, it was intolerably dreary there, and she longed for companionship. "Someone with an interest," she said. "Someone who loves the same things that I do, who cares for me, and for my pursuits. Someone like Sophia Maybury. Oh! how I should have liked to spend my last days with Sophia! What keeps Dr. Maybury alive so, I can't imagine. If he had only—gone to his rest," said the good woman, "Sophia and I could join our forces and live together in clover. And how we should enjoy it! We could talk together, read together, sew together. No more long, dull evenings and lonely nights listening to the mice. But a friend, a dear sister, constantly at hand! Sophia was the gentlest young woman, the prettiest,—oh, how I loved her in those days! She was a part of my youth. I love her just as much now. I wish she could come and live here. She might, if there weren't any Dr. Maybury. I can't stand this solitude. Why did fate make me such a social old body, and then set me here all alone?"

If Sophia was the prettiest young woman in those days, she was an exceedingly pretty old woman in these, with her fresh face and her bright eyes, and if her hair was not all her own, she had companions in bangs. Dr. Maybury made a darling of her all his lifetime, and when he died he left her what he had; not much—the rent of the Webster House—but enough.

But there had always been a pea-hen in Mrs. Maybury's lot. It was all very well to have an adoring husband—but to have no home! The Doctor had insisted for years upon living in the tavern, which he owned, and if there was one thing that his wife detested more than another, it was life in a tavern. The strange faces, the strange voices, the going and coming, the dreary halls, the soiled table-cloths, the thick crockery, the damp napkins, the flies, the tiresome *menu*—every roast tasting of every other, no gravy to any—the all outdoors feeling of the whole business, your affairs in everybody's mouth, the banging doors, the restless feet, the stamping of horses in the not distant stable, the pandemonium of it all! She tried to make a little home in the corner of it; but it was useless. And when one day Dr. Maybury suddenly died, missing him and mourning him, and half distracted as she was, a thrill shot across the darkness for half a thought,—now at any rate she could have a home of her own! But presently she saw the folly of the thought,— a home without a husband! She staid on at the tavern, and took no pleasure in life.

But with Dr. Maybury's departure, the thought recurred again and again to Mrs. Cairnes of her and Sophia's old dream of living together. "We used to say, when we were girls, that we should keep house together, for neither of us would ever marry. And it's a great, great pity we did! I dare say, though, she's been very happy. I know she has, in fact. But then if she hadn't been so happy with him, she wouldn't be so unhappy without him. So it evens up. Well, it's half a century gone; but perhaps she'll remember it. I should like to have her come here. I never could bear Dr. Maybury, it's true; but then I could avoid the subject with her. I mean to try. What a sweet, comfortable, peaceful time we should have of it!"

A sweet, comfortable, peaceful time! Well; you shall see. For Mrs. Maybury came; of course she came. Her dear, old friend Julia! Oh, if anything could make up for Dr. Maybury's loss, it would be living with Julia! What castles they used to build about living together and working with the heathen around home. And Julia always went to the old East Church, too; and they had believed just the same things, the same election, and predestination and damnation and all; at one time they had thought of going out missionaries together to the Polynesian Island, but that had been before Julia took Captain Cairnes for better or worse, principally worse, and before she herself undertook all she could in converting Dr. Maybury,—a perfect Penelope's web of a work; for Dr. Maybury died as he had lived, holding her fondest beliefs to be old wives' fables, but not quarreling with her fidelity to them, any more than with her finger-rings or her false bangs, her ribbons, and what she considered her folderols in general. And how kind, she went on in her thoughts, it was of Julia to want her now! what comfort they would be to each other! Go?—of course she would!

She took Allida with her; Allida who had been her maid so long that she was a part of herself; and who, for the sake of still being with her mistress, agreed to do the cooking at Mrs. Cairnes's and help in the house-work. The house was warm and light on the night she arrived; other friends had dropped in to receive her, too; there were flowers on the table in the cosy red dining-room, delicate slices of ham that had been stuffed with olives and sweet herbs, a cold queen's pudding rich with frosting, a mold of coffee jelly in a basin of whipped cream, and little thin bread-and-butter sandwiches.

"Oh, how delightful, how homelike!" cried Mrs. Maybury. How unlike the great barn of a dining-room at the Webster House! What delicious bread and butter! Julia had always been such a famous cook! "Oh, this is home indeed, Julia!" she cried.

Alas! The queen's pudding appeared in one shape or another till it lost all resemblance to itself, and that ham after a fortnight became too familiar for respect.

Mrs. Cairnes, when all was reestablished and at rights, Sophia in the best bedroom, Allida in the kitchen, Sophia's board paying Allida's wages and all extra expense, Sophia's bird singing like a little fountain of melody in the distance, Mrs. Cairnes then felt that after a long life of nothingness, fate was smiling on her; here was friendship, interest, comfort, company, content. No more lonesomeness now. Here was a motive for coming home; here was somebody to come home to! And she straightway put the thing to touch, by coming home from her prayer-meeting, her bible-class, her Ladies' Circle, her First Charitable, and taking in a whole world of pleasure in Sophia's waiting presence, her welcoming smile, her voice asking for the news. And if Sophia were asking for the news, news there must be to give Sophia! And she went about with fresh eagerness, and dropped in here, there, and everywhere, and picked up items at every corner to retail to Sophia.

She found it a little difficult to please Sophia about the table. Used to all the variety of a public-house, Mrs. Maybury did not take very kindly to the simple fare, did not quite understand why three people must be a whole week getting through with a roast,— a roast that, served underdone, served overdone, served cold, served warmed up with herbs, served in a pie, made five dinners; she didn't quite see why one must have salt fish on every Saturday, and baked beans on Sunday; she hankered after the flesh-pots that, when she had them, she had found tiresome, and then which she had frequently remarked she would rather have the simplest home-made bread and butter. Apples, too. Mrs. Cairnes's three apple-trees had been turned to great account in her larder always; but now—Mrs. Maybury never touched apple-sauce, disliked apple-jelly, thought apple-pie unfit for human digestion, apple-pudding worse; would have nothing with apples in it, except the very little in mincepie which she liked as rich as brandy and sherry and costly spices could make it.

"No profit in this sort of boarder," thought the thrifty Mrs. Cairnes. But then she didn't have Sophia for profit, only for friendliness and companionship; and of course there must be some little drawbacks. Sophia was not at all slow in expressing her likes and dislikes. Well, Mrs. Cairnes meant she should have no more dislikes to express than need be. Nevertheless, it made Mrs. Cairnes quite nervous with apprehension concerning Mrs. Maybury's face on coming to the dinner-table; she left off having roasts, and had a slice of steak; chops and tomato-sauce; a young chicken. But even that chicken had to make its reappearance till it might have been an old hen. "I declare," said Mrs. Cairnes, in the privacy of her own emotions, "when I lived by myself I had only one person to please! If Sophia had ever been any sort of a housekeeper herself—it's easy to see why Dr. Maybury chose to live at a hotel!" Still the gentle face opposite her at the table, the lively warmth of a greeting when she opened the door, the delight of someone with whom to talk things over, the source of life and movement in the house; all this far outweighed the necessity of having to plan for variety in the little dinners.

"I really shall starve to death if this thing does on," Mrs. Maybury had meanwhile said to herself. "It isn't that I care so much for what I have to eat; but I really can't eat enough here to keep me alive. If I went out as Julia does, walking and talking all over town, I daresay I could get up the same sort of appetite for sole-leather. But I haven't the heart for it. I can't do it. I have to sit at home and haven't any relish for anything. I really will see if Allida can't start something different." But Allida could not make bricks without straw; she could only prepare what Mrs. Cairnes provided, and as Mrs. Cairnes had never had a servant before, she looked on the whole tribe of them as marauders and natural enemies, and doled out everything from a locked store-room at so much a head.

"Well," sighed Mrs. Maybury, "perhaps I shall get used to it." From which it will be seen that Julia's efforts after all were not particularly successful. But if Mrs. Cairnes had been lonely before Mrs. Maybury came, Mrs. Maybury was intolerably lonely, having come; the greater part of the time, Allida being in the kitchen, or out herself, and no one in the house but the sunshine, the cat, and the bird; and she detested cats, and had a shudder if one touched her. However, this was Julia's cat, this great black and white evil spirit, looking like an imp of darkness; she would be kind to it if it didn't touch her. But if it touched her—she shivered at the thought—she couldn't answer for the consequences. Julia was so good in taking her into her house, and listening to her woes, and trying to make her comfortable,—only if this monster tried to kill her bird—Mrs. Maybury, sitting by herself, wept at the thought.

How early it was dark now, too! She didn't see what kept Julia so,—really she was doing too much at her age. She hinted that gently to Julia when Mrs. Cairnes did return. And Mrs. Cairnes could not quite have told what it was that was so unpleasant in the remark. "My age," she said, laughing. "Why, I am as young as ever I was, and as full of life. I could start on an exploring expedition to Africa, tomorrow!" But she began to experience a novel sense of bondage,—she who had all her life been responsible to no one. And presently, whenever she went out, she had a dim consciousness in her mental background of Sophia's eyes following her, of Sophia's thoughts upon her trail, of Sophia's face peering from the bay-window as she went from one door to another. She begged some slips, and put a half dozen new flower-pots on a bracket-shelf in the window, in order to obscure the casual view, and left the inner curtain drawn.

She came in one day, and there was that inner curtain strung wide open, and the sun pouring through the plants in a broad radiance. Before she took off her bonnet she stepped to the window and drew the curtain.

"Oh!" cried Mrs. Maybury, "what made you do that? The sunshine is so pleasant."

"I can't have the sun streaming in here and taking all the color out of my carpet, Sophia!" said Julia, with some asperity.

"But the sun is so very healthy," urged Mrs. Maybury.

"Oh, well! I can't be getting a new carpet every day."

"You feel," said Mrs. Maybury, turning away wrath, "as you did when you were a little girl, and the teacher told you to lay your wet slate in your lap: 'It'll take the fade out of my gown,' said you. How long ago is it! Does it seem as if it were you and I?"

"I don't know," said Julia tartly. "I don't bother myself much with abstractions. I know it is you and I." And she put her things on the hall-rack, as she was going out again in the afternoon to bible-class.

She had no sooner gone out than Mrs. Maybury went and strung up every curtain in the house where the sun was shining, and sat down triumphantly and rocked contentedly for five minutes in the glow, when her conscience overcame her, and she put them all down again, and went out into the kitchen for a little comfort from Allida. But Allida had gone out, too; so she came back to the sitting-room, and longed for the stir and bustle and frequent faces of the tavern, and welcomed a book-canvasser presently as if she had been a dear friend.

Perhaps Julia's conscience stirred a little, too; for she came home earlier than usual, put away her wraps, lighted an extra lamp, and said, "Now we'll have a long, cosy evening to ourselves."

"We might have a little game of cards," said Sophia, timidly. "I know a capital double solitaire—"

"Cards!" cried Julia.

"Why—why not?"

"Cards! And I just came from bible-class!"

"What in the world has that got to do with it?"

"Everything!"

"Why, the Doctor and I used—"

"That doesn't make it any better."

"Why, Julia, you can't possibly mean that there's any! harm—that—that it's wicked—"

"I think we'd better drop the subject, Sophia," said Julia loftily.

"But I don't want to drop the subject!" exclaimed Mrs. Maybury. "I don't want you to think that the Doctor would—"

"I can't help what the Doctor did. I think cards are wicked! And that's enough for me!"

"Well!" cried Mrs. Maybury, then in great dudgeon. "I'm not a member of the old East Church in good and regular standing for forty years to be told what's right and what's wrong by anyone now!"

"If you're in good and regular standing, then the church is very lax in its discipline, Sophia; that's all I've got to say."

"But, Julia, things have been very much liberalized of late years. The minister's own daughter has been to dancing-school." The toss of Julia's head, and her snort of contempt only said, "So much the worse for the minister's daughter!"

"Nobody believes in infant damnation now," continued Mrs. Maybury.

"I do."

"O Julia!" cried Mrs. Maybury, for the moment quite faint, "that is because," she said, as soon as she had rallied, and breaking the dreadful silence, "you never had any little babies of your own, Julia." This was adding insult to injury, and still there was silence. "I don't believe it of you, Julia," she continued, "your kind heart—"

"I don't know what a kind heart has to do with the immutable decrees of an offended deity!" cried the exasperated Julia. "And this only goes to show what forty years' association with a free-thinking—"

"You were right in the beginning, Julia; we had better drop the subject," said Mrs. Maybury; and she gathered up her Afghan wools gently, and went to her room.

Mrs. Maybury came down, however, when tea was ready, and all was serene again, especially as Susan Peyster came in to tell the news about Dean Hampton's defalcation at the village bank, and had a seat at the table. "But I don't understand what on earth he has done with the money," said Mrs. Maybury.

"Gambled," said Susan.

"Cards," said Mrs. Cairnes. "You see?'

"Not that sort of gambling!" cried Susan. "But stocks and that."

"It's the same thing," said Mrs. Cairnes.

"And that's the least part of it! They do say," said Susan, balancing her teaspoon as if in doubt about speaking.

"They say what?" cried Mrs. Cairnes.

But for our part, as we don't know Mr. Dean Hampton, and, therefore, can not relish his misdoings with the same zest as if we did, we will not waste time on what was said. Only when Susan had gone, Mrs. Maybury rose, too, and said, "I must say, Julia, that I think this dreadful conversation is infinitely worse and more wicked than any game of cards could be!"

"What are you talking about?" said Julia, jocosely, and quite good-humored again.

"And the amount of shocking gossip of this description that I've heard since I've been in your house is already more than I've heard in the whole course of my life! Dr. Maybury would never allow a word of gossip in our rooms." And she went to bed.

"You shall never have another word in mine!" said the thunder-stricken Julia to herself. And if she had heard that the North Pole had tipped all its ice off into space, she wouldn't have told her a syllable about it all that week.

But in the course of a fortnight, a particularly choice bit of news having turned up, and the edge of her resentment having worn away, Mrs. Cairnes could not keep it to herself. And poor Mrs. Maybury, famishing now for some object of interest, received it so kindly that things returned to their former footing. Perhaps not quite to their former footing, for Julia had now a feeling of restraint about her news, and didn't tell the most piquant, and winked to her visitors if the details trenched too much on what had better be unspoken. "Not that it was really so very—so very—but then Mrs. Maybury, you know," she said afterward. But she had never been accustomed to this restraint, and she didn't like it.

In fact Mrs. Cairnes found herself under restraints that were amounting to a mild bondage. She must be at home for meals, of course; she had been in the habit of being at home or not as she chose, and often of taking the bite and sup at other houses, which precluded the necessity of preparing anything at home. She must have the meals to suit another and very different palate, which was irksome and troublesome. She must exercise a carefulness concerning her conversation, and that of her gossips, too, which destroyed both zest and freedom. She strongly suspected that in her absence the curtains were up and the sun was allowed to play havoc with her carpets. She was remonstrated with on her goings and comings, she who had had the largest liberty for two score years. And then, when the minister came to see her, she never had the least good of the call, so much of it was absorbed by Mrs. Maybury. And Mrs. Maybury's health was delicate, she fussed and complained and whined; she cared for the things that Mrs. Cairnes didn't care for, and didn't care for the things that Mrs. Cairnes did care for; Mrs. Cairnes was conscious of her unspoken surprise at much that she said and did, and resented the somewhat superior gentleness and refinement of her old friend as much as the old friend resented her superior strength and liveliness.

"What has changed Sophia so? It isn't Sophia at all! And I thought so much of her, and I looked forward to spending my old age with her so happily!" murmured Julia. "But perhaps it will come right," she reasoned cheerily. "I may get used to it. I didn't suppose there'd be any rubbing of corners. But as there is, the sooner they're rubbed off the better, and we shall settle down into comfort again, at last instead of at first, as I had hoped in the beginning."

Alas! "I really can't stand these plants of yours, Julia, dear," said Mrs. Maybury, soon afterward. "I've tried to. I've said nothing. I've waited, to be very sure. But I never have been able to have plants about me. They act like poison to me. They always make me sneeze so. And you see I'm all stuffed up—"

Her plants! Almost as dear to her as children might have been! The chief ornament of her parlors! And just ready to bloom! This was really asking too much. "I don't believe it's the plants at all," said Julia. "That's sheer nonsense. Anybody living on this green and vegetating earth to be poisoned by plants in a window! I don't suppose they trouble you any more than your lamp all night does me; but I've never said anything about that. I can't bear lamplight at night; I want it perfectly dark, and the light streams out of your room—"

"Why don't you shut the door, then?"

"Because I never shut my door. I want to hear if anything disturbs the house. Why don't you shut yours?"

"I never do, either. I've always had several rooms, and kept the doors open between. It isn't healthy to sleep with closed doors."

"Healthy! Healthy! I don't hear anything else from morning till night when I'm in the house."

"You can't hear very much of it, then."

"I should think, Sophia Maybury, you wanted to live forever!"

"Goodness knows I don't!" cried Mrs. Maybury, bursting into tears. And that night she shut her bedroom door and opened the window, and sneezed worse than ever all day afterward, in spite of the fact that Mrs. Cairnes had put all her cherished plants into the dining-room alcove.

"I can't imagine what has changed Julia so," sighed Mrs. Maybury. "She used to be so bright and sweet and good-tempered. And now I really don't know what sort of an answer I'm to have to anything I say. It keeps my nerves stretched on the *qui vive* all day. I am so disappointed. I am sure the Doctor would be very unhappy if he knew how I felt."

But Mrs. Maybury had need to pity herself; Julia didn't pity her. "She's been made a baby of so long," said Julia, "that now she really can't go alone." And perhaps she was a little bitterer about it than she would have been had Captain Cairnes ever made a baby of her in the least, at any time.

They were sitting together one afternoon, a thunderstorm of unusual severity having detained Mrs. Cairnes at home, and the conversation had been more or less acrimonious, as often of late. Just before dusk there came a great burst of sun, and the whole heavens were suffused with splendor.

"O Julia! Come here, come quick, and see this sunset!" cried Mrs. Maybury. But Julia did not come. "Oh! I can't bear to have you lose it," urged the philanthropic lover of nature again. "There! It's streaming up the very zenith. I never saw such color—do come."

"Mercy, Sophia! You're always wanting people to leave what they're about and see something! My lap's full of worsteds."

"Well," said Sophia. "It's for your own sake. I don't know that it will do me any good. Only if one enjoys beautiful sights."

"Dear me! Well, there! Is that all? I don't see anything remarkable. The idea of making one get up to see that!" And as she took her seat, up jumped the great black and white cat to look out in his turn. Mrs. Maybury would have been more than human if she had not said "Scat! scat! scat!" and she did say it, shaking herself in horror.

It was the last straw. Mrs. Cairnes took her cat in her arms and moved majestically out of the room, put on her rubbers, and went out to tea, and did not come home till the light upstairs told her that Mrs. Maybury had gone to her room.

Where was it all going to end? Mrs. Cairnes could not send Sophia away after all the protestations she had made. Mrs. Maybury could never put such a slight on Julia as to go away without more overt cause for displeasure. It seemed as though they would have to fight it out in the union.

But that night a glare lit the sky which quite outdid the sunset; the fire-bells and clattering engines called attention to it much more loudly than Sophia had announced the larger conflagration. And in the morning it was found that the Webster House was in ashes. All of Mrs. Maybury's property was in the building. The insurance had run out the week before, and meaning to attend to it every day she had let it go, and here she was penniless.

But no one need commiserate with her. Instead of any terror at her situation a wild joy sprang up within her. Relief and freedom clapped their wings above her.

It was Mrs. Cairnes who felt that she herself needed pity. A lamp at nights, oceans of fresh air careering round the house, the everlast-ing canary-bird's singing to bear, her plants exiled, her table revo-lutionized, her movements watched, her conversation restrained, her cat abused, the board of two people and the wages of one to come out of her narrow hoard. But she rose to the emergency. Sophia was penniless. Sophia was homeless. The things which it was the ashes of bitterness to allow her as a right, she could well give her as a benefactress. Sophia was welcome to all she had. She went into the room, meaning to overwhelm the weeping, helpless Sophia with her benevolence. Sophia was not there.

Mrs. Maybury came in some hours later, a carriage and a job-wagon presently following her to the door. "You are very good, Julia," said she, when Julia received her with the rapid sentences of welcome and assurance that she had been accumulating. "And you mustn't think I'm not sensible of all your kindness. I am. But my husband gave the institution advice for nothing for forty years, and I think I have rights there now without feeling under obliga-tions to any. I've visited the directors, and I've had a meeting called and attended,—I've had all your energy, Julia, and have hurried things along in quite your own fashion. And as I had just one hundred dollars in my purse after I sold my watch this morn-ing, I've paid it over for the entrance-fee, and I've been admitted and am going to spend the rest of my days in the Old Ladies' Home. I've the upper corner front room, and I hope you will come and see me there."

"Sophia!"

"Don't speak! Don't say one word! My mind was made up irrevocably when I went out. Nothing you, nothing any one, can say, will change it. I'm one of the old ladies now."

Mrs. Cairnes brought all her plants back into the parlor, pulled down the shades, drew the inside curtain, had the cat's cushion again in its familiar corner, and gave Allida warning, within half an hour. She looked about a little while and luxuriated in her freedom,—no one to supervise her conversation, her movements, her opinions, her food. Never mind the empty rooms, or the echoes there! She read an angry psalm or two, looked over some texts denouncing pharisees and hypocrites, thought indignantly of the ingratitude there was in the world, felt that any way, and on the whole, she was where she was before Sophia came, and went out to spend the evening, and came in at the nine-o'clock bell-ringing with such a sense of freedom, that she sat up till midnight to enjoy it.

And Sophia spent the day putting her multitudinous belongings into place, hanging up her bird-cage, arranging her books and her bureau-drawers, setting up a stocking, and making the acquaintance of the old ladies next her. She taught one of them to play double solitaire that very evening. And then she talked a little while concerning Dr. Maybury, about whom Julia had never seemed willing to hear a word; and then she read, "Come unto me, all ye that labor and are heavy laden, and I will give you rest," and went to bed perfectly happy.

Julia came to see her the next day, and Sophia received her with open arms. Everyone knew that Julia had begged her to stay and live with her always, and share what she had. Julia goes now to see her every day of her life, rain or snow, storm or shine; and the whole village says that the friendship between those two old women is something ideal.

SOURCE: *The Ten Books of the Merrymakers*. Edited by Marshall Pinckney Wilder. Volume 9. New York: The Circle Publishing Company, 1909.

THE RANSOM OF RED CHIEF (1910)

O. Henry (William Sydney Porter)

William Sydney Porter (1862–1910) served three years in prison for embezzlement from the bank where he worked in Texas. In 1901 he began a new career for himself in New York City as a short story writer, taking the pseudonym O. Henry. Within the decade, he became America's favorite author of clever tales.

IT LOOKED LIKE a good thing: but wait till I tell you. We were down South, in Alabama—Bill Driscoll and myself—when this kidnapping idea struck us. It was, as Bill afterward expressed it, "during a moment of temporary mental apparition"; but we didn't find that out till later.

There was a town down there, as flat as a flannel-cake, and called Summit, of course. It contained inhabitants of as undeleterious and self-satisfied a class of peasantry as ever clustered around a Maypole.

Bill and me had a joint capital of about six hundred dollars, and we needed just two thousand dollars more to pull off a fraudulent town-lot scheme in Western Illinois with. We talked it over on the front steps of the hotel. Philoprogenitiveness, says we, is strong in semi-rural communities therefore, and for other reasons, a kidnapping project ought to do better there than in the radius of newspapers that send reporters out in plain clothes to stir up talk about such things. We knew that Summit couldn't get after us with anything stronger than constables and, maybe, some lackadaisical bloodhounds and a diatribe or two in the *Weekly Farmers' Budget*. So, it looked good.

We selected for our victim the only child of a prominent citizen named Ebenezer Dorset. The father was respectable and tight, a

164

mortgage fancier and a stern, upright collection-plate passer and
forecloser. The kid was a boy of ten, with bas-relief freckles, and
hair the color of the cover of the magazine you buy at the news-
stand when you want to catch a train. Bill and me figured that
Ebenezer would melt down for a ransom of two thousand dollars
to a cent. But wait till I tell you.

About two miles from Summit was a little mountain, covered
with a dense cedar brake. On the rear elevation of this mountain
was a cave. There we stored provisions.

One evening after sundown, we drove in a buggy past old
Dorset's house. The kid was in the street, throwing rocks at a kitten
on the opposite fence.

"Hey, little boy!" says Bill, "would you like to have a bag of
candy and a nice ride?"

The boy catches Bill neatly in the eye with a piece of brick.

"That will cost the old man an extra five hundred dollars," says
Bill, climbing over the wheel.

That boy put up a fight like a welter-weight cinnamon bear; but,
at last, we got him down in the bottom of the buggy and drove
away. We took him up to the cave, and I hitched the horse in the
cedar brake. After dark I drove the buggy to the little village, three
miles away, where we had hired it, and walked back to the
mountain.

Bill was pasting court-plaster over the scratches and bruises on his
features. There was a fire burning behind the big rock at the
entrance of the cave, and the boy was watching a pot of boiling
coffee, with two buzzard tail-feathers stuck in his red hair. He
points a stick at me when I come up, and says:

"Ha! cursed paleface, do you dare to enter the camp of Red
Chief, the terror of the plains?"

"He's all right now," says Bill, rolling up his trousers and examin-
ing some bruises on his shins. "We're playing Indian. We're making
Buffalo Bill's show look like magic-lantern views of Palestine in the
town hall. I'm Old Hank, the Trapper, Red Chief's captive, and I'm
to be scalped at daybreak. By Geronimo! that kid can kick hard."

Yes, sir, that boy seemed to be having the time of his life. The
fun of camping out in a cave had made him forget that he was a
captive himself. He immediately christened me Snake-eye, the Spy,
and announced that, when his braves returned from the warpath, I
was to be broiled at the stake at the rising of the sun.

Then we had supper; and he filled his mouth full of bacon and bread and gravy, and began to talk. He made a during-dinner speech something like this:

"I like this fine. I never camped out before; but I had a pet 'possum once, and I was nine last birthday. I hate to go to school. Rats ate up sixteen of Jimmy Talbot's aunt's speckled hen's eggs. Are there any real Indians in these woods? I want some more gravy. Does the trees moving make the wind blow? We had five puppies. What makes your nose so red, Hank? My father has lots of money. Are the stars hot? I whipped Ed Walker twice, Saturday. I don't like girls. You dassent catch toads unless with a string. Do oxen make any noise? Why are oranges round? Have you got beds to sleep on in this cave? Amos Murray has got six toes. A parrot can talk, but a monkey or a fish can't. How many does it take to make twelve?"

Every few minutes he would remember that he was a pesky redskin, and pick up his stick rifle and tiptoe to the mouth of the cave to rubber for the scouts of the hated paleface. Now and then he would let out a war-whoop that made Old Hank the Trapper shiver. That boy had Bill terrorized from the start.

"Red Chief," says I to the kid, "would you like to go home?"

"Aw, what for?" says he. "I don't have any fun at home. I hate to go to school. I like to camp out. You won't take me back home again, Snake-eye, will you?"

"Not right away," says I. "We'll stay here in the cave a while."

"All right!" says he. "That'll be fine. I never had such fun in all my life."

We went to bed about eleven o'clock. We spread down some wide blankets and quilts and put Red Chief between us. We weren't afraid he'd run away. He kept us awake for three hours, jumping up and reaching for his rifle and screeching: "Hist! pard," in mine and Bill's ears, as the fancied crackle of a twig or the rustle of a leaf revealed to his young imagination the stealthy approach of the outlaw band. At last, I fell into a troubled sleep, and dreamed that I had been kidnapped and chained to a tree by a ferocious pirate with red hair.

Just at daybreak, I was awakened by a series of awful screams from Bill. They weren't yells, or howls, or shouts, or whoops, or yawps, such as you'd expect from a manly set of vocal organs—they were simply indecent, terrifying, humiliating screams, such as women emit when they see ghosts or caterpillars. It's an awful thing to hear a strong, desperate, fat man scream incontinently in a cave at daybreak.

I jumped up to see what the matter was. Red Chief was sitting on Bill's chest, with one hand twined in Bill's hair. In the other he had the sharp case-knife we used for slicing bacon; and he was industriously and realistically trying to take Bill's scalp, according to the sentence that had been pronounced upon him the evening before.

I got the knife away from the kid and made him lie down again. But, from that moment, Bill's spirit was broken. He laid down on his side of the bed, but he never closed an eye again in sleep as long as that boy was with us. I dozed off for a while, but along toward sun-up I remembered that Red Chief had said I was to be burned at the stake at the rising of the sun. I wasn't nervous or afraid; but I sat up and lit my pipe and leaned against a rock.

"What you getting up so soon for, Sam?" asked Bill.

"Me?" says I. "Oh, I got a kind of a pain in my shoulder. I thought sitting up would rest it."

"You're a liar!" says Bill. "You're afraid. You was to be burned at sunrise, and you was afraid he'd do it. And he would, too, if he could find a match. Ain't it awful, Sam? Do you think anybody will pay out money to get a little imp like that back home?"

"Sure," said I. "A rowdy kid like that is just the kind that parents dote on. Now, you and the Chief get up and cook breakfast, while I go up on the top of this mountain and reconnoiter."

I went up on the peak of the little mountain and ran my eye over the contiguous vicinity. Over toward Summit I expected to see the sturdy yeomanry of the village armed with scythes and pitchforks beating the countryside for the dastardly kidnappers. But what I saw was a peaceful landscape dotted with one man plowing with a dun mule. Nobody was dragging the creek; no couriers dashed hither and yon, bringing tidings of no news to the distracted parents. There was a sylvan attitude of somnolent sleepiness pervading that section of the external outward surface of Alabama that lay exposed to my view. "Perhaps," says I to myself, "it has not yet been discovered that the wolves have borne away the tender lambkin from the fold. Heaven help the wolves!" says I, and I went down the mountain to breakfast.

When I got to the cave I found Bill backed up against the side of it, breathing hard, and the boy threatening to smash him with a rock half as big as a cocoanut.

"He put a red-hot boiled potato down my back," explained Bill, "and then mashed it with his foot; and I boxed his ears. Have you got a gun about you, Sam?"

I took the rock away from the boy and kind of patched up the argument. "I'll fix you," says the kid to Bill. "No man ever yet struck the Red Chief but what he got paid for it. You better beware!"

After breakfast the kid takes a piece of leather with strings wrapped around it out of his pocket and goes outside the cave unwinding it.

"What's he up to now?" says Bill, anxiously. "You don't think he'll run away, do you, Sam?"

"No fear of it," says I. "He don't seem to be much of a home body. But we've got to fix up some plan about the ransom. There don't seem to be much excitement around Summit on account of his disappearance; but maybe they haven't realized yet that he's gone. His folks may think he's spending the night with Aunt Jane or one of the neighbors. Anyhow, he'll be missed today. Tonight we must get a message to his father demanding the two thousand dollars for his return."

Just then we heard a kind of war-whoop, such as David might have emitted when he knocked out the champion Goliath. It was a sling that Red Chief had pulled out of his pocket, and he was whirling it around his head.

I dodged, and heard a heavy thud and a kind of a sigh from Bill, like a horse gives out when you take his saddle off. A niggerhead rock the size of an egg had caught Bill just behind his left ear. He loosened himself all over and fell in the fire across the frying pan of hot water for washing the dishes. I dragged him out and poured cold water on his head for half an hour.

By and by, Bill sits up and feels behind his ear and says: "Sam, do you know who my favorite Biblical character is?"

"Take it easy," says I. "You'll come to your senses presently."

"King Herod," says he. "You won't go away and leave me here alone, will you, Sam?"

I went out and caught that boy and shook him until his freckles rattled.

"If you don't behave," says I, "I'll take you straight home. Now, are you going to be good, or not?"

"I was only funning," says he sullenly. "I didn't mean to hurt Old Hank. But what did he hit me for? I'll behave, Snake-eye, if you won't send me home, and if you'll let me play the Black Scout today."

"I don't know the game," says I. "That's for you and Mr. Bill to decide. He's your playmate for the day. I'm going away for a while, on business. Now, you come in and make friends with him and say you are sorry for hurting him, or home you go, at once."

I made him and Bill shake hands, and then I took Bill aside and told him I was going to Poplar Cove, a little village three miles from the cave, and find out what I could about how the kidnapping had been regarded in Summit. Also, I thought it best to send a peremptory letter to old man Dorset that day, demanding the ransom and dictating how it should be paid.

"You know, Sam," says Bill, "I've stood by you without batting an eye in earthquakes, fire and flood—in poker games, dynamite outrages, police raids, train robberies and cyclones. I never lost my nerve yet till we kidnapped that two-legged skyrocket of a kid. He's got me going. You won't leave me long with him, will you, Sam?"

"I'll be back some time this afternoon," says I. "You must keep the boy amused and quiet till I return. And now we'll write the letter to old Dorset."

Bill and I got paper and pencil and worked on the letter while Red Chief, with a blanket wrapped around him, strutted up and down, guarding the mouth of the cave. Bill begged me tearfully to make the ransom fifteen hundred dollars instead of two thousand. "I ain't attempting," says he, "to decry the celebrated moral aspect of parental affection, but we're dealing with humans, and it ain't human for anybody to give up two thousand dollars for that forty-pound chunk of freckled wildcat. I'm willing to take a chance at fifteen hundred dollars. You can charge the difference up to me."

So, to relieve Bill, I acceded, and we collaborated a letter that ran this way:

Ebenezer Dorset, Esq.:
    We have your boy concealed in a place far from Summit. It is useless for you or the most skilful detectives to attempt to find him. Absolutely, the only terms on which you can have him restored to you are these: We demand fifteen hundred dollars in large bills for his return; the money to be left at midnight to-night at the same spot and in the same box as your reply—as hereinafter described. If you agree to these terms, send your answer in writing by a solitary messenger to-night at half-past eight o'clock. After crossing Owl Creek,

on the road to Poplar Cove, there are three large trees about a hundred yards apart, close to the fence of the wheat field on the right-hand side. At the bottom of the fence-post, opposite the third tree, will be found a small pasteboard box.

The messenger will place the answer in this box and return immediately to Summit.

If you attempt any treachery or fail to comply with our demand as stated, you will never see your boy again.

If you pay the money as demanded, he will be returned to you safe and well within three hours. These terms are final, and if you do not accede to them no further communication will be attempted.

Two Desperate Men

I addressed this letter to Dorset, and put it in my pocket. As I was about to start, the kid comes up to me and says: "Aw, Snake-eye, you said I could play the Black Scout while you was gone."

"Play it, of course," says I. "Mr. Bill will play with you. What kind of a game is it?"

"I'm the Black Scout," says Red Chief, "and I have to ride to the stockade to warn the settlers that the Indians are coming. I'm tired of playing Indian myself. I want to be the Black Scout."

"All right," says I. "It sounds harmless to me. I guess Mr. Bill will help you foil the pesky savages."

"What am I to do?" asks Bill, looking at the kid suspiciously.

"You are the hoss," says Black Scout. "Get down on your hands and knees. How can I ride to the stockade without a hoss?"

"You'd better keep him interested," said I, "till we get the scheme going. Loosen up."

Bill gets down on his all fours, and a look comes in his eye like a rabbit's when you catch it in a trap.

"How far is it to the stockade, kid?" he asks, in a husky manner of voice.

"Ninety miles," says the Black Scout. "And you have to hump yourself to get there on time. Whoa, now!"

The Black Scout jumps on Bill's back and digs his heels in his side.

"For Heaven's sake," says Bill, "hurry back, Sam, as soon as you can. I wish we hadn't made the ransom more than a thousand. Say, you quit kicking me or I'll get up and warm you good."

I walked over to Poplar Cove and sat around the post office and store, talking with the chawbacons that came in to trade. One whiskerando says that he hears Summit is all upset on account of

Elder Ebenezer Dorset's boy having been lost or stolen. That was all I wanted to know. I bought some smoking tobacco, referred casually to the price of black-eyed peas, posted my letter surreptitiously and came away. The postmaster said the mail-carrier would come by in an hour to take the mail on to Summit.

When I got back to the cave Bill and the boy were not to be found. I explored the vicinity of the cave, and risked a yodel or two, but there was no response.

So I lighted my pipe and sat down on a mossy bank to await developments.

In about half an hour I heard the bushes rustle, and Bill wabbled out into the little glade in front of the cave. Behind him was the kid, stepping softly like a scout, with a broad grin on his face. Bill stopped, took off his hat and wiped his face with a red handkerchief. The kid stopped about eight feet behind him.

"Sam," says Bill, "I suppose you'll think I'm a renegade, but I couldn't help it. I'm a grown person with masculine proclivities and habits of self-defense, but there is a time when all systems of egotism and predominance fail. The boy is gone. I have sent him home. All is off. There was martyrs in old times," goes on Bill, "that suffered death rather than give up the particular graft they enjoyed. None of 'em ever was subjugated to such supernatural tortures as I have been. I tried to be faithful to our articles of depredation; but there came a limit."

"What's the trouble, Bill?" I asks him.

"I was rode," says Bill, "the ninety miles to the stockade, not barring an inch. Then, when the settlers was rescued, I was given oats. Sand ain't a palatable substitute. And then, for an hour I had to try to explain to him why there was nothin' in holes, how a road can run both ways and what makes the grass green. I tell you, Sam, a human can only stand so much. I takes him by the neck of his clothes and drags him down the mountain. On the way he kicks my legs black-and-blue from the knees down; and I've got two or three bites on my thumb and hand cauterized.

"But he's gone"—continues Bill—"gone home. I showed him the road to Summit and kicked him about eight feet nearer there at one kick. I'm sorry we lose the ransom; but it was either that or Bill Driscoll to the madhouse."

Bill is puffing and blowing, but there is a look of ineffable peace and growing content on his rose-pink features.

"Bill," says I, "there isn't any heart disease in your family, is there?"

"No," says Bill, "nothing chronic except malaria and accidents. Why?"

"Then you might turn around," says I, "and have a look behind you."

Bill turns and sees the boy, and loses his complexion and sits down plump on the ground and begins to pluck aimlessly at grass and little sticks. For an hour I was afraid for his mind. And then I told him that my scheme was to put the whole job through immediately and that we would get the ransom and be off with it by midnight if old Dorset fell in with our proposition. So Bill braced up enough to give the kid a weak sort of a smile and a promise to play the Russian in a Japanese war with him as soon as he felt a little better.

I had a scheme for collecting that ransom without danger of being caught by counterplots that ought to commend itself to professional kidnappers. The tree under which the answer was to be left—and the money later on—was close to the road fence with big, bare fields on all sides. If a gang of constables should be watching for any one to come for the note they could see him a long way off crossing the fields or in the road. But no, sirree! At half-past eight I was up in that tree as well hidden as a tree toad, waiting for the messenger to arrive.

Exactly on time, a half-grown boy rides up the road on a bicycle, locates the pasteboard box at the foot of the fencepost, slips a folded piece of paper into it and pedals away again back toward Summit.

I waited an hour and then concluded the thing was square. I slid down the tree, got the note, slipped along the fence till I struck the woods, and was back at the cave in another half an hour. I opened the note, got near the lantern and read it to Bill. It was written with a pen in a crabbed hand, and the sum and substance of it was this:

Two Desperate Men:

 Gentlemen: I received your letter today by post, in regard to the ransom you ask for the return of my son. I think you are a little high in your demands, and I hereby make you a counter-proposition, which I am inclined to believe you will accept. You bring Johnny home and pay me two hundred and fifty dollars in cash, and I agree to take him off your hands. You had better come at night, for the neighbors believe he is lost, and I couldn't be responsible for what they would do to anybody they saw bringing him back.

Very respectfully,
Ebenezer Dorset

"Great pirates of Penzance!" says I; "of all the impudent—"

But I glanced at Bill, and hesitated. He had the most appealing look in his eyes I ever saw on the face of a dumb or a talking brute.

"Sam," says he, "what's two hundred and fifty dollars, after all? We've got the money. One more night of this kid will send me to a bed in Bedlam. Besides being a thorough gentleman, I think Mr. Dorset is a spendthrift for making us such a liberal offer. You ain't going to let the chance go, are you?"

"Tell you the truth, Bill," says I, "this little he ewe lamb has somewhat got on my nerves too. We'll take him home, pay the ransom and make our get-away."

We took him home that night. We got him to go by telling him that his father had bought a silver-mounted rifle and a pair of moccasins for him, and we were going to hunt bears the next day.

It was just twelve o'clock when we knocked at Ebenezer's front door. Just at the moment when I should have been abstracting the fifteen hundred dollars from the box under the tree, according to the original proposition, Bill was counting out two hundred and fifty dollars into Dorset's hand.

When the kid found out we were going to leave him at home he started up a howl like a calliope and fastened himself as tight as a leech to Bill's leg. His father peeled him away gradually, like a porous plaster.

"How long can you hold him?" asks Bill.

"I'm not as strong as I used to be," says old Dorset, "but I think I can promise you ten minutes."

"Enough," says Bill. "In ten minutes I shall cross the Central, Southern and Middle Western States, and be legging it trippingly for the Canadian border."

And, as dark as it was, and as fat as Bill was, and as good a runner as I am, he was a good mile and a half out of summit before I could catch up with him.

SOURCE: O. Henry. *Whirligigs*. New York: Doubleday, Page and Company, 1910.

THE GOLDEN HONEYMOON (1922)

Ring Lardner

Ringgold Wilmer Lardner (1885–1933) was a renowned sportswriter and a great and popular writer of short fiction. His most famous book is You Know Me, Al, *a collection of fictional letters by a fictional baseball player, Jack Keefe. The hero-narrator of this story is a retired gentleman from New Jersey.*

MOTHER SAYS THAT when I start talking I never know when to stop. But I tell her the only time I get a chance is when she ain't around, so I have to make the most of it. I guess the fact is neither one of us would be welcome in a Quaker meeting, but as I tell Mother, what did God give us tongues for if He didn't want we should use them? Only she says He didn't give them to us to say the same thing over and over again, like I do, and repeat myself. But I say:

"Well, Mother," I say, "when people is like you and I and been married fifty years, do you expect everything I say will be something you ain't heard me say before? But it may be new to others, as they ain't nobody else lived with me as long as you have."

So she says:

"You can bet they ain't, as they couldn't nobody else stand you that long."

"Well," I tell her, "you look pretty healthy."

"Maybe I do," she will say, "but I looked even healthier before I married you."

You can't get ahead of Mother.

Yes, sir, we was married just fifty years ago the seventeenth day of last December and my daughter and son-in-law was over from

174

Trenton to help us celebrate the Golden Wedding. My son-in-law is John H. Kramer, the real estate man. He made $12,000 one year and is pretty well thought of around Trenton; a good, steady, hard worker. The Rotarians was after him a long time to join, but he kept telling them his home was his club. But Edie finally made him join. That's my daughter.

Well, anyway, they come over to help us celebrate the Golden Wedding and it was pretty crimpy weather and the furnace don't seem to heat up no more like it used to and Mother made the remark that she hoped this winter wouldn't be as cold as the last, referring to the winter previous. So Edie said if she was us, and nothing to keep us home, she certainly wouldn't spend no more winters up here and why didn't we just shut off the water and close up the house and go down to Tampa, Florida? You know we was there four winters ago and staid five weeks, but it cost us over three hundred and fifty dollars for hotel bill alone. So Mother said we wasn't going no place to be robbed. So my son-in-law spoke up and said that Tampa wasn't the only place in the South, and besides we didn't have to stop at no high price hotel but could rent us a couple rooms and board out somewheres, and he had heard that St. Petersburg, Florida, was the spot and if we said the word he would write down there and make inquiries.

Well, to make a long story short, we decided to do it and Edie said it would be our Golden Honeymoon and for a present my son-in-law paid the difference between a section and a compartment so as we could have a compartment and have more privatecy. In a compartment you have an upper and lower berth just like the regular sleeper, but it is a shut in room by itself and got a wash bowl. The car we went in was all compartments and no regular berths at all. It was all compartments.

We went to Trenton the night before and staid at my daughter and son-in-law and we left Trenton the next afternoon at 3:23 p.m.

This was the twelfth day of January. Mother set facing the front of the train, as it makes her giddy to ride backwards. I set facing her, which does not affect me. We reached North Philadelphia at 4:03 p.m. and we reached West Philadelphia at 4:14, but did not go into Broad Street. We reached Baltimore at 6:30 and Washington, D.C., at 7:25. Our train laid over in Washington two hours till another train come along to pick us up and I got out and strolled up the platform and into the Union Station. When I come back, our car had been switched on to another track, but I remembered the name of it, the La Belle, as I had once visited my aunt out in Oconomowoc, Wisconsin, where there was a lake of that name, so I had no difficulty in getting located. But Mother had nearly fretted herself sick for fear I would be left.

"Well," I said, "I would of followed you on the next train."

"You could of," said Mother, and she pointed out that she had the money.

"Well," I said, "we are in Washington and I could of borrowed from the United States Treasury. I would of pretended I was an Englishman."

Mother caught the point and laughed heartily.

Our train pulled out of Washington at 9:40 p.m. and Mother and I turned in early, I taking the upper. During the night we passed through the green fields of old Virginia, though it was too dark to tell if they was green or what color. When we got up in the morning, we was at Fayetteville, North Carolina. We had breakfast in the dining car and after breakfast I got in conversation with the man in the next compartment to ours. He was from Lebanon, New Hampshire, and a man about eighty years of age. His wife was with him, and two unmarried daughters and I made the remark that I should think the four of them would be crowded in one compartment, but he said they had made the trip every winter for fifteen years and knowed how to keep out of each other's way. He said they was bound for Tarpon Springs.

We reached Charleston, South Carolina, at 12:50 p.m. and arrived at Savannah, Georgia, at 4:20. We reached Jacksonville, Florida, at 8:45 p.m. and had an hour and a quarter to lay over there, but Mother made a fuss about me getting off the train, so we had the darky make up our berths and retired before we left Jacksonville. I didn't sleep good as the train done a lot of hemming and hawing, and Mother never sleeps good on a train as she says she is always worrying that I will fall out. She says she would rather have the upper herself, as then she would not have to worry about me, but I tell her I can't take the risk of having it get out that I allowed my wife to sleep in an upper berth. It would make talk.

We was up in the morning in time to see our friends from New Hampshire get off at Tarpon Springs, which we reached at 6:53 a.m.

Several of our fellow passengers got off at Clearwater and some at Belleair, where the train backs right up to the door of the mammoth hotel. Belleair is the winter headquarters for the golf dudes and everybody that got off there had their bag of sticks, as many as ten and twelve in a bag. Women and all. When I was a young man we called it shinny and only needed one club to play with and about one game of it would of been a-plenty for some of these dudes, the way we played it.

The train pulled into St. Petersburg at 8:20 and when we got off the train you would think they was a riot, what with all the darkies barking for the different hotels.

I said to Mother, I said:

"It is a good thing we have got a place picked out to go to and don't have to choose a hotel, as it would be hard to choose amongst them if every one of them is the best."

She laughed.

We found a jitney and I give him the address of the room my son-in-law had got for us and soon we was there and introduced ourselves to the lady that owns the house, a young widow about forty-eight years of age. She showed us our room, which was light and airy with a comfortable bed and bureau and washstand. It was twelve dollars a week, but the location was good, only three blocks from Williams Park.

St. Pete is what folks calls the town, though they also call it the Sunshine City, as they claim they's no other place in the country where they's fewer days when Old Sol don't smile down on Mother Earth, and one of the newspapers gives away all their copies free every day when the sun don't shine. They claim to of only give them away some sixty-odd times in the last eleven years. Another nickname they have got for the town is "the Poor Man's Palm Beach," but I guess they's men that comes there that could borrow as much from the bank as some of the Willie boys over to the other Palm Beach.

During our stay we paid a visit to the Lewis Tent City, which is the headquarters for the Tin Can Tourists. But maybe you ain't heard about them. Well, they are an organization that takes their vacation trips by auto and carries everything with them. That is, they bring along their tents to sleep in and cook in and they don't patronize no hotels or cafeterias, but they have got to be bona fide auto campers or they can't belong to the organization.

They tell me they's over 200,000 members to it and they call themselves the Tin Canners on account of most of their food being put up in tin cans. One couple we seen in the Tent City was a couple from Brady, Texas, named Mr. and Mrs. Pence, which the old man is over eighty years of age and they had come in their auto all the way from home, a distance of 1,641 miles. They took five weeks for the trip, Mr. Pence driving the entire distance.

The Tin Canners hails from every State in the Union and in the summer time they visit places like New England and the Great Lakes region, but in the winter the most of them comes to Florida and scatters all over the State. While we was down there, they was a national convention of them at Gainesville, Florida, and they elected a Fredonia, New York, man as their president. His title is Royal Tin Can Opener of the World. They have got a song wrote up which everybody has got to learn it before they are a member:

> The tin can forever! Hurrah, boys! Hurrah!
> Up with the tin can! Down with the foe!
> We will rally round the campfire, we'll rally once again,
> Shouting, "We auto camp forever!"

That is something like it. And the members has also got to have a tin can fastened on to the front of their machine.

I asked Mother how she would like to travel around that way and she said:

"Fine, but not with an old rattle brain like you driving."

"Well," I said, "I am eight years younger than this Mr. Pence who drove here from Texas."

"Yes," she said, "but he is old enough to not be skittish."

You can't get ahead of Mother.

Well, one of the first things we done in St. Petersburg was to go to the Chamber of Commerce and register our names and where we was from as they's great rivalry amongst the different States in regards to the number of their citizens visiting in town and of course our little State don't stand much of a show, but still every little bit helps, as the fella says. All and all, the man told us, they was eleven thousand names registered, Ohio leading with some fifteen hundred-odd and New York State next with twelve hundred. Then come Michigan, Pennsylvania and so on down, with one man each from Cuba and Nevada.

The first night we was there, they was a meeting of the New York-New Jersey Society at the Congregational Church and a man from Ogdensburg, New York State, made the talk. His subject was Rainbow Chasing. He is a Rotarian and a very convicting speaker, though I forget his name.

Our first business, of course, was to find a place to eat and after trying several places we run on to a cafeteria on Central Avenue that suited us up and down. We eat pretty near all our meals there and it averaged about two dollars per day for the two of us, but the food was well cooked and everything nice and clean. A man don't mind paying the price if things is clean and well cooked.

On the third day of February, which is Mother's birthday, we spread ourselves and eat supper at the Poinsettia Hotel and they charged us seventy-five cents for a sirloin steak that wasn't hardly big enough for one.

I said to Mother: "Well," I said, "I guess it's a good thing every day ain't your birthday or we would be in the poorhouse."

"No," says Mother, "because if every day was my birthday, I would be old enough by this time to of been in my grave long ago."

You can't get ahead of Mother.

In the hotel they had a card-room where they was several men and ladies playing five hundred and this new fangled whist bridge. We also seen a place where they was dancing, so I asked Mother would she like to trip the light fantastic too and she said no, she was too old to squirm like you have got to do now days. We watched some of the young folks at it awhile till Mother got disgusted and said we would have to see a good movie to take the taste out of our mouth. Mother is a great movie heroyne and we go twice a week here at home.

But I want to tell you about the Park. The second day we was there we visited the Park, which is a good deal like the one in Tampa, only bigger, and they's more fun goes on here every day than you could shake a stick at. In the middle they's a big bandstand and chairs for the folks to set and listen to the concerts, which they give you music for all tastes, from Dixie up to classical pieces like Hearts and Flowers.

Then all around they's places marked off for different sports and games—chess and checkers and dominoes for folks that enjoys those kind of games, and roque and horse-shoes for the nimbler

ones. I used to pitch a pretty fair shoe myself, but ain't done much
of it in the last twenty years.

Well, anyway, we bought a membership ticket in the club which
costs one dollar for the season, and they tell me that up to a couple
years ago it was fifty cents, but they had to raise it to keep out the
riff-raff.

Well, Mother and I put in a great day watching the pitchers and
she wanted I should get in the game, but I told her I was all out of
practice and would make a fool of myself, though I seen several
men pitching who I guess I could take their measure without no
practice. However, they was some good pitchers, too, and one boy
from Akron, Ohio, who could certainly throw a pretty shoe. They
told me it looked like he would win them championship of the
United States in the February tournament. We come away a few
days before they held that and I never did hear if he win. I forget
his name, but he was a clean cut young fella and he has got a
brother in Cleveland that's a Rotarian.

Well, we just stood around and watched the different games for
two or three days and finally I set down in a checker game with a
man named Weaver from Danville, Illinois. He was a pretty fair
checker player, but he wasn't no match for me, and I hope that
don't sound like bragging. But I always could hold my own on a
checker-board and the folks around here will tell you the same
thing. I played with this Weaver pretty near all morning for two or
three mornings and he beat me one game and the only other time
it looked like he had a chance, the noon whistle blowed and we
had to quit and go to dinner.

While I was playing checkers, Mother would set and listen to the
band, as she loves music, classical or no matter what kind, but anyway she was setting there one day and between selections the
woman next to her opened up a conversation. She was a woman
about Mother's own age, seventy or seventy-one, and finally she
asked Mother's name and Mother told her her name and where she
was from and Mother asked her the same question, and who do
you think the woman was?

Well, sir, it was the wife of Frank M. Hartsell, the man who was
engaged to Mother till I stepped in and cut him out, fifty-two
years ago!

Yes, sir!

You can imagine Mother's surprise! And Mrs. Hartsell was surprised, too, when Mother told her she had once been friends with her husband, though Mother didn't say how close friends they had been, or that Mother and I was the cause of Hartsell going out West. But that's what we was. Hartsell left his town a month after the engagement was broke off and ain't never been back since. He had went out to Michigan and become a veterinary, and that is where he had settled down, in Hillsdale, Michigan, and finally married his wife.

Well, Mother screwed up her courage to ask if Frank was still living and Mrs. Hartsell took her over to where they was pitching horse-shoes and there was old Frank, waiting his turn. And he knowed Mother as soon as he seen her, though it was over fifty years. He said he knowed her by her eyes.

"Why, it's Lucy Frost!" he says, and he throwed down his shoes and quit the game.

Then they come over and hunted me up and I will confess I wouldn't of knowed him. Him and I is the same age to the month, but he seems to show it more, some way. He is balder for one thing. And his beard is all white, where mine has still got a streak of brown in it. The very first thing I said to him, I said:

"Well, Frank, that beard of yours makes me feel like I was back north. It looks like a regular blizzard."

"Well," he said, "I guess yourn would be just as white if you had it dry cleaned."

But Mother wouldn't stand that.

"Is that so!" she said to Frank. "Well, Charley ain't had no tobacco in his mouth for over ten years!"

And I ain't!

Well, I excused myself from the checker game and it was pretty close to noon, so we decided to all have dinner together and they was nothing for it only we must try their cafeteria on Third Avenue. It was a little more expensive than ours and not near as good, I thought. I and Mother had about the same dinner we had been having every day and our bill was $1.10. Frank's check was $1.20 for he and his wife. The same meal wouldn't of cost them more than a dollar at our place.

After dinner we made them come up to our house and we all set in the parlor, which the young woman had give us the use of to entertain company. We begun talking over old times and Mother said she was a-scared Mrs. Hartsell would find it tiresome listening to we three talk over old times, but as it turned out they wasn't much chance for nobody else to talk with Mrs. Hartsell in the company. I have heard lots of women that could go it, but Hartsell's wife takes the cake of all the women I ever seen. She told us the family history of everybody in the State of Michigan and bragged for a half hour about her son, who she said is in the drug business in Grand Rapids, and a Rotarian.

When I and Hartsell could get a word in edgeways we joked one another back and forth and I chafed him about being a horse doctor.

"Well, Frank," I said, "you look pretty prosperous, so I suppose they's been plenty of glanders around Hillsdale."

"Well," he said, "I've managed to make more than a fair living. But I've worked pretty hard."

"Yes," I said, "and I suppose you get called out all hours of the night to attend births and so on."

Mother made me shut up.

Well, I thought they wouldn't never go home and I and Mother was in misery trying to keep awake, as the both of us generally always takes a nap after dinner. Finally they went, after we had made an engagement to meet them in the Park the next morning, and Mrs. Hartsell also invited us to come to their place the next night and play five hundred. But she had forgot that they was a meeting of the Michigan Society that evening, so it was not till two evenings later that we had our first card game.

Hartsell and his wife lived in a house on Third Avenue North and had a private setting room besides their bedroom. Mrs. Hartsell couldn't quit talking about their private setting room like it was something wonderful. We played cards with them, with Mother and Hartsell partners against his wife and I. Mrs. Hartsell is a miserable card player and we certainly got the worst of it.

After the game she brought out a dish of oranges and we had to pretend it was just what we wanted, though oranges down there is like a young man's whiskers; you enjoy them at first, but they get to be a pesky nuisance.

We played cards again the next night at our place with the same partners and I and Mrs. Hartsell was beat again. Mother and Hartsell was full of compliments for each other on what a good team they made, but the both of them knowed well enough where the secret of their success laid. I guess all and all we must of played ten different evenings and they was only one night when Mrs. Hartsell and I come out ahead. And that one night wasn't no fault of hern.

When we had been down there about two weeks, we spent one evening as their guest in the Congregational Church, at a social give by the Michigan Society. A talk was made by a man named Bitting of Detroit, Michigan, on "How I Was Cured of Story Telling." He is a big man in the Rotarians and give a witty talk.

A woman named Mrs. Oxford rendered some selections which Mrs. Hartsell said was grand opera music, but whatever they was my daughter Edie could of give her cards and spades and not made such a hullaballoo about it neither.

Then they was a ventriloquist from Grand Rapids and a young woman about forty-five years of age that mimicked different kinds of birds. I whispered to Mother that they all sounded like a chicken, but she nudged me to shut up.

After the show we stopped in a drug store and I set up the refreshments and it was pretty close to ten o'clock before we finally turned in. Mother and I would of preferred tending the movies, but Mother said we mustn't offend Mrs. Hartsell, though I asked her had we came to Florida to enjoy ourselves or to just not offend an old chatter-box from Michigan.

I felt sorry for Hartsell one morning. The women folks both had an engagement down to the chiropodist's and I run across Hartsell in the Park and he foolishly offered to play me checkers.

It was him that suggested it, not me, and I guess he repented himself before we had played one game. But he was too stubborn to give up and set there while I beat him game after game and the worst part of it was that a crowd of folks had got in the habit of watching me play and there they all was, hooking on, and finally they seen what a fool Frank was making of himself, and they began to chafe him and pass remarks. Like one of them said: "Who ever told you you was a checker player!"

And: "You might maybe be good for tiddle-de-winks, but not checkers!"

I almost felt like letting him beat me a couple games. But the crowd would of knowed it was a put up job.

Well, the women folks joined us in the Park and I wasn't going to mention our little game, but Hartsell told about it himself and admitted he wasn't no match for me.

"Well," said Mrs. Hartsell, "checkers ain't much of a game anyway, is it?" She said: "It's more of a children's game, ain't it? At least, I know my boy's children used to play it a good deal."

"Yes, ma'am," I said. "It's a children's game the way your husband plays it, too."

Mother wanted to smooth things over, so she said: "Maybe they's other games where Frank can beat you."

"Yes," said Mrs. Hartsell, "and I bet he could beat you pitching horse-shoes."

"Well," I said, "I would give him a chance to try, only I ain't pitched a shoe in over sixteen years."

"Well," said Hartsell, "I ain't played checkers in twenty years."

"You ain't never played it," I said.

"Anyway," says Frank, "Lucy and I is your master at five hundred."

Well, I could of told him why that was, but had decency enough to hold my tongue.

It had got so now that he wanted to play cards every night and when I or Mother wanted to go to a movie, any one of us would have to pretend we had a headache and then trust to goodness that they wouldn't see us sneak into the theater. I don't mind playing cards when my partner keeps their mind on the game, but you take a woman like Hartsell's wife and how can they play cards when they have got to stop every couple seconds and brag about their son in Grand Rapids?

Well, the New York-New Jersey Society announced that they was goin' to give a social evening too and I said to Mother, I said: "Well, that is one evening when we will have an excuse not to play five hundred."

"Yes," she said, "but we will have to ask Frank and his wife to go to the social with us as they asked us to go to the Michigan social."

"Well," I said, "I had rather stay home than drag that chatterbox everywheres we go."

So Mother said: "You are getting too cranky. Maybe she does talk a little too much but she is good hearted. And Frank is always good company."

So I said: "I suppose if he is such good company you wished you had of married him."

Mother laughed and said I sounded like I was jealous. Jealous of a cow doctor!

Anyway we had to drag them along to the social and I will say that we give them a much better entertainment than they had given us.

Judge Lane of Paterson made a fine talk on business conditions and a Mrs. Newell of Westfield imitated birds, only you could really tell what they was the way she done it. Two young women from Red Bank sung a choral selection and we clapped them back and they gave us "Home to Our Mountains," and Mother and Mrs. Hartsell both had tears in their eyes. And Hartsell, too.

Well, some way or another the chairman got wind that I was there and asked me to make a talk and I wasn't even going to get up, but Mother made me, so I got up and said:

"Ladies and gentlemen," I said. "I didn't expect to be called on for a speech on an occasion like this or no other occasion as I do not set myself up as a speech maker, so will have to do the best I can, which I often say is the best anybody can do."

Then I told them the story about Pat and the motorcycle, using the brogue, and it seemed to tickle them and I told them one or two other stories, but altogether I wasn't on my feet more than twenty or twenty-five minutes and you ought to of heard the clapping and hollering when I set down. Even Mrs. Hartsell admitted that I am quite a speechifier and said if I ever went to Grand Rapids, Michigan, her son would make me talk to the Rotarians.

When it was over, Hartsell wanted we should go to their house and play cards, but his wife reminded him that it was after 9:30 p.m., rather a late hour to start a card game, but he had went crazy on the subject of cards, probably because he didn't have to play partners with his wife. Anyway, we got rid of them and went home to bed.

It was the next morning, when we met over to the Park, that Mrs. Hartsell made the remark that she wasn't getting no exercise so I suggested that why didn't she take part in the roque game.

She said she had not played a game of roque in twenty years, but if Mother would play she would play. Well, at first Mother wouldn't hear of it, but finally consented, more to please Mrs. Hartsell than anything else.

Well, they had a game with a Mrs. Ryan from Eagle, Nebraska, and a young Mrs. Morse from Rutland, Vermont, who Mother had met down to the chiropodist's. Well, Mother couldn't hit a flea and they all laughed at her and I couldn't help from laughing at her myself and finally she quit and said her back was too lame to stoop over. So they got another lady and kept on playing and soon Mrs. Hartsell was the one everybody was laughing at, as she had a long shot to hit the black ball, and as she made the effort her teeth fell out on to the court. I never seen a woman so flustered in my life. And I never heard so much laughing, only Mrs. Hartsell didn't join in and she was madder than a hornet and wouldn't play no more, so the game broke up.

Mrs. Hartsell went home without speaking to nobody, but Hartsell stayed around and finally he said to me, he said: "Well, I played you checkers the other day and you beat me bad and now what do you say if you and me play a game of horseshoes?"

I told him I hadn't pitched a shoe in sixteen years, but Mother said: "Go ahead and play. You used to be good at it and maybe it will come back to you."

Well, to make a long story short, I give in. I oughtn't to of never tried it, as I hadn't pitched a shoe in sixteen years, and I only done it to humor Hartsell.

Before we started, Mother patted me on the back and told me to do my best, so we started in and I seen right off that I was in for it, as I hadn't pitched a shoe in sixteen years and didn't have my distance. And besides, the plating had wore off the shoes so that they was points right where they stuck into my thumb and I hadn't throwed more than two or three times when my thumb was raw and it pretty near killed me to hang on to the shoe, let alone pitch it.

Well, Hartsell throws the awkwardest shoe I ever seen pitched and to see him pitch you wouldn't think he would ever come nowheres near, but he is also the luckiest pitcher I ever seen and he made some pitches where the shoe lit five and six feet short and then schoonered up and was a ringer. They's no use trying to beat that kind of luck.

They was a pretty fair size crowd watching us and four or five other ladies besides Mother, and it seems like, when Hartsell pitches, he has got to chew and it kept the ladies on the anxious seat as he don't seem to care which way he is facing when he leaves go.

You would think a man as old as him would of learnt more manners.

Well, to make a long story short, I was just beginning to get my distance when I had to give up on account of my thumb, which I showed it to Hartsell and he seen I couldn't go on, as it was raw and bleeding. Even if I could of stood it to go on myself, Mother wouldn't of allowed it after she seen my thumb. So anyway I quit and Hartsell said the score was nineteen to six, but I don't know what it was. Or don't care, neither.

Well, Mother and I went home and I said I hoped we was through with the Hartsells as I was sick and tired of them, but it seemed like she had promised we would go over to their house that evening for another game of their everlasting cards.

Well, my thumb was giving me considerable pain and I felt kind of out of sorts and I guess maybe I forgot myself, but anyway, when we was about through playing Hartsell made the remark that he wouldn't never lose a game of cards if he could always have Mother for a partner.

So I said: "Well, you had a chance fifty years ago to always have her for a partner, but you wasn't man enough to keep her."

I was sorry the minute I had said it and Hartsell didn't know what to say and for once his wife couldn't say nothing. Mother tried to smooth things over by making the remark that I must of had something stronger than tea or I wouldn't talk so silly. But Mrs. Hartsell had froze up like an iceberg and hardly said good night to us and I bet her and Frank put in a pleasant hour after we was gone.

As we was leaving, Mother said to him: "Never mind Charley's nonsense, Frank. He is just mad because you beat him all hollow pitching horseshoes and playing cards."

She said that to make up for my slip, but at the same time she certainly riled me. I tried to keep ahold of myself, but as soon as we was out of the house she had to open up the subject and begun to scold me for the break I had made.

Well, I wasn't in no mood to be scolded. So I said: "I guess he is such a wonderful pitcher and card player that you wished you had married him."

"Well," she said, "at least he ain't a baby to give up pitching because his thumb has got a few scratches."

"And how about you," I said, "making a fool of yourself on the roque court and then pretending your back is lame and you can't play no more!"

"Yes," she said, "but when you hurt your thumb I didn't laugh at you, and why did you laugh at me when I sprained my back?"

"Who could help from laughing!" I said.

"Well," she said, "Frank Hartsell didn't laugh."

"Well," I said, "why didn't you marry him?"

"Well," said Mother, "I almost wished I had!"

"And I wished so, too!" I said.

"I'll remember that!" said Mother, and that's the last word she said to me for two days.

We seen the Hartsells the next day in the Park and I was willing to apologize, but they just nodded to us. And a couple days later we heard they had left for Orlando, where they have got relatives.

I wished they had went there in the first place.

Mother and I made it up setting on a bench.

"Listen, Charley," she said. "This is our Golden Honeymoon and we don't want the whole thing spoilt with a silly old quarrel."

"Well," I said, "did you mean that about wishing you had married Hartsell?"

"Of course not," she said, "that is, if you didn't mean that you wished I had, too." So I said:

"I was just tired and all wrought up. I thank God you chose me instead of him as they's no other woman in the world who I could of lived with all these years."

"How about Mrs. Hartsell?" says Mother.

"Good gracious!" I said. "Imagine being married to a woman that plays five hundred like she does and drops her teeth on the roque court!"

"Well," said Mother, "it wouldn't be no worse than being married to a man that expectorates towards ladies and is such a fool in a checker game."

So I put my arm around her shoulder and she stroked my hand and I guess we got kind of spoony.

They was two days left of our stay in St. Petersburg and the next to the last day Mother introduced me to a Mrs. Kendall from Kingston, Rhode Island, who she had met at the chiropodist's.

Mrs. Kendall made us acquainted with her husband, who is in the grocery business. They have got two sons and five grandchildren and one great-grandchild. One of their sons lives in Providence and is way up in the Elks as well as a Rotarian.

We found them very congenial people and we played cards with them the last two nights we was there. They was both experts and I only wished we had met them sooner instead of running into the

Hartsells. But the Kendalls will be there again next winter and we will see more of them, that is, if we decide to make the trip again.

We left the Sunshine City on the eleventh day of February, at 11 a.m. This give us a day trip through Florida and we seen all the country we had passed through at night on the way down.

We reached Jacksonville at 7 p.m. and pulled out of there at 8:10 p.m. We reached Fayetteville, North Carolina, at nine o'clock the following morning, and reached Washington, D.C., at 6:30 p.m., laying over there half an hour.

We reached Trenton at 11:01 p.m. and had wired ahead to my daughter and son-in-law and they met us at the train and we went to their house and they put us up for the night. John would of made us stay up all night, telling about our trip, but Edie said we must be tired and made us go to bed. That's my daughter.

The next day we took our train for home and arrived safe and sound, having been gone just one month and a day.

Here comes Mother, so I guess I better shut up.

SOURCE: *Cosmopolitan*. Volume 73. New York, July 1922.

A TELEPHONE CALL (1928)

Dorothy Parker

Parker (1893–1967) was the fast-talking New Yorker whose voice of simultaneous toughness and vulnerability has influenced more female American humorists than anyone else. She was a founding member of the hard-drinking, hard-joking Algonquin Round Table.

PLEASE, GOD, LET him telephone me now. Dear God, let him call me now. I won't ask anything else of You, truly I won't. It isn't very much to ask. It would be so little to You, God, such a little, little thing. Only let him telephone now. Please, God. Please, please, please.

If I didn't think about it, maybe the telephone might ring. Sometimes it does that. If I could think of something else. If I could think of something else. Maybe if I counted five hundred by fives, it might ring by that time. I'll count slowly. I won't cheat. And if it rings when I get to three hundred, I won't stop; I won't answer it until I get to five hundred. Five, ten, fifteen, twenty, twenty-five, thirty, thirty-five, forty, forty-five, fifty . . . Oh, please ring. Please.

This is the last time I'll look at the clock. I will not look at it again. It's ten minutes past seven. He said he would telephone at five o'clock. "I'll call you at five, darling." I think that's where he said "darling." I'm almost sure he said it there. I know he called me "darling" twice, and the other time was when he said good-by. "Good-by, darling." He was busy, and he can't say much in the office, but he called me "darling" twice. He couldn't have minded my calling him up. I know you shouldn't keep telephoning them— I know they don't like that. When you do that they know you are thinking about them and wanting them, and that makes them hate you. But I hadn't talked to him in three days—not in three days. And all I did was ask him how he was; it was just the way anybody might have called him up. He couldn't have minded that. He couldn't have thought I was bothering him. "No, of course you're not," he said. And he said he'd telephone me. He didn't have to say that. I didn't ask him to, truly I didn't. I'm sure I didn't. I don't think he would say he'd telephone me, and then just never do it. Please don't let him do that, God. Please don't.

"I'll call you at five, darling." "Good-by, darling." He was busy, and he was in a hurry, and there were people around him, but he called me "darling" twice. That's mine, that's mine. I have that, even if I never see him again. Oh, but that's so little. That isn't enough. Nothing's enough, if I never see him again. Please let me see him again, God. Please, I want him so much. I want him so much. I'll be good, God. I will try to be better, I will, if you will let me see him again. If You will let him telephone me. Oh, let him telephone me now.

Ah, don't let my prayer seem too little to You, God. You sit up there, so white and old, with all the angels about You and the stars slipping by. And I come to You with a prayer about a telephone call. Ah, don't laugh, God. You see, You don't know how it feels. You're so safe, there on Your throne, with the blue swirling under You. Nothing can touch You; no one can twist Your heart in his hands. This is suffering, God, this is bad, bad suffering. Won't You help me? For Your Son's sake, help me. You said You would do whatever was asked of You in His name. Oh, God, in the name of Thine only beloved Son, Jesus Christ, our Lord, let him telephone me now.

I must stop this. I mustn't be this way. Look. Suppose a young man says he'll call a girl up, and then something happens, and he doesn't. That isn't so terrible, is it? Why, it's going on all over the world, right this minute. Oh, what do I care what's going on all over the world? Why can't that telephone ring? Why can't it, why can't it? Couldn't you ring? Ah, please, couldn't you? You damned, ugly, shiny thing. It would hurt you to ring, wouldn't it? Oh, that would hurt you. Damn you, I'll pull your filthy roots out of the wall, I'll smash your smug black face in little bits. Damn you to hell.

No, no, no. I must stop. I must think about something else. This is what I'll do. I'll put the clock in the other room. Then I can't look at it. If I do have to look at it, then I'll have to walk into the bedroom, and that will be something to do. Maybe, before I look at it again, he will call me. I'll be so sweet to him, if he calls me. If he says he can't see me tonight, I'll say, "Why, that's all right, dear. Why, of course it's all right." I'll be the way I was when I first met him. Then maybe he'll like me again. I was always sweet, at first. Oh, it's so easy to be sweet to people before you love them.

I think he must still like me a little. He couldn't have called me "darling" twice today, if he didn't still like me a little. It isn't all gone, if he still likes me a little; even if it's only a little, little bit. You see, God, if You would just let him telephone me, I wouldn't have to ask You anything more. I would be sweet to him, I would be gay, I would be just the way I used to be, and then he would love me again. And then I would never have to ask You for anything more. Don't You see, God? So won't You please let him telephone me? Won't You please, please, please? Are You punishing me, God, because I've been bad? Are You angry with me because I did that? Oh, but, God, there are so many bad people— You could not be hard only to me. And it wasn't very bad; it couldn't have been bad. We didn't hurt anybody, God. Things are only bad when they hurt people. We didn't hurt one single soul; You know that. You know it wasn't bad, don't You, God? So won't You let him telephone me now?

If he doesn't telephone me, I'll know God is angry with me. I'll count five hundred by fives, and if he hasn't called me then, I will know God isn't going to help me, ever again. That will be the sign. Five, ten, fifteen, twenty, twenty-five, thirty, thirty-five, forty, forty-five, fifty, fifty-five. . . It was bad. I knew it was bad. All right, God, send me to hell. You think You're frightening me with Your hell, don't You? You think Your hell is worse than mine.

I mustn't. I mustn't do this. Suppose he's a little late calling me up—that's nothing to get hysterical about. Maybe he isn't going to call—maybe he's coming straight up here without telephoning. He'll be cross if he sees I have been crying. They don't like you to cry. He doesn't cry. I wish to God I could make him cry. I wish I could make him cry and tread the floor and feel his heart heavy and big and festering in him. I wish I could hurt him like hell.

He doesn't wish that about me. I don't think he even knows how he makes me feel. I wish he could know, without my telling him. They don't like you to tell them they've made you cry. They don't like you to tell them you're unhappy because of them. If you do, they think you're possessive and exacting. And then they hate you. They hate you whenever you say anything you really think. You always have to keep playing little games. Oh, I thought we didn't have to; I thought this was so big I could say whatever I meant. I guess you can't, ever. I guess there isn't ever anything big enough for that. Oh, if he would just telephone, I wouldn't tell him I had been sad about him. They hate sad people. I would be so sweet and so gay, he couldn't help but like me. If he would only telephone. If he would only telephone.

Maybe that's what he is doing. Maybe he is coming on here without calling me up. Maybe he's on his way now. Something might have happened to him. No, nothing could ever happen to him. I can't picture anything happening to him. I never picture him run over. I never see him lying still and long and dead. I wish he were dead. That's a terrible wish. That's a lovely wish. If he were dead, he would be mine. If he were dead, I would never think of now and the last few weeks. I would remember only the lovely times. It would be all beautiful. I wish he were dead. I wish he were dead, dead, dead. This is silly. It's silly to go wishing people were dead just because they don't call you up the very minute they said they would. Maybe the clock's fast; I don't know whether it's right. Maybe he's hardly late at all. Anything could have made him a little late. Maybe he had to stay at his office. Maybe he went home, to call me up from there, and somebody came in. He doesn't like to telephone me in front of people. Maybe he's worried, just a little, little bit, about keeping me waiting. He might even hope that I would call him up. I could do that. I could telephone him.

I mustn't. I mustn't, I mustn't. Oh, God, please don't let me telephone him. Please keep me from doing that. I know, God, just as well as You do, that if he were worried about me, he'd telephone no matter where he was or how many people there were around him. Please make me know that, God. I don't ask You to make it easy for me—You can't do that, for all that You could make a world. Only let me know it, God. Don't let me go on hoping. Don't let me say comforting things to myself. Please don't let me hope, dear God. Please don't.

I won't telephone him. I'll never telephone him again as long as I live. He'll rot in hell, before I'll call him up. You don't have to give me strength, God; I have it myself. If he wanted me, he could get me. He knows where I am. He knows I'm waiting here. He's so sure of me, so sure. I wonder why they hate you, as soon as they are sure of you. I should think it would be so sweet to be sure. It would be so easy to telephone him. Then I'd know. Maybe it wouldn't be a foolish thing to do. Maybe he wouldn't mind. Maybe he'd like it. Maybe he has been trying to get me. Sometimes people try and try to get you on the telephone, and they say the number doesn't answer. I'm not just saying that to help myself; that really happens. You know that really happens, God. Oh, God, keep me away from that telephone. Keep me away. Let me still have just a little bit of pride. I think I'm going to need it, God. I think it will be all I'll have.

Oh, what does pride matter, when I can't stand it if I don't talk to him? Pride like that is such a silly, shabby little thing. The real pride, the big pride, is in having no pride. I'm not saying that just because I want to call him. I am not. That's true, I know that's true. I will be big. I will be beyond little prides.

Please, God, keep me from, telephoning him. Please, God.

I don't see what pride has to do with it. This is such a little thing, for me to be bringing in pride, for me to be making such a fuss about. I may have misunderstood him. Maybe he said for me to call him up, at five. "Call me at five, darling." He could have said that, perfectly well. It's so possible that I didn't hear him right. "Call me at five, darling." I'm almost sure that's what he said. God, don't let me talk this way to myself. Make me know, please make me know.

I'll think about something else. I'll just sit quietly. If I could sit still. If I could sit still. Maybe I could read. Oh, all the books are about people who love each other, truly and sweetly. What do they want to write about that for? Don't they know it isn't true? Don't they know it's a lie, it's a God damned lie? What do they have to tell about that for, when they know how it hurts? Damn them, damn them, damn them.

I won't. I'll be quiet. This is nothing to get excited about. Look. Suppose he were someone I didn't know very well. Suppose he were another girl. Then I'd just telephone and say, "Well, for goodness' sake, what happened to you?" That's what I'd do, and I'd never even think about it. Why can't I be casual and natural, just because I love him? I can be. Honestly, I can be. I'll call him up, and be so easy and pleasant. You see if I won't, God. Oh, don't let me call him. Don't, don't, don't.

God, aren't You really going to let him call me? Are You sure, God? Couldn't You please relent? Couldn't You? I don't even ask You to let him telephone me this minute, God; only let him do it in a little while. I'll count five hundred by fives. I'll do it so slowly and so fairly. If he hasn't telephoned then, I'll call him. I will. Oh, please, dear God, dear kind God, my blessed Father in Heaven, let him call before then. Please, God. Please.

Five, ten, fifteen, twenty, twenty-five, thirty, thirty-five. . . .

SOURCE: *The Portable Dorothy Parker.* Revised and enlarged edition. New York: Viking Press, 1981.

THE SECRET LIFE OF WALTER MITTY
(1939)

James Thurber

Born in Columbus, Ohio, James Thurber (1894–1961) moved to New York in 1926 and became a writer and cartoonist at The New Yorker *magazine. Thurber's humor has been collected in over thirty volumes of essays, stories, fables, plays, drawings, and cartoons. His work has been adapted for stage, TV, and film—two films alone are based on "The Secret Life of Walter Mitty." Visit* www.ThurberHouse.org.

"WE'RE GOING THROUGH!" The Commander's voice was like thin ice breaking. He wore his full-dress uniform, with the heavily braided white cap pulled down rakishly over one cold gray eye. "We can't make it, sir. It's spoiling for a hurricane, if you ask me." "I'm not asking you, Lieutenant Berg," said the Commander. "Throw on the power lights! Rev her up to 8500! We're going through!" The pounding of the cylinders increased: ta-pocketa-pocketa-pocketa-pocketa-pocketa. The Commander stared at the ice forming on the pilot window. He walked over and twisted a row of complicated dials. "Switch on No. 8 auxiliary!" he shouted. "Switch on No. 8 auxiliary!" repeated Lieutenant Berg. "Full strength in No. 3 turret!" shouted the Commander. "Full strength in No. 3 turret!" The crew, bending to their various tasks in the huge, hurtling eight-engined Navy hydroplane, looked at each other and grinned. "The Old Man'll get us through," they said to one another. "The Old Man ain't afraid of hell!" . . .

"Not so fast! You're driving too fast!" said Mrs. Mitty. "What are you driving so fast for?"

"Hmm?" said Walter Mitty. He looked at his wife, in the seat beside him, with shocked astonishment. She seemed grossly unfamiliar, like a strange woman who had yelled at him in a crowd. "You were up to fifty-five," she said. "You know I don't like to go more than forty. You were up to fifty-five." Walter Mitty drove on toward Waterbury in silence, the roaring of the SN202 through the worst storm in twenty years of Navy flying fading in the remote, intimate airways of his mind. "You're tensed up again," said Mrs. Mitty. "It's one of your days. I wish you'd let Dr. Renshaw look you over."

Walter Mitty stopped the car in front of the building where his wife went to have her hair done. "Remember to get those overshoes while I'm having my hair done," she said. "I don't need overshoes," said Mitty. She put her mirror back into her bag. "We've been all through that," she said, getting out of the car. "You're not a young man any longer." He raced the engine a little. "Why don't you wear your gloves? Have you lost your gloves?" Walter Mitty reached in a pocket and brought out the gloves. He put them on, but after she had turned and gone into the building and he had driven on to a red light, he took them off again. "Pick it up, brother!" snapped a cop as the light changed, and Mitty hastily pulled on his gloves and lurched ahead. He drove around the streets aimlessly for a time, and then he drove past the hospital on his way to the parking lot.

. . . "It's the millionaire banker, Wellington McMillan," said the pretty nurse. "Yes?" said Walter Mitty, removing his gloves slowly. "Who has the case?" "Dr. Renshaw and Dr. Benbow, but there are two specialists here, Dr. Remington from New York and Dr. Pritchard-Mitford from London. He flew over." A door opened down a long, cool corridor and Dr. Renshaw came out. He looked distraught and haggard. "Hello, Mitty," he said. "We're having the devil's own time with McMillan, the millionaire banker and close personal friend of Roosevelt. Obstreosis of the ductal tract. Tertiary. Wish you'd take a look at him." "Glad to," said Mitty.

In the operating room there were whispered introductions: "Dr. Remington, Dr. Mitty. Dr. Pritchard-Mitford, Dr. Mitty." "I've read your book on streptothricosis," said Pritchard-Mitford, shaking hands. "A brilliant performance, sir." "Thank you," said Walter Mitty. "Didn't know you were in the States, Mitty," grumbled Remington. "Coals to Newcastle, bringing Mitford and me up here for a tertiary." "You are very kind," said Mitty. A huge, complicated machine, connected to the operating table, with many tubes and wires, began at this moment to go pocketa-pocketa-pocketa. "The new anesthetizer is giving away!" shouted an intern. "There is no one in the East who knows how to fix it!" "Quiet, man!" said Mitty, in a low, cool voice. He sprang to the machine, which was now going pocketa-pocketa-queep-pocketa-queep . He began fingering delicately a row of glistening dials. "Give me a fountain pen!" he snapped. Someone handed him a fountain pen. He pulled a faulty piston out of the machine and inserted the pen in its place. "That will hold for ten minutes," he said. "Get on with the operation." A nurse hurried over and whispered to Renshaw, and Mitty saw the man turn pale. "Coreopsis has set in," said Renshaw nervously. "If you would take over, Mitty?" Mitty looked at him and at the craven figure of Benbow, who drank, and at the grave, uncertain faces of the two great specialists. "If you wish," he said. They slipped a white gown on him, he adjusted a mask and drew on thin gloves; nurses handed him shining . . .

"Back it up, Mac! Look out for that Buick!" Walter Mitty jammed on the brakes. "Wrong lane, Mac," said the parking-lot attendant, looking at Mitty closely. "Gee. Yeh," muttered Mitty. He began cautiously to back out of the lane marked "Exit Only." "Leave her sit there," said the attendant. "I'll put her away." Mitty got out of the car. "Hey, better leave the key." "Oh," said Mitty, handing the man the ignition key. The attendant vaulted into the car, backed it up with insolent skill, and put it where it belonged.

They're so damn cocky, thought Walter Mitty, walking along Main Street; they think they know everything. Once he had tried to take his chains off, outside New Milford, and he had got them wound around the axles. A man had had to come out in a wrecking car and unwind them, a young, grinning garageman. Since then Mrs. Mitty always made him drive to a garage to have the chains taken off. The next time, he thought, I'll wear my right arm in a sling; they won't grin at me then. I'll have my right arm in a sling and they'll see I couldn't possibly take the chains off myself. He kicked at the slush on the sidewalk. "Overshoes," he said to himself, and he began looking for a shoe store.

When he came out into the street again, with the overshoes in a box under his arm, Walter Mitty began to wonder what the other thing was his wife had told him to get. She had told him, twice before they set out from their house for Waterbury. In a way he hated these weekly trips to town—he was always getting something wrong. Kleenex, he thought, Squibb's, razor blades? No. Toothpaste, toothbrush, bicarbonate, Carborundum, initiative and referendum? He gave it up. But she would remember it. "Where's the what's-its-name?" she would ask. "Don't tell me you forgot the what's-its-name." A newsboy went by shouting something about the Waterbury trial.

. . . "Perhaps this will refresh your memory." The District Attorney suddenly thrust a heavy automatic at the quiet figure on the witness stand. "Have you ever seen this before?" Walter Mitty took the gun and examined it expertly. "This is my Webley-Vickers 50.80," he said calmly. An excited buzz ran around the courtroom. The Judge rapped for order. "You are a crack shot with any sort of firearms, I believe?" said the District Attorney, insinuatingly. "Objection!" shouted Mitty's attorney. "We have shown that the defendant could not have fired the shot. We have shown that he wore his right arm in a sling on the night of the fourteenth of July." Walter Mitty raised his hand briefly and the bickering attorneys were stilled. "With any known make of gun," he said evenly, "I could have killed Gregory Fitzhurst at three hundred feet *with my left hand*." Pandemonium broke loose in the courtroom. A woman's scream rose above the bedlam and suddenly a lovely, dark-haired girl was in Walter Mitty's arms. The District Attorney struck at her savagely. Without rising from his chair, Mitty let the man have it on the point of the chin. "You miserable cur!" . . .

"Puppy biscuit," said Walter Mitty. He stopped walking and the buildings of Waterbury rose up out of the misty courtroom and surrounded him again. A woman who was passing laughed. "He said 'Puppy biscuit,'" she said to her companion. "That man said 'Puppy biscuit' to himself." Walter Mitty hurried on. He went into an A. & P., not the first one he came to but a smaller one farther up the street. "I want some biscuit for small, young dogs," he said to the clerk. "Any special brand, sir?" The greatest pistol shot in the world thought a moment. "It says 'Puppies Bark for It' on the box," said Walter Mitty.

His wife would be through at the hairdresser's in fifteen minutes, Mitty saw in looking at his watch, unless they had trouble drying it; sometimes they had trouble drying it. She didn't like to get to the hotel first, she would want him to be there waiting for her as usual. He found a big leather chair in the lobby, facing a window, and he put the overshoes and the puppy biscuit on the floor beside it. He picked up an old copy of *Liberty* and sank down into the chair. "Can Germany Conquer the World Through the Air?" Walter Mitty looked at the pictures of bombing planes and of ruined streets.

. . . "The cannonading has got the wind up in young Raleigh, sir," said the sergeant. Captain Mitty looked up at him through tousled hair. "Get him to bed," he said wearily, "with the others. I'll fly alone." "But you can't, sir," said the sergeant anxiously. "It takes two men to handle that bomber and the Archies are pounding hell out of the air. Von Richtman's circus is between here and Saulier." "Somebody's got to get that ammunition dump," said Mitty. "I'm going over. Spot of brandy?" He poured a drink for the sergeant and one for himself. War thundered and whined around the dugout and battered at the door. There was a rending of wood and splinters flew through the room. "A bit of a near thing," said Captain Mitty carelessly. "The box barrage is closing in," said the sergeant. "We only live once, Sergeant," said Mitty, with his faint, fleeting smile. "Or do we?" He poured another brandy and tossed it off. "I never see a man could hold his brandy like you, sir," said the sergeant. "Begging your pardon, sir." Captain Mitty stood up and strapped on his huge Webley-Vickers automatic. "It's forty kilometers through hell, sir," said the sergeant. Mitty finished one last brandy. "After all," he said softly, "what isn't?" The pounding of the cannon increased; there was the rat-tat-tatting of machine guns, and from somewhere came the menacing pocketa-pocketa-pocketa of the new flame-throwers. Walter Mitty walked to the door of the dugout humming "Aupres de Ma Blonde." He turned and waved to the sergeant. "Cheerio!" he said. . . .

Something struck his shoulder. "I've been looking all over this hotel for you," said Mrs. Mitty. "Why do you have to hide in this old chair? How did you expect me to find you?" "Things close in," said Walter Mitty vaguely. "What?" Mrs. Mitty said. "Did you get the what's-its-name? The puppy biscuit? What's in that box?" "Overshoes," said Mitty. "Couldn't you have put them on in the store?" "I was thinking," said Walter Mitty. "Does it ever occur to you that I am sometimes thinking?" She looked at him. "I'm going to take your temperature when I get you home," she said.

They went out through the revolving doors that made a faintly derisive whistling sound when you pushed them. It was two blocks to the parking lot. At the drugstore on the corner she said, "Wait here for me. I forgot something. I won't be a minute." She was more than a minute. Walter Mitty lighted a cigarette. It began to rain, rain with sleet in it. He stood up against the wall of the drugstore, smoking. . . . He put his shoulders back and his heels together. "To hell with the handkerchief," said Walter Mitty scornfully. He took one last drag on his cigarette and snapped it away. Then, with that faint, fleeting smile playing about his lips, he faced the firing squad; erect and motionless, proud and disdainful, Walter Mitty the Undefeated, inscrutable to the last.

SOURCE: *The New Yorker,* March 18, 1939.

WOOING THE MUSE (1950)

Langston Hughes

Hughes (1902–1967) was born in Missouri but made his way to New York City as a young man, where he flourished as a poet and writer in the Harlem Renaissance. In a series of columns for a black newspaper chain, Hughes created and developed the character of Simple, a native of Virginia, who also discovered racial and personal freedom and energy in New York City's predominantly African-American neighborhood. The narrator of the hundreds of Simple stories is Simple's uptight, straight-arrow straight-man, not, as some commentators have suggested, Hughes himself. The columns, begun in the early 1940s and continued into the '60s, were so popular Hughes collected and revised them into several short-story collections as well as into a Broadway musical.

"Hey, now!" said Simple one hot Monday evening. "Man, I had a *fine* weekend."

"What did you do?"

"Me and Joyce went to Orchard Beach."

"Good bathing?"

"I don't know. I didn't take a bath. I don't take to cold water."

"What did you do then, just lie in the sun?"

"I did not," said Simple. "I don't like violent rays tampering with my complexion. I just laid back in the shade while Joyce sported on the beach wetting her toes to show off her pretty white bathing suit."

"In other words, you relaxed."

"Relaxed is right," said Simple. "I had myself a great big nice cool quart of beer so I just laid back in the shade and relaxed. I also wrote myself some poetries."

"Poetry!" I said.

"Yes," said Simple. "Want to hear it?"

"Indeed I do."

"I will read you Number One. Here it is:

> *Sitting under the trees*
> *With the birds and the bees*
> *Watching the girls go by*

How do you like it?"

"Is that all?"

"That's enough!" said Simple.

"You ought to have another rhyme," I said. "*By* ought to rhyme with *sky* or something."

"I was not looking at no sky, as I told you in the poem. I was looking at the girls."

"Well, anyhow, what else did you write?"

"This next one is a killer," said Simple. "It's serious. I got to thinking about how if I didn't have to ride Jim Crow, I might go down home for my vacation. And I looked around me out yonder at Orchard Beach and almost everybody on that beach, besides me and Joyce, was foreigners—New York foreigners. They was speaking Italian, German, Yiddish, Spanish, Puerto Rican, and everything but English. So I got to thinking how any one of them foreigners could visit my home state down South and ride anywhere they want to on the trains—except with me. So I wrote this poem which I will now read it to you. Listen:

> *I wonder how it can be*
> *That Greeks, Germans, Jews,*
> *Italians, Mexicans,*
> *And everybody but me*
> *Down South can ride in the trains,*
> *Streetcars and busses*
> *Without any fusses.*
>
> *But when I come along—*
> *Pure American—*
> *They got a sign up*
> *For me to ride behind:*
>
> COLORED

> *My folks and my folks' folkses*
> *And their folkses before*
> *Have been here 300 years or more—*
> *Yet any foreigner from Polish to Dutch*
> *Rides anywhere he wants to*
> *And is not subject to such*
> *Treatments as my fellow-men give me*
> *In this Land of the Free.*
>
>
> *Dixie, you ought to get wise*
> *And be civilized!*
> *And take down that COLORED sign*
> *For Americans to ride behind!*

Signed, *Jesse B. Semple.* How do you like that?"

"Did you write it yourself, or did Joyce help you?"

"Every word of it I writ myself," said Simple. "Joyce wanted me to change *folkses* and say *peoples,* but I did not have an eraser. It would have been longer, too, but Joyce made me stop and go with her to get some hot dogs."

"It's long enough," I said.

"It's not as long as Jim Crow," said Simple.

"You didn't write any nature poems at all?" I asked.

"What do you mean, nature poems?"

"I mean about the great out-of-doors—the flowers, the birds, the trees, the country."

"To tell the truth, I never was much on country," said Simple. "I had enough of it when I was down home. Besides, in the country flies bother you, bees sting you, mosquitoes bite you, and snakes hide in the grass. No, I do not like the country—except a riverbank to fish near town."

"It's better than staying in the city," I said, "and spending your money around these Harlem bars."

"At least I am welcome in these bars—run by white folks though they are," said Simple, "but I do not know no place in the country where I am welcome. If you're driving, every little roadhouse you stop at, they look at you like was a varmint and say, 'We don't serve colored,' I tell you I do not want no parts of the country in this country."

"You do not go to the country to drink," I said.

"What am I gonna do, hibernate?"

"You could lie in a hammock and read a book, then go in the house and eat chicken."

"I do not know anybody in the country around here, and you know these summer resort places up North don't admit colored. Besides, the last time I was laying out in a hammock reading the funnies in the country down in Virginia, it were in the cool of evening and, man, a snake as long as you are tall come whipping through the grass, grabbed a frog right in front of my eyes, and started to choking it down."

"What did you do?"

"Mighty near fell out of that hammock!" said Simple. "If that snake had not been so near, I would've fell out. As it were, I stepped down quick on the other side and went to find myself a stone."

"Did you kill it?"

"My nerves were bad and my aim was off. I hit the frog instead of the snake. I knocked that frog right out of his mouth."

"What did the snake do?"

"Runned and hid his self in the grass. I was scared to go outdoors all the rest of the time I was in the country."

"You are that scared of a snake?" I said.

"As scared of a snake as a Russian was of a Nazi. I would go to as much trouble to kill one as Stalin did to kill Hitler. Besides, that poor little frog were not bothering that snake. Frogs eat mosquitoes and mosquitoes eat me. So I am for letting that frog live and not be et. But a snake would chaw on my leg as quick as he would a frog, so I am for letting a snake die. Anything that bites me must die—snakes, bedbugs, bees, mosquitoes, or bears. I don't even much like for a woman to bite me, though I would not go so far as to kill her. But of all the things that bites, two is worst—a mad dog and a snake. But I would take the dog. I never could understand how in the Bible Eve got near enough to a snake to take an apple."

"Snakes did not bite in those days," I said. "That was the Age of Innocence."

"It was only after Eve got hold of the apple that everything got wrong, huh? Snakes started to bite, women to fight, men to paying, and Christians to praying," said Simple. "It were awful after Eve approached that snake and accepted that apple! It takes a woman to do a fool thing like that."

"Adam ate it, too, didn't he?"

"A woman can make a fool out of a man," said Simple. "But don't let's start talking about women. We have talked about enough unpleasant things for one night. Will you kindly invite me into the bar to have a beer? This sidewalk is hot to my feet. And as a thank-you for a drink, the next time I write a poem, I will give you a copy. But it won't be about the country, neither about nature."

"As much beer as you drink, it will probably be about a bar," I said. "When are you going to wake up, fellow, get wise to yourself, settle down, marry Joyce, and stop gallivanting all over Harlem every night? You're old enough to know better."

"I might be old enough to know better, but I am not old enough to *do* better," said Simple. "Come on in the bar and I will say you a toast I made up the last time somebody told me just what you are saying now about doing better. . . . That's right, bartender, two beers for two steers. . . . Thank you! . . . Pay for them, chum! . . . Now, here goes. Listen fluently:

> *When I get to be ninety-one*
> *And my running days is done,*
> *Then I will do better.*

> *When I get to be ninety-two*
> *And just CAN'T do,*
> *I'll do better.*

> *When I get to be ninety-three*
> *If the womens don't love me,*
> *Then I must do better.*

> *When I get to be ninety-four*
> *And can't jive no more,*
> *I'll have to do better.*

> *When I get to be ninety-five,*
> *More dead than alive,*
> *It'll be necessary to do better.*

> *When I get to be ninety-six*
> *And don't know no more tricks,*
> *I reckon I'll do better.*

When I get to be ninety-seven
And on my way to Heaven,
I'll try and do better.

When I get to be ninety-eight
And see Saint Peter at the gate,
I know I'll do better.

When I get to be ninety-nine,
Remembering it were fine,
Then I'll do better.

But even when I'm a hundred and one,
If I'm still having fun,
I'll start all over again
Just like I begun—
Because what could be better?"

SOURCE: Langston Hughes. *Simple Speaks His Mind*. New York: Simon and Schuster, 1950.

THE CONVERSION OF THE JEWS (1958)

Philip Roth

Roth, born in Newark in 1933, has been one of America's leading authors of fiction for decades, ever since his debut collection, Goodbye, Columbus and Five Short Stories *(1959), which contained this story.*

"YOU'RE A REAL one for opening your mouth in the first place," Itzie said. "What do you open your mouth all the time for?"

"I didn't bring it up, Itz, I didn't," Ozzie said.

"What do you care about Jesus Christ for anyway?"

"I didn't bring up Jesus Christ. He did. I didn't even know what he was talking about. Jesus is historical, he kept saying. Jesus is historical." Ozzie mimicked the monumental voice of Rabbi Binder.

"Jesus was a person that lived like you and me," Ozzie continued. "That's what Binder said—"

"Yeah? . . . So what? What do I give two cents whether he lived or not. And what do you gotta open your mouth!" Itzie Lieberman favored closed-mouthedness, especially when it came to Ozzie Freedman's questions. Mrs. Freedman had to see Rabbi Binder twice before about Ozzie's questions and this Wednesday at four-thirty would be the third time. Itzie preferred to keep *his* mother in the kitchen; he settled for behind-the-back subtleties such as gestures, faces, snarls and other less delicate barnyard noises.

"He was a real person, Jesus, but he wasn't like God, and we don't believe he is God." Slowly, Ozzie was explaining Rabbi Binder's position to Itzie, who had been absent from Hebrew School the previous afternoon.

"The Catholics," Itzie said helpfully, "they believe in Jesus Christ, that he's God." Itzie Lieberman used "the Catholics" in its broadest sense—to include the Protestants.

Ozzie received Itzie's remark with a tiny head bob, as though it were a footnote, and went on. "His mother was Mary, and his father probably was Joseph," Ozzie said. "But the New Testament says his real father was God."

"His *real* father?"

"Yeah," Ozzie said, "that's the big thing, his father's supposed to be God."

"Bull."

"That's what Rabbi Binder says, that it's impossible—"

"Sure it's impossible. That stuff's all bull. To have a baby you gotta get laid," Itzie theologized. "Mary hadda get laid."

"That's what Binder says: 'The only way a woman can have a baby is to have intercourse with a man.'"

"He said *that,* Ozz?" For a moment it appeared that Itzie had put the theological question aside. "He said that, intercourse?" A little curled smile shaped itself in the lower half of Itzie's face like a pink mustache. "What you guys do, Ozz, you laugh or something?"

"I raised my hand."

"Yeah? Whatja say?"

"That's when I asked the question."

Itzie's face lit up. "Whatja ask about—intercourse?"

"No, I asked the question about God, how if He could create the heaven and earth in six days, and make all the animals and the fish and the light in six days—the light especially, that's what always gets me, that He could make the light. Making fish and animals, that's pretty good—"

"That's damn good." Itzie's appreciation was honest but unimaginative: it was as though God had just pitched a one-hitter.

"But making light . . . I mean when you think about it, it's really something," Ozzie said. "Anyway, I asked Binder if He could make all that in six days, and He could pick the six days he wanted right out of nowhere, why couldn't He let a woman have a baby without having intercourse."

"You said intercourse, Ozz, to Binder?"

"Yeah."

"Right in class?"

"Yeah."

Itzie smacked the side of his head.

"I mean, no kidding around," Ozzie said, "that'd really be nothing. After all that other stuff, that'd practically be nothing."

Itzie considered a moment. "What'd Binder say?"

"He started all over again explaining how Jesus was historical and how he lived like you and me but he wasn't God. So I said I *understood* that. What I wanted to know was different."

What Ozzie wanted to know was always different. The first time he had wanted to know how Rabbi Binder could call the Jews "The Chosen People" if the Declaration of Independence claimed all men to be created equal. Rabbi Binder tried to distinguish for him between political equality and spiritual legitimacy, but what Ozzie wanted to know, he insisted vehemently, was different. That was the first time his mother had to come.

Then there was the plane crash. Fifty-eight people had been killed in a plane crash at La Guardia. In studying a casualty list in the newspaper his mother had discovered among the list of those dead eight Jewish names (his grandmother had nine but she counted Miller as a Jewish name); because of the eight she said the plane crash was "a tragedy." During free-discussion time on Wednesday Ozzie had brought to Rabbi Binder's attention this matter of "some of his relations" always picking out the Jewish names. Rabbi Binder had begun to explain cultural unity and some other things when Ozzie stood up at his seat and said that what he wanted to know was different. Rabbi Binder insisted that he sit down and it was then that Ozzie shouted that he wished all fifty-eight were Jews. That was the second time his mother came.

"And he kept explaining about Jesus being historical, and so I kept asking him. No kidding, Itz, he was trying to make me look stupid."

"So what he finally do?"

"Finally he starts screaming that I was deliberately simple-minded and a wise guy, and that my mother had to come, and this was the last time. And that I'd never get bar-mitzvahed if he could help it. Then, Itz, then he starts talking in that voice like a statue, real slow and deep, and he says that I better think over what I said about the Lord. He told me to go to his office and think it over." Ozzie leaned his body towards Itzie. "Itz. I thought it over for a solid hour, and now I'm convinced God could do it."

Ozzie had planned to confess his latest transgression to his mother as soon as she came home from work. But it was a Friday night in November and already dark, and when Mrs. Freedman came through the door she tossed off her coat, kissed Ozzie quickly on the face and went to the kitchen table to light the three yellow candles, two for the Sabbath and one for Ozzie's father.

When his mother lit the candles she would move her two arms slowly towards her, dragging them through the air, as though persuading people whose minds were half made up. And her eyes would get glassy with tears. Even when his father was alive Ozzie remembered that her eyes had gotten glassy, so it didn't have anything to do with his dying. It had something to do with lighting the candles.

As she touched the flaming match to the unlit wick of a Sabbath candle, the phone rang, and Ozzie, standing only a foot from it, plucked it off the receiver and held it muffled to his chest. When his mother lit candles Ozzie felt there should be no noise; even breathing, if you could manage it, should be softened. Ozzie pressed the phone to his breast and watched his mother dragging whatever she was dragging, and he felt his own eyes get glassy. His mother was a round, tired, gray-haired penguin of a woman whose frail skin had begun to feel the tug of gravity and the weight of her own history. Even when she was dressed up she didn't look like a chosen person. But when she lit candles she looked like something better; like a woman who knew momentarily that God could do anything.

After a few mysterious minutes she was finished. Ozzie hung up the phone and walked to the kitchen table where she was beginning to lay the two places for the four-course Sabbath meal. He told her that she would have to see Rabbi Binder next Wednesday at four-thirty, and then he told her why. For the first time in their life together she hit Ozzie across the face with her hand.

All through the chopped liver and chicken soup part of the dinner Ozzie cried; he didn't have an appetite for the rest.

On Wednesday, in the largest of the three basement classrooms of the synagogue, Rabbi Marvin Binder, a tall, handsome, broad-shouldered man of thirty with thick strong-fibered black hair, removed his watch from his pocket and saw that it was four o'clock. At the rear of the room Yakov Blotnik, the seventy-one-year-old custodian, slowly polished the large window, mumbling to himself: unaware that it was four o'clock or six o'clock, Monday or Wednesday. To most of the students Yakov Blotnik's mumbling, along with his brown curly beard, scythe nose, and two heel-trailing black cats, made of him an object of wonder, a foreigner, a relic, towards whom they were alternately fearful and disrespectful. To Ozzie the mumbling had always seemed a monotonous, curious prayer; what made it curious was that old Blotnik had been mumbling so steadily for so many years, Ozzie suspected he had memorized the prayers and forgotten all about God.

"It is now free-discussion time," Rabbi Binder said. "Feel free to talk about any Jewish matter at all—religion, family, politics, sports—"

There was silence. It was a gusty, clouded November afternoon and it did not seem as though there ever was or could be a thing called baseball. So nobody this week said a word about that hero from the past, Hank Greenberg—which limited free discussion considerably.

And the soul-battering Ozzie Freedman had just received from Rabbi Binder had imposed its limitation. When it was Ozzie's turn to read aloud from the Hebrew book the rabbi had asked him petulantly why he didn't read more rapidly. He was showing no progress. Ozzie said he could read faster but that if he did he was sure not to understand what he was reading. Nevertheless, at the rabbi's repeated suggestion Ozzie tried, and showed a great talent, but in the midst of a long passage he stopped short and said he didn't understand a word he was reading, and started in again at a dragfooted pace. Then came the soul-battering.

Consequently when free-discussion time rolled around none of the students felt too free. The rabbi's invitation was answered only by the mumbling of feeble old Blotnik.

"Isn't there anything at all you would like to discuss?" Rabbi Binder asked again, looking at his watch. "No questions or comments?"

There was a small grumble from the third row. The rabbi requested that Ozzie rise and give the rest of the class the advantage of his thought.

Ozzie rose. "I forget it now," he said, and sat down in his place.

Rabbi Binder advanced a seat towards Ozzie and poised himself on the edge of the desk. It was Itzie's desk and the rabbi's frame only a dagger's-length away from his face snapped him to sitting attention.

"Stand up again, Oscar," Rabbi Binder said calmly, "and try to assemble your thoughts."

Ozzie stood up. All his classmates turned in their seats and watched as he gave an unconvincing scratch to his forehead.

"I can't assemble any," he announced, and plunked himself down.

"Stand up!" Rabbi Binder advanced from Itzie's desk to the one directly in front of Ozzie; when the rabbinical back was turned Itzie gave it five-fingers off the tip of his nose, causing a small titter in the room. Rabbi Binder was too absorbed in squelching Ozzie's nonsense once and for all to bother with titters. "Stand up, Oscar. What's your question about?"

Ozzie pulled a word out of the air. It was the handiest word "Religion."

"Oh, now you remember?"

"Yes."

"What is it?"

Trapped, Ozzie blurted the first thing that came to him. "Why can't He make anything He wants to make?"

As Rabbi Binder prepared an answer, a final answer, Itzie, ten feet behind him, raised one finger on his left hand, gestured it meaningfully towards the rabbi's back, and brought the house down.

Binder twisted quickly to see what had happened and in the midst of the commotion Ozzie shouted into the rabbi's back what he couldn't have shouted to his face. It was a loud, toneless sound that had the timbre of something stored inside for about six days.

"You don't know! You don't know anything about God!"

The rabbi spun back towards Ozzie, "What?"

"You don't know—you don't—"

"Apologize, Oscar, apologize!" It was a threat.

"You don't—" Rabbi Binder's hand flicked out at Ozzie's cheek. Perhaps it had only been meant to clamp the boy's mouth shut, but Ozzie ducked and the palm caught him squarely on the nose.

The blood came in a short, red spurt on to Ozzie's shirt front.

The next moment was all confusion. Ozzie screamed, "You bastard, you bastard!" and broke for the classroom door. Rabbi

Binder lurched a step backwards, as though his own blood had started flowing violently in the opposite direction, then gave a clumsy lurch forward and bolted out the door after Ozzie. The class followed after the rabbi's huge blue-suited back, and before old Blotnik could turn from his window, the room was empty and everyone was headed full speed up the three flights leading to the roof.

If one should compare the light of day to the life of man: sunrise to birth; sunset—the dropping down over the edge—to death; then as Ozzie Freedman wiggled through the trapdoor of the synagogue roof, his feet kicking backwards bronco-style at Rabbi Binder's outstretched arms—at that moment the day was fifty years old. As a rule, fifty or fifty-five reflects accurately the age of late afternoons in November, for it is in that month, during those hours, that one's awareness of light seems no longer a matter of seeing, but of hearing: light begins clicking away. In fact, as Ozzie locked shut the trapdoor in the rabbi's face, the sharp click of the bolt into the lock might momentarily have been mistaken for the sound of the heavier gray that had just throbbed through the sky.

With all his weight Ozzie kneeled on the locked door: any instant he was certain that Rabbi Binder's shoulder would fling it open, splintering the wood into shrapnel and catapulting his body into the sky, But the door did not move and below him he heard only the rumble of feet, first loud then dim, like thunder rolling away.

A question shot through his brain. "Can this be *me*?" For a thirteen-year-old who had just labeled his religious leader a bastard, twice, it was not an improper question.

Louder and louder the question came to him—"Is it me? Is it me?"—until he discovered himself no longer kneeling, but racing crazily towards the edge of the roof, his eyes crying, his throat screaming, and his arms flying every which way as though not his own.

"Is it me? Is it me ME ME ME ME! It has to be me—but is it?"

It is the question a thief must ask himself the night he jimmies open his first window, and it is said to be the question with which bridegrooms quiz themselves before the altar.

In the few wild seconds it took Ozzie's body to propel him to the edge of the roof, his self-examination began to grow fuzzy. Gazing down at the street, he became confused as to the problem beneath the question. Was it, is-it-me-who-called-Binder-a-bastard? or, is-it-me-prancing-around-on-the-roof? However, the scene below settled all, for there is an instant in any action when whether it is you or somebody else is academic. The thief crams the money in his pockets and scoots out the window. The bridegroom signs the hotel register for two. And the boy on the roof finds a street-full of people gaping at him, necks stretched backwards, faces up, as though he were the ceiling of the Hayden Planetarium. Suddenly you know it's you.

"Oscar! Oscar Freedman!" A voice rose from the center of the crowd, a voice that, could it have been seen, would have looked like the writing on a scroll. "Oscar Freedman, get down from there. Immediately!" Rabbi Binder was pointing one arm stiffly up at him; and at the end of that arm, one finger aimed menacingly. It was the attitude of a dictator, but one—the eyes confessed all—whose personal valet had spit neatly in his face.

Ozzie didn't answer. Only for a blink's length did he look towards Rabbi Binder. Instead his eyes began to fit together the world beneath him, to sort out people from places, friends from enemies, participants from spectators. In little jagged star-like clusters his friends stood around Rabbi Binder—who was still pointing. The topmost point on a star compounded not of angels but of five adolescent boys with Itzie. What a world it was, with those stars below, Rabbi Binder below . . . Ozzie, who a moment earlier hadn't been able to control his own body, started to feel the meaning of the word control: he felt Peace and he felt Power.

"Oscar Freedman, I'll give you three to come down."

Few dictators give their subjects three to do anything; but, as always, Rabbi Binder only looked dictatorial.

"Are you ready, Oscar?"

Ozzie nodded his head yes, although he had no intention in the world—the lower one or the celestial one he'd just entered—of coming down even if Rabbi Binder should give him a million.

"All right then," said Rabbi Binder. He ran a hand through his black Samson hair as though it were the gesture prescribed for uttering the first digit. Then, with his other hand cutting a circle out of the small piece of sky around him, he spoke. "One!"

There was no thunder. On the contrary, at that moment, as though "one" was the cue for which he had been waiting, the world's least thunderous person appeared on the synagogue steps.

He did not so much come out the synagogue door as lean out, onto
the darkening air. He clutched at the doorknob with one hand and
looked up at the roof.

"Oy!"

Yakov Blotnik's old mind hobbled slowly, as if on crutches, and
though he couldn't decide precisely what the boy was doing on the
roof: he knew it wasn't good—that is, it wasn't-good-for-the-Jews.
For Yakov Blotnik life had fractionated itself simply: things were
either good-for-the-Jews or no-good-for-the-Jews.

He smacked his free hand to his in-sucked cheek, gently. "Oy,
Gut!" And then quickly as he was able, he jacked down his head and
surveyed the street. There was Rabbi Binder (like a man at an auction
with only three dollars in his pocket, he had just delivered a shaky
"Two"); there were the students—and that was all. So far it-wasn't-
so-bad-for-the-Jews. But the boy had to come down immediately,
before anybody saw. The problem: how to get the boy off the roof?

Anybody who has ever had a cat on the roof knows how to get
him down. You call the fire department. Or first you call the
operator and you ask her for the fire department. And the next
thing there is great jamming of brakes and clanging of bells and
shouting of instructions. And then the cat is off the roof. You do
the same thing to get a boy off the roof.

That is, you do the same thing if you are Yakov Blotnik and you
once had a cat on the roof.

When the engines, all four of them, arrived, Rabbi Binder had
four times given Ozzie the count of three. The big hook-and-ladder
swung around the corner and one of the firemen leaped from it,
plunging headlong towards the yellow fire hydrant in front of the
synagogue. With a huge wrench he began to unscrew the top nozzle. Rabbi Binder raced over to him and pulled at his shoulder.

"There's no fire . . ."

The fireman mumbled back over his shoulder and, heatedly,
continued working at the nozzle.

"But there's no fire. There's no fire . . ." Binder shouted. When
the fireman mumbled again, the rabbi grasped his face with both his
hands and pointed it up at the roof.

To Ozzie it looked as though Rabbi Binder was trying to tug the
fireman's head out of his body, like a cork from a bottle. He had to
giggle at the picture they made: it was a family portrait—rabbi in
black skullcap, fireman in red fire hat, and the little yellow hydrant

squatting beside like a kid brother, bareheaded. From the edge of the roof Ozzie waved at the portrait, a one-handed, flapping, mocking wave; in doing it his right foot slipped from under him. Rabbi Binder covered his eyes with his hands.

Firemen work fast. Before Ozzie had even regained his balance, a big, round, yellowed net was being held on the synagogue wall. The firemen who held it looked up at Ozzie with stern, feelingless faces.

One of the firemen turned his head towards Rabbi Binder. "What, is the kid nuts or something?"

Rabbi Binder unpeeled his hand, from his eyes, slowly, painfully, as if they were tape. Then he checked: nothing on the sidewalk, no dents in the net.

"Is he gonna jump or what?" the fireman shouted.

In a voice not at all like a statue, Rabbi Binder finally answered. "Yes, yes, I think so . . . He's been threatening to . . ."

Threatening to? Why, the reason he was on the roof, Ozzie remembered, was to get away; he hadn't even thought about jumping. He had just run to get away and the truth was that he hadn't really headed for the roof as much as he'd been chased there.

"What's his name, the kid?"

"Freedman," Rabbi Binder answered. "Oscar Freedman."

The fireman looked up at Ozzie. "What is it with you, Oscar? You gonna jump or what?"

Ozzie did not answer. Frankly, the question had just arisen.

"Look, Oscar. If you're gonna jump, jump—and if you're not gonna jump, don't jump. But don't waste our time, willya?"

Ozzie looked at the fireman and then at Rabbi Binder. He wanted to see Rabbi Binder cover his eyes one more time.

"I'm going to jump."

And then he scampered around the edge of the roof to the corner, where there was no net below, and he flapped his arms at his sides, swishing the air and smacking his palms to his trousers on the downbeat. He began screaming like some kind of engine, "Wheeeee: wheeeee," and leaning way out over the edge with the upper half of his body. The firemen whipped around to cover the ground with the net. Rabbi Binder mumbled a few words to Somebody and covered his eyes. Everything happened quickly, jerkily, as in a silent movie. The crowd, which had arrived with the fire engines, gave out a long, Fourth-of-July fireworks oooh-aahhh. In the excitement no one had paid the crowd much heed, except, of course, Yakov Blotnik, who swung from the doorknob counting heads. "Fier und tsvansik . . . finf und tsvantsik . . . Oy, Gut!" It wasn't like this with the cat.

Rabbi Binder peeked through his fingers, checked the sidewalk and net. Empty. But there was Ozzie racing to the other corner. The firemen raced with him but were unable to keep up. Whenever Ozzie wanted to he might jump and splatter himself upon the sidewalk, and by the time the firemen scooted to the spot all they could do with their net would be to cover the mess.

"Wheeeee . . . wheeeee . . ."

"Hey, Oscar," the winded fireman yelled, "What the hell is this, a game or something?"

"Wheeeee . . . wheeeee . . ."

"Hey, Oscar—"

But he was off now to the other corner, flapping his wings fiercely. Rabbi Binder couldn't take it any longer—the fire engines from nowhere, the screaming, suicidal boy, the net. He fell to his knees, exhausted, and with his hands curled together in front of his chest, like a little dome, he pleaded, "Oscar, stop it, Oscar. Don't jump, Oscar. Please come down . . . Please don't jump."

And further back in the crowd a single voice, a single young voice, shouted a lone word to the boy on the roof.

"Jump!"

It was Itzie. Ozzie momentarily stopped flapping.

"Go ahead, Ozz—jump!"

Itzie broke off his point of the star and courageously, with the inspiration not of a wise-guy but of a disciple, stood alone. "Jump, Ozz, jump!"

Still on his knees, his hands still curled, Rabbi Binder twisted his body back. He looked at Itzie, then, agonizingly, back to Ozzie.

"OSCAR, DON'T JUMP! PLEASE, DON'T JUMP . . . please please . . ."

"Jump!" This time it wasn't Itzie but another point of the star. By the time Mrs. Freedman arrived to keep her four-thirty appointment with Rabbi Binder, the whole little upside down heaven was shouting and pleading for Ozzie to jump, and Rabbi Binder no longer was pleading with him not to jump, but was crying into the dome of his hands.

Understandably Mrs. Freedman couldn't figure out what her son was doing on the roof. So she asked.

"Ozzie, my Ozzie, what are you doing? My Ozzie, what is it?"

Ozzie stopped wheeeeeing and slowed his arms down to a cruising flap, the kind birds use in soft winds, but he did not answer. He stood against the low clouded, darkening sky—light clicked down swiftly now as on a small gear—flapping softly and gazing down at the small bundle of a woman who was his mother.

"What are you doing, Ozzie?" She turned towards the kneeling Rabbi Binder and rushed so close that only a paper-thickness of dusk lay between her stomach and his shoulders.

"What is my baby doing?"

Rabbi Binder gaped up at her but he too was mute. All that moved was the dome of his hands; it shook back and forth like a weak pulse.

"Rabbi, get him down! He'll kill himself. Get him down, my only baby . . ."

"I can't," Rabbi Binder said, "I can't . . ." and he turned his handsome head towards the crowd of boys behind him. "It's them. Listen to them."

And for the first time Mrs. Freedman saw the crowd of boys, and she heard what they were yelling.

"He's doing it for them. He won't listen to me. It's them." Rabbi Binder spoke like one in a trance.

"For them?"

"Yes."

"Why for them?"

"They want him to . . ."

Mrs. Freedman raised her two arms upward as though she were conducting the sky. "For them he's doing it!" And then in a gesture older than pyramids, older than prophets and floods, her arms came slapping down to her sides. "A martyr I have. Look!" She tilted her head to the roof. Ozzie was still flapping softly. "My martyr."

"Oscar, come down, *please*," Rabbi Binder groaned.

In a startlingly even voice Mrs. Freedman called to the boy on the roof. "Ozzie, come down, Ozzie. Don't be a martyr, my baby."

As though it were a litany, Rabbi Binder repeated her words. "Don't be martyr, my baby. Don't be a martyr."

"Gawhead, Ozz—be a Martin!" It was Itzie. "Be a Martin, be a Martin," and all the voices joined in singing for Martindom, whatever it was. "Be a Martin, be a Martin . . ."

Somehow when you're on a roof the darker it gets the less you can hear. All Ozzie knew was that two groups wanted two new things: his friends were spirited and musical about what they wanted; his mother and the rabbi were even-toned, chanting, about what they didn't want. The rabbi's voice was without tears now and so was his mother's.

The big net stared up at Ozzie like a sightless eye. The big, clouded sky pushed down. From beneath it looked like a gray corrugated board. Suddenly, looking up into that unsympathetic sky, Ozzie realized all the strangeness of what these people, his friends, were asking: they wanted him to jump, to kill himself; they were singing about it now—it made them that happy. And there was an even greater strangeness: Rabbi Binder was on his knees, trembling. If there was a question to be asked now it was not "Is it me?" but rather "Is it us? . . . Is it us?"

Being on the roof, it turned out, was a serious thing. If he jumped would the singing become dancing? Would it? What would jumping stop? Yearningly, Ozzie wished he could rip open the sky, plunge his hands through, and pull out the sun; and on the sun, like a coin, would be stamped JUMP or DON'T JUMP.

Ozzie's knees rocked and sagged a little under him as though they were setting him for a dive. His arms tightened, stiffened, froze, from shoulders to fingernails. He felt as if each part of his body were going to vote as to whether he should kill himself or not—and each part as though it were independent of *him*.

The light took an unexpected click down and the new darkness, like a gag, hushed the friends singing for this and the mother and rabbi chanting for that.

Ozzie stopped counting votes, and in a curiously high voice, like one who wasn't prepared for speech, he spoke.

"Mamma?"

"Yes, Oscar."

"Mamma, get down on your knees, like Rabbi Binder."

"Oscar—"

"Get down on your knees," he said, "Or I'll jump."

Ozzie heard a whimper, then a quick rustling, and when he looked down where his mother had stood he saw the top of a head and beneath that a circle of dress. She was kneeling beside Rabbi Binder.

He spoke again. "Everybody kneel." There was the sound of everybody kneeling.

Ozzie looked around, with one hand he pointed towards the synagogue entrance. "Make *him* kneel."

There was a noise, not of kneeling, but of body-and-cloth stretching. Ozzie could hear Rabbi Binder saying in a gruff whisper, ". . . or he'll *kill* himself," and when next he looked there was Yakov Blotnik off the doorknob and for the first time in his life upon his knees in the Gentile posture of prayer.

As for the firemen—it was not as difficult as one might imagine to hold a net taut while you are kneeling.

Ozzie looked around again; and then he called to Rabbi Binder. "Rabbi?"

"Yes, Oscar."

"Rabbi Binder, do you believe in God?"

"Yes."

"Do you believe God can do anything?" Ozzie leaned his head out into the darkness. "Anything?"

"Oscar, I think—"

"Tell me you believe God can do Anything."

There was a second's hesitation. Then: "God can do Anything."

"Tell me you believe God can make a child without intercourse."

"He can."

"Tell me!"

"God," Rabbi Binder admitted, "can make a child without intercourse."

"Mamma, you tell me."

"God can make a child without intercourse," his mother said.

"Make *him* tell me." There was no doubt who *him* was.

In a few moments Ozzie heard an old comical voice say something to the increasing darkness about God.

Next, Ozzie made everybody say it. And then he made them all say they believed in Jesus Christ—first one at a time, then all together.

When the catechizing was through it was the beginning of evening. From the street it sounded as if the boy on the roof might have sighed.

"Ozzie?" A woman's voice dared to speak. "You'll come down now?"

There was no answer, but the woman waited, and when a voice finally did speak it was thin and crying, and exhausted as that of an old man who has just finished pulling the bells.

"Mamma, don't you see—you shouldn't hit me. He shouldn't hit me. You shouldn't hit me about God, Mamma. You should never hit anybody about God—"

"Ozzie, please come down now."

"Promise me, promise me you'll never hit anybody about God."

He had asked only his mother, but for some reason everyone kneeling in the street promised he would never hit anybody about God.

Once again there was silence.

"I can come down now, Mamma," the boy on the roof finally said. He turned his head both ways as though checking the traffic lights. "Now I can come down . . ."

And he did, right into the center of the yellow net that glowed in the evening's edge like an overgrown halo.

SOURCE: *The Paris Review.* New York. Spring 1958.

HARRISON BERGERON (1961)

Kurt Vonnegut, Jr.

Vonnegut (1922–2007), was born and raised in Indiana. He served in the U.S. Army in World War II and began his writing career after his return from being a prisoner of war. Many of his novels are sharp and satiric, delivered in his characteristic dead-pan casual voice. "Harrison Bergeron" is perhaps the most famous of his short stories.

THE YEAR WAS 2081, and everybody was finally equal. They weren't only equal before God and the law. They were equal every which way. Nobody was smarter than anybody else. Nobody was better looking than anybody else. Nobody was stronger or quicker than anybody else. All this equality was due to the 211th, 212th, and 213th Amendments to the Constitution, and to the unceasing vigilance of agents of the United States Handicapper General.

Some things about living still weren't quite right, though. April, for instance, still drove people crazy by not being springtime. And it was in that clammy month that the H-G men took George and Hazel Bergeron's fourteen-year-old son, Harrison, away.

It was tragic, all right, but George and Hazel couldn't think about it very hard. Hazel had a perfectly average intelligence, which meant she couldn't think about anything except in short bursts. And George, while his intelligence was way above normal, had a little mental handicap radio in his ear. He was required by law to wear it at all times. It was tuned to a government transmitter. Every twenty seconds or so, the transmitter would send out some sharp noise to keep people like George from taking unfair advantage of their brains.

George and Hazel were watching television. There were tears on Hazel's cheeks, but she'd forgotten for the moment what they were about.

On the television screen were ballerinas.

A buzzer sounded in George's head. His thoughts fled in panic, like bandits from a burglar alarm.

"That was a real pretty dance, that dance they just did," said Hazel.

"Huh" said George.

"That dance-it was nice," said Hazel.

"Yup," said George. He tried to think a little about the ballerinas. They weren't really very good—no better than anybody else would have been, anyway. They were burdened with sashweights and bags of birdshot, and their faces were masked, so that no one, seeing a free and graceful gesture or a pretty face, would feel like something the cat drug in. George was toying with the vague notion that maybe dancers shouldn't be handicapped. But he didn't get very far with it before another noise in his ear radio scattered his thoughts.

George winced. So did two out of the eight ballerinas.

Hazel saw him wince. Having no mental handicap herself, she had to ask George what the latest sound had been.

"Sounded like somebody hitting a milk bottle with a ball peen hammer," said George.

"I'd think it would be real interesting, hearing all the different sounds," said Hazel a little envious. "All the things they think up."

"Um," said George.

"Only, if I was Handicapper General, you know what I would do?" said Hazel. Hazel, as a matter of fact, bore a strong resemblance to the Handicapper General, a woman named Diana Moon Glampers. "If I was Diana Moon Glampers," said Hazel, "I'd have chimes on Sunday—just chimes. Kind of in honor of religion."

"I could think, if it was just chimes," said George.

"Well—maybe make 'em real loud," said Hazel. "I think I'd make a good Handicapper General."

"Good as anybody else," said George.

"Who knows better than I do what normal is?" said Hazel.

"Right," said George. He began to think glimmeringly about his abnormal son who was now in jail, about Harrison, but a twenty-one-gun salute in his head stopped that.

"Boy!" said Hazel, "that was a doozy, wasn't it?"

It was such a doozy that George was white and trembling, and tears stood on the rims of his red eyes. Two of of the eight ballerinas had collapsed to the studio floor, were holding their temples.

"All of a sudden you look so tired," said Hazel. "Why don't you stretch out on the sofa, so's you can rest your handicap bag on the pillows, honeybunch." She was referring to the forty-seven pounds of birdshot in a canvas bag, which was padlocked around George's neck. "Go on and rest the bag for a little while," she said. "I don't care if you're not equal to me for a while."

George weighed the bag with his hands. "I don't mind it," he said. "I don't notice it any more. It's just a part of me."

"You been so tired lately—kind of wore out," said Hazel. "If there was just some way we could make a little hole in the bottom of the bag, and just take out a few of them lead balls. Just a few."

"Two years in prison and two thousand dollars fine for every ball I took out," said George. "I don't call that a bargain."

"If you could just take a few out when you came home from work," said Hazel. "I mean—you don't compete with anybody around here. You just sit around."

"If I tried to get away with it," said George, "then other people'd get away with it—and pretty soon we'd be right back to the dark ages again, with everybody competing against everybody else. You wouldn't like that, would you?"

"I'd hate it," said Hazel.

"There you are," said George. "The minute people start cheating on laws, what do you think happens to society?"

If Hazel hadn't been able to come up with an answer to this question, George couldn't have supplied one. A siren was going off in his head.

"Reckon it'd fall all apart," said Hazel.

"What would?" said George blankly.

"Society," said Hazel uncertainly. "Wasn't that what you just said?"

"Who knows?" said George.

The television program was suddenly interrupted for a news bulletin. It wasn't clear at first as to what the bulletin was about, since the announcer, like all announcers, had a serious speech impediment. For about half a minute, and in a state of high excitement, the announcer tried to say, "Ladies and Gentlemen."

He finally gave up, handed the bulletin to a ballerina to read.

"That's all right," Hazel said of the announcer, "he tried. That's the big thing. He tried to do the best he could with what God gave him. He should get a nice raise for trying so hard."

"Ladies and Gentlemen," said the ballerina, reading the bulletin. She must have been extraordinarily beautiful, because the mask she wore was hideous. And it was easy to see that she was the strongest and most graceful of all the dancers, for her handicap bags were as big as those worn by two-hundred pound men.

And she had to apologize at once for her voice, which was a very unfair voice for a woman to use. Her voice was a warm, luminous, timeless melody. "Excuse me!" she said, and she began again, making her voice absolutely uncompetitive.

"Harrison Bergeron, age fourteen," she said in a grackle squawk, "has just escaped from jail, where he was held on suspicion of plotting to overthrow the government. He is a genius and an athlete, is under-handicapped, and should be regarded as extremely dangerous."

A police photograph of Harrison Bergeron was flashed on the screen—upside down, then sideways, upside down again, then right side up. The picture showed the full length of Harrison against a background calibrated in feet and inches. He was exactly seven feet tall.

The rest of Harrison's appearance was Halloween and hardware. Nobody had ever born heavier handicaps. He had outgrown hindrances faster than the H-G men could think them up. Instead of a little ear radio for a mental handicap, he wore a tremendous pair of earphones, and spectacles with thick wavy lenses. The spectacles were intended to make him not only half blind, but to give him whanging headaches besides.

Scrap metal was hung all over him. Ordinarily, there was a certain symmetry, a military neatness to the handicaps issued to strong people, but Harrison looked like a walking junkyard. In the race of life, Harrison carried three hundred pounds.

And to offset his good looks, the H-G men required that he wear at all times a red rubber ball for a nose, keep his eyebrows shaved off, and cover his even white teeth with black caps at snaggle-tooth random.

"If you see this boy," said the ballerina, "do not—I repeat, do not—try to reason with him."

There was the shriek of a door being torn from its hinges.

Screams and barking cries of consternation came from the television set. The photograph of Harrison Bergeron on the screen jumped again and again, as though dancing to the tune of an earthquake.

George Bergeron correctly identified the earthquake, and well he might have—for many was the time his own home had danced to the same crashing tune. "My God—" said George, "that must be Harrison!"

The realization was blasted from his mind instantly by the sound of an automobile collision in his head.

When George could open his eyes again, the photograph of Harrison was gone. A living, breathing Harrison filled the screen.

Clanking, clownish, and huge, Harrison stood in the center of the studio. The knob of the uprooted studio door was still in his hand. Ballerinas, technicians, musicians, and announcers cowered on their knees before him, expecting to die.

"I am the Emperor!" cried Harrison. "Do you hear? I am the Emperor! Everybody must do what I say at once!" He stamped his foot and the studio shook.

"Even as I stand here" he bellowed, "crippled, hobbled, sickened—I am a greater ruler than any man who ever lived! Now watch me become what I can become!"

Harrison tore the straps of his handicap harness like wet tissue paper, tore straps guaranteed to support five thousand pounds.

Harrison's scrap-iron handicaps crashed to the floor.

Harrison thrust his thumbs under the bar of the padlock that secured his head harness. The bar snapped like celery. Harrison smashed his headphones and spectacles against the wall.

He flung away his rubber-ball nose, revealed a man that would have awed Thor, the god of thunder.

"I shall now select my Empress!" he said, looking down on the cowering people. "Let the first woman who dares rise to her feet claim her mate and her throne!"

A moment passed, and then a ballerina arose, swaying like a willow.

Harrison plucked the mental handicap from her ear, snapped off her physical handicaps with marvelous delicacy. Last of all he removed her mask.

She was blindingly beautiful.

"Now," said Harrison, taking her hand, "shall we show the people the meaning of the word dance? Music!" he commanded.

The musicians scrambled back into their chairs, and Harrison stripped them of their handicaps, too. "Play your best," he told them, "and I'll make you barons and dukes and earls."

The music began. It was normal at first—cheap, silly, false. But Harrison snatched two musicians from their chairs, waved them like batons as he sang the music as he wanted it played. He slammed them back into their chairs.

The music began again and was much improved.

Harrison and his Empress merely listened to the music for a while—listened gravely, as though synchronizing their heartbeats with it.

They shifted their weights to their toes.

Harrison placed his big hands on the girl's tiny waist, letting her sense the weightlessness that would soon be hers.

And then, in an explosion of joy and grace, into the air they sprang!

Not only were the laws of the land abandoned, but the law of gravity and the laws of motion as well.

They reeled, whirled, swiveled, flounced, capered, gamboled, and spun.

They leaped like deer on the moon.

The studio ceiling was thirty feet high, but each leap brought the dancers nearer to it.

It became their obvious intention to kiss the ceiling. They kissed it.

And then, neutraling gravity with love and pure will, they remained suspended in air inches below the ceiling, and they kissed each other for a long, long time.

It was then that Diana Moon Glampers, the Handicapper General, came into the studio with a double-barreled ten-gauge shotgun. She fired twice, and the Emperor and the Empress were dead before they hit the floor.

Diana Moon Glampers loaded the gun again. She aimed it at the musicians and told them they had ten seconds to get their handicaps back on.

It was then that the Bergerons' television tube burned out.

Hazel turned to comment about the blackout to George. But George had gone out into the kitchen for a can of beer.

George came back in with the beer, paused while a handicap signal shook him up. And then he sat down again. "You been crying," he said to Hazel.

"Yup," she said.

"What about?" he said.

"I forget," she said. "Something real sad on television."

"What was it?" he said.

"It's all kind of mixed up in my mind," said Hazel.

"Forget sad things," said George.

"I always do," said Hazel.

"That's my girl," said George. He winced. There was the sound of a rivetting gun in his head.

"Gee—I could tell that one was a doozy," said Hazel.

"You can say that again," said George.

"Gee—" said Hazel, "I could tell that one was a doozy."

THE GIFT (1979)

Kia Penso

Born in New York City in 1959, and raised in Kingston, Jamaica, Penso has been a professor of English, a journalist, and a newspaper editor. This story of a Jamaican grandmother visiting her grown-up child in America was her first publication. Penso now works as an editor in Washington, D.C.

MISS GLADYS' MARRIED daughter Annetta had been living in Miami almost four years. Since they had left Jamaica, Annetta and her husband and three children had not been back, and Miss Gladys had not been able to go and visit them until now.

The trip was in the middle of July, the mango season. This had been very important to Miss Gladys, because if she carried nothing else for her daughter, she had to take a St. Julian mango from the big tree in the back yard. As it was, she had spent half the night before her departure cooking up ackee and saltfish, roasting a breadfruit, and making up two quarts of rum punch, and a few other things to take for Annetta and the family. She was convinced that they had to be suffering for the lack of them.

Bright and early the next morning, her young son Errol climbed the big Julie mango tree and picked the mango. It was one that Miss Gladys had been watching for weeks. Every day she went outside to check and make sure that neither the birds nor the neighborhood children had got to it. It was finally in her possession, perfect. It was big, and smooth and green with a pale hint of yellow on one of the cheeks. It weighed about a pound and a half, and the flesh under the skin was firm but not hard, under the tight skin. She noticed that the stem had not bled when the mango was picked, which meant that it was very ripe indeed. It was elegantly shaped, like a teardrop, but round at the top. And the smell! If anyone wanted to know what a mango was and could be, they had only to smell this one. The smell almost made Miss Gladys weep for joy with the beauty of it.

The mango was king. Oh, yes, there were oranges and tangerines and bananas, water coconuts and star apples and rose apples and naseberries and guavas. There were countless other fruits, but the mango was King, and the St. Julian mango was King of the mangoes. It wasn't too sweet or too cloying, or too stringy, like some commoner types. It was a high class mango, a whole meal of a mango.

Miss Gladys wrapped up the mango with tenderest care, first in a plastic bag, then in a hand towel, and packed it firmly in the shopping bag with the other foodstuffs.

She walked heavily through the corridors of Miami airport, loaded down with two shopping bags. One was filled with gifts from the Victoria Crafts Market, and the other was filled with the food, and the mango. She felt pleasure in the presence of it, and thought of Annetta.

The customs man saw her coming. He saw her with her two big shopping bags and the enormous suitcase she had brought from the baggage claim area. He thought she had probably never traveled before. Miss Gladys put the shopping bags on the conveyor belt at the customs desk. There was a low, sudden murmur of machinery, and the belt leaped forward, carrying the bags. The customs man smiled at the surprise on Miss Gladys' face.

"Okay, let's see, what have we got here?" he grinned, and looked inside one of the shopping bags.

"Is just some little presents I bringing for me daughter children, sir." She said this politely, covering her resentment at the invasion of her privacy.

"And what's in here?" He had moved to the other shopping bag, the one with the food in it.

"Just some food I cook up for me daughter, sir. She can't buy it here, so I did bring it for her. Is long time now she don't eat none."

He took the roast breadfruit out of the bag, and unwrapped it. It was a big, black, charred thing the size of a bowling ball, and it left soot all over his hands. Obviously cooked, no problem there. He examined the pot of ackee and saltfish, and saw that that was cooked. The same procedure for the curried goat, the rum punch (which he did not open), the escoveitch fish. He took one whiff of the fish and his eyes started to water. He saw in the bottom of the bag a little round bundle in a hand towel. He took it out.

Miss Gladys was furious. Her jaw was set, but she spoke politely when he asked her what it was.

"Nothing, sir." He frowned and unwrapped the mango. The smell hit the air, and lust suddenly shone in the eyes of the customs man.

"You know that it is not permitted to bring fresh fruit into the United States?"

"No, I never know, sir. Is just the one so-so mango I did was bringing for me married daughter, four year now I don't see her. You going to take it weh from me, sir?"

"I'm sorry, but we will have to confiscate this." He caressed the mango.

Miss Gladys' eyes grew moist, and her lower lip trembled. "All right, sir, I beg you just to please let me hold it one time. Just for me daughter, sir?"

The man handed it to her reluctantly. "It's not really allowed, but . . ."

He didn't get to finish his sentence, because Miss Gladys had sunk her teeth into the top of the mango. The smell rose when the golden meat of the mango was exposed. Miss Gladys peeled the skin off in strips with her teeth. It came off smoothly, and she held the strips in her hand. She bit into the firm meat and juice poured down her chin, but she couldn't stop now to clean it up. The juice ran down her arm and dripped to the floor where her elbow was bent. Miss Gladys ate that mango with a vengeance. She ate it for love of Annetta, she ate it for hatred of the greedy little man watching her. She saw her young son Errol up in the mango tree, climbing down, handing her the mango, smiling at her over the mango. The juice was everywhere; on her nose, her cheeks, her chin, the front of her dress, her arm. It shined up in little golden drops on the floor. And the smell spoke for all the enjoyment that was in it. When Miss Gladys was finished, there was no juice left on the mango; the seed was white. She handed the skin and the big, flat seed to the customs man, and with her clean hand reached into the sleeve of her dress and pulled out a dainty handkerchief. She mopped her face delicately, and moistened one corner of the hand-kerchief in her mouth and rubbed at the spots on the front of her dress. She wiped her arm and her hand, and called a porter. She packed the other food carefully in the shopping bag, and made the porter carry the suitcase and the bag from the crafts market. She could see Annetta waiting worriedly at the exit to the customs area. She walked towards her, and then turned and spoke to the customs man, loudly, for everyone to hear.

"You wicked brute, you. You think I never know sey dat did want eat it you'self. Eh? You think I never know when you damn ol' eye dem was a shine like when mawga dag deh in a butcher shop? If it wasn't das me married daughter was here me woulda dis tun round same time go home a mi yard. Damn likkle red boy like you, though."

Miss Gladys turned and proudly took the arm of her married daughter.

SOURCE: Originally published in *Spectrum*, Volume 21. University of California, Santa Barbara, 1979.

FLIGHT CONTROL (1981)

Jervey Tervalon

Raised in South Central Los Angeles, Tervalon (born in 1958) is a novelist and essayist who earned his master's degree in creative writing from the University of California, Irvine. He teaches literature and writing at various colleges.

"So when you think she'll be getting back?" Frank asked Garvy.

"Sometime tonight. It'll be too late for me to see her tonight, but first thing tomorrow."

"Well, I'm glad you're getting over all that broken-hearted crap."

"Yeah, I'm happy, Frank, that you're happy for *me*." Garvy turned away from Frank and waved at Ronnie.

"Say, Ron, why don't you hand me one of those beers?"

Ronnie, lying comfortably on the thick grass of Garvy's front yard, wasn't going to hop up and hand Garvy a beer. It took a real effort for him to unclasp his hands that were pillowing his head and point towards the beer.

"Get it yourself, big boy."

Garvy stood up, muttering about doggish partners, and reached for a beer. He grabbed one and sat down again on the porch step.

"Why don't you go with her mama and meet Debra at the airport?" Frank said to Garvy.

"You know how families are. Her mama ain't gonna want me standing around when Debra and her are hugging."

Frank nodded his agreement. Garvy leaned back on the steps and rested his beer on his stomach.

"Have you seen Cindy today? Is she going to pick Debra up too?" Garvy asked Frank.

"No, I haven't seen Cindy in a while."

"You two get in a fight?"

"No, I've just been playing too much chess to see her."

Frank stood up and bounced his basketball a couple of times. Then he practiced his jump-shot until he got tired.

"You know, these last couple of days went by so slow. You know how it is when your lady raises up on you," Garvy said to nobody in particular.

Ronnie nodded to be polite, but Frank sat down and looked at Garvy like he was observing a patient.

"Damn, man, she's only been gone a week and a couple of days and you been bitching since day one. You must be in love for *days*."

"Yeah, I am. But you wouldn't understand none of that. You see, when you're away from the person that you're sharing your love with, it's just like missing an arm or something, and unless you're on the inside, you wouldn't understand," Garvy said righteously.

"Garvy, you're tripping. You're so in love, it's hard to talk to you. If you're gonna be that in love, you oughta keep it to yourself."

Garvy sat quietly a while and then started talking again.

"Yeah, I bet sometime today her plane flies over my house."

"Well, her plane won't be going over your house. She's coming from back east. She'd be coming from that direction." Frank pointed towards the mountains.

"You don't know, Frank."

"Maybe not."

Garvy looked down at Ronnie and noticed that he hadn't moved for a while. Sleeping away, he thought. It was warm and not too smoggy, a pretty good day for sleeping on the lawn. He didn't want to wake Ronnie, but he wanted to talk, and it was almost too much work talking to Frank. He must be in an evil mood, Garvy thought. So Garvy sat there quietly sipping his beer and staring at the planes that occasionally flew overhead. After the fifth plane, Garvy had to say something to somebody.

"Yeah, I'll be glad when that plane comes in."

"How do you know it's gonna come in?" Frank asked.

"It's supposed to! What kind of question is that?"

"Suppose something happened?" Frank said.

"Ain't nothing gonna happen."

"Suppose it did?" Frank said.

"You act like you want her plane to crash."

"I do."

Garvy was quiet for a long moment. He noticed that Ronnie was sitting up now, looking on with interest.

"You mean you want her plane to crash?"

"Yeah."

"You want her to die?"

"I didn't say that," Frank said.

Garvy was crying mad. He tried not to show it, but he was. He looked at Frank a long time and said, "If her plane crashes, I'm gonna kill you."

Ronnie was watching with his head on his knees, he was wondering about his friends.

"What do you mean you're gonna kill *me*. I can't make her plane crash."

"But you want it to happen. If it does, I'm gonna kill you."

Frank smiled at Garvy, but Garvy didn't smile back. After a while, Garvy went into his house and left them on the porch. They both knew he was upset. He never left them on the porch. He stayed outside till they left him or came into his house.

Ronnie stood up to stretch. Frank was about to ring the doorbell.

"Naw, Frank, leave Garvy alone. You two do some weird shit. And that was some of the weirdest shit I've seen in a while. I'll call him up later and patch things up."

"I didn't mean to upset him like that. I didn't know he'd get that crazy. Shit, now he got me worrying about that plane crashing."

The next day Debra came by Garvy's house. She brought him a cup with a whistle built into the handle and some words on the front saying "Whistle if you got to pee." Garvy thought it didn't make too much sense, but he liked it anyway. And he never had a cup he could scare his brother with by whistling it loud and sharp at the breakfast table. Garvy and Debra sat on his front porch in the good summer heat, passing the time lazily—Garvy admiring Debra's skinny legs and Debra enjoying the attention that Garvy was paying her. After a while the heat got the better of them, so Garvy went into the house to get some lemonade. When he came out, Ronnie and Frank were on the porch. Debra was happy to see them and they were politely returning her affection. After they talked a while to Debra, Frank turned to Garvy.

"Hey, I have something for you." He pulled out of his back pocket a roll of comics and handed them to Garvy.

Garvy took them and sat down next to Debra.

"Thanks, Frank," Garvy said.

Frank turned to Debra. "You know, Deb, I'm happy you're back."

Debra called to Ronnie, who was lying on the lawn again: "Ronnie, they've been at each other again?"

"Yeah. I don't think they can find nothing better to do."

SOURCE: Jervey Tervalon. *Living for the City*. San Diego: Incommunicado Press. 1998. Originally published in *Spectrum*, Volume 23, 1981.

HOW TO FIGHT WITH YOUR WIFE
(1996)

Howard Kaplan

Kaplan, born in 1953, in San Francisco, has written for the New York Times, *the* Daily News, The New Yorker, *and* Vanity Fair, *but was best known as a columnist for the* New York Press, *especially for "The Howie Chronicles," which were presented as "transcriptions" of the title-character's weekly visits to his psychologist. This piece is from his later "How to Fight with Your Wife" column, a fictional diary of social and familial dilemmas.*

SUNDAY, JUNE 2

I had a slight turn this morning. The two of us, Jean and I, were busy in the kitchen when I noticed a bowl of half-eaten cereal on the counter. I shot a nervous look at Jean. When had she poured herself the cereal and dipped in?

She was moving about briskly. That was a relief. Was it possible this wasn't the same cereal I thought it was?

I glanced back at the counter. No, I was right, I knew what I was looking at. These were the same round kernels, small as buck-shot, that I—without telling Jean—had shied away from trying after breaking open the box and finding the pouch unsealed. Not completely unsealed but still enough to make me hesitate. It doesn't take much to put me on my guard. There were kernels in the pocket between the cardboard and pouch. That's the kind of thing you shouldn't have to see until later, until after you've helped yourself to at least the first serving. I closed up the box and put it back on the shelf. That was a full two weeks ago. I haven't touched it since.

It never crossed my mind that Jean might try the cereal. "Health cereal" and "soy milk," written in my hand, are two items that appear week to week on our shopping list. If I haven't jotted one or the other down, Jean will ask about it. I'm the only one who really uses these goods. And yet I like to leave Jean a certain latitude in shopping for me. It's her decision which particular "health cereal" to get.

This is how we came to have the box of Nutty Wheat. Did I murmur my approval when I saw what she had bought? I truly like the whole Nutty line, which Jean herself discovered. Nutty Wheat, Nutty Corn, Nutty Rice—I've tried them all.

And yet perhaps I do overdo it just a little. I know Jean is looking to hear nice words from me. And not just about whichever "health cereal" she brings home to me, but also about the food shopping in general for that day. If I suggest not getting dried pears again soon, say, Jean gets offended by it, she feels I'm being critical. "Everything I buy," she says, "I buy with you in mind." Or maybe I'll question why she chose a certain box of cookies. "*You're* doing the shopping next week," Jean will shoot back.

What would she say if I told her straight out that I was leery of the Nutty Wheat cereal she had bought because I wasn't quite comfortable with the pouch being partly open? Isn't this too much? Wouldn't she take it personally? Wouldn't she threaten yet again not to do the shopping?

I decided not to find out. I didn't want to risk it. I put the box back undisturbed, and kept quiet about it.

Perhaps one day, after a decent amount of time had passed, I might have eased the box out the door while Jean's back was turned. It wouldn't be the first time I pulled such a stunt. But only now am I putting it so clearly to myself. I didn't really think it through before. I'd acted on impulse. I can't even swear that I wouldn't have had second thoughts and finally chanced putting down a spoonful or two. I knew in my heart that there was nothing wrong with the cereal.

Still, it gave me a turn this morning to see it in that bowl of milk, to see it gotten into. I threw a quick glance at Jean. She looked quite normal. It was I, rather, for just a second, who didn't look himself. I was suddenly in the position of a man who comes to the realization he might have just accidentally poisoned his wife. I'm not often in this predicament. Was this the first time in fact? The alarm I could have predicted, but not the degree of furtiveness. The furtiveness was there in equal measure to the alarm. And then shame at my furtiveness: I wasn't going to warn her. Either everything was absolutely fine—as I was sure it was—or something really was the matter, in which case it was too late. In either case, it seemed to me best to keep quiet.

Still, I was so ashamed I actually had half a mind to put a bowl of the cereal in my system right with her.

But then I thought of Guy and Dora. I had to act responsibly. If something happened to both of us, who would watch over them?

I felt very guilty. I imagined the box of cereal causing Jean's death after all and the police coming by later to ask me a few questions.

Of course, while making every effort to appear neutral, in reality they'd be working from the assumption that I'd killed her. We all start from that assumption. The husband probably did it.

Given the world's attitude, wouldn't it look better if I didn't mention my own prior doubts about the cereal? I could hear one of the detectives saying, "Excuse me, I'm sorry, I don't understand. You mean you actually put the box of cereal back inside the cabinet and didn't bother telling your wife you thought it might have been tampered with?"

My mind was made up. I wouldn't say a word about opening up the box on my own and all the rest of it. I never touched the box. It was the only way to get me off the hook with these people.

I suddenly stopped myself. What on earth was I thinking? When suspects are picked up, they often give stories out that the cops have no trouble at all shooting holes through. I get so annoyed with these suspects I read about. Don't they realize it's just a matter of time before the cops trip them up in their futile little deceits? In their place, I tell myself, I'd come clean right away.

But look what I was doing now! I was falling into the same trap! How was my thinking any different from a criminal's?

I vowed then and there I'd tell the cops everything.

SOURCE: *New York Press.* June 19, 1996.

CENTER OF THE UNIVERSE (2012)

Simon Rich

Born and raised in New York City, Rich (b. 1984) went to Harvard and became editor of the Harvard Lampoon. *He has published two collections of humor pieces, two novels, and a book of short stories since graduating in 2007.*

ON THE FIRST day, God created the heavens and the earth.

"Let there be light," He said, and there was light. And God saw that it was good. And there was evening—the first night.

On the second day, God separated the oceans from the sky. "Let there be a horizon," He said. And lo: a horizon appeared and God saw that it was good. And there was evening—the second night.

On the third day, God's girlfriend came over and said that He'd been acting distant lately.

"I'm sorry," God said. "Things have been crazy this week at work."

He smiled at her, but she did not smile back. And God saw that it was not good.

"I never see you," she said.

"That's not true," God said. "We went to the movies just last week."

And she said, "Lo. That was last *month*."

And there was evening—a tense night.

On the fourth day, God created stars, to divide the light from the darkness. He was almost finished when He looked at His cell phone and realized that it was almost nine-thirty.

"Fuck," He said. "Kate's going to kill me."

He finished the star He was working on and cabbed it back to the apartment.

"Sorry I'm late!" He said.

And lo: she did not even respond.

"Are you hungry?" He asked. "Let there be yogurt!" And there was that weird lo-cal yogurt that she liked.

"That's not going to work this time," she said.

"Look," God said, "I know we're going through a hard time right now. But this job is only temporary. As soon as I pay off my student loans, I'm going to switch to something with better hours."

And she said unto Him, "*I* work a full-time job and *I* still make time for you."

And He said unto her, "Yeah, but your job's different."

And lo: He knew immediately that He had made a terrible mistake.

"You think my job's less important than yours?" she said.

"No!" God said. "Of course not! I know how difficult it is to work in retail—I'm totally impressed by what you do!"

"Today I had to talk to fourteen buyers, because it's Fashion Week. And I didn't even have time to eat lunch."

"That's so hard," God said. "You work so hard."

"How would you know? You never even ask about my day! You just talk about your work, for hours and hours, like you're the center of the universe!"

"Let there be a back rub," God said.

And He started giving her a back rub.

And she said unto Him, "Can you please take the day off tomorrow?"

And He said unto her, "Don't *you* have to work tomorrow? I thought it was Fashion Week."

"I can call in sick."

And God felt like saying to her, "If your job is so important, how come you can just take days off whenever you feel like it?" But He knew that was a bad idea. So He said unto her, "I'm off Sunday. We can hang out Sunday."

On the fifth day, God created fish and fowl to swim in the sea and fly through the air, each according to its kind. Then, to score some points, He closed the door to His office and called up Kate.

"I'm so happy to hear your voice," she said. "I'm having the hardest day."

"Tell me all about it," God said.

"Caitlin is throwing this party next week for Jenny, but Jenny is, like, being so weird about it that I'm not even sure that it's going to happen."

"That's crazy," God said.

And she continued to tell Him about her friends, who had all said hurtful things to one another, each according to her kind. And while she was repeating something that Jenny had said to Caitlin God came up with an idea for creatures that roam the earth. He couldn't get off the phone, though, because Kate was still talking. So He covered the receiver and whispered, "Let there be elephants." And there were elephants and God saw that they were good.

But lo: she had heard Him create the elephants.

"Oh, my God," she said. "You're not even listening to me."

"Kate . . ."

"It's so obvious!" she said. "You care more about your stupid planet thing than you do about me!"

God wanted to correct her. It wasn't just a planet He was creating; it was an entire universe. He knew, though, that it would be a bad idea to say something like that right now.

He said, "Listen. I'm really sorry, O.K.?"

But lo: she had already hung up on Him.

On the sixth day, God called in sick and surprised Kate at her store in Chelsea. She was in the back, reading a magazine.

"What are you doing here?" she asked.

"I blew off work," He said. "I want to spend the day with you."

"Really?" she said.

"*Really*," He said.

And she smiled at Him so brightly that He knew He had made the right decision.

They bought some beers at a bodega and drank them on a bench in Prospect Park. And Kate introduced Him to a game her friend Jenny had taught her, called Would You Rather?

"I don't know if I want to play a game," God said. But she made Him play anyway, and after a few rounds He saw that it was good. They played all afternoon, laughing at each other's responses. When it got cold, God rubbed her shoulders and she kissed Him on the neck.

"You know what I kind of want to do right now?" Kate said. God tensed up.

"What?"

"See a movie," she said.

And God laughed, because it was exactly what He wanted to do.

They decided to see *The Muppets*, because they had heard that it was good. They had a great time, and when it was over God paid for a cab so they wouldn't have to wait all night for the L train.

"I love you," Kate said, as she nodded off in the back seat. "I love you so much."

"I love you, too," God said.

And both of them saw that it was good.

On the seventh day, God quit His job. He never finished the earth.

SOURCE: *The New Yorker.* January 9, 2012.